EDGE
OF THE
STORM

Also by Valerie Geary

Crooked River

Everything We Lost

Brett Buchanan Mystery Series:
On A Dark Tide (Book 1)
The Ophelia Killer (A Prequel)
Edge of the Storm (Book 2)

EDGE OF THE STORM

A BRETT BUCHANAN MYSTERY

VALERIE GEARY

BROKEN BRANCH

EDGE OF THE STORM
Copyright © 2022 by Valerie Geary
Broken Branch Books
Portland, OR

Firs edition May 2022

ISBN 978-1-954815-06-3

www.valeriegeary.com

For Alisa —
Trust her to find the perfect ending.

EDGE
OF THE
STORM

CHAPTER 1

If the stars had been visible that night, Lizzie would have stuck with their plan. If the clouds had not smothered the moon, she would have waited with Daniel and June as long as it took until Adam showed. The four of them could have left Crestwood together, gone anywhere they wanted, and been halfway to a new life by morning.

"Where is he?" Lizzie checked her cheap plastic watch, but it was too dark to see the dial. "Give me some light?"

Daniel swung the flashlight toward her.

"We said midnight, right?" Lizzie frowned. "It's 12:05."

"Give him ten more minutes," June said.

"I don't think he's coming."

"He said he'd be here." June lifted the Polaroid camera she carried around with her everywhere and took a picture of Daniel's hand as he turned the flashlight toward a break in the trees surrounding the large clearing.

The old dirt road that cut through the forest was the only way to get to the ruins. Seconds passed. A minute. Then another, but Adam didn't materialize from the shadows.

A cool wind swept across the headland. The clouds shifted, expanding the already deep pockets of darkness. The scent of rain drifted in with the salt-smell of the ocean. Lizzie didn't suppress the shudder that rolled through her as she tugged her jacket tighter.

"Let's go without him," she said.

Daniel and June stood close to one another, their arms brushing. They exchanged a glance, and Daniel said, "Adam's the one with the car, remember?"

"We can take the bus," said Lizzie.

Daniel shook his head. "We don't have enough for tickets. And no buses are running right now anyway."

"We can't leave Adam behind. Stick together, that's what you said, right, Lizzie?" June tipped her head to one side, her white-blond hair shimmering in the dark. "Don't worry. He promised he'd be here, so he'll be here."

She turned to watch the road, ever the optimist. Daniel stood guard beside her. His fingers tapped a loose rhythm against his thigh.

Lizzie turned her gaze to the steep drop-off that bottomed out at the edge of Sculpin Bay. In the dark, it would be easy to walk in the wrong direction, lose your footing, and tumble to certain death on the sharp rocks below where the ocean would then suck you into its infinite black depths, never to be seen again. She felt dizzy thinking about it.

A clatter of falling stones drew her attention to the crumbling ruins opposite the cliff.

Kids at school said this place was haunted. It used to be a psychiatric hospital where doctors ran experiments, locking up patients and cutting out parts of their brains. Rumor had it that people had died here, either from experiments gone wrong or from throwing themselves off the cliff to end their own suffering.

Lizzie took a small step toward the ruins. What was once an expansive, multi-storied building now lay half-demolished and strewn in pieces, a jagged and smudged charcoal silhouette.

A faint voice floated from the crumbled stones. Lizzie squinted at an empty doorway leading into the building. The shadows there moved. She swore they did. A piece of night splintered off and slid deeper into the ruins.

"I'm going now." Her words echoed too loudly for this dead and quiet place.

She tightened her grip on her backpack and stepped toward the path, but June grabbed her elbow. "Lizzie, please wait. It hasn't been that long."

"He's not coming." She tried to wiggle free.

June held on tight. "This was your idea. Leave together or don't leave at all. Isn't that what you said?"

"I'm here," Lizzie said. "And you two are here. So, where is he?"

"Give him a few more minutes," June pleaded. She flicked a glance at Daniel, clearly wanting him to help convince Lizzie to stay, but Daniel shook his head. "If she wants to go, let her go."

"I'm sorry. I just—I can't." Lizzie broke free of her best friend's grasp and took off running along the dirt track that would eventually lead to the highway. As she stumbled through the trees, she heard June calling for her to come back.

CHAPTER 2

Detective Brett Buchanan pushed a stack of files out of the way and spread a map across her desk. "Okay, so where am I headed?"

Irving Winters jabbed his finger at a spot near Deadman's Point. His tie swung forward, brushing over the roads and rivers. It was the same tie he wore every Friday. A grinning, pink flamingo in sunglasses stood crooked against a brightly colored, tropical background. The bird held a martini glass in one of its webbed feet.

"There's a path through some bushes near the restrooms," Irving said. "But it can be tricky to find. You might want to go by Ed's house first and have him show you."

Laughter erupted from a small group of officers huddled around a nearby desk. They had been lurking there, whispering together when Brett arrived at the precinct fifteen minutes ago to start her shift and found the report waiting on her desk.

Irving shot the officers a mean look, which stifled their laughter for a few seconds, until one of them piped up, saying, "Be careful out there, Princess. Old Eddy can be a handful."

"If he doesn't grab a hand full first," another officer muttered, staring pointedly at her breasts.

The men roared together.

Irving rolled his eyes. "Ignore those idiots. Are you sure you don't want me to come along? Ed knows me. We'll be able to clear this faster if it's the two of us. My smash and grab can wait."

Irving had more than a burglary investigation waiting for him. Ever since their old sergeant, Stan Harcourt, became their new chief, every cold or dead end case—anything that wasn't closed within the first two weeks—was reassigned to Irving. In the past six weeks, his once high closure rate had taken a severe nosedive. He spent most of his shifts digging himself out of a never-ending avalanche of paperwork.

Brett was the reason Irving was drowning in crap cases. He'd sided with her on a big case last year instead of siding with Stan, which in Stan's mind was the ultimate betrayal.

Stan had trained Irving. The two men had worked together for over twenty years, as officers and later, as detectives. It couldn't have been easy for Irving to turn his back on his friend, not with that kind of history and certainly not with the delicate balance he'd struck as the department's first and only African-American officer.

He had a lot to lose when he chose to help Brett last year. The least she could do now to show her appreciation was to not drag him along with her on a follow-up call she, and everyone else in this room, knew was a complete waste of time. She'd been working as a detective in Crestwood, Washington since last June, almost a year and a half now, but she'd heard enough stories about Crazy Old Ed Shoal to know this case wouldn't be worth the ink she used to write up her notes later.

"I appreciate the offer," Brett said to Irving. "But I don't need a babysitter."

The older man bristled, straightening his shoulders and smoothing his tie. "I never said—"

"Oh, stop hassling her, Irv!" One of the other officers called out. "Princess is up next on the rotation. So, she takes this case. No more favorites, remember?"

It was a poorly kept secret that most of the men on this squad thought Brett was only wearing a Crestwood PD badge because their last chief, Henry Bascom, was a longtime friend of her grandmother's. It was 1985, and women all over the country were joining departments and demanding fair treatment and equal pay. In some places, women were even being promoted to lieutenants and captains. But Crestwood PD was slow to catch up, and the men here still chafed at Brett's presence. They didn't see her as a peer so much as a nuisance, and when Henry was chief, they were under the impression, however wrong, that he coddled her.

But Henry was gone now, forced to retire six weeks ago. Ever since Stan Harcourt took his place, the squad had been testing Brett, trying to measure her toughness and loyalty. If she kept her head down and did her work, eventually they'd figure out she wasn't going anywhere. They'd get bored and back off. At least, that's what she kept hoping would happen.

Brett folded the map and stacked it on top of the initial report, then grabbed her jacket off the back of her chair and slipped it over her shoulders. The nylon fabric was still damp from this morning's short walk across the parking lot. She turned off the lamp on her desk and walked toward the front door with Irving trailing after her.

"You're carrying more than your fair share around here already, you know that, right?" He spoke in a low voice. "How many cases are you working on right now?"

Crestwood was a mid-sized town with a population that hovered around forty-thousand for most of the year, doubling during the summer when flocks of tourists arrived to enjoy cool ocean breezes and experience the great outdoors mere steps from their rental houses. Most of Brett's cases were property related—vandalism, burglaries, neighbor disputes that had taken a bad turn. She had a few open cases involving more complicated crimes, but nothing she couldn't handle. She was busy—who wasn't, there were always new cases coming in—but she wasn't too busy to take care of this Ed Shoal business.

"It's fine," she said. "I'll go out and talk to the guy for a few minutes, look around, make sure everything is where it should be, and then I'm done. It's an easy close."

Brett slowed as she approached their detective sergeant's corner office. Wes Harris had been promoted three weeks ago and was still getting used to being in charge. Even though it was a waste of time and completely unnecessary, he insisted on being briefed on all new cases as soon as possible. Brett was hoping to tell him about this Ed Shoal thing before heading to Deadman's Point, but the lights in his office were off. She'd deal with her sergeant later. Hopefully by the time she talked to him, she'd already have the case closed.

Irving continued to trail her out of the precinct. He stopped under the eaves and glared at the gray clouds roiling overhead. "You could at least wait to go until this rain lets up."

The storm had made landfall overnight and didn't look to be moving on anytime soon. A crow flew past them, seeking shelter in a nearby tree.

"I've got my rain jacket." Brett pulled up the hood. "And a tarp in the trunk if it gets worse."

She tucked the file and map under her jacket and stepped into the driving rain.

———————

Twenty minutes later, Brett pulled the blue sedan borrowed from the detective pool into the parking lot at Deadman's Point. It didn't matter if it was gloomy and raining like today, or sunny and sparkling blue skies like last week, she got chills every time she came to this spot.

Last year, a man had been stabbed to death on the public dock with its rickety boards and tilted pylons. His body was then rolled into the waves below, where the tide dragged him three miles north before washing up on the beach near Brett's grandmother's house.

Since then, the parks department had all but abandoned Deadman's Point. The bathrooms were locked, the grass had grown waist-high. Someone had put up Danger signs around the dock, which was missing even more boards now and tilting at an even sharper angle toward the water. Wind gusts buffeted the pylons. Loose boards groaned against rusted nails. The whole dock shuddered above the churning waves as if seconds away from being swept out to sea.

Considering the park's history and how rundown it was now, it didn't surprise Brett one bit that Crazy Old Ed Shoal was seeing ghosts out here.

She grabbed the case file off the passenger seat of her car and opened it to read the initial report again. There wasn't much. It listed Ed Shoal as the caller, along with the date and time the phone call had been made: 11/1/1985, 1:42 AM. In small, slanting script, the dispatcher had written that Ed reported seeing two people dressed in white walking along the headland near Deadman's Point. According to Ed, the couple leaped over the edge of the cliff together and disappeared. Before the dispatcher could get any more information, Ed abruptly hung up the phone. The dispatcher had sent a patrol officer to follow-up, but the responding officer, Eli Miller, had found nothing interesting at Deadman's Point, and certainly nothing to verify what Ed Shoal had reported in his initial call to the police.

The second report written by Officer Miller offered a few additional details: *Officer arrived at Deadman's Point approximately 2:04 AM and searched the area for about fifteen minutes but could not locate Mr. Shoal or anyone else in the vicinity. No vehicles in the parking lot. No sign of recent visitors to the park. Officer drove by Mr. Shoal's house around 2:30 AM. Mr. Shoal presented himself at the front door in pajamas and a robe. He seemed in good health, though his mental state may have been compromised as he did not remember making the initial phone call to police, nor did he recall being anywhere near the park this evening. Mr. Shoal said he had been inside his house all night. He said, "I don't go outside on All Hallows' Eve. That's when the dead come walking." Recommending case to detective for follow up due to report of third party involvement.*

Brett closed the file and tossed it onto the seat.

Last night was Halloween. Some bored kids probably thought it would be fun to call the police station pretending to be Ed Shoal. Or maybe Ed Shoal had been out here, and had seen someone walking in the dark, but his eyesight wasn't great and he'd mistaken something innocuous for trouble.

There were ruins on the other side of those trees, an abandoned building where kids came to drink and smoke and escape their parents. If Ed saw anyone out last night, it was probably teenagers messing around, daring each other to walk close to the cliffs.

Brett toyed with the idea of driving back to the police station without even getting out of her car, writing up some half-assed report to satisfy her superiors, shoving the file in with the rest of the closed cases in the records room, and calling it a day. Another detective might have been able to get away with that kind of shoddy work, but not Brett. Her new chief was breathing down her neck, double-checking every pencil scratch and phone call, hoping to catch her slacking off so he'd have an excuse to fire her.

She sighed, zipped her jacket, and pulled up the hood. She'd come all the way out here, so she might as well have a look around.

Mud squelched under her boots as she walked along the unpaved road in the direction of the ruins and the clearing where Ed Shoal claimed to have seen the people jump off a cliff. She scanned the ground as she walked, though she had no idea what she was looking for. An arrow pointing her in the right direction would be nice.

The tree canopy did little to block the torrential rain. Her pants quickly became sopping wet. It wouldn't be long before her jacket was saturated to the point of being useless. Even with her hood up, rain streamed into her face, stinging her eyes. A chill crept over her skin as the damp began to soak through her clothes. She felt ridiculous. The guys back at the station were going to have a good laugh about this later—Detective Brett Buchanan, as crazy as Old Ed Shoal, shambling through an empty forest, drenched by the worst storm in years, with no clue where she was headed, chasing ghosts.

She was seconds away from turning around and going back to the parking lot when the road opened onto a grassy headland with a breathtaking view of Sculpin Bay and the Pacific Ocean beyond. If not for the storm, a person could have seen all the way to the other side of the world from up here. Today, low clouds melted with the water, vanishing the horizon and streaking the world gray.

Brett turned from the ocean to face a crumbling brick building. Dense woods surrounded the headland and crowded the back side of the building, making the broad peninsula seem cut off from the rest of the world.

Much of the building's front section was missing, revealing its once grand foyer with a large stone fireplace and a staircase leading to nowhere. Graffiti covered the walls that were still standing. Brett picked her way carefully through the rubble, stepping over a low stone wall and up a set of broken concrete steps to what used to be the main floor of the ruins. Someone had dragged in a raggedy couch and dumped it in front of the fireplace. Stuffing poked from the cushions. The wooden legs looked like they'd been chewed by some sharp-toothed creature.

Behind the fireplace, a wooden staircase that might have been breathtaking once, now leaned badly to one side. The landing hovered in space, leading to the remnants of a second-floor. Brett doubted the structural integrity of the beams stretching overhead. One strong wind could bring what was left of the ruins crashing down around her.

The shadows under the staircase shifted, and a hooded figure stepped into the foyer.

He was dressed in chest-high waders, rubber boots, and a hooded poncho, everything he wore a different shade of gray. The rain coming through the large holes in the ceiling slicked off him, making him seem more apparition than man.

He leaned against a hooked wooden cane as he shuffled a few steps closer.

Brett recognized him and lifted her hand in a wave. "Mr. Shoal? I'm Detective Buchanan. I'm following up on a phone call you made to the police station last night. You said there were two people messing around on the cliffs out here?"

It was difficult to see the man's face underneath his hood. He was little more than shadows and a stern grimace. His voice was gruff and low, barely audible above the deafening hiss of the waves slamming against rocks nearby.

"You shouldn't go walking at night," he said.

"You spoke to Officer Miller last night," Brett tried again. "He stopped by your house. Do you remember?"

The man tapped his cane once on the stone floor, then swept his arm through the air, gesturing toward the north wing of the building. "She's over there."

Before Brett could ask any follow-up questions, Ed Shoal turned and shuffled in that direction.

"Mr. Shoal, wait," Brett called after him.

The click of his cane grew fainter as he disappeared down a darkened hallway. He moved quickly for a man of his age. Afraid he'd disappear on her completely, Brett hurried after him.

He led her down a long hallway lined with empty rooms. Shafts of light beamed through holes that used to be windows. Puddles gathered on the floor where the rain streamed in through the rotted boards. The air was heavy, thick with the scent of mold and decay, a trace of old cigar smoke, and something sweet, a cloying on the back of her tongue.

As she walked, she tried to pull information from Ed. "What time were you out here last night, Mr. Shoal?"

"What time is it? I don't know." He shook his head in frustration, tapping his cane faster as he quickened his pace.

"No, what time last night? You said you saw two people walking around?"

Ed stopped so quickly, Brett almost ran into the back of him.

He twisted his head around, scowling at her from beneath the dripping hood of his poncho. "No, we don't go walking at night. Not at night. Not here."

"Then, when did you see them?" Brett asked.

His eyes were awash with confusion. His face twisted to a baffled and terrified expression that reminded Brett of her grandmother. Anita Wilson had recently been diagnosed with dementia and, on her worst days, forgot where she was in time, who in her long and well-lived life was still alive, and who had passed on decades ago. Ed, too, seemed to be struggling to separate fiction from reality, his ghost memories from his more recent ones.

"A lot of people died here." Ed's voice creaked like a rusty door hinge. He squinted at a bulge in the ceiling, brown with water damage, that looked like it was about to pop. "Terrible, horrible deaths."

"Mr. Shoal, why don't I take you home?" Brett suggested, reaching for his elbow. "We can make some tea and talk out of the rain."

There really was no point in questioning the poor man in weather like this, in a crumbled down old building that was on the verge of collapse. The questions she needed to ask could wait until they were in a warm room with hot drinks in hand.

But Ed shook her off. "Quickly now, before they take her eyes."

He spun away and shuffled through an opening at the end of the hall that used to be a doorway. Brett hurried after him, worried now that he might hurt himself, so deeply was he immersed in his own strange fantasy.

She noticed the birds when she stepped outside again. They circled like black kites against the ash-dull clouds, tracing wide loops above a nearby stand of trees. Brett had spent enough time birdwatching with Irving over the past year to know that these were turkey vultures. A bird that typically fed on carrion, vultures were drawn to a location by the scent of something freshly dead. Two more appeared, materializing from the gray mist and sweeping in on silent wings to join the others.

The rain didn't seem to bother them.

The rain didn't seem to bother the flies either.

As Brett stepped into the clump of pine trees, the air turned thick with their rising and falling peppercorn bodies. The sound of their wings was a persistent and high-pitched drone. One fly landed on Brett's arm and crawled toward her elbow. She swatted it away.

A knot formed in her stomach as she moved closer to where Ed had stopped to look at something lying at his feet.

Brett didn't need to touch the girl to know she was dead, but she knelt anyway and pressed two fingers to ice cold skin. The flies were here, too, crawling over the girl's marbled hands and blue-veined face, slipping through the narrow gap of her violet lips, avoiding the fat rain drops splashing down around them.

The girl was lying on her back in the dirt. A black scarf covered her eyes. A white rose with delicate, red-trimmed petals had been laid across her chest where blood blossomed through her light-blue shirt. Her hands lay at her side, spread open, facing the sky. Mud streaked her jeans. One shoelace had come untied.

"I didn't touch her."

Ed's voice startled Brett.

She was so focused on the body and the details, she forgot he was even standing there. She rose to her feet again, her knees popping. Her mind whirred with the myriad tasks she needed to do in the next few hours: secure the scene, call for backup, call the medical examiner, identify the victim, find out what the hell happened out here last night. First, she needed to get Ed somewhere safe and dry.

She took the older man by the arm and guided him away from the body, back to the ruins where he could take shelter out of the rain until another officer could come and take him home. As they walked, Brett unclipped her radio from her belt and called in the code to dispatch.

"Do you feel that?" Ed asked as Brett got him settled in a room with an intact ceiling and four solid walls. It looked like it might have been an office once, not so long ago. There was an empty filing cabinet in one corner and a metal folding chair that creaked when Ed sat down, but held firm under his weight.

"Feel what, Mr. Shoal?" Brett asked. The only thing she felt right now was a damp chill all the way to her underwear from standing too long in the rain and a sickening dread growing in the pit of her stomach over how quickly this day had turned sour.

Ed Shoal looked over her shoulder like someone had entered the room behind her, but when she turned, the doorway stood empty.

"You must feel that." He breathed out a white puff of air and said, "She's still with us." He pressed one finger to his lips. "If you're quiet you can hear her rage."

Outside, the wind howled through the trees.

CHAPTER 3

Officer Eli Miller was the first to arrive on scene. Over the radio, Brett gave him directions for where to find her. While she waited, she studied the ground around the body, noting two different boot prints pressed into the fresh mud, protected from the worst of the rain by a thick canopy of pine branches. There were also several drag marks leading from the ruins into the trees. She'd have Eli place markers on the prints first thing when he arrived with the equipment.

She walked deeper into the trees, looking for other evidence as well as for trails or access roads a person could use to get to this part of the peninsula. The underbrush quickly tangled underfoot, becoming impassable.

The radio on her hip crackled, and Eli's voice pierced the silence, "I'm here. Where are you?"

Brett walked back to where Eli waited near the body. He held a roll of yellow tape in one hand and a tarp in the other. An opaque poncho billowed around his broad shoulders. The hem of the poncho hit a few inches above his knees. Below that, mud splattered his dark slacks and caked the heels of his boots. He wore a Crestwood PD navy ball cap pulled low over his eyes.

"God, this is miserable." He squinted at the clouds, then dropped his gaze back to Brett, the hint of a smile forming on his lips as he leaned in to try and kiss her.

Brett took a step back and held her hand out to stop him. "I told you already. Not while we're at work."

He blushed and ducked his head. Twin dimples creased his lightly-tanned cheeks as his smile widened. "I'm sorry. I can't stop thinking about last weekend."

She glanced around, grateful to see it was still just the two of them.

Any second this peninsula would be crawling with cops, and the last thing Brett wanted was for everyone in the department to find out she was dating one of them. Sort of dating. If hanging out with a guy twice and kissing him once could be considered dating. Whatever she and Eli were doing, no one else needed to know about it. Especially not today, not here, with a dead girl lying steps from where they were standing.

She grabbed the tape from Eli and began tying a perimeter. "Get that tarp up before we lose any more evidence. And watch where you put your feet."

Keeping his eyes fixed on the ground, he carried the tarp over to the body.

"O'Reilly, Billy, and Ennis are a few minutes behind me," he said, referring to three dayshift patrol officers Brett knew in passing. "Charlie was across town when dispatch called it in, but he said he'd get here as soon as he could."

Charlie was Charles Hadley, the medical examiner, a man who had been tending to Whatcom County's dead for nearly half a century. The body would need to be protected as best as possible until he arrived. Brett finished stringing the perimeter and went to help Eli. She grabbed rope from a pile of equipment he'd brought with him and looped it between two trees while Eli shook out the tarp. Then she grabbed one end, and with Eli on the other, they stretched the plastic carefully over the rope to form a rudimentary tent.

"I'm not sure what good this is going to do us now." Eli frowned at the body. "She's probably been out here all night."

"You came out here, though, didn't you?" Brett tugged the tarp to make sure it was tight and didn't slip off the rope in a gust of wind.

"Not here, no," he admitted. "I stayed in the parking lot and just searched that area of the park. The report that came in last night was that Ed Shoal saw someone at Deadman's Point. And when I talked to Ed, well, he acted like I was the crazy one. I didn't even know this spot was back here." He glanced over his shoulder at the ruins where Ed Shoal waited, silhouetted in an empty window frame and still as stone. "What did Ed have to say?"

"Not much," Brett said.

She tried asking him a few questions about the dead girl—*Did he know her? Had he been here when she died?*—but this made him more agitated. He rambled on about ghosts and fog and how people shouldn't go walking at night. Nothing that was of any use to the case.

Brett hadn't pushed him.

Ed Shoal saw something out here last night—that much was obvious. But whether he was experiencing health issues that made it hard to separate facts from the haze of his fantasies or being deliberately stubborn were not questions Brett wanted to delve into while the rain washed away good evidence. Sorting through Ed's convoluted memories would have to wait until she was in a warm, dry room, with a hot cup of coffee in her hands.

"He seems confused," Brett told Eli. "I don't think he had anything to do with this, but we'll need to question him some more, see if we can figure out exactly what he saw last night. If he saw anything we can separate from his ghost stories. Do you know if he has family around?"

Eli shook his head. "I think he has a son who lives on the East Coast or in Florida or something. As far as I know, he lives alone. You think there was any truth to his original call? About seeing two people walk off the cliff?"

They left the trees and crossed to where the land fell into the ocean. Monster waves rose, churning foam and pummeling the jagged rocks below.

"If this storm ever lets up, we can send a boat out to see if there's anyone down there," Eli suggested.

Though they both knew that if anyone had gone over the edge last night, they wouldn't have survived; the body would have been sucked out to sea in seconds.

Loud voices echoed across the peninsula as three patrol officers appeared, pushing through the brush and cursing the rain. They wore ponchos and hats and carried more equipment.

Brett and Eli greeted them in front of the ruins.

One of the men said, "Sergeant Harris and Detective Winters are right behind us with Charlie."

Seconds later, the three older men appeared in the clearing, hurrying to join the rest of the group. They were a study in contrasts. Irving Winters was the tallest, darkest, and thickest around the middle. His face was clean-shaven, his rich brown skin damp with rain. Droplets clung to his short, black hair and turned the dusting of gray at his temples a shimmering platinum. Wes Harris was about a foot shorter than Irving, with a ruddy, beige complexion and wavy, auburn hair. His shoulders were broad, but his waist was slim. He smoothed stubby fingers over a thick, but neatly-trimmed painters' mustache that covered most of his upper lip. Then there was Charles Hadley, the oldest of the group, the shortest, the skinniest, and the palest, a man pushing seventy with a crown of frizzy white hair perched atop a deeply lined face. He wore a windbreaker and khaki pants and carried something that looked like a tackle box.

"Let's hurry up with this one," Charlie said, his voice scratchy. "I don't want to be out in this torrent any longer than I have to be. I just got over a bad bout of pneumonia, sure as heck don't need another."

He stepped under the yellow tape. Brett, Irving, and Wes followed him. The four patrol officers, including Eli, stayed outside the perimeter.

When they reached the body, Wes was the first to speak.

"Ah, hell." The two words seemed to slip out by accident.

Charlie set his kit down and pulled out several pairs of latex gloves, which he handed around to everyone. "Anyone take pictures yet?"

Irving took a 35mm Canon from under his gray trench coat where he'd been keeping it protected from the rain. Shutter clicks filled the silence as he moved around the body, taking multiple pictures from different angles. When he was finished with the body, he started taking pictures of the surrounding area, including the shoe prints and drag marks Brett had noticed earlier.

Charlie pulled on his gloves and crouched beside the body.

Wes slipped his gloves on, too, and cleared his throat. "I hate this part."

Charlie removed the scarf from her face.

Brett hadn't realized until this very second that she'd been hoping the victim would be from out of town, someone she didn't know, a tourist or a hitchhiker who found herself in the wrong place at the wrong time. She didn't want this body to be local. Local meant personal, and personal meant complicated, and complicated was exactly what this case was going to be.

Brett wasn't the only one who recognized the girl.

Wes sucked in a sharp breath and turned away. Irving, who had come back to take pictures of her face, muttered something—a prayer or a curse—under his breath, and his hands shook as he snapped a few close-up shots.

So much for an easy close, Brett thought as she swatted away another fly.

Gloves on, she took the scarf from Charlie and bagged it. He handed her the rose, too, which went into its own bag. Each new piece twisted the case into something ever more complicated.

"She was shot through the chest," Charlie said bluntly, pointing at the dark stain dampening her shirt. "I suppose that's what killed her, but don't go putting that into any official reports until I finish my examination." He studied the body for a minute, then added, "I guess we can be happy about one thing."

"What's that?" Wes asked.

"All of her clothes are still on, buttoned and tied and cinched," Charlie said. "Whoever did this to her, it doesn't appear to be sexually motivated. 'Course, I could be wrong about that, too. The body will tell us the story."

He went back to work, picking up bugs with tweezers and putting them into small jars, scanning for other injuries or evidence. He unfolded a body bag and spread it on the ground beside the girl.

"Well, Buchanan..." Sergeant Harris called his officers by their last names whether they liked it or not. "Why don't you start from the beginning since you didn't bother briefing me about this case before you left this morning."

Welcoming the distraction, Brett didn't bother pointing out the fact that she had stopped by his office, but he wasn't there. She wanted a better relationship with her new sergeant than she had with her old one, she wanted an ally not an enemy, and that meant letting go of small things like this—even if she was right.

Brett detailed her actions from the minute she left the precinct all the way to Sergeant Harris' arrival on the scene.

Wes listened closely. When she mentioned Ed Shoal, his eyes flicked over her shoulder to the ruins where Ed was still waiting for someone to talk with him. "Did he see anything?"

"We're trying to figure that out."

"He's being uncooperative?"

"Not exactly." Brett explained how Ed Shoal might be suffering from some kind of memory loss or delusional hallucinations.

"So, he's saying a ghost did this? Is that what you're telling me?" Wes' mustache twitched when he frowned.

"He saw something out here last night," Brett said. "But he's having a hard time sorting out what's reality and what's not."

"Well, let's get him home and get him warmed up, see if that doesn't help shake something loose." Wes snapped his fingers at one of the patrol officers. He met the young man at the perimeter tape and spoke quietly to him, gesturing to where Ed Shoal waited.

The patrol officer nodded and trotted off to collect the older man and take him home.

Wes turned to the other officers still waiting. "Cooper and Jones, I want you to help Charlie carry the body out to the van, then I want you back here scouring these woods for anything that looks like evidence. Miller, I want you and Winters to go through that building inch by inch. You know the routine. Take pictures of everything. Holler if you find something important. It would be great if we could find the gun before it gets dark." He scanned the sky then checked his watch. "We've got about five hours of daylight, six before we'll need flashlights. Let's not waste any more time picking the lint from our navels, right?"

He clapped his hands, and the men got to work.

Wes snapped his back attention to Brett. "I need you to inform the family. Can you do that?"

She nodded, already dreading the conversation with the girl's parents, but happy to have an excuse to finally get out of the incessant rain.

"Handle them like porcelain for now, until we have more concrete answers. And see if you can find out the last time anyone saw her alive," Wes said. "When you're done there, head back to the station and start setting up a conference room. I want us three steps ahead on this one. I'll radio the chief, let him know what's coming."

He glanced to where Charlie was zipping the girl into the body bag. The medical examiner worked carefully, tucking away the white-blond strands of her hair to keep them from snagging in the metallic teeth.

"What a fucking waste," Wes said through gritted teeth. He jerked his chin at Brett. "Well, what the hell are you standing around here for? A girl is dead, Buchanan. If that doesn't light a fire under your ass, I'm not sure what will."

By the time Brett got to the parking lot, she was shivering. She turned the heater on full blast and sat a minute waiting for the ice in her bones to thaw. Her thoughts kept returning to the image of the girl stretched out on her back, her eyes covered, a rose resting on her chest, her white-blond hair in stark contrast to the muddy earth.

It was all so familiar.

Another shiver ran through Brett, but this time it had nothing to do with the cold. Somewhere in the back of her mind, she'd always known there was something wrong with this town. Crestwood seemed friendly enough from the outside, but a closer look revealed the whole place was rotten straight through to its core.

Before she could put the car in reverse and head back into town, the radio on her belt crackled. The dispatcher's voice came through loud and clear. "Detective Buchanan, are you on?"

"I'm here, Freddie. Go ahead."

He had Brett switch to a private channel before he said, "I've got the principal from Crestwood High on hold. I was going to have her leave you a message, but it seems like something that can't wait."

There was a pause, a flood of static, then the dispatcher continued, "She says your grandmother's there right now, at the school, waiting to be picked up?"

He sounded confused.

Brett didn't explain anything to him. She said, "Okay, yeah. Tell Principal London I'll be there in a few minutes. I'm headed back from Deadman's Point right now. Thanks, Freddie."

She signed off before the dispatcher could ask any more questions.

Amma had been completely fine this morning when Brett left for work. She'd been humming a song as she made coffee, chatting happily with their little dog Pistol who pranced underfoot hoping for treats. Everything seemed normal, but her grandmother's moods could change quickly. One minute, she'd be walking into the kitchen to make a sandwich; the next, Brett would find her plopped down on the floor surrounded by spoons and screaming about how someone had come in and stolen their silver. With each passing day, Amma was becoming more and more like the ocean, tempestuous and unpredictable.

There wasn't a single, good reason that Brett could think of for why Amma would be at the high school today. Which meant somewhere in the three hours since Brett had left for work, Amma had gotten lost in her own mind and wandered away from home. The fact that she'd ended up somewhere safe like the high school, with someone who was well-practiced at handling small emergencies, was a minor miracle. But Brett couldn't leave Amma there. Principal London had better things to do than babysit a confused old woman.

Brett thumped her hands on the steering wheel in frustration. Amma couldn't have picked a worse time to need her.

CHAPTER 4

Lizzie Trudeau pulled down a handful of orange and black Halloween streamers hanging above June's locker. She crumpled the fragile paper in her fist as she waited for her best friend to appear around the corner. Cardboard jack-o-lanterns covered the walls and tissue-paper ghosts floated from the ceiling. The school janitors would take down the decorations over the weekend, and eventually the hallways would become a mess of colorful fall leaves and overflowing Thanksgiving cornucopias, but for one more day Crestwood High could stay spun out on candy and ghost stories.

Leaning against June's locker, Lizzie drew the hood of her sweatshirt up to block the too-bright fluorescent lights and the clamor of students starting to fill the hallways.

Last night, after she left June and Daniel at the ruins, she'd been too much of a coward to skip town on her own. She'd gone home thinking the rest of them would eventually do the same.

Leave together or don't leave at all—that had always been their plan.

But the longer Lizzie waited for June by her locker, the more she worried that Adam had shown up after she bailed and the three of them had gone to Seattle without her.

A burst of laughter drew Lizzie's attention to the far end of the hall where five girls walked together in a crowded pack. They layered on lip gloss and flipped their hair as they giggled about something. They were all dressed the same, in high-waisted blue jeans and brightly colored pullovers with sleeves slouching off their shoulders. Their hair was varying shades of blond and crimped or teased high. It was hard to tell one Barbie from another.

As they got closer to Lizzie, their eyes swept over her. They tilted their heads together, whispering quietly. Lizzie pressed herself against the locker. They were predators. If she didn't move, maybe they'd leave her alone.

They brushed past, and Lizzie thought she'd gotten off easy today until a girl wearing hot pink cowboy boots called over her shoulder, "Hey, Lizard Breath, have you killed anyone today?"

"Be careful, Mariah," another Barbie said to the girl in pink cowboy boots. "You know what happens when she tattles to Mommy Dearest."

The girl laughed and made a slashing motion through the air like she was stabbing someone with a knife. The other girls exploded in a fit of giggles. One held up her fingers in a cross shape and pointed it at Lizzie.

They knew her mother was dead. It had been all over the news and the only thing anyone in this stupid town wanted to talk about for months. Clara Trudeau, the killer housewife, Mommy Dearest. Clara Trudeau, who stabbed two men and almost got away with it. Her mother, who'd lived a lie for twenty years and would have gone on pretending for her entire life if the rest of the world hadn't discovered her dark secrets first.

The girls' laughter echoed down the hall for a long time after they walked away.

When it was clear they weren't coming back to torment her more, Lizzie lifted her fingers to her hair, tugging on the short strands. She'd taken a dull pair of scissors to it two months ago, hacking off a foot of the chestnut brown locks she'd been growing out since she was a kid. The drugstore hair dye stained the sink and her hands a purplish-black. Her grandmother cried when she saw what Lizzie had done. June had made a whimpering sound and said, *Oh, Lizzie, why would you do that to yourself? Your hair was so beautiful.*

But Lizzie liked it better this way. She thought the jagged ends and ink-black sheen made her look bad ass. Like a girl who could go anywhere, do anything, be anyone. A girl with plans and a life outside of this pathetic, fish-gut town. She was a girl reborn, one who looked nothing like her mother.

Some people thought Lizzie and her father should have known what kind of monster they were living with day after day; other people thought, *Like mother, like daughter.* And nothing Lizzie said or did could convince them how wrong they were about her. About all of it.

The first bell clattered. The noise in the hallway rose as students rushed to get to their homerooms. Lockers slammed. Shoes squeaked across the dingy, beige linoleum tiles. Voices clamored over top of each other, but none of them called out to Lizzie. In that moment, in the hum and sugar buzz of a post-Halloween Friday morning, Lizzie realized she could walk out of this school and no one would even miss her.

She shoved away from the locker and walked in the direction of the nearest exit.

As she passed the art room, she took a quick glance inside. Students filed in, but Daniel Yoon wasn't among them, which was odd. He was usually the first one at his desk every morning. His mom dropped him off on her way to work so he could spend an unbothered hour before class drawing his comics. The art room was the first place Lizzie looked when she wanted to find Daniel; before today, he'd never not been here.

Mr. Cadden wasn't at his desk yet either, which was less surprising. In addition to being Crestwood High School's most popular art teacher, Mr. Cadden was also the assistant soccer coach, and during the fall, the team had conditioning practice before school.

Lizzie had quit soccer last year, and while she had no regrets, sometimes she missed it. The smell of a fresh-cut field and the shrill *blat* of a referee's whistle. She missed the physicality of it, too, the sweat slicking her skin, her eyes tracking the ball, her muscles stretching as she moved her body to protect the goal, and hearing the cheers when she blocked a kick. Most of all, she missed being part of a team, of feeling like there was some place in this world she belonged. What she didn't miss, though, were conditioning practices, where Mr. Cadden leered from the bleachers and Coach Lansing ran them rain or shine, searing heat or blinding snow, until someone puked. She didn't miss that at all.

It occurred to Lizzie that the reason June hadn't been at her locker this morning was because of soccer practice. She'd stuck with the team even after Lizzie quit, and she was probably out there now, finishing up her laps, grabbing her gear and heading to the locker room to change. Lizzie didn't know why she hadn't thought of it earlier. June would never leave Crestwood unless Lizzie was by her side.

She hurried away from the art room, racing to the locker rooms instead, desperate in that moment to find her friend and confirm she hadn't been left behind.

Lost in thought, Lizzie didn't notice the teacher striding past her, hurrying to get to his classroom before the final bell rang.

"Elizabeth?" Mr. Cadden still called her by her full name, even though she asked him not to multiple times.

She stopped being Elizabeth last year when everything bad happened. Elizabeth was a girl she didn't recognize anymore. Elizabeth was from Before. She was Lizzie now—only Lizzie. Lizzie was who came After.

She stopped walking and turned to face him.

"Where are you going? Shouldn't you be in class right now?" As he said it, the bell clattered overhead.

From somewhere inside the school, a door slammed, and silence settled over them.

He stared at her, waiting for a response.

"Was June at practice this morning?" Lizzie asked.

A strange expression crossed over Mr. Cadden's face. "Do you have a hall pass? If you don't have a hall pass, I'm afraid I'm going to have to—"

Before he could finish the sentence, Lizzie turned away from him and continued her rush to the locker room. But Mr. Cadden was quick to catch up. He grabbed her arm.

"Don't touch me." Lizzie wrenched free.

"Let me see your hall pass." Mr. Cadden stared at her empty hands. His eyes flicked over her chest and down to her pants, eyeing her pockets. "You do have a pass, right? That's the only reason I can think of as to why you'd be trying to leave school before first period has even started."

Mr. Cadden was the youngest teacher at Crestwood High. He wore his jet-black hair slicked back at the sides with a devil-may-care swirl that fell across the middle of his forehead. He reminded Lizzie of Danny Zuko from the movie *Grease*. His green eyes were the color of moss that grew in sidewalk cracks, the color of the trees in summer. Lizzie had a crush on him once, like every other girl in this school, but not anymore. Now, she knew what a creep he was. Now, she wanted nothing to do with him.

"Come with me." He grabbed her elbow again, firmer this time, and dragged her away from the gymnasium, moving quickly toward the front of the school.

She struggled against him for a few seconds, then gave up. "Where are you taking me?"

"You want to act like a delinquent, then I'm going to treat you like a delinquent." He pulled her through the empty hallways toward the principal's office.

———————————

Lizzie waited in one of three chairs pressed against the wall of the reception area, where she was partially hidden from view by a large filing cabinet. From behind the principal's closed door, she could hear the murmur of voices. One she recognized as Principal London's voice—firm but calm. The other voice was unfamiliar, but sounded agitated.

Lizzie kicked her feet back and forth, scuffing her shoes across the linoleum. Mrs. Sharp, the school receptionist, glared at her over the tall stacks of paper piled on her desk. Lizzie sighed loudly and stopped kicking. She stared at the ceiling.

She could do it. She could still leave Crestwood. She didn't need Daniel or Adam or even June. She had a little money saved from birthdays and Christmases and doing barn chores for Grandpa. It wasn't much, but it was enough for a one-way bus ticket plus a little extra to keep her going for a few days until she found a job. She'd have to lie on applications, tell them she was sixteen instead of fifteen. But, so what? People lied all the time, and she'd do anything for the chance to start over in a place where no one knew her name and no one knew her mother.

Almost anything.

After close to an hour, Principal London's office door finally swung open. An ancient and fragile-looking woman shuffled into the reception area. Her short, silver hair stuck out in all directions, making her look a little like Einstein. The plush, navy-blue bathrobe and matching slippers she wore were damp and flecked with mud. Her brow rumpled with confusion when she saw Lizzie, and she turned to look at Principal London who was exiting the office behind her.

"You said my daughter wasn't here today." The old woman's voice crackled.

Principal London glanced at Lizzie, but didn't acknowledge her.

She kept a gentle hand on the old woman's elbow as she guided her through the office into the main hallway. "Like I said a few minutes ago, Mrs. Wilson, your *granddaughter* is coming to get you and take you home."

The old woman craned her neck around, her salt-blue eyes fixing on Lizzie again. "You have to be careful with those boys, Lydia. I've told you time and time again."

Lizzie slumped in the chair and dropped her gaze to her shoes, embarrassed for the old woman who had called her by someone else's name and didn't seem to be all there.

"Here we go, Mrs. Wilson." Principal London pulled her through the doorway. "Here's Brett now. Nothing to worry about, didn't I tell you?"

Lizzie raised her head. The filing cabinet blocked her view of the main office entry area, but if she leaned slightly forward, she could see out the open door. Water dripped from the detective's raincoat and mannish, brown slacks. Her hair was kinked in a funny way. Even though Lizzie hadn't seen Detective Buchanan in a few months, she recognized her right away. She would never forget the face of the woman who'd ruined her life.

Technically, what happened to her parents wasn't the detective's fault. She was just doing her job—that's what the psychologist Lizzie went to last year said anyway. The psychologist Grandma insisted Lizzie go to; the psychologist she saw for a sum total of three sessions before she realized what a huge waste of time it was.

Your parents made choices, the psychologist reminded her during every visit with a nasally voice that made Lizzie want to claw her ears off. *And choices have consequences. Blame should be reserved for the people who choose to do the wrong things, not the people trying to right those wrongs.*

Lizzie didn't care what the psychologist or her grandparents said. She could blame whomever she wanted. Detective Buchanan was there when her father was arrested and later sentenced to two years in prison; she was there when her mother went under the waves. No one in this town would have even known about all the terrible things Lizzie's mother had done if Detective Buchanan had minded her own business. They could have all gone on pretending to be happy.

"Thank you, Effy," Detective Buchanan said to Principal London in a breathless rush. "I would have gotten here sooner but I was tied up at work. I hope she wasn't too much trouble."

"No trouble at all," Principal London said, using the voice she used when talking to parents. "Just got a little turned around I think, isn't that right, Mrs. Wilson?"

The old woman muttered something Lizzie couldn't hear.

Detective Buchanan cleared her throat. "While I'm here, can I ask you to check a student's attendance records for me?"

"Certainly," Principal London said. "I hope everything's okay?"

The three women came back inside the office.

Lizzie pressed herself against the wall so that she was hidden behind the filing cabinet again, though neither Detective Buchanan nor Principal London bothered a glance in her direction. She couldn't see Mrs. Wilson from where she sat, but she could hear the older woman sigh loudly and ask how long this would take.

"I need a few more minutes, Amma," Detective Buchanan said.

"Mrs. Sharp." Principal London leaned one elbow on the front desk. "We need you to look up the records for..." She raised her eyebrows at Detective Buchanan. "Which student is it?"

"June Newmark."

Lizzie's heart sped up and her stomach somersaulted. She pressed back hard against the wall, trying to make herself even more invisible than she already was.

Mrs. Sharp rustled some papers on the desk.

"June Newmark? Are you sure that's right?" Concern edged Principal London's voice. "June is one of our best students. She never misses class."

Detective Buchanan ignored the principal's protests. "Can you tell me if she attended all her classes yesterday?"

"Yes," Mrs. Sharp said. "She was here all day. But…now…this is strange. Ms. Perkins marked her absent from homeroom this morning."

Principal London's neatly plucked eyebrows shot up. "There must be some mistake. Let me send someone to double-check. Which class is she supposed to be in right now, Mrs. Sharp?"

"That won't be necessary," Detective Buchanan spoke before Mrs. Sharp could answer. "And if I could also get her home address and phone number while I'm here, that would really save me some time."

There was something in the sound of her voice that raced chills through Lizzie. Principal London must have heard it, too, because her whole body went stiff.

"I don't like the look on your face, Detective," she said. "And I don't like these questions. Has something happened to June?"

Lizzie's leg bounced uncontrollably. She pressed her hand on her knee, and it stopped. She dropped her gaze to the floor. Her shoes were caked in mud, and bits of dirt were now sprinkled over the white tile.

"I'm afraid there's not much I can tell you right now," Detective Buchanan said with a formality that reminded Lizzie of the cops on television. "We still need to talk to her family."

"Oh!" The principal chirped like a startled bird.

Lizzie lifted her gaze. The room had turned colorless and

blurred, stuttering like an old movie. Mrs. Sharp grabbed a different folder from the shelf, opened it, and scribbled something onto a piece of paper. Principal London smoothed her hands down her pinstriped skirt and rolled her shoulders straight. She fussed with her raven-colored and ironed-straight bob, as if having every hair in place would help bring her emotions under control.

"How? Did it happen this morning? Should we…?" She looked around the office like she was missing something important. Her eyes skipped right over Lizzie for the third time that morning. "Are there any other students hurt?"

"As far as we know, there's no need to worry about any of the other students," Detective Buchanan reassured her. "Though, we may need to talk to some of them. To June's friends specifically. But that can wait until later. Right now—"

"But what happened?" Principal London cut her off, her voice sounding frantic. "They'll have questions. What should I tell them?" She fluttered her hand at Mrs. Sharp. "Get Shep down here. I think he still has a stack of grief brochures from last year with Zach. He'll know what to do."

Shep was the school guidance counselor and the teacher every girl had a crush on before Mr. Cadden showed up mid-semester last spring. Zach was a senior who—Zach was nobody to Lizzie anymore. After what he did to her at last year's Halloween party, she wasn't going to pretend to be upset he was dead.

"Slow down, Effy." Detective Buchanan's voice was firm as she put one hand on Principal London's shoulder, steadying the other woman. "It's best if you don't say or do anything right now. It's a delicate situation. The chief will probably hold a press conference in the next day or so. If you could hold off on planning anything or telling the kids anything until after that, it would really help me out here."

Principal London nodded and tugged her blouse straight. "Right, yes, of course. Whatever you need. I would like to prepare my staff at some point. We weren't prepared last year with Zach, and it turned into a huge mess."

"There'll be time for that," Detective Buchanan said. "But right now, I think what's most important is giving the family some space to grieve. And giving the rest of us some time to get organized. It would be nice to get our feet under us with this investigation first and have a few answers before the public starts asking questions."

"Investigation?" Principal London's voice pitched to panic again. "Wait, this wasn't an accident? I thought—" All the breath seemed to rush from her at once. "Not again. Do you know who? Do you have someone in custody already? Poor girl. That poor, poor girl."

"I'm sorry. There's nothing else I can share right now." Detective Buchanan took the scrap of paper Mrs. Sharp had laid on the desk between them and started to turn away. "And I really do need to get going. I need to get my grandmother home and get back to work. Thank you for your help today. With her. With everything."

At the last second, Principal London reached and grabbed the detective's hand. "You find whoever did this, okay? You find them."

Their eyes locked for a beat before they broke apart. Detective Buchanan led her grandmother out of the office. The sound of their shoes squeaking over the linoleum echoed for a few seconds after they were gone.

Finally, Mrs. Sharp's shrill voice broke the spell. "Effy, I don't understand. What's happening? What's happened with June?"

Principal London leaned both elbows on the counter and buried her face in her hands. "She's dead, Barb. June Newmark is dead."

———

Somehow Lizzie managed to rise on legs made of stone. Somehow she stumbled out of the front office without anyone noticing and made it to the nearest bathroom before she puked. Somehow she flushed the toilet and washed her face and walked out of the school and walked all four miles to her grandparents' ranch on the edge of town and in through the front door and up the staircase to her bedroom on the second floor before collapsing onto her bed. Somehow she fell asleep, and when she woke up again, her grandfather was sitting beside her, stroking her back and asking her what was wrong.

"Lizbug, are you sick?"

"No." The pillow muffled her voice.

"Kids picking on you again?"

She turned her head away from him. "I just want to be alone right now."

Rain slammed against the window pane like it was trying to break in.

She felt the bed shift as Grandpa rose to his feet with a groan. "These old knees."

She listened as he shuffled across the plush carpet to the door.

"Well, you know where to find me if you change your mind about talking," he said.

She waited to hear the sound of his slippers in the hallway, but he hovered in the doorway a few seconds longer, giving her time to tell him why she was curled up in bed during the middle of a school day, drenched through to the skin and shivering from cold.

When she said nothing, he sighed, shuffled back to her, and pulled a blanket around her shoulders, tucking it tight.

"I'll tell your grandmother you've got a stomach bug," he said as he left.

Lizzie watched the rain carve jagged lines down the window pane.

June Newmark is dead. She kept repeating the words, turning them over in her head, but no matter how many times she said it, she couldn't convince herself it was true.

Not June. June couldn't be dead. Not her June. Her best friend since kindergarten. The one person who really knew her. Who knew the Elizabeth Before, the happy girl who made daisy chains after soccer practice, sang into hairbrushes, and wore her long hair in pigtails, and only watched scary movies if she already knew the ending. And who knew the Lizzie After, a girl-monster made of broken glass and rusty nails and bitter nightmares, a hollowed-out creature who probably wasn't worth saving, but whom June loved anyway.

You couldn't get rid of me even if you tried.

Lizzie punched her fist into her pillow, then pressed her face into the soft middle to muffle her screams. It wasn't supposed to happen like this. The four of them wanted a fresh start. No one should have ended up dead.

CHAPTER 5

Amma didn't say a word to Brett until they pulled up to the house on Bayshore Drive. Her eyes were fixed on the ocean, when she said, "Looks like the gods woke up on the wrong side of the bed today."

The section of Sculpin Bay visible from the driveway was a churning cauldron of gray water and foaming, dark waves. The sky matched the waves, roiling gray and black and streaked with rain. Lightning flickered in the distance. The seagulls that usually hung out on the boathouse roof and dock pylons had done the smart thing and headed inland. The copper, whale-shaped wind vane that had been perched on the roof of Amma's house since before Brett was born, whirled in a frenzy, set in motion by strong onshore winds.

The storm seemed to be getting worse.

"Let's get you inside." Brett helped Amma out of the car.

It wasn't a very long walk to the front door, but they both ended up drenched.

Inside the house, a crooked-eared Chihuahua greeted them. Brett had adopted Pistol last year from a woman who wasn't taking good care of him. Adopted was a generous term. The truth was she'd taken the dog without asking. At the time it had felt like a way to grab back some small amount of control from a case that was spiraling into chaos. Later, feeling guilty, she tried to return the dog, but the woman didn't want him back. Instead, Brett had given her twenty dollars as payment, out of some sort of misplaced guilt about taking him in the first place.

Brett looked down at the little tan dog with the white star on his forehead, who was now dancing happily around their feet, wagging his tail furiously. It was the best twenty dollars Brett had ever spent.

Amma scooped Pistol into her arms and carried him to the kitchen. Brett shucked off her dripping wet jacket and muddy shoes before following them. She didn't have a lot of time to waste before her sergeant would start to wonder where she was, but she couldn't exactly leave Amma home alone now. Not after the adventure she'd been on this morning.

With half her body shoved inside the fridge, Amma rummaged through stacks of Tupperware and foil-wrapped foods. She grabbed a container of shredded chicken, opened it, and offered a piece to Pistol who snapped the meat from her fingers like he was starving. He wasn't. Brett had fed him a generous scoop of kibble this morning before she left for work.

"Have you eaten anything today?" Brett reached around Amma to grab a container of leftover spaghetti from the fridge. She'd had a quick piece of toast on her way out the door earlier, but hadn't eaten anything since and didn't know when she'd get a chance to eat again.

"I had coffee this morning," Amma said.

"That's not food."

"I know that." Her words were clipped.

Amma fed Pistol a second bite of chicken, then ate a piece herself. She didn't seem to notice that she'd left the refrigerator door standing open.

Brett shut it and put the leftover spaghetti in the microwave. As she waited for the food to reheat, she walked to the telephone hanging on the wall and dialed a number she knew by heart. "I'm going to see if Henry can come over this afternoon. I need to get back to work."

There were only a few people in Crestwood who knew about her grandmother's dementia, and even fewer Brett trusted to take care of her when she was having a bad day. Ex-police chief Henry Bascom was one of the people she trusted. He was the first to notice Amma's symptoms over a year ago, and the reason Brett had returned to Crestwood, even though it was the last place she ever thought she'd find herself. Henry had been helping out a lot with Amma since his forced retirement.

"Come on, Henry, pick up." Brett wasn't sure what she'd do if he didn't answer the phone. She couldn't stay home; not with the homicide that had just landed on her desk.

Amma's new doctor had warned Brett about trying to do all of this alone. *You're going to feel isolated, embarrassed, you're going to want to retreat. Don't. Let people in. Don't be afraid to ask for help.* She had shrugged off his advice, thinking she wouldn't need it yet, thinking they had months left, years even, before Amma would need more comprehensive care. Now, Brett wished she'd been more proactive about finding a nurse or someone else she could trust to stay with Amma while she was at work.

Just when Brett thought she'd have to take her grandmother with her to the precinct, Henry picked up. He promised he could be at the house in a half hour, which wasn't as fast as she'd hoped, but better than nothing.

After she hung up with Henry, she dialed the station's main number. "Freddie, are Sergeant Harris and the others back from Deadman's Point yet?"

"Nope." Freddie had an easy way of talking, like nothing in the world bothered him.

"Listen, can you get a conference room ready for that homicide we picked up this morning? Snag the good one, if it's open. Sergeant Harris asked me to do it after I spoke to the family, but I'm running a little late over here, and if the guys get back before I do, I want them going full speed on this one."

"Yeah, sure thing, no problem." There was a scratching sound like he was making notes on a piece of paper. Then he said, "While I've got you... A call came in about an hour ago. A woman says her son's missing. I tried sending a car over, but everyone is either tied up at Deadman's or responding to other calls. I wouldn't bother except he's a minor."

Brett's shoulders tensed. "How old?"

"Seventeen."

She relaxed slightly. A missing teenager was a very different kind of case than that of a missing toddler. "I'll swing by after I talk to the Newmark's. Maybe he'll be home by then. What's the name and address?"

She wrote both down and hung up the phone.

Amma, who had been standing behind her listening the whole time, said, "It was a full moon last week."

The microwave beeped. Brett pulled the leftovers from the microwave and divided the reheated food onto two plates. "What?"

"Bad things happen on a full moon." Amma set Pistol on the floor, but the dog stuck close to her heels. "I don't need a babysitter, by the way."

She flapped her hand at the phone.

"Henry's not a babysitter. He's your friend." Brett offered her a plate of steaming spaghetti, but Amma refused to take it.

"I know who he is," Amma snapped, opening the fridge again to look for something else to eat. "And I know he's not coming over here just to play Scrabble and watch soaps with me because he has nothing better to do."

"Remember what the doctor said, Amma? It's good to ask for help. And today we need help. Besides, you like Henry."

"I know I like Henry. I don't need you constantly reminding me about everything. I remember a lot. I remember more than you think I do." She pulled her head out of the fridge, forgetting again to shut the door, and shuffled out of the kitchen toward the stairs. As she headed up to her room, she called out, "You can't keep me a prisoner in this house forever."

Brett stepped over Pistol, who had plopped down at her feet to beg for food, and closed the fridge door for the second time.

Her gaze skimmed over a dozen, colorful paper scraps stuck with magnets to the white door. *Brush teeth after breakfast; take Pistol for a walk before lunch; Pistol gets a half scoop of food every day; buy milk, bread, and sponges; the mailman comes in the afternoon, except on Sundays; if you get confused, call Brett.* The phone number for the precinct was scrawled next to that one.

Amma had started leaving these reminders for herself a few months ago, but it was an imperfect system. Notes were added frequently but never removed because Amma was afraid of forgetting something, and if Brett tried to take down any that were no longer relevant, her grandmother would fly into a panic.

Brett brushed her fingers over a note she hadn't seen before: *Jimmy called for Brett.*

The message was written on a scrap of paper that had been hiding under a note about what to do with wilted lettuce, and Brett only saw it because when she closed the refrigerator door, one of the magnets shifted, revealing Jimmy's message.

Amma hadn't written down the date or time or why Jimmy called or whether he was expecting a call back. He could have called a day ago, a week ago, a month. And if it was that long ago and he'd been expecting a call back, then Brett had screwed up. Again.

Jimmy Eagan was a reporter for the *Oregonian* and Brett's best friend, or at least he used to be.

After saving her life last year, Jimmy had confessed he had

feelings for her that went beyond friendship. He'd offered to move to Crestwood, permanently, for her, for them, to start some kind of relationship. Brett cared deeply about Jimmy—there was no doubt in her mind about that. But she wasn't sure she could give him what he needed. She wasn't sure she was good relationship material for anyone, but especially not a nice guy like Jimmy. So she told him no, and sent him away, and ever since, things between them had been awkward.

They used to talk over the phone all the time—every week, sometimes twice—but it had been months since she'd heard his voice. She told herself it was because Jimmy was currently on the road, promoting his new book, and that once his life slowed down again, things between them could go back to how they used to be. But doubt tugged on her heart every day that passed not hearing from him. She was starting to believe he was deliberately avoiding her.

Now, finally, he'd called, and even though Brett didn't know when he'd called or what he was calling about, it felt like a step in the right direction. She pulled the note off the fridge and tucked it into her pocket. As soon as she had a minute to herself, she'd call Jimmy back.

She ate her lunch standing over the sink, staring out the window at the storm. Rain lashed the glass. The trees planted along the property line between Amma and the neighbor's house whipped back and forth. The normally docile bay looked angry enough to break free of its confines and devour the land. *Someday this will all be gone,* Brett thought. Someday the ocean would push back hard enough and win.

Henry arrived thirty minutes later, exactly when he said he would. He knocked on the front door twice, then let himself in. Pistol gave a few excited barks and rushed to greet the man.

When Brett came into the living room, she found Henry crouched on the floor, scratching Pistol behind the ears and cooing in a high-pitched voice. She cleared her throat. Henry flushed red all the way to the dome of his bald head. He rose and straightened the flannel shirt he was wearing.

"You're looking good, Henry." She said the same thing every time she saw him, whether he was dressed up or dressed down or had crumbs on the front of his shirt like he did today.

Retirement suited him. His movements were loose, his shoulders relaxed. He smiled more than he ever had when he was Chief of Police and laughed with the ease of someone who no longer bore the weight of a town on his shoulders.

Brett had worked under Henry for less than a year, but she had known him since she was a kid. Two decades older than her, Brett thought of Henry as an uncle. Neither of her parents had any siblings, and Henry's parents had been good friends with Amma and Pop. Over decades, the two families had become close. After his own parents died, Henry continued to spend weekends with Pop, sailing and fishing. Then, after Pop's heart attack, Henry started to check on Amma, taking her out for dinner or for strolls along the boardwalk when the weather was nice.

Henry was the first to notice Amma acting differently, the first to worry. Last year, he had called Brett to share his concerns and offer her a job. She'd moved here because of Henry. Because of Amma, technically, but she wasn't sure she would have even considered it if Henry hadn't offered her a transfer.

Brett still bristled over the argument they had last year where Henry confessed her title as detective was little more than window dressing, that he'd given her the job, not because he thought she deserved it, but because he knew she wouldn't have moved to Crestwood otherwise.

He wasn't wrong, but she didn't have to be happy about it.

She'd mostly forgiven him since. She was still a detective, wasn't she? She had a job that for the most part was interesting and challenging and offered her a steady paycheck. Not that she had many bills these days living with Amma, but it felt good to watch her savings grow. She didn't know what she was going to spend the money on, but it was nice to know it was there if she needed it.

Henry earned a little more forgiveness from her, too, every time he helped out with Amma. It didn't seem to matter what time she called—middle of the day, middle of the night, early mornings, weekends, holidays. If she asked for his help, Henry showed up. It was hard to stay mad at a man who was that reliable.

"How is she?" Henry gave Pistol one last scratch before rising to his feet again.

"No harm done. Except I think we're all feeling a little embarrassed. She's resting now."

"She walked all the way to the high school?"

"Apparently."

Henry let out a low whistle and stroked the ends of his white mustache. His eyes darted toward the staircase. "Did she tell you why she thought she needed to be there?"

"Not yet. She hasn't said much to me about it at all. Maybe you can get something more out of her." Brett shrugged. "I'm not sure the 'why' matters very much, though. The doctor warned us that the things she does will start to make less and less sense to us the more she deteriorates."

Amma was seeing a neurologist out of Seattle. There wasn't much he could tell them beyond the obvious diagnosis of age-related dementia. And he didn't have much to recommend in the way of treatment. Establishing routines, simplifying tasks, exercise. There'd been some discussion that her dementia might be related to Alzheimer's, but it was hard to know for certain. Not that there was treatment for that either. The medical community was barely scratching the surface as far as research and treatment options for the disease, but the doctor was hopeful. Every day they were learning something new and trials were being conducted for new medications. If Amma could hold on until there was some miracle breakthrough, perhaps they could slow her symptoms. But to what end, Brett sometimes wondered.

Amma was in her eighties. She'd lived a long life, a good life for the most part. She had survived so much. Two World Wars. The Great Depression. Her own illnesses and tragedies—her granddaughter murdered, her daughter dead five years after that, her husband passed after sixty long years of marriage. But there had been victories too, happy memories to brush light through the dark. Brett didn't know how much longer her grandmother had left on this earth, but she wished those years could be something more than this slow decline.

Keep her calm, the doctor recommended. *Try not to fight with her. Give her tasks to stay busy. Try to keep her connected to the present as much as you can.* It wasn't much as far as advice went, but it was something. And at least Amma was seeing a doctor now. Last year, Brett couldn't even get her to acknowledge there was a problem. So they were making progress, however slow.

Henry slipped off his shoes and hung his windbreaker next to Brett's jacket. Water dripped off the sleeves.

"It's really coming down out there." He squinted out the living room window to the gray sheets streaming off the eaves. "Haven't seen a storm blow up like this in years."

The second-floor landing creaked, and Amma appeared at the top of the stairs. She'd showered and changed into a nice blouse and slacks. She used the handrail to make her way down to where Henry was waiting with one arm extended to take her elbow and guide her like a debutante across a dance floor. He swept her into the living room and settled her on the couch, spreading a blanket over her lap and tucking it around her legs.

"I heard you had quite the adventure this morning, Anita."

Amma patted her hair, which she'd combed into a neat side part. "The doctor told me to take more walks."

"Did he now?" Henry turned on the television and changed it to Amma's favorite station, then scooped up Pistol and set the dog on Amma's lap. Pistol curled into a ball and fell asleep.

"How about some peppermint tea?" Henry asked her.

"I think I would prefer hot cocoa," Amma said.

"Hot cocoa it is." Henry started toward the kitchen, calling over his shoulder, "With marshmallows?"

"If you even have to ask, I'm not sure I want you coming over here anymore," Amma teased him.

In the kitchen, Henry moved around Brett like he was the one who lived here, not her. He filled the kettle with water, dug through a cupboard for cocoa powder, and knew exactly where to find marshmallows Brett didn't even know they had.

"I suppose her wandering off in the middle of the day is better than the night walks she was going on last month," Henry spoke in a quiet voice as he prepared the cocoa.

"I don't know." Brett leaned against the counter and folded her arms over her chest. "At night, at least, I'm here with her. So she never gets too far."

She thought of last year, when Amma's symptoms weren't as bad as they were now and she'd wandered off for the first time. Eli had found her walking along the side of the highway, being buffeted by semi-trucks, weaving into traffic. She'd come close to being killed then. Brett wondered how close to death she'd been today.

Henry laid his hand on Brett's shoulder. "You're doing the best you can."

Brett laughed quietly and shook her head. "If this is my best, I don't want to see my worst."

"You're doing fine," he insisted, the pressure of his hand

growing heavier. Then he lifted it and turned back to the kettle heating on the stove. He changed the subject. "How's the new boss?"

"Which one?"

"Well, both I guess." He poured boiling water into the cups with a splash of warm milk and stirred the cocoa powder smooth.

"I think Wes Harris and I will get along fine," Brett said. "He seems like he knows what he's doing. And he doesn't immediately dismiss me because I'm a woman." Then she shrugged. "You already know my feelings about Stan."

Henry grunted in a sympathetic way.

The newly elected mayor came down hard on Henry last year after new details surrounding the Margot Buchanan case came to light. The original investigation in 1964 was filled with missteps and oversights. The work was sloppy. Even Henry admitted that. A murderer had lived among the residents of Crestwood undetected for twenty years; and that entire time Henry Bascom had been working as Chief of Police. Failing as Chief of Police, was what the mayor had told the *Crestwood Tribune*.

Henry had been moving toward retirement anyway, but he could have worked a few more years if the mayor hadn't pushed him out early under the pretense of wanting to establish a safer community.

We need someone running the department who is going to take law and order as seriously as I do, the mayor had stated when word came down that Henry was leaving the position of chief and Stan Harcourt was stepping in to take his place.

The irony wasn't lost on Brett that the mayor promoted the very same man who had bungled her sister's case so badly twenty years ago. Stan Harcourt didn't give two shits about law and order. But he did play golf with the mayor, and their wives attended the same book club, and, apparently, that was all the experience you needed to get a promotion in this town.

"Is he treating you okay?" Henry asked.

"Stan?"

Henry nodded.

"He ignores me most of the time, which honestly, is preferable. I've seen the kind of shit he's shoveling in Irving's direction, and I think I'm getting off pretty easy."

She darted a glance at her wristwatch, a gift from her grandparents on her fourteenth birthday, the same year her sister died. It was a simple gold band with small diamonds surrounding the bezel and a mother-of-pearl dial, each tick reminding her that bad days didn't last forever. The good days didn't last, though, either, did they? Every minute marching into the next with barely a second to breathe.

"Speaking of work," she said. "I really have to get back. We caught a bad one this morning."

Henry arched his eyebrows. "Anyone I know?"

"It's still too early to talk about it."

"What? You think I'm going to run straight to the papers with it?" He snorted as he dropped a handful of marshmallows into Amma's mug. "You know I can't stand those scavengers, ripping into people's lives the way they do."

Brett thought of the vultures circling June Newmark's body, the damage they would have done if Brett hadn't found her.

Henry must have recognized something in her expression, because he said, "What are you standing around here for, then? If this is as important of a case as your face says it is, you should have left five minutes ago."

He grabbed the mugs of hot cocoa and herded Brett toward the front door. "Don't worry a stitch about us old folks. Anita here will keep an eye on me and see that I stay out of trouble. Isn't that right, Anita?"

Amma sniffed a disgruntled laugh and took a sip of cocoa. "You can start by getting me more marshmallows."

CHAPTER 6

Shirley Newmark took one look at Brett standing on the porch of her idyllic brick mansion and said, "It's June, isn't it? Something's happened to my baby."

Brett barely managed to get the words out before Shirley crumpled to the floor, screaming. The sound of her breaking heart ricocheted through the grand foyer, echoing off the cold tile.

Brett crouched beside the smaller woman and stroked her heaving shoulders. "Is there someone I can call?"

Shirley just kept crying, choking on her grief, inconsolable.

A plump woman in a gray dress and white apron came running from another room, her eyes wide with panic at the sight of her employer crushed under the weight of such immense grief, sprawled over the front stoop like a broken doll.

"Help me get her inside." Brett grabbed Shirley under one arm and gestured for the housekeeper to do the same.

They half-dragged, half-carried the sobbing woman into the closest room and laid her down on an expensive-looking sofa.

"Is there anyone else home?" Brett asked the housekeeper who was wringing her hands in her apron.

The woman shook her head.

"Mr. Newmark?" Brett asked.

"At work. I'll call him." The housekeeper disappeared into another room.

Brett kneeled beside the couch and tried to get Shirley to talk to her. "The sooner we find out where June was last night and who she was with, the sooner we'll be able to find out what happened to her."

The words made Shirley sob harder. She turned her head away and buried her face into a velvet throw pillow.

Brett rose to her feet and went to look for the housekeeper, meeting her coming down the hallway.

"Mr. Newmark is on his way," the woman said primly, tilting her chin up as if to keep herself from crying.

"Do you live here, too?" Brett asked her.

The woman shook her head. "I come in the mornings to help Mrs. Newmark around the house. I leave in the afternoon whenever she runs out of things for me to do."

"What time did you leave yesterday?"

"One-thirty," the housekeeper answered. The woman didn't seem to know what to do or how to stand. She kept shifting her weight on the balls of her feet, rising up on her toes and falling down again, twisting at the hips like there were bugs in her stockings making her itch.

"Did you interact with June at all yesterday?" Brett asked. "Did you talk to her? See her? Do you know where she was supposed to be last night? If she was going out with friends?"

The housekeeper shook her head and, with bitterness in her voice, said, "I hardly ever see that child. She's off to school before I get here and doesn't come home until well after I'm already gone. I was hired to clean and cook, not keep track of everyone's comings and goings."

"Do you clean her room?"

The housekeeper shook her head a second time. "Mr. New-mark wants his children to learn responsibility."

Brett checked her watch. It was almost 3:00 PM, and she still needed to talk to the mother who'd reported her son missing before heading back to the station. She hoped the rest of the team was having better luck than she was.

It didn't sound like the sobbing in the other room would be slowing down anytime soon. Shirley Newmark was impossible to talk to in her current state and holding her hand while she cried wasn't going to help the woman feel any better about the loss of her child. What she needed was answers. The best thing Brett could do for this shattered woman right now was go out and find the person who killed her daughter.

Brett slipped a business card from her pocket and handed it to the housekeeper. "Will you please tell Mr. Newmark that we'll be sending someone over later today to talk with him and his wife?"

The housekeeper looked horrified at the thought of being left alone with the wailing mother, but took the business card and nodded politely before showing Brett to the door.

———

Patricia Yoon's house was on the exact opposite side of town as the Newmark's. It was a duplex with a small, fenced yard and a beige sedan parked in the driveway. The front door opened as soon as Brett parked on the curb, and a short woman wearing a lilac skirt and matching lilac blazer stepped onto the small, concrete porch. Her smooth brow furrowed with suspicion as Brett came up the walkway.

Brett was in plain clothes, brown slacks and a collared shirt beneath a bulky rain jacket, and the badge she wore on her belt was hidden somewhere underneath all that, too. She knew she wasn't who people expected to show up on their doorsteps when they called the police for help.

"Hi, there. I'm Detective Buchanan," Brett spoke first, then stuck out her hand.

The woman ignored the gesture, her scowl deepening.

Brett fumbled under her jacket for her badge. Only when she held that out, did the woman nod once and step into the house, gesturing for Brett to follow her inside.

"Thank you for coming." Her voice was stiff, almost formal. She had a slight accent. "My son did not come home last night, and I am worried something's happened to him."

Patricia led Brett into the dimly lit house. It was small, the walls close, the ceiling low, but there was a coziness to it, a feeling of being in a warm cabin on a rainy day. The furniture was minimalist beige and tan with pops of color. A bright red throw pillow. A floral orange and pink blanket. A painting hanging in a prominent place above the couch drew Brett's gaze.

A sprawling apple tree was painted in the center of a green and purple field. The branches were heavy with bright red apples. The play of shadow, light, and color gave the effect of motion, as if the branches were swaying, the clouds passing overhead, the grass rustling. Brett could almost hear the birds, the sigh of wind, the shout of a child just out of sight, a mother humming as she walked toward the tree, a basket for picking slung over one arm.

"Daniel painted that. My son," Patricia said. Her chin tilted as she spoke, her voice was thick with pride. "It is the tree that grew behind our house when we lived in Yakima. He has an eye for the light and shadow, his teachers say. He has always been talented this way. Even as a young boy."

Patricia seemed to remember why Brett was here. She clasped her hands together at her waist. "Please, sit down. Can I get you something to drink?"

Brett shook her head and lowered herself onto the couch, taking her notebook from her pocket and opening it to a blank page, eager to get this done so she could get back to the precinct and find out if any progress had been made with June Newmark's case. "Why don't you tell me about your son, why you think he's missing?"

Patricia perched on the chair opposite Brett. She sat with her shoulders rigid and her feet neatly crossed at the ankles. Her lilac skirt inched up to mid-calf revealing a small tear in her beige nylons. "I went to wake him for school this morning, and he wasn't there."

"When did you see him last?"

"Last night," Patricia said. "He works at the Blue Whale Diner. His shift ends at eight. He was home by eight-fifteen. He brought me a slice of cherry pie. He always brings me cherry pie. He knows it's my favorite."

"So, he brought the pie home around eight-fifteen and then what?"

Brett jotted notes as Patricia spoke. "I ate the pie. We watched *Cheers* together. When the show ended, he went to his bedroom."

"Did you see him again after that?"

Patricia shook her head. "The light under his door was on when I went to my bedroom later. I tapped and told him not to stay up too late."

"Did he answer you?"

She shook her head again and stared at her lap in despair. "I thought he had fallen asleep with the light on."

"You didn't open the door to check?"

"I had no reason to think he wasn't there. He's never done anything like this before. He's a good boy. He follows the rules. It was a school night. He does not go out on school nights." She twisted a gold band around the ring finger on her left hand as she spoke.

"His father," Brett asked, "is he around? Could Daniel have gone somewhere with him?"

Patricia covered her ring with one hand. "No."

Brett waited for her to elaborate, but she stared at the worn carpet at her feet and said nothing.

"Tell me about this morning," Brett prompted her. "You said you went to wake him up for school, and that's when you realized he wasn't in his room?"

"Normally, I take him to school on my way to work," Patricia said. "He likes to go early and draw before classes start. And he is good about waking himself and getting ready so I am not late. But this morning, he did not come out of his bedroom to shower at his usual time. He did not come into the kitchen for breakfast. It was time to go, and Daniel was not ready. I went into his room to wake him up, but he wasn't there. His bed was made. It looked like he hadn't even slept in it. The light was still on. I don't think he ever turned it off."

"And he didn't tell you he was going out last night?" Brett asked. "Or that he was going to get up early and leave before you did?"

"I wouldn't have called the police if he had." Her words were sharp with impatience. "This is not like Daniel. He is a good boy. He does not stay out late at night. He does not go places without telling me where and when he'll be back."

Most parents who thought their children were good knew nothing about what their children actually did all day or the kind of mischief they so easily got into.

"Does Daniel have a car, Mrs. Yoon?" Brett asked. "Does he drive?"

"No. He walks. Or I give him rides. Sometimes he takes the bus. He is saving money for school. He's going to Harvard." The last sentence was said with immense pride in her voice.

"What about friends?" Brett asked. "Have you called any of them to see if he stayed over last night?"

"I called a few parents of boys Daniel has brought to the house before, but no one has seen him," Patricia said. "I called the school, too. He wasn't there. I called the diner. He is nowhere. After that, I called the police because this is not like Daniel. He would tell me if he was going to be staying with someone else. He always tells me where he is."

"He's a student at Crestwood High?"

Patricia nodded. "A senior. He skipped second grade. He's a very smart boy."

Brett rested the pen across her notebook and leaned slightly forward, keeping her voice as neutral as possible, knowing she needed to ask but doubting she'd get the answer she wanted. "Mrs. Yoon, do you know a girl named June Newmark?"

The woman's brow furrowed in thought. She shook her head. "I have never heard that name, no."

"And Daniel doesn't have a girlfriend? No one he's dating?"

Patricia shook her head even harder, the sleek black strands of her neat bob swishing around her chin. "No. No, girlfriend. He does not have time for dating. He is focused on school, on his art. He is too young for a girlfriend."

Her voice quavered. She touched her fingers to her throat. "Please, can you find him? I have a bad feeling." She pressed her knuckles into her stomach as her eyes drifted to the small window that looked almost directly into a neighbor's house. "If he was fine, he would call. He would not let me worry like this."

Before Brett could respond, Patricia rose to her feet and crossed to a small credenza pushed against the wall. She took something off the top and returned to Brett.

"You will need a picture? For the poster? So people will know what he looks like?

The photograph was wallet-sized and fit in the palm of Brett's hand. It was a professional shot, the kind taken during the first week of school. Daniel looked like his mother with high cheekbones and a straight nose, thick eyebrows and full lips. His thick, dark hair was brushed to one side, with a slight curl above the left eye. His expression was serious and moody. In the photo, he wore a chocolate brown suit and tie. The shoulders of the jacket were too big for his narrow frame. He had a small mole on his left temple.

"That is for you to keep," Patricia said, sitting back down in the chair. "You will start looking today?"

Brett tucked the picture into her notebook. "Mrs. Yoon, you said Daniel is seventeen, is that right?"

"Yes, he will turn eighteen in March."

"He's almost an adult then," Brett said, hoping the woman would understand what she as hinting at without actually having to say the words aloud.

"Yes." Patricia gave a small shake of her head, and her lips pursed. She began to twist her wedding ring around her finger again. "I do not understand what difference that makes. He is still a child. He is not where he is supposed to be. I called the police so that he can be found."

"Mrs. Yoon..." Brett closed her notebook with the pen and photograph of Daniel tucked inside. "Was there anything missing from Daniel's room when you looked in there? Clothes? A backpack? Or are you missing anything from your purse? Money?"

"He would not steal from me." Patricia's cheeks flushed bright pink. "He would not run away either. If that's what you mean. Something is wrong. Something has happened to him."

"Do you have any reason to believe someone might have wanted to hurt him?" Brett asked.

Patricia sucked her lower lip between her teeth. Her eyes drifted to the window again, losing focus as she thought about the answer. When she finally returned her attention to Brett, her expression was one of disappointment, of a woman who had learned not to hope for much in this world.

"Please." Her earlier determination was fading. "There must be something you can do. Somewhere you can look."

Brett rose from the couch, adjusted her jacket and tucked the notebook in her pocket. "I'll write up a report. We'll have our patrol units keep an eye out for him, but I have to tell you, Mrs. Yoon, boys this age, sometimes they need time to themselves. They go off for a few days, and then they come back, and it's like nothing happened. I'll make some calls, check in at the school and at his work, but it's just as likely he'll come home on his own. Try not to worry."

Brett left Patricia Yoon with her business card.

As she drove back to the precinct, Brett searched the faces in every car she passed and the people walking along the sidewalks, hoping one of them would be Daniel. But with every mile that passed, dread knotted her stomach—like Patricia, she had a bad feeling. Because what were the odds of one kid turning up dead and another turning up missing on the very same day?

———————————

Brett tried to sneak into the conference room unnoticed, but the hinges squealed when she pushed the door open, and two dozen pairs of eyes swung in her direction. She offered an apologetic smile and mouthed 'Sorry' to Irving who stood with Sergeant Wes Harris and Chief Stan Harcourt at the front of the room.

Stan had been talking, but he stopped mid-sentence when she entered and waited silently, his eyes tracking her as she made her way to an empty seat in the corner farthest from the door. A smirk twisted his thin lips.

"Nice of you to finally join us, Princess. Now, as I was saying..."

He scanned the room. "Once the news about June Newmark is public, things are going to turn into a real shit show around here. We're going to have everyone and their mother breathing down our necks to make an arrest. So, let's do as much as we can to make something happen before the news gets out. June Newmark is everyone's priority now. We'll still be assigning new cases as they come in, but unless someone is bleeding or about to bleed, those cases can get pushed to the back burner. And don't even think about futzing around with cold cases. Anything that's more than two months old can wait until we catch the bastard who killed this poor girl. Am I making myself clear?"

A smattering of 'yessirs' echoed through the room. Chairs creaked. Uniforms rustled. Someone coughed. The cramped space reeked of wet wool, old leather, and rank armpits.

"Good." Stan folded his arms over his chest. He was a thin man, all sharp edges and elbows. "I want Irving running point on this one."

Murmurs rippled through the room. Technically, the case should have been Brett's. She was the one who responded to the initial call and found the body. She'd done the hard work of telling the family. She should be the one to see it through to the end, but if the chief wanted Irving to handle it, then Irving would handle it. Brett wasn't going to argue with the decision; not when a teenage girl lay on a cold slab a few blocks down the street in the hospital morgue. Irving Winters was their most experienced detective. Brett had no doubts he'd handle this investigation the right way.

"Everything comes through Irving," Stan said. "He'll be handing out assignments and making sure you're all getting your shit done. He'll be reporting to me and to Sergeant Harris, so don't think you can get away with any of your usual bull crap."

The noise in the room rose. Mutters and grunts, the shifting of bodies, men anxious to start tracking a killer.

Stan nodded to Irving. "Go ahead, Irv. Put these men to work." His eyes darted to Brett, his lips twisting again into a sour pucker. "These people, I mean."

Stan sat in an empty chair, and Irving stepped forward, taking control of the meeting.

"It's still early, and we don't know much." His voice was serious and measured. "Like Chief Harcourt said, it appears June Newmark was shot, and while we're still waiting for the official autopsy report, we're treating this as a homicide. We found evidence of blood in two different locations. One where her body was found, and one several feet away, closer to the structure. We're sending it to the lab to see if the blood matches, but we believe whoever killed June may have shot her near the building, then dragged her into the woods, perhaps because that location was more hidden. We found two separate shoe prints in the mud nearby. Small miracles, they're mostly intact despite the rain. They both appear to be too big to belong to our victim, so it's possible one might be our killer."

Irving shuffled some papers that were sitting on the table in front of him. "We won't know the official time of death until Charlie finishes the autopsy, but from the state of the body, we don't believe she was out there for too long. Ed Shoal's call about seeing people out in that vicinity came in around about a quarter to two this morning. Officer Eli Miller responded to Deadman's Point a little after that, but he didn't search the area where June was found. Brett, you talked to the parents? What did they have to say?"

"The mother was the only one home when I arrived," Brett said. "As you can imagine, she was upset. Too upset to tell me anything useful. I'd like to speak with her again at some point, after she's had a chance to calm down, and we still need to talk with the father. But I was able to confirm with the school that June attended all her classes yesterday. The last class ended around three. After that, her movements are, as of right now, unaccounted for."

Irving nodded and continued, "So, we need to establish a timeline for June Newmark's whereabouts yesterday after she left school. Who was she with? What was she doing? Who was the last person to see her alive? In addition to interviewing her parents, we should follow up with friends, classmates, teachers, anyone who has regular contact with her. And we need to re-interview Ed. Compare his shoe size to what we found at the scene. He's the one who made the initial report of trespassing. He also led Detective Buchanan to the body, so he may have additional information useful to our investigation. Billy, did you get anything else out of him after you took him home?"

The young patrolman shook his head slowly and scratched at a spot behind his ear. "I'm not sure you're going to get anything but ghost stories and bullshit out of that man."

"Well, let's send someone out tomorrow to try again. Maybe a good night's sleep will help him remember something." Irving ran his hand along the back of his neck. "We found what we believe to be June's backpack at the scene. Her school ID was in the pocket along with some clothes and cash. Even so, we'd still like to have one of the parents identify the body. And we'll need someone to attend the autopsy."

"I'll do it," Sergeant Harris spoke before the silence grew uncomfortable.

A collective sigh of relief rose from the group. No one liked autopsies, but the ones involving children or young adults were especially difficult.

Irving nodded his thanks and then asked, "Does anyone have anything else to add before we get to work?"

Brett raised her hand. When Irving gestured for her to go ahead, she said, "Right before I got here, I was following up on a call that came in this morning about a missing kid. He's seventeen and goes to the same high school as June. His mother saw him last night around eight-thirty but when she went to wake him for school this morning, he was gone."

She had the room's attention now.

"Did he know June?" Irving asked.

"His mother didn't recognize her name, but I think it's worth following up on."

Stan snorted. "Seems to me we've got bigger things to worry about than looking for some kid who decided to sleep off his hangover at a friend's house."

But Irving ignored the chief's comment and said, "Let's see what the Newmarks have to say, if they know this kid...what's his name?"

"Daniel Yoon." Brett rose from the chair and walked to the front of the room, handing Irving the school photograph Patricia had given her.

Irving studied it a moment, then handed it back. As she returned to her seat, he said, "Make copies of this. For now, we'll treat these as two separate cases, so we're going to build two different files, but let's try and find out where they overlap."

"If they overlap." Stan slapped his hands on the table and hauled himself to his feet again. "Let's get this meeting wrapped up, Irv. I need to get started on a press release, and it would be great if you could get me something I can use to reassure folks before they go into full blown panic mode over this dead kid."

Irving began assigning tasks. The conference room turned noisy and chaotic. Brett moved against the flow of bodies, pushing her way to the front of the room where Irving gathered loose papers and tucked them into a manila folder.

"What took you so long to get back?" he asked. "I thought for sure you'd beat us here."

"Amma needed me," she explained. "Then this Daniel Yoon thing came up."

"Everything okay? With your grandmother?"

Brett nodded. "No worse than before. But honestly, it's probably a good thing Stan assigned you lead on this case. That girl deserves someone who can give her their undivided attention."

"That's not why he did it, you know," Irving said, keeping his voice low even though they were the only two left in the room. "This case isn't going to be an easy close, and he wants a fall guy. Someone to blame when it all turns to shit."

Before Brett could respond, a tap at the conference room door interrupted them. Freddie, the front desk officer, peeked his head inside and jerked his thumb over his shoulder. "I've got Peter Newmark on hold. He wants to know if we're going to send someone over to his house or if he's going to have to, and I quote, 'come down here and do your damn jobs for you.'"

Irving adjusted the knot of his tie and yanked up the collar of his trench coat. He gathered June Newmark's file under one arm. "Tell him we're on our way."

CHAPTER 7

Brett and Irving followed Peter Newmark into the living room of the three-story, brick house where his wife, Shirley, lay catatonic on the same rose-pink sofa where Brett had left her four hours ago. The couple's eldest daughter, Marcie fussed over her mother, tucking a blanket around her bare feet and stroking her arm, asking if there was anything she could do.

"I can make some chamomile tea, if you want," Marcie spoke quietly to her mother.

A single, high-pitched wail escaped Shirley's lips, a sound that rang too sharply in Brett's ears. An involuntary shudder rolled through her shoulders, which she tried to hide by taking off her jacket. But Irving noticed, and his brow pinched in the shape of a question. She ignored him, folded her jacket over one arm, and focused her gaze on the husband, a well-dressed man with silver hair trimmed neat.

"We're so very sorry for your loss, Mr. Newmark," she said. "We can't imagine how difficult this must be for your family, but we appreciate you taking the time to talk to us. The more information we gather about June now, the faster we can move forward with the investigation and get your family some answers."

Another whimper rose from the couch. Marcie kneeled beside

her mother, trying to comfort her, but Shirley shrugged away and rolled so her face was pressed against the cushions with her back to the room. Marcie lifted her eyes to her father, who helped the girl to her feet. He kept his arm around Marcie's waist as he gestured for Brett and Irving to follow them deeper into the house.

"She's been like that ever since I got home," Peter said, his baritone voice dampened by a thick, burgundy carpet running the length of the long hallway. "The doctor prescribed some tranquilizers to help calm her down, but so far they don't seem to be working."

They stepped into a kitchen that was triple the size of the living room. Copper pots hung from a rack over a large, granite-topped island. There were two ovens and so many cabinets that Brett wondered how a person managed to find anything. But Marcie walked straight to a cabinet that was filled with mugs and glasses. She pulled out five cups, then paused, staring at them a few seconds before putting one back.

"Please, sit." Peter waved his hand at a line of barstools pushed close to the kitchen island.

Brett perched herself on one. Irving stayed standing. He took a pen and notebook from his jacket pocket and flipped to a page in the center.

During the twenty-minute ride from the downtown police station to the Newmark's house tucked in the foothills of the Cascades and surrounded by old-growth forest, Irving had given Brett a brief history of the family. She knew Peter Newmark only as the defense attorney who'd represented Marshall Trudeau last year after he was charged with false imprisonment and accessory after the fact for his involvement in two murders and a kidnapping. It was Peter who'd bargained the prosecutor down to a deal of two years in prison plus three years' probation in exchange for Marshall's guilty plea—a light sentence considering the damage Marshall had inflicted.

According to Irving, in addition to being the best and most expensive defense attorney in the county, perhaps even the state, Peter Newmark was also a philanthropist. He donated thousands of dollars a year to multiple charities and sat on multiple boards, including the library and hospital. He was also a vocal advocate for the Crestwood Revitalization Committee and had purchased and renovated or was in the process of renovating several historic homes in the area. In short, Peter Newmark was a beloved, important, and very rich, long-standing member of the community. He was also golfing buddies with the mayor and the new police chief. Which meant this case was to be handled with the utmost delicacy and discretion and every available resource. It also meant the police department would be under a microscope; there could be no mistakes.

"What can you tell me so far?" Peter turned his keen, hazel eyes onto Irving. "Do you have anyone in custody?"

"Not yet," Irving said. "Right now we're trying to establish a timeline. Find out who may have had opportunity."

"And motive," Peter added. He flexed his hands where they rested on the granite countertop. "Yes, I know how this works, Irving. This isn't my first homicide."

There was a loud clatter as Marcie fumbled with the kettle, dropping it onto the stove. Water splashed from the spout.

Irving's gaze moved to Marcie and then back to Peter. "Mr. Newmark, perhaps we should speak in private."

"My daughter can stay," Peter said. "She's an adult now. Whatever you need to say to me, you can say in front of her. She's studying to become a lawyer, so she should learn how this stuff works anyway. Isn't that right, sweetheart?"

Marcie gave her father a tight-lipped smile. Her cheeks were pale, her hand still shaking as she moved the kettle onto the burner and started up the gas flame.

"Marcie's a freshman at the University of Washington this year on full scholarship," Peter said, his voice brimming with pride.

"I drove up as soon as I heard what happened to June." Her words were choked with grief.

"Got here about twenty minutes before you did," Peter added, arching his eyebrows at Brett and Irving, then smiling again at his daughter. "I don't even think she packed. She just hopped in the car and drove. That's how close this family is."

"When was the last time you spoke with your sister?" Irving asked.

Marcie shook her head. "A couple of weeks ago, I think. I came up for the weekend to do laundry and see old friends."

"She was home for two days," Peter said. "October twelfth and the thirteenth. Saturday and Sunday. We had dinner as a family at Morton's Steakhouse."

Brett was impressed by how much detail he could remember without referencing any kind of day planner or notes.

"We were done around seven-thirty," he said. "And Marcie drove back to Seattle straight from the restaurant. We said good-bye to her in the parking lot. We listened to Elvis Presley on the way home." He looked at his daughter. "It's the details that make or break a case, Marcella, my love. If you want to be a defense attorney one day, a great one like your old man, then you've got to start paying better attention."

Marcie flinched, then said, "Right, the parking lot. I guess that's when I talked to June last. That weekend. But we didn't talk about anything important. I've got a full course load this year, and June's busy with her own life, so we don't really talk on the phone or anything. We weren't great about staying in touch." Her voice trembled.

The kettle whistled on the stove. Marcie snapped off the burner and carried it to where the mugs were lined up on the counter.

"Let's talk about yesterday," Irving said, shifting his attention back to Peter. "When was the last time you saw June?"

"Yesterday morning before she left for school," Peter said. "She's an early bird like me, so we eat breakfast together sometimes. Yesterday we had eggs benedict and cantaloupe from six-thirty to seven. I had coffee. She had a glass of milk. I kissed her goodbye at seven-fifteen."

Irving wrote it all down. Then asked, "Was she acting differently? Anything out of the ordinary?"

For the first time since they started talking, Peter's professional demeanor slipped. A painful expression passed over his face. His hands tightened to fists, and he swallowed hard, as if suddenly sick to his stomach. His eyes fluttered closed. For several seconds, no one said anything, then Peter opened his eyes again, cleared his throat, and shook off the grief, returning to the stiff posture of a defense attorney offering his opening arguments in court.

"There was nothing wrong. Nothing she told me about. Nothing I could see. June was a good student, a nice girl. She got along with everyone. She was getting good grades. She had a lot of friends. I can't think of any reason someone might kill her. It has to be random," he said. "It's the only thing that makes sense to me."

"Here, Daddy." Marcie set a steaming cup of chamomile tea in front of her father. She looked at Brett and Irving. "I can make you some, too, if you want."

Irving shook his head. "No, thank you."

"Me neither. Thank you, though." Brett watched Marcie cross to the counter where the cups and tea kettle waited.

She had interviewed Marcie for a different case last year when the girl was still a senior at Crestwood High School. She didn't know very much about her except that she was June's older sister and had poor taste in the boys she chose to date.

Marcie put the unused cups back in the cabinet, then leaned

against the counter. Her fingers twisted strands of her long, dark hair, tugging absentmindedly as she listened to them talk.

"And you didn't see her again yesterday?" Irving asked. "After school? Family dinner?"

"No, I'm afraid not." A frown tugged on Peter's mouth. "Shirley and I attended the Miller's Halloween Party last night, the same as we do every year. I went straight to the Miller's house from my office after work yesterday. I got there around seven. I met Shirley at the party and then, around eleven, we left the party and drove to the Harbor Court Hotel." His eyes flickered in the direction of the living room. "We've been going through a bit of a rocky patch so I rented us an expensive hotel room for the night. Like I said, we got there some time after eleven. We paid with a credit card, ordered room service around midnight. Burgers and champagne. When I left the hotel this morning around six, Shirley was still sleeping. I went straight to work from the hotel. I didn't know anything was wrong until the housekeeper called a few hours ago."

"So June was home alone last night?" Brett asked.

"She made plans with friends to go out trick-or-treating," Peter explained. "She was meeting up with them around eight o'clock. They were going to go around our neighborhood, a few others. June has a curfew on school nights, so Shirley called the house last night when we got to the hotel to check in. That was around eleven-thirty, I think. They spoke for a few minutes. Everything seemed fine."

"You weren't worried about her being home by herself all night?"

"She's done it before," Peter said with a quick shrug. "She's a responsible girl. Besides, she wasn't entirely alone. A friend was spending the night."

"Which friend?" Irving asked.

Peter thought for a minute, then answered, "I believe it was Elizabeth Trudeau."

"Dad!" Marcie sounded upset. "Please tell me you're not still letting them hang out."

Peter frowned at her. "She's June's best friend, Marcie. And she's harmless. Besides, June is fifteen now. She's perfectly capable of making her own decisions about who she wants to be friends with."

Marcie groaned and buried her face in her hands.

Irving and Brett exchanged a glance. Brett wanted to push the line of questioning further, but before she had a chance, Irving asked, "Mr. Newmark, do you know if June was dating anyone?"

"Not that she told me," Peter said. "But her mother would know more about all of that."

"And the name Daniel Yoon?" Irving flipped a page in his notebook. "Is that familiar to you?"

Peter looked surprised. "His father was a client of mine. Why? Is he involved in this?"

Instead of answering the question, Irving said, "We're following up on several leads right now. There's no indication Daniel was involved in June's death, but we're going to need as much information from you as possible about your relationship with his father."

"Certainly, of course, anything you need. I can call Sally and have her make a copy of Randall's file for you. If you think it will help."

"Thank you," Irving said. "Have her send it over to the station whenever it's ready." Then he slipped a photograph out from the pages of his notebook and handed it to Peter. "We found this at the scene. Do you recognize it?"

Peter studied the photograph a moment before handing it back, nodding, and saying, "Yes, that's June's backpack."

"There were clothes inside and a significant amount of cash, along with some other personal effects." Irving paused to give Peter time to process what he was saying, then asked, "Can you think of any reason why June would be running away?"

Peter choked on his tea. He sputtered and wiped the back of his hand across his mouth. "I'm certain she wasn't. She has no reason to. She has a good home. A bright future. Her mother and I love her very much. She wants for nothing." He gestured to the large house. "Who would run away from this? Maybe the clothes were Elizabeth's."

"And the money?"

"For pizza, candy, earrings. I don't know what girls buy these days." Peter's expression tightened. "Have you spoken with Elizabeth?"

"Not yet," Irving answered.

"Well, it seems to me that's who you should talk to next since June was supposed to be with her last night. If anyone knows something, it's bound to be her, right?"

Marcie stared at her father with fury in her eyes. Her knuckles had gone pale from gripping the counter so tight. Peter paid her no attention.

He sighed loudly, tapped one finger on the countertop, and said, "I suspect you'll want to search June's room."

"If you have no objections," Irving said.

"Go ahead." He turned to his older daughter. "Marcie, can you show them where it's at? I'm going to go check on your mother and put that call in to Sally."

Marcie's footsteps trudged heavily up the stairs as she led Brett and Irving to June's bedroom on the second floor. The room was large and filled with expensive-looking furniture, including a canopy bed decorated with over a dozen pink and glittery throw pillows. Stuffed animals hung from a cloth hammock in a corner above the bed. One wall was covered in band posters and partic-ipation ribbons from soccer, track, and choir. A shelf on another wall displayed a large collection of plastic dolls, fake make-up kits, and other toys. The room seemed to be going through a transition, much like June herself had been—from a little girl who played with dolls and daydreamed about being a princess to a teenager who crushed on boys and kept secrets from her parents.

As Irving moved in a slow circle around the room, inspecting items on the dresser, pulling open drawers, examining pictures taped to the wall, Brett hung back in the doorway with Marcie. She had a feeling that the girl might be more willing to talk now that her father wasn't around to hear.

"Was something going on with Elizabeth Trudeau?" Brett asked. "In the kitchen, you seemed pretty upset that June was hanging out with her."

Marcie chewed on the corner of her lip. She tracked Irving's movements with her eyes, reluctant to say anything bad about her sister. Brett knew exactly what it felt like to be the one who survived, the sister who was left behind. After Margot's body was found that terrible summer when Brett turned fourteen, the police and her parents had asked her so many questions, she'd lost track of how many of her sister's secrets she'd revealed. Every answer felt like a betrayal.

"You're not going to help her by staying silent," Brett said, as gently as she could.

"I'm not going to help her if I say anything, either." Her tone matched her father's, efficient and slightly bored. "She's dead, isn't she? No one can help her."

"But you can help us find the person who did this to her. You can help her get justice."

Marcie snorted a laugh and snapped her gaze to Brett. Her eyes were crystal blue and unflinching. "You do know who my father is, right? Do you know what he says about justice? What he likes to tell me? He's always saying, 'Listen to me, Marcella. Justice is bull-shit. Justice is a sack of fool's gold sold to the highest bidder.' He bought his Jaguar off the money he makes seeing justice served."

Another laugh, filled with disgust. "He bought my Jaguar with that fool's gold, too."

Irving took a Polaroid picture off the wall. He crossed the room and handed the picture to Brett. Four teenagers stood in a line with their arms slung around one another's shoulders. June Newmark and Elizabeth Trudeau stood beside each other in the middle. A boy with curly brown hair and a too-eager grin flanked June. Brett recognized him from the half dozen times he'd come into the station after school to talk to his father. She couldn't remember his first name and had never been formally introduced, but Brett could easily see the family resemblance. The boy had the same square head and faded-blue eyes as Wes Harris. The same dimpled chin and strong nose. He was still growing into some of his features, so his ears stuck out too far and his cheeks were plump with baby fat. Acne mottled his jawline, which was not yet defined like his father's, but even with the subtle differences, it was obvious who he belonged to.

Brett recognized the boy standing on the other side of Elizabeth, too, though she'd only seen him for the first time today. He was smiling in this picture and wearing a leather jacket that fit perfectly, but the mole was in the exact spot on his left temple and he had the same flip of hair over one eye and Asian features that matched his mother's.

Marcie glared at the photograph. "Those are Lizzie's friends. June shouldn't even be hanging out with them."

"Why not?" Brett asked.

"That one—" She pointed to Daniel Yoon. "That's the kid you asked about. Daniel. His dad's in prison for drugs or something. Dad tried to get him a deal, but he wouldn't take it. And him." This time she pointed at Wes Harris' son. "He's a creep. I saw him after school once carrying this dead cat through the football field."

Irving's eyebrows arched high, but he didn't speak. He took the photograph back from Brett and tucked it into his notebook.

"His dad's a cop," Marcie added, then shrugged and leaned her head against the door jamb. She stared at the ceiling, and it was obvious she was trying to keep herself from crying. "Dad doesn't see it. June's always been his perfect little girl. In his eyes, she can do no wrong. Mom's always saying he wears June-colored glasses. But the truth is, she's been acting differently for months."

"Different how?" Brett pressed her.

Marcie dropped her gaze to the floor. "Moody. Short-tempered. Withdrawn. She quit soccer. She loves soccer. Soccer's practically her whole life. Soccer and Lizzie. That's the problem. Lizzie quit soccer, and then June quit, too. Lizzie dyed her hair black, and then June tried, but thank God Mom caught her before she actually went through with it. It's like, I love my sister, but when it comes to Lizzie, she's an idiot. Dad thinks Lizzie's harmless, and June thinks the world revolves around her, but if you ask me, she's dangerous. We all know who her mother is. What she did to Zach last year. I'm just saying, Lizzie isn't the poor, innocent victim everyone thinks she is. She can't be. Not with a mother like that."

"Do you think Lizzie would be capable of hurting June? Her own best friend?" Brett asked.

Marcie swept her hand through her hair. The dark locks a near inversion of her sister's white-blond hair. A sad smile crept onto her face when she said, "Yes, I do. I think Elizabeth Trudeau is capable of anything."

CHAPTER 8

Lizzie waited until after dinner when her grandparents retreated to the den to watch television. They were hard of hearing and turned the volume up so loud, it was easy for her to sneak downstairs and out the front door without them noticing. She dragged her bicycle from the garage, threw her leg over the saddle, and pedaled up the driveway toward the road.

The ride to Adam's house was almost entirely downhill. It was dark, but she knew where she was going, and once she reached the city limits, there were street lights on every corner, illuminating the gray.

Adam lived with his parents at the end of a cul-de-sac halfway between the Trudeau ranch and the high school. The house was long, L-shaped, with a detached garage off to one side and huge pine trees shading the backyard. Lizzie had never been inside, but she knew which window was Adam's.

She leaned her bike against a tree, crept across the grass, and crouched in the shadow of a large rose bush that grew beneath his window. The light was on, and the curtains were open. She could hear people arguing inside, but the words were too muffled for Lizzie to tell what they were fighting about. Rising on her toes, she peered over the window ledge straight into Adam's bedroom. She let out a breath, relieved to find him home.

Adam sat hunched at his desk with his face buried in his hands. His father loomed in the doorway, gesturing in a way that made Lizzie flinch. She'd never met Mr. Harris in person, but had heard enough of Adam's stories to be scared of him.

She ducked back into the shadows. As she did, her hand brushed against the rose bush, and a prick of pain flared through her. She brought the pad of her thumb to her mouth, sucking at the scratch, and her mouth filled with the taste of blood. Her shoes squelched in the muddy flower bed as she shifted her weight, trying to get comfortable. She wasn't leaving until she talked to Adam.

The voices continued arguing for a few minutes, then a door slammed shut, rattling the window frame. Lizzie listened to heavy footsteps pound through the house. She waited a few more seconds, then reached up and rapped her knuckles on the glass.

Adam appeared in the window almost instantly. She moved into the light so he could see it was her. His eyes widened in surprise, then he flicked a glance over his shoulder as if expecting his father to reappear in the doorway behind him. When he turned back to the window, he was frowning. His cheeks were red, like he'd been crying. He jerked his head to one side, then ducked away from the window.

Lizzie made her way across the yard to their meeting spot behind the garage, which was out of sight of the house and dark enough that even if someone did happen to look in this direction, they would have a hard time seeing anything through the thick shadows. She tucked herself under the overhanging eaves and out of the rain. A few minutes later, footsteps rustled the damp grass, and Adam rounded the corner. He leaned against the wall beside her. The two of them stared out at the trees that edged the back side of the Harris property, though there was nothing to see beyond the darkness.

"What are you doing here?" Adam whispered.

"I looked for you at school, but you weren't there," Lizzie said.

He shrugged, but offered no explanation for his absence.

"What happened last night?" She pressed her palms flat against the garage wall. It was cool and slightly damp, but comforting in its solidness. She couldn't drift away if she was holding onto something real. The scratch on her hand throbbed.

Instead of answering her question, Adam said, "June's dead."

"I know," she said, and Adam stiffened beside her.

Realizing he probably had the wrong idea about what she meant, she explained, "I overheard Principal London talking to a cop about it at school. It's true, then?"

"My dad just told me." His voice shook with emotion. "He says they found her body this morning."

"Do they know what happened?"

"You saw her last night, didn't you?" Adam stared at the ground when he spoke. "You were meeting up at the ruins."

"We were all supposed to be meeting there, remember? But you didn't show." She didn't care if she sounded angry, or if she hurt his feelings. She wanted someone else to blame for June, someone other than herself. "We waited forever."

"I was grounded. I couldn't come."

"We all agreed," Lizzie said. "We promised each other. We made plans."

When they were first talking about leaving, Lizzie had given June an out. She'd warned her. She'd said, *If you knew what was good for you, you would stay the hell away from me.* But June hadn't listened. She'd taken Lizzie's hand, leaned into her, and said, *I'm not letting you go anywhere without me. Wherever you go, I go. Best friends forever, that's what we promised. You couldn't get rid of me even if you tried.* Lizzie should have been more forceful with June. She should have insisted.

"Plans change." Adam tilted his head to watch the rain drip from the eaves.

"So you didn't come?" Lizzie asked. "Not at all?"

"Nope." He shoved his hands into his pockets. "But you already know that."

Now he was the one accusing her.

"I left," Lizzie said. "I got tired of waiting for you, and I left her and Daniel there and walked home. You didn't show up after that?"

"No," he said. "I told you, I wasn't there. You know more than I do."

Lizzie's voice rang sharp when she said, "The last time I saw her, she was still alive."

They both turned to look at each other at the same time. In the dark, Adam's eyes looked full-black, hollow and deep enough to fall into.

"You left her alone with him?" He pushed his face into hers, so close she could smell garlic on his breath from whatever he ate for dinner.

She stepped back. "We were all supposed to leave together. You're the one who bailed on us at the last minute."

"Lizzie. Fuck." He dropped his head back against the wall. "You can't tell anyone you were there, you know that, right?"

"But—"

"No. Lizzie, listen to me." He grabbed her by the shoulders. "This is serious. No one can know you were there with her. What do you think would happen if they found out?"

She tried to break free of his grip, but he squeezed tighter.

"They're going to think you did it," he said. "Maybe they already do."

"I didn't kill her. I swear, I didn't. She was alive—you believe me right?"

"Of course, I believe you." He released her and started to walk away, talking over his shoulder as he rounded the corner of the garage. "But no one else will."

———————————————

Daniel's house was on the other side of town, and before Lizzie was even halfway there, her legs were ready to quit. But she kept pedaling, pushing herself through the rain. She needed to talk to him before the police did.

The Yoon's duplex was smaller than the Harris' house and shared a wall with a neighbor. The front porch light was on, but the rest of the house was dark. Lizzie dropped her bike on the sidewalk, hopped a low fence, and trotted around to the back of the house.

She snuck to Daniel's window and rapped her knuckles on the glass using the same pattern she'd used with Adam. She held her breath, listening, but the house was quiet, and the room stayed dark. She waited, counting the seconds in her head.

When she reached sixty, she knocked on the window again.

A light switched on in the room, and her heart leaped. She started to rise from where she was crouched against the side of the house, but the figure moving toward the window wasn't Daniel. She ducked back down again.

A shadow passed through the square of light spilling from the window. A few seconds later, there was a pop, and the sound of the window being slid open in its frame. Lizzie stayed completely still, barely breathing. She waited for Mrs. Yoon to start shouting at her, but apparently Lizzie was hidden well enough that Mrs. Yoon didn't notice her. The night stayed quiet, filled with the gentle patter of rain.

Several minutes passed, with Mrs. Yoon standing in front of the open window, casting a long shadow over Lizzie. If she moved, she'd be caught. Her legs were starting to tingle. She gritted her teeth and closed her eyes, willing Mrs. Yoon to go away.

"Daniel?" Mrs. Yoon's voice trembled through the dark. "Daniel? Are you out there?"

His mother listened for another minute, then slid the window shut. A few seconds later, the light clicked off, and darkness descended over the backyard.

Lizzie rose on shaking legs, stumbled toward the street, grabbed her bike, and pedaled home as fast as she could.

CHAPTER 9

By the time Brett finally got home Friday night, it was late, almost 9:00 PM, and she was running on fumes.

She'd wanted to drive straight from the Newmark's house in the hills to Robert and Victoria Trudeau's ranch on the flatter, south end of Crestwood to talk to Elizabeth, but Irving had taken one look at her and said, "Absolutely not. We've been at this all day, and I don't know about you, but my brain is fried, and my wife is probably worried I drove off a cliff chasing a bird. Plus, we both stink like the underside of a goose, so I'm taking you back to the precinct and then I'm going home. I suggest you do the same. We can pick it up again in the morning."

Brett almost went to see Elizabeth by herself, but when Irving dropped her at the precinct, the adrenaline that had been keeping her going all day flickered down to nothing, and exhaustion took over. She'd been awake since 5:00 that morning, but it felt longer. She didn't even enter the precinct. She darted through the rain to her car and drove home with the windows cracked, cold air blasting to help her stay awake.

Twenty minutes later, she stumbled into the house on Bayshore Drive.

Amma and Henry were still on the couch watching television in almost the exact positions as when Brett had left them earlier that day. Pistol hopped off Amma's lap and trotted over to greet Brett. She pet the little dog as he sniffed her muddy pant cuffs.

"Everything okay here?" She raised her voice to be heard over the television.

"No complaints." Henry pushed up from the couch with a groan.

"Henry knew all the answers to *Jeopardy* tonight." Amma readjusted the blanket on her lap as Pistol hopped back up on the couch to cuddle with her.

"Almost." Henry winked at Brett.

"You should fly down to Los Angeles and try out for the show," Amma said. "Don't give me that look, Henry, I'm being serious. You're too smart to waste your time here making sure I don't set the house on fire."

Brett leaned over and kissed Amma on the top of her head. Her grandmother blinked at her with a startled look on her face. "What happened to you?"

Brett touched her cheeks, suddenly self-conscious. "What do you mean 'what happened?' I was at work—"

"You look like you've been through the wringer and then spat out by a cat."

Henry snorted a laugh.

Brett rolled her eyes. She walked across the living room to a mirror hanging above the fireplace. Her grandmother was right— she looked like a mangy rat that had barely survived a shipwreck.

After spending hours in the rain, her brown hair was a frazzled mess of kinks and coils. She had the kind of hair that curled when she didn't want it to and otherwise hung lanky and thin around her face. Normally at work, she wore it in a ponytail or low bun, but over the past few hours that ponytail had worked itself into a frizzy mess. The cowlick she'd had since birth stuck up over her left brow. She pushed it down, but it sprang up again. Dark circles formed shadows under her puffy eyes. There was a streak of mud across the left side of her jaw. She rubbed at it with the sleeve of her shirt as she moved toward the kitchen.

"I'm starving," she said. "Did you two eat?"

"We ordered Chinese a few hours ago," Henry said.

"I got you that kung pao chicken you like so much," Amma added.

Brett's stomach growled loudly. She took the leftovers from the fridge, scooped them into a bowl, and started the microwave. As the food reheated, she found the expensive Irish whiskey her grandmother kept hidden under the sink and poured herself a shot. She added two ice cubes, which clinked against the glass as she dropped them in.

"You better not be drinking my whiskey!" Amma shouted.

"I wouldn't dare!" Brett shouted back. She took a sip, then raised the glass toward Henry who had followed her into the kitchen. "Want some?"

He shook his head. "I snuck a nip while she was watching *Wheel of Fortune*."

He studied her with an intensity that raised the hairs on the back of her neck.

"What is it, Henry?"

"I called the precinct this afternoon to figure out when you'd be home."

"I'm sorry." Guilt rose in her chest. "I should have called. I didn't mean to be gone this long, but this case—"

"Yes, about this case—are you sure you should be working on it?"

Irving had asked the same question after they'd left the Newmark's. Brett hadn't understood at first, thinking he was asking her about Amma. But then he clarified, "You see it, don't you? How similar this is to your sister's case."

A teenager killed, her body dumped in the woods, her sister left behind to pick up the pieces of her shattered family.

Everyone in the department knew about Margot Buchanan by now. The ones who hadn't been told the story in-person had read about it in a newspaper. Twenty-one years ago, Brett's older sister was murdered in Crestwood, her body dumped in the woods near Lake Chastain. Stan Harcourt had been the lead detective and, because of his incompetence, the case had gone unsolved for over a decade. If not for Jimmy Eagan, a reporter for the *Statesman Journal* at the time and a friend of Brett's, the case would have kept gathering dust in the evidence room indefinitely. But even with Jimmy's help, it had taken another few years and Brett moving to Crestwood before she finally learned the truth about what happened to Margot. Most of the truth. Brett still had a lot of questions, but Margot's killer was gone now, which meant the answers she wanted were gone, too, rotting somewhere on the bottom of the ocean.

Brett took another sip of whiskey, not enjoying it as much as she wanted to.

She told Henry the same thing she told Irving, "There are similarities between this case and my sister's case, sure, but it's been over twenty years, and I'm not a kid anymore, Henry. I know how to separate my personal feelings from the job. Don't worry. If I feel like it's going to be an issue, I'll step back."

The microwave beeped. Brett took the bowl of rice and chicken to the kitchen table and sat down. Henry sat beside her. He tugged at his mustache, and his brow furrowed with concern.

"I'm not talking about that," he said. "I have every confidence in your abilities to properly investigate a case, no matter how challenging or close to home it may be."

"Then what are you talking about?"

"Anita," he said her grandmother's name quietly.

"What about her?" Brett shoveled food into her mouth, hardly tasting it.

"Brett," Henry chided. "You left her alone all day."

"She wasn't alone. She was with you."

"And don't get me wrong, I'm happy to help. I love your grandmother, and I enjoy spending time with her, but I have my own life that needs taking care of, too. And a wife who's bugging me about driving cross-country to visit the National Parks now that I'm retired."

"Well, don't hang around on our account. Go if you want to go." Brett hated the petulant way her voice sounded.

Henry frowned at her. "I'm not trying to start a fight. I'm just checking in, making sure you know what's really going on around here so you can make the best decision for how to care for Anita. She asked about you at least a dozen times today. She keeps forgetting that you're an adult with a job. She kept asking if you'd gone out to the beach to swim with Margot. She asked about your mother a few times, too." He sighed. "Every time I gave her a straight answer, she became very agitated. After the first few times, I started making stuff up to keep her calm. I don't like lying to her, Brett."

Brett shifted her gaze to the double french doors that led to the backyard. It was too dark to see the ocean or anything else through the glass, but she could hear the waves and rain tap-dancing on stones. She scraped the last bite of kung pao chicken into her mouth. It had already gone cold again.

"Have you thought any more about a nursing home?" Henry asked. "I've heard about some really nice facilities opening up in Seattle."

Brett rose from the table and dumped the dirty dishes into the sink. She was too tired to wash them tonight, and too tired to have this conversation with Henry.

"Or what about hiring someone to come over during the day

when you're at work," he pushed. "It's only going to get harder to care for her on your own."

She gripped the edge of the sink and stared into the window, seeing her haggard reflection looking back. It startled her how much she looked like her mother now. As a girl, everyone told her she looked exactly like her father. These days, all she saw was the ghost of a woman who hadn't been able to unravel herself from her own grief. Five years after Margot's death, Lydia Buchanan had given up, given in, drank herself to oblivion, and driven herself straight into a highway barrier. Brett still hadn't forgiven her mother for leaving her like that.

"Go home, Henry." Her words were weighted with exhaustion.

"Brett—" The chair scraped against the floor as he pushed back from the table. "I didn't mean to upset you."

"It's been a really long day. That's all." She spun to face him, offering an olive branch in the form of a smile. "Thank you for coming over. Really. I know it's not easy taking care of her, and I appreciate you being here when I can't be. But I get it. You need a break. You need to get back to your own life."

He started to protest, "That's not what I meant."

But she held up her hand to keep him from saying anything else. "I can handle it from here on out. We'll be fine. Don't worry."

He gave her a stern look, so she added, "And if I can't, if it gets to be too much, I promise, I'll look into hiring someone. Okay?"

He nodded, satisfied for now, then gathered his things, said goodbye to Amma and Pistol, and left.

Brett checked on Amma, then she went upstairs to shower and change into dry clothes. Under the stream of scalding water, she started to relax, the tight knots in her shoulders untwisting.

Henry was right to be concerned. Not about Brett, but about Amma. She was getting worse. Brett had noticed it, too, even if she wasn't ready to admit it to anyone but herself. Acknowledging how bad things were getting felt like giving up, and Brett didn't want to give up on Amma. Not when Amma had never given up on her.

Brett had been an angry teenager. Mad at her parents, at her sister, at herself. If not for Amma's constant love and reminders that things would get better, Brett might have burned down the whole world. But Amma had been right, and things had gotten better. Brett's anger morphed into a stubborn determination that she could do good in this world, that she could make things better for other people the way Amma had made things better for her.

Realistically, Amma probably only had a few years left on this earth, but Brett wasn't going to let any of that time go to waste. She refused to send Amma away to rot with a bunch of strangers who didn't know the first thing about what made her happy. Not when she had a perfectly good home right here in Crestwood.

Amma had lived a full and vibrant life in this house with its ocean views and the smell of salt trapped in the floorboards. She'd loved in this house, raised children in this house, lost family and grieved those losses in this house. Brett wasn't going to take away an entire lifetime of memories and comfort when her grandmother needed it most. No, Amma was staying right where she was. The two of them would figure out a way to make it work the way they always did.

Brett met Amma on the second-story landing. She had Pistol tucked under one arm. She passed the dog over to Brett, wished them both goodnight, and walked into her bedroom. The neurologist had said not to baby Amma, that if she didn't need help, Brett shouldn't force her to take it. *Be there when she needs you, but don't smother her.*

Brett set Pistol on the floor and went back downstairs to check that the doors were locked and the lights turned off. The dog followed closely on her heels. In the kitchen, Brett eyed the bottle of whiskey sitting on the counter. Another drink would be nice, but she worried the booze would have too much of a numbing effect, and she wouldn't hear Amma if she decided to take another one of her night walks. Brett put the bottle back under the sink where it belonged.

She turned off the last light downstairs and headed up to her room. She paused on the second-floor landing at the base of a narrow staircase that twisted into the house's single, ridiculous turret. When her grandfather was alive, he used the room at the top as his study. Amma never went up here, but Brett did—for the view and for privacy. She crept up the staircase now, lifting Pistol and carrying him under one arm because the steps were an inch too high for him to climb up on his own. Once inside the study, she set him down on the worn carpet. He sniffed in a circle, ending up where he always ended up—on a tufted green pillow Brett left for him under the desk.

Brett sat in her grandfather's old leather chair and turned on the desk lamp. A warm pool of light spread over the smooth wood.

Her mind ran in circles as she thought of June Newmark and how much work still needed to be done, of who might have done this and why and thinking, too, *Not again.*

The last thing Crestwood needed was another dead girl.

She picked up the phone that sat on the corner near her elbow and dialed a number she still knew by heart even though she hadn't called in months.

After four rings, a man answered, his voice thick with sleep. "Hello?"

"Jimmy, it's me."

"Hey, Brett. It's pretty late." He sounded more awake with each word.

"It's barely eleven," she teased him.

"Is everything okay? Amma's okay?" Fear bracketed his words.

"We're fine," she reassured him. "I finally have a few minutes to myself so I'm returning your message."

There was a brief moment of silence, then he laughed. "Oh, right. I called two weeks ago." Another laugh, strained and uncertain. "I thought you were avoiding me."

"I didn't even see it until this morning. I swear. Amma was hiding it from me, I guess."

"She would never." His tone was lighter now, easy the way they used to be together. "Other than being the world's worst secretary, is everything good with her?"

"Sure, same as before. Why? Did she say something to you?"

"No, not in so many words. She did call me Frank, though."

Frank was Amma's late-husband and Brett's grandfather. He died of a heart attack over six years ago. Jimmy had never gotten a chance to meet him.

"Well, I think that's a compliment," Brett said. "How's Trixie?"

"Still a little monster," Jimmy said, his voice filled with love for the five-year-old bmeagle he'd raised from a puppy. "She got into a tussle with a skunk the other day. Took me seven baths and twenty cans of tomato sauce to get the stink out."

Brett laughed. "Pistol brought me a piece of seaweed last week. That's about as adventurous as we get around here."

"Trust me, Bretty. You do not want this level of adventure. Be grateful for your seaweed."

This time the silence between their words was comforting and familiar. The study was warm. The sound of the rain, a lullaby. Brett could have fallen asleep in her grandfather's chair listening to Jimmy breathe, but she knew if she did, she'd wake up more tired than before, with a crick in her neck and an exorbitant long-distance bill, so she said, "Are you going to tell me why you called or what?"

"You called me."

She couldn't tell if he was teasing her or not. "I mean, are you going to tell me why you called two weeks ago? Was it something specific or—?"

"Yes, Bretty, I know what you meant. I just...God, it's good to hear your voice."

"It's good to hear yours, too." She tugged her fingers through her still-damp hair. "I've missed this."

"I've missed us." The words were tentative, questioning.

She didn't want to say the wrong thing, but Jimmy must have heard rejection in her silence because he rushed ahead, "Never mind. Forget I said anything."

She could hear the hurt in his voice, but he didn't give her a chance to stick up for herself or explain. He rambled on, "So, my publisher set up a signing event at a bookstore in Seattle, and I was thinking, since we were going to be so close anyway, Trixie and I could swing by to stay with you and Amma for a couple of days after."

"When's the event?" she asked.

It had been about a year since she'd seen Jimmy in person. He hadn't been back to Crestwood since last November after she rejected his romantic advances. Between writing and promoting his book, *Murder Your Darlings: The True Story of the Ophelia Killer*, which detailed his hunt for serial killer Archer French, and continuing to write feature-length articles for the *Oregonian*, he hadn't exactly had time for a vacation. Not that Brett went out of her way to drive to Portland to visit either. She'd been busy, too, with work and Amma and trying to avoid awkward conversations like this one.

"Well," Jimmy said hesitantly. "It's on Sunday."

"This Sunday? As in two days from now?"

"Yes, but I called to tell you about it two weeks ago, so it's not entirely my fault that it's turning into such a last minute thing."

Brett turned her head to look outside as a gust of wind whipped rain against the windows. There was nothing to see but the blackest of nights.

"Are you still there, Bretty?" Jimmy sounded so far away, his voice a thin thread spanning the miles between them.

"I'm here," she said. "Look, Jimmy. I would love to see you, and I know Amma would, too, but it's tough right now. We had this huge case drop into our laps this morning. It's an all hands on deck kind of thing, and I don't think it's going to get wrapped up by Sunday. Plus, things with Amma…" She trailed off for a few seconds, then added, "There's a lot going on, that's all. I'm not sure we'd be very good company for you."

Brett had known Jimmy going on five years now, and she knew him well enough to read his silences. This one was filled with disappointment and edged with anger. But he forced an understanding smile into his voice when he said, "Yeah, sure, I get it. I understand."

Another beat passed, then he said, "You could come to Seattle. Just for the day, for the event. It would mean a lot to have you there."

Usually Sunday and Monday were Brett's days off, and Seattle was less than a two-hour drive from Crestwood. It wouldn't be hard to go down for the day, attend the event, grab dinner with Jimmy, and drive home.

"I might be able to make that happen," she said, not wanting to promise him too much. There were a lot of things that could make it impossible for her to drive to Seattle on Sunday—work, Amma, mudslides, flooded roads—but she would try to be there. It was the best she could offer him.

"You can bring Amma, of course," Jimmy said.

"Of course."

"And Pistol. I'll put him on Trixie's VIP list."

Brett laughed softly and reached under the desk to scratch the Chihuahua's ear. Pistol licked her finger.

"And you can bring your new boyfriend, too, if you want." His words danced on a knife's edge.

Brett couldn't tell if he was serious or joking, upset or curious. For the first time in a long time, she was unable to read Jimmy's silence.

"My boyfriend?" Her voice cracked, betraying her. "I don't have a boyfriend."

She was glad they were talking on the phone so he couldn't see her cheeks flush red. She brushed her fingertips to her neck, then dropped her hand quickly, remembering that was the exact spot Eli Miller had kissed her last weekend. Her cheeks flushed hotter, thinking of the way his hands had roamed, and how she'd sparked under his touch.

"Oh. I mean, I guess I just assumed." Jimmy's voice was stiff, bordering on polite. "When I called, Amma mentioned you were out on a date."

Brett thought she had been discreet. She hadn't told Amma where she was going when she left. No, that wasn't true. She'd told Amma she was going to a friend's house for dinner and she'd written down Eli's phone number on a piece of paper and stuck it to the fridge door, in case there was an emergency. Amma had connected the dots on her own.

Jimmy spoke into her silence, "It's okay, you know. If you do have a boyfriend. It's not like we're—" He cut himself off. "We're still friends, Bretty. And I want you to be happy."

She heard his unspoken words this time: *I want you to be happy... even if it's not with me.*

When she and Jimmy kissed for the first and only time on his balcony overlooking the Willamette River a year and a half ago, it was nice. More than nice. It had felt like coming home and slipping into a comfy pair of slippers. She didn't know why that wasn't enough for her. She wanted it to be enough. But then she thought of the way Eli had lifted her onto the countertop without asking permission, how he'd nipped at her skin hard enough to leave a small bruise, how it had taken all of her restraint to push him away and go home alone.

She'd known Eli since they were children. Their worlds orbited every summer she spent with Amma and Pop at the house on Bayshore Drive. And now that she was here permanently, and an adult, they were finally colliding. Brett didn't know if what she was doing with Eli was a fling or if it would turn into something more, but she at least owed herself a chance to see how it might play out.

"It's late, Jimmy." She echoed the words he'd said to her earlier. "I really should—"

"Go get your beauty rest," he cut her off. "I'll see you Sunday."

"Jimmy, I can't promise I'll be there—" But he'd already hung up on her.

Brett reached under the desk, scooped Pistol into her arms, and carried him to her bedroom. She was certain she'd be up all night tossing and turning, thinking about June's case, replaying her conversation with Jimmy, feeling guilty for letting him down. Again. But the long day and the incessant rain had sucked every last drop of energy from her. The blankets were heavy, the bed was warm, and the second her head hit the pillow, Brett was fast asleep.

Brett startled from a half-remembered nightmare of water rushing into her mouth as she tried to scream. She woke with a gasp, shivering in a pool of her own sweat, and squinted at the clock radio next to her bed. 3:33 AM.

The hallway floorboards outside her bedroom creaked. Pistol, who had been sleeping curled in a ball tucked behind Brett's knees, let out a low woof, hopped off the bed, and trotted over to the closed door. He snuffled his nose under the crack and woofed again.

Brett groaned and pulled the blankets over her head. She'd slept only a few hours and desperately needed a few more if she was going to function properly later today.

Pistol barked again, louder now, more demanding.

"Okay, I hear you." Brett threw the covers off and swung her feet to the floor.

Heavy rain drummed on the roof and tapped against the windows. She snapped on the bedside lamp, and light flooded the room. Pistol whimpered and scratched at the door, his tail wagging. His glittering obsidian eyes followed Brett as she shoved her feet into a pair of slippers and walked over to him.

She opened the door expecting him to race downstairs. Instead, he trotted to Amma's room. Brett hurried after him, afraid Pistol would bark again. These days, even the smallest sounds could wake Amma from the deepest sleep. But Pistol could have howled and yapped and played the tuba, and it wouldn't have mattered. The door to Amma's bedroom stood wide open. Her bed was empty, the covers shoved to the floor.

Brett swallowed down rising panic. It wasn't unusual for Amma to wake in the middle of the night and go downstairs to make a cup of tea or watch television. More recently, though, she'd been getting up in the middle of the night to do stranger activities, like painting, starting a load of laundry, or organizing her record collection. Once last month, Brett found her sitting cross-legged on the front driveway staring up at the stars like she was waiting for someone to come take her away. Brett cocked her head now, to see if she could hear where in the house her grandmother had wandered off to, but all she heard was the rain's hiss and ocean's roar.

"Amma?" There was something about this early morning hour that made everything sound different. The house felt emptier, abandoned, and Brett's voice rang sharply through the hall, loud even though she was barely speaking above a whisper.

When she got no response, she started toward the staircase. Pistol, done sniffing in Amma's room, trotted past Brett again, moving in front of her and tripping his way to the first floor. He went straight to the kitchen where the french doors stood wide open. Rain blew in from outside.

Pistol stopped in the doorway, and Brett could have sworn, from the expression on his face, that he was asking if she was going to take care of this or should he?

From where they stood, they could see Amma, a dark silhouette against the ink-black ocean. She stood with her back to the house on the pebbled beach a few steps from the dock and close enough to the water that small waves rolled over her feet.

"Amma, what are you doing?" Brett called as she raced across the yard.

Pistol stayed in the house, offering a couple of encouraging barks to spur her on.

Brett stepped onto the beach, knocking stones loose and sending them clattering toward the water, but Amma didn't turn around. Her head was tilted, staring down at her feet, and the scene was eerily similar to last October when they found Nathan Andress floating dead in the water in that exact spot. For a second, with the night crushing around them, and the waves hissing against the stones, Brett thought another body had washed up. But when she reached her grandmother's side, she saw there was nothing on the beach but rocks, strings of seaweed, and broken shells.

Amma shivered uncontrollably. She wore nothing but a thin, cotton nightgown that hung an inch below her knobby knees. The fabric was drenched through to the skin.

Brett approached her grandmother carefully, uncertain if she was awake or asleep, not wanting to startle her too much, but needing to get her inside before she caught her death. Before they both did. The cold rain stung when it hit Brett's bare skin.

She brushed her fingers across Amma's arm, and a shudder ran through her whole body.

She turned toward Brett. Her eyes were unfocused, confusion etching deep lines into her face. "Where's my boat?"

For their fiftieth wedding anniversary, Pop had given Amma a fourteen-foot wooden skiff he'd named after her. The *Anita Horizon* was a sturdy daysailer, small enough for one person to handle on their own. Amma had spent hundreds of hours over the past decade skimming alone across Sculpin Bay, the wind in her hair, chasing sunsets. She used to sail it often enough that leaving it tied in the water made sense, but Brett thought it was too dangerous now for her to go out alone, and Brett herself was a fair-weather sailor. So with summer's end and the first fall storm, Brett had moved the boat into the boathouse, hoisting it onto the dry dock until next summer when the waters were calmer and the winds weren't gale force.

"I pulled it out of the water a few weeks ago. Remember?" Brett said.

And it's a good thing she did. If the boat had still been tied to the dock, it would have taken a severe pummeling against the pylons during this most recent storm.

"Don't worry, Amma. The boat's fine." Brett put her arm around her grandmother's shoulders, noticing how thin she'd become over the past few months. She steered Amma away from the water. "We can take her out for a jaunt when this storm clears up, if you want."

Amma nodded, then leaned her weight against Brett and allowed herself to be led back inside the house.

CHAPTER 10

Leaving Crestwood should have been easy. From the downtown Greyhound station, Lizzie had a few options. There were three buses and three main routes. South to Seattle, north to Vancouver, or east to Boise. All she needed to do was get to one of those bigger cities, and then she could go anywhere she wanted. Anywhere in the entire world. Niagara Falls, the snow-capped peaks of the Rockies, the deserts of New Mexico. Anywhere but another ocean. Anywhere as long as it didn't taste like salt and remind her of how much she'd lost. She had enough money, all she needed was a ticket and then she'd be gone, but the man behind the ticket counter was being impossible.

"Your parent or legal guardian has to buy your ticket," he drawled in a bored tone as he slid a piece of paper across the counter. "And fill out this form."

The words **UNACCOMPANIED CHILD** took up most of the top half of the page.

"I'm eighteen," Lizzie lied.

The man laughed and scratched his nose. "Yeah, and I'm Robert Redford." He tapped the form sitting on the counter in front of her. "Get them to fill this out and you can go anywhere you want, but until then, I'm afraid I'm going to have to ask you to step out of line so I can help the next person."

The crowd behind her was small, but growing, and several people stared at her with exasperated expressions. Lizzie stepped out of line and walked toward a bench that was out of the flow of people moving through the terminal.

She dropped her backpack on the bench and then dropped herself beside it. Running her fingers through her hair, she stared out the glass-fronted entrance through the streaks of gray rain, trying to come up with a plan. She unzipped her backpack and felt for the roll of cash stuffed in the bottom. Maybe she could talk someone into buying her a ticket.

As she scanned the terminal for someone she might be able to manipulate, her eyes caught on a newspaper stand. June smiled at her from behind smeared glass. Lizzie's pulse quickened. She dug a dime from the front pocket of her backpack where she kept loose change, walked over to the box, and bought a copy of the latest Saturday edition of the *Crestwood Tribune*.

The headline took up half the front page: **LOCAL TEENAGER FOUND MURDERED AT DEADMAN'S POINT.**

June's school picture was printed beneath that. Her smile was all teeth. Her eyes were wide and sparkling, like the photographer had caught her mid-laugh. Lizzie's heart clenched in her chest. She gripped the paper so tightly, the edges crumpled. The article gave almost no useful information. *15-year-old June Newmark, daughter of prominent Whatcom County defense attorney, was killed on Halloween night in a secluded area near Deadman's Point. Police are investigating the circumstances surrounding her death and asking anyone with information to please come forward. A tip line has been set up for this purpose.*

A phone number was listed, along with additional information about the Newmark family. How June played soccer and sang in the school choir. How she had an older sister who was attending the University of Washington on a full-ride academic scholarship. How Peter Newmark was the county's best criminal defense attorney and sat on several charity boards. How Shirley Newmark had raised over $50,000 last year for the Crestwood Community Theater. There was nothing about Adam, nothing about Daniel, nothing about Lizzie, nothing about the four of them together.

Here it was, then, in black and white, which made it official. June Newmark, her best friend since kindergarten, attached at the hip, practically sisters, June was dead, and there was nothing Lizzie could do to change that fact.

She stuffed the newspaper into her backpack. Her stomach was in knots, and she regretted eating breakfast before leaving the house this morning.

She couldn't stop thinking about Daniel's mother calling out for her son in the dark. The newspaper and Adam and the detective and even Principal London, they all said June was dead. Not June and Daniel. Not June and another kid. Not two students, just one. Just June.

Lizzie hadn't seen or heard from Daniel since Halloween when she left him and June at the ruins alone. She knew two things for certain: when she walked away that night, June was very much alive, and now she wasn't. There was a third thing that Lizzie knew she needed to consider but she didn't want to. Because if she'd thought for even a minute that Daniel was capable of killing someone, she would have never started hanging out with him.

But she hadn't believed her mother to be capable of murder either—until it was too late. She'd been wrong once; she could be wrong again.

It felt like a betrayal to even think the words, but they kept floating through her mind. *When I left the woods, June was alive and Daniel was with her. Now June is dead, and Daniel is missing.*

Adam's voice rang in her head. *You left her alone with him?*

She had to find Daniel. If she found him, she could ask him point blank: *Did you kill June? Did you kill my best friend?*

The next bus to Seattle left in twenty minutes, and Lizzie needed to be on it. She had no idea if Daniel would be at his cousin's, but that was where they'd planned to go Thursday night, so it was at least a place to start.

A group of people gathered near the front doors, preparing to board.

Lizzie stood and shrugged her backpack over her shoulders. She stepped toward the crowd, thinking she might be able to slip by the bus driver if she pretended to be someone's daughter. A hand grabbed her elbow and yanked her out of line.

She whipped her head around, prepared to fight, but the adrenaline fled her body when she saw it was her grandfather.

They spoke at the same time.

She asked, "How did you know I was here?"

And he asked, "Where are you going, Lizbug?"

She shrugged and stared at her feet.

"Lizzie..." Grandpa's voice was kind and calm. "Lizzie, look at me."

His eyes were gray-blue, the color of the sky before the sun came up. He looked sad when he asked, "Why didn't you tell me about June?"

Lizzie threw herself against her grandfather, burying her face in his sturdy chest. He rubbed her back, saying nothing for a minute, before finally murmuring, "Come on, Lizbug. Let's get you home."

She stiffened and pulled away from him, shaking her head. "I can't. I can't be here anymore."

"Because of June?"

"Because of everything. I hate this place."

Grandpa's jaw tensed. He kept one hand on her shoulder, the weight of him keeping her steady. "How about this? How about you come home with me today, and then, if you still feel like leaving tomorrow, I'll bring you back here myself. I'll buy you a ticket wherever you want to go, no questions asked."

He would spend the next twenty-four hours trying to talk her out of leaving, and he'd probably do it, too. He'd offer her a thousand reasons why a fifteen-year-old couldn't live on her own; he'd probably offer her money to stay; and he'd tell Grandma what she was planning and Grandma would step in with her guilt and her sorrow-filled eyes, reminding her that family was all they had. Family was what saved you.

June was Lizzie's family. A hell of a lot of good that had done.

Lizzie gave in and let Grandpa guide her to where his car waited in the parking lot.

He didn't try to talk to her again until they were parked in the driveway in front of the sprawling ranch house. He kept the engine running, the heater on full-blast. Lizzie could tell by the way he gripped the wheel that he had something important to say, but needed a few seconds to work up to it. He cleared his throat.

Here it comes. She fixed her gaze on the pasture, where small ponds were starting to form in the low spots. The horses were tucked inside the barn safe and dry.

Grandpa cleared his throat again and said, "Listen, Lizbug. We need to talk about the other night..."

But before he could continue, a red VW Beetle pulled into the driveway and parked behind them. They both recognized the car and the driver climbing out, even though her hand was raised to protect her face from the pouring rain.

Grandpa frowned into the rearview mirror. "Now, what's she doing here?"

He got out of the car to intercept Detective Buchanan before she made it to the front door. He snapped open a large black umbrella he seemed to have pulled out of nowhere and held it over the detective's head, offering her a tight smile as he politely asked, "How's Anita doing these days? Victoria and I don't see her much at the club anymore."

Even though Lizzie was still in the car, she could hear what they were saying. She hunched low in her seat, trying to make herself invisible.

"She's doing well," Detective Buchanan said, her tone and shoulders stiff. "We're staying busy." She gestured to Grandpa's car. "I actually stopped by to talk to your granddaughter. I'm sure you read in the paper this morning about what happened at Deadman's Point?"

Grandpa nodded.

"Well, that's why I'm here. I need to ask Elizabeth a few questions about her friend June."

They both turned to look at her. Lizzie dropped her gaze to her lap, pretending she hadn't heard a single word, but neither Grandpa nor Detective Buchanan were that stupid.

"Come on out, Lizbug," Grandpa called. "Let's go inside and get this over with."

CHAPTER 11

"Tell me about June." The wicker chair creaked underneath Brett as she tried to get comfortable.

Elizabeth—she went by Lizzie now apparently—sat in a wicker loveseat across from Brett. She twisted her hands in her lap and shrugged. "I don't know what you want me to say."

"Why don't you start by telling me where you were on Thursday night? On Halloween?"

Lizzie released a heavy sigh and snuck a side glance at her grandfather who sat on the loveseat beside her. The older man nodded at her, encouraging her to answer Brett's questions, but Lizzie squirmed in her seat, twisting her hands harder, saying nothing.

"Were you with June?" Brett prompted.

It was strange to be interviewing Elizabeth Trudeau in the same room where she'd interviewed the girl's father a year ago. Plants crowded the small sun porch. Floor to ceiling windows overlooked expansive pastures and stables, though no horses were out today. In this very room last year, Marshall Trudeau had confessed his part in Clara Trudeau's crimes. He'd stopped lying and told the truth. Brett hoped Lizzie would now do the same today—tell the truth about her best friend June.

"I didn't kill her." Lizzie lifted her chin defiantly, but Brett saw through her false bravado. The girl was scared.

"I never said you did." Brett leaned forward. "Look, Lizzie, I'm not here to accuse you of anything or get you in trouble. But your friend is dead."

Lizzie flinched at the words, but Brett pressed on. This girl had been through a lot over the past year, but there was no time to coddle her, not if they were going to find June's killer.

"Sometime on Halloween, June was murdered," Brett said. "She was shot. And I want to find out how that happened, but I need your help, okay? You were her best friend, weren't you?"

Lizzie bit her lip and nodded.

"Do you know who killed her?"

The girl shook her head so fiercely, Brett believed her, but she still had a job to do. She was all too familiar with how easy it was for people to lie—especially the people in this family. To get to the truth, she'd need more from Lizzie than a simple denial of guilt.

"But you want us to find out who did, right?" Brett asked.

She expected a similar kind of enthusiastic response as before, but Lizzie simply shrugged and shifted her gaze to the window as if hoping the answers could be found in the falling rain.

After a beat of silence, Brett tried again. "I spoke with June's dad and sister."

Lizzie's gaze returned to Brett. The fifteen-year-old had changed so much over the past year. Her cheek bones had sharpened. Her eyes were rimmed in black liner, making her seem older. Her hair, too, once long and flowing chestnut, was hacked off at the chin and dyed a raven-black, making her pale skin even more so.

The word 'haunted' flitted through Brett's mind. She pushed it away and said, "Mr. Newmark said you and June were going out trick-or-treating on Halloween. Is that what you did?"

"We're too old for trick-or-treating."

"But you two were together Thursday night?"

Lizzie nodded, but added no further information.

"If you weren't trick-or-treating, then what were you doing?" Brett asked.

Lizzie rolled her eyes toward the window again, refusing to answer the question.

"Lizzie…" Her grandfather rested his hand on her knee, but Lizzie ignored him. Her lips pursed tighter, giving every indication that even if she did know something about what happened to June, she wasn't going to tell Brett.

Irving had volunteered to take the harder of the two interviews today: talking to their sergeant about his son's connections to June. Talking to Lizzie should have been easy considering Brett already had rapport with her from their interactions over the past year. She wasn't a stranger, not a mean woman with a badge and a list of questions to check off. Brett cared about Lizzie, and about June. And yes, she was here because it was her job, but she also understood what it was like to lose a piece of your heart, how difficult it was to grieve when you didn't have any answers.

Brett had seen the two girls together and knew how close they were, like sisters. Naively, she'd thought that because of this Lizzie would want to do anything she could to help find June's killer. There was no reason for her to keep quiet unless she had something to hide.

"Were you and June fighting?" Brett asked.

Red spots flared in Lizzie's cheeks, and her eyes narrowed. She crossed her arms over her chest. "No."

"Was June upset about anything? Was she scared of someone?"

"No."

One-word answers were better than silence, Brett supposed. Plus, Lizzie wasn't as good at keeping her secrets as she thought she was. She wore her emotions in the tilt of her mouth, the heat blossoming across her cheeks and chest, the way her eyes darted to the left when she was lying about something, like they did when she said June wasn't scared of someone.

Brett slipped the Polaroid picture Irving had found in June's room from the notebook resting on her lap. She held the photograph out for Lizzie to see.

"The four of you look pretty close in this picture."

Lizzie's brow crumpled, and her lower lip trembled. She looked like she was trying to hold back her emotions, but couldn't. Her hand lifted, taking the picture from Brett and setting it on her knee. With one finger, she traced a heart around June's face.

"We were going to drive to Seattle." Her voice was a scratch above a whisper.

Brett let the silence settle, knowing that sometimes waiting people out was enough for an entire story to shake loose. But Lizzie was stubborn and didn't seem to care about the bloated silence or the way her grandfather shifted in his chair, readjusting his slacks, clearly uncomfortable.

She stared at the picture and said nothing.

Brett spoke first, trying to draw more out of her. "Who was going to drive to Seattle? You and June with these two boys?"

Without lifting her eyes from the photograph, Lizzie nodded. "We were going to leave on Halloween. We were just going to stay the weekend," she added quickly, her head finally lifting as her eyes swiveled to her grandfather. "Daniel has a cousin there. We were going to stay at his apartment, do some sightseeing stuff. We were bored. We were..." Her gaze dropped again, focusing on her lap this time, her hands folded together. "We wanted a break."

"You weren't planning to run away?" Brett asked.

Lizzie swallowed hard enough for Brett to hear a faint clicking sound at the back of her throat. "No. We were going to come back after a few days." But her eyes darted to the left with the lie.

"Daniel..." Brett tapped her finger on the picture. "This is him, right?"

Lizzie nodded.

"Is he June's boyfriend?"

Lizzie's brow furrowed. "No. June doesn't have a boyfriend."

"And him..." Brett moved her finger to the other boy in the picture. "This is Adam Harris, is that right?"

Another nod.

"So none of you were dating or hooking up or anything like that?" Brett asked.

Lizzie scrunched her nose like something smelled bad, but she didn't answer the question.

Brett shifted focus away from the group's dynamics and asked about their plans for that night instead. "Was Daniel going to drive you?"

"Adam was."

"And you were meeting at Deadman's Point?"

Lizzie's leg bounced as she glanced at the door with a panicked look on her face.

"What time did you and June get there?" Brett pressed.

Lizzie shrugged, and Brett thought she wasn't going to say anything else, but then the words slipped out like she didn't have any control. "Around midnight." And once she started, she couldn't stop herself. "We were supposed to meet at the old ruins out on the headland. June and I got there first a little before midnight. Then Daniel showed up a few minutes later. But Adam wasn't there. Adam never came and he was our ride. We couldn't go without him. I didn't want to stay there. That place freaks me out. So I told them I wanted to leave."

"You left together?" Brett asked.

Lizzie reached to tug on a chunk of her hair. She wrapped it tight around her finger, and her eyes lifted to the ceiling. "No," she finally said. "Just me. I left June and Daniel there alone."

"What time did you leave?"

"It was like twelve-thirty, I think."

"And you came straight home?"

She nodded and shifted her gaze to her grandfather.

Robert Trudeau cleared his throat and sat up a little taller. "I heard her come in through the back door around one-thirty. I went to check on her. She was in her room, listening to music. I left her there and went to bed. When I came down to breakfast the next morning, she was already making herself something to eat. She was dressed and ready for school. Nothing seemed wrong."

"Did you two talk?" Brett asked. "Did she tell you where she'd been?"

He looked disappointed in himself when he shook his head. "I should have asked."

Brett turned her attention back to Lizzie, keeping her tone neutral when she asked, "Have you seen or spoken to Daniel since Thursday night?"

Lizzie whipped back from the words, her whole body going tense. "He wouldn't hurt her. I know that's what you're thinking, but Daniel would never do something like that. Someone else must have come while they were still there. Someone could have followed us into the woods—"

"Lizzie," Brett interrupted her before the girl spun completely out of control. "Please answer my question. Have you seen or spoken to Daniel since Thursday?"

Her shoulders collapsed forward as she let out a meek, "No."

Then she seemed to remember something important because she snapped straight again, and the flush returned to her cheeks. "Have you talked to Mr. Cadden?"

"Who's that?" Brett jotted the name down in the notebook.

"He's an art teacher. And the assistant soccer coach. He comes across as this nice guy, but really he's a creep."

"What do you mean by 'creep?'" Brett asked.

A look of concern passed across Robert Trudeau's face. Lizzie's cheeks flushed a deeper red, as if she were embarrassed to be talking about this kind of thing in front of him.

"He was always really touchy-feely with everyone on the team," Lizzie explained. "Always patting our shoulders, giving high fives and hugs, getting real close to us. And he gave us flowers after our games. Everyone got a single red rose whether we won or lost. I don't know, he creeped me out. And he seemed to be kind of obsessed with June. He was always staring at her more than the other girls and offering to give her a ride home after practice."

"Is that why you both quit soccer?" It was a good reason, but apparently not one June had given her parents as they seemed quite upset by her leaving the sport so abruptly.

The surprise in Lizzie's voice was genuine when she said, "June didn't quit soccer."

Before Brett could continue the interview, Victoria Trudeau bustled into the sunroom holding a cordless phone. The sleeves of her flowery blouse billowed as she waved the phone at her husband.

"It's Marshall." Then she noticed Brett. Her whole body stiffened, and she clutched the phone tight against her bosom. "What are you doing here?"

"Don't get upset, Victoria," Robert said, rising to his feet. "She needed to ask Lizzie a few questions about June, that's all."

Anger flickered across the older woman's stern features. "My granddaughter had nothing to do with that poor girl's death, and next time you feel the need to interrogate a member of my family, you can save yourself the trip out here and call our lawyer."

Brett didn't bother pointing out that it was their lawyer's daughter who was missing, their lawyer who had told her to talk to Lizzie in the first place. If Peter Newmark was no longer able to protect the Trudeau's interests, they could easily hire someone who could.

Victoria Trudeau's smile was a sliver of broken glass as she gestured toward the door. "If you'll excuse us, Detective, we'd like to be left alone. I think you know the way out?"

Brett rose and gathered her things. She thanked Lizzie for her help and shook hands with Robert who gave her an apologetic look.

"If you think of anything else that might be important, you know how to reach me," Brett said before showing herself out of the room with the icy hatred of Victoria's stare burning the back of her neck.

Instead of heading straight to the front door, Brett lingered. If anyone asked, she wasn't eavesdropping, she was just putting her notebook and pen back in her pocket. But she could admit to herself that her curiosity had been piqued. She idled near the door for a few seconds, long enough to hear Victoria say, "Marshall? Yes, here he is." And then, with bright relief, "Our prayers have been answered, Elizabeth. Your father's coming home early."

CHAPTER 12

Brett was so angry hearing the news about Marshall Trudeau's early release that she ordered the wrong sandwich. She lifted the top slice of sourdough, scowled at the bright pink ham slapped between two soggy lettuce leaves and a limp piece of American cheese, and sighed. She'd meant to get turkey with no mayonnaise. At least she'd gotten Irving's order right. He chomped down happily on his meatball sub. Sauce squirted out and landed with a splat on the napkin he wore tucked into his shirt collar to protect his tie. Today it was a simple one: tan fabric with a silhouetted mourning dove embroidered on the tip.

The briefing to discuss progress with the Newmark case wasn't scheduled to start for another half hour, so for the moment, they had the conference room to themselves. They'd needed two tables to spread out all their paperwork.

"I can't believe he's getting out already." Brett took a small bite of the ham sandwich and forced herself to swallow. She had to eat something, and the vending machine in the break room was broken again. "Two years was a light sentence to begin with, and now he's free after just ten months. Jimmy still uses a cane, you know."

"Marshall didn't shoot him, though. Clara did," Irving said, eating the last of his sandwich.

"I remember. I was there. But I blame Marshall, too."

"Why?" Irving wiped his fingers on a napkin.

"He knew about Clara and never came forward."

"He says he didn't know," Irving argued.

"Yeah, well, I think he did." She bit off another chunk of sandwich.

"And how's that working out for you?" Irving arched his eyebrows high.

The ham sandwich landed like a stone in Brett's stomach, but Irving was right. It didn't matter what Brett believed about Marshall's involvement in his wife's crimes, the parole board had decided he was not a significant risk to the general population and therefore eligible for early release, and there wasn't a damn thing she could do about it.

"Tell me what you found out from talking with Elizabeth," Irving said, turning the subject back to more important matters.

Brett told Irving everything she'd learned from her interview with Lizzie Trudeau. "She was reluctant to talk. If you ask me, she's protecting someone."

"And you think it could be this Daniel kid?"

"Maybe. What did Wes have to say?"

"Not much," Irving said. "According to him, the family was home together all night, and Adam never left the house."

"You're kidding me. It's Halloween, and you're telling me this kid spent it at home with his parents? Willingly?"

"Well, he spent it with his parents. I'm not sure if it was willingly. Wes says Adam's been struggling in school recently. He brought home an F in Spanish so they grounded him."

"Because of an F?"

"Because he talked back, threw a fit, whatever it is kids do."

Irving wadded up the empty sandwich paper, twisted in his chair, aimed, and tossed the paper ball at the trash can in the corner of the room. It bounced off the rim and skittered across the floor. He grunted as he rose from his chair to go pick it up and throw it away properly. As he sat down again, he asked, "Do you ever want kids, Brett?"

"What kind of question is that?"

"Just curious. You don't seem like you're in any hurry."

She wasn't, not really. Taking care of Amma was almost like taking care of a kid, and she was barely managing that.

Last night, after getting Amma inside, changed into dry clothes, and tucked back into bed, Amma had grabbed Brett's hand. Her panicked eyes drifted to the large bay window across from her bed where the lamp's reflection distorted the dark and the ocean crashed relentlessly against the shore.

"Where is Lydia?" Amma had asked.

Brett flinched at the sound of her mother's name. With a bitter taste in her mouth, she'd said, "Lydia's dead, Amma, remember. She died fifteen years ago? In a car accident?" If drinking a fifth of vodka and then getting on the freeway could be called an accident.

Amma's lips had pinched, and she burrowed deeper beneath the blankets, shaking her head, as if she could keep Brett's words from breaching whatever memory she was living in where her daughter was still alive.

"Don't let her play too close to the water," Amma said in a hushed voice. "She shouldn't go near the water."

Brett had sighed and made sure the blankets were tight around Amma's thin frame. She'd been too tired to fight with her. "I'll make sure she stays on the beach. Don't worry about Lydia. I'll make sure she's safe."

Amma nodded, satisfied with that answer, and her eyes fluttered closed. Brett had fallen asleep in the high-backed chair in the corner of the room. She'd been too afraid to go back to her own bed, worried that Amma would sneak out again. This morning, she'd woken with a kink in her neck and the beginning of a headache.

Did she want kids? She didn't know. Not now, but maybe someday. She had turned thirty-four this year, and knew if she did want kids, she couldn't keep saying someday and shrugging it off. Already, she felt too old to start trying. Of course, even if she did want kids right now, it's not like she had a lot of prospects in the husband/father department.

As she thought it, the door to the conference room opened, and Eli walked in. He flashed Brett a smile, his twin dimples quickening her pulse. He was a good-looking man, who had still managed to hold onto some boyish charm, even at thirty-eight. When he sat down in the chair next to her, he bumped his leg against hers in a way that felt intentional.

Brett grabbed the paper coffee cup sitting in front of her and tipped the dredges to her lips to cover the sudden blush rising in her cheeks. The coffee was lukewarm and sludgy. She swallowed it anyway.

"How's it going in here?" Eli tapped his fingers lightly on the tabletop. "Stan wants to do another press conference this afternoon. He's hoping you'll have something more substantial for him this time."

Irving filled Eli in on what they'd uncovered so far.

"Wes' story fits with what Lizzie told me," Brett said. "According to her, Adam never showed up at Deadman's Point, even though he was their ride out of town."

"You really buy this story that they were going to Seattle just for the weekend?" Eli pointed at the uneaten half of her ham sandwich. "Are you going to finish that?"

She shoved it over to him. He ate it in three bites.

"I'm not sure it matters whether they were going to be there for a weekend or the rest of their lives," Irving pointed out. "They didn't make it there. They never left Crestwood."

"June and Lizzie and Adam didn't," Brett said. "But Daniel... he's still our unknown factor here."

"So that's who we need to focus on first, right?" Eli asked. "This Daniel Yoon kid?"

Irving nodded, shuffling through some papers until he found what he was looking for.

Brett said, "We need to track him down as soon as possible, especially since it seems he may have been the last one to see June alive."

"And considering who his father is." Irving pushed the paper across the table to Brett.

It was an arrest report for Randall Yoon. Randall was a known felon, in and out of prison for almost a decade for various misdemeanors. He was considered a small-time criminal until last year when he was caught with over a pound of cocaine, two pounds of marijuana, and three unregistered guns hidden in the trunk of his car as he was trying to cross the border into Canada. Hoping to catch a bigger fish, the prosecutor's office tried to cut Randall Yoon a plea deal if he rolled on his bosses, but Yoon kept his mouth shut. The judge had sentenced him to fifteen years.

"You think Daniel picked up where his father left off?" Brett asked.

"I think it's interesting that the daughter of the lawyer who represented Randall Yoon is dead and now Randall Yoon's son is nowhere to be found," Irving said.

"It's a small town," Brett countered.

"Not that small," said Eli.

"Daniel doesn't have any criminal history, though, right?" Brett asked, passing the rap sheet back to Irving.

"Nothing that we've caught him for yet anyway."

Brett found that to be a cynical viewpoint: innocent until we catch you being guilty. Not everyone broke the law. But she understood, too, how easy it could be for a son to follow in his father's footsteps once the path was laid.

"When you talked to his mother, did she mention being worried about Daniel?" Irving asked.

"She was worried because he was missing, sure, but no, she didn't say anything about his father. Or any kind of criminal behavior."

"Do we think he's on the run, or do we think there's another body out there?" Eli asked.

"Like a murder-suicide? Is that what you're thinking?" Brett asked.

The weather hadn't cleared up enough to send boats to check the rocks around Deadman's Point, but so far there hadn't been any evidence to suggest Daniel was dead, too. Except for Ed Shoal's strange report of a couple jumping off the cliff. June hadn't gone over, but maybe Daniel had.

Eli shrugged. "Or maybe the crew Randall was working for tried to recruit his son and Daniel wanted nothing to do with them? Maybe that's why he was leaving with the other kids? Maybe he had some dirt on the crew? Maybe they didn't like the idea of him leaving, knowing what he might have known? Maybe they followed him out to the peninsula, and June got caught in the crossfire. I don't know. I'm throwing things at the wall here, hoping something will stick."

Brett and Irving exchanged a glance. Eli had been working for the Crestwood Police Department as a patrol officer for over ten years. He'd applied for a promotion to detective the year before Brett was hired. There was no doubt in her mind he would have gotten the spot, too, if Henry hadn't asked for her transfer. Eli Miller was the kind of officer who paid attention and thought outside the box, plus he got along with everyone. Brett was sure he'd be wearing a detective's badge in no time, as soon as a spot opened up again.

"He has a cousin in Seattle," Brett said. "So let's start there. Find out what he knows."

"And if Daniel's not there?" Eli asked.

"We send out a bulletin," Irving said, jotting notes. "Then we get his mother on television asking him to come home. See if we can bring him out of hiding."

"And if he's not hiding?" Brett asked, not needing to say the rest out loud.

"Then we head back to Deadman's Point with cadaver dogs and see if they turn up anything." Irving's voice was strained.

Brett hoped it wouldn't come to that either.

"What about Peter Newmark?" she asked.

Irving and Eli both looked at her like she'd spoken gibberish.

"What about him?" Irving asked.

"He was oddly specific with details when we interviewed him yesterday," she said. "Like he was trying a little too hard to give us an alibi, you know?"

"He's a lawyer," Irving said. "His whole career depends on details."

"He's June's father," Eli added. "What's the motive there? Why murder your own daughter?"

"Maybe it was an accident," Brett suggested.

Eli gave her a doubtful look, then leaned forward in the chair, to check the notes sitting on the table. He tapped one of the papers. "What about this teacher? This Mr. Cadden? It seems like there could be something there, right?"

"It's definitely worth checking out," Brett said, going along with his train of thought. The last thing she wanted was for Peter Newmark to be their prime suspect; she was happy to chase other theories first, but early in a case like this one, all options needed to be considered. Even the ones that seemed implausible.

"We need to find out when he saw June last," Brett said. "And if there was anything going on between them, any truth to what Lizzie told us about his behavior with the girls on the soccer team.

Maybe he knows why June quit playing. We should talk to the other girls on the team, too. See if she confided in any of them."

Irving continued to make notes. "What's the status of the autopsy? Do we have that yet?"

"Last I heard, we're still waiting," Eli said. "There was some big accident yesterday on the highway headed toward Mount Baker. Really nasty crash. Several fatalities. Three bodies came into the morgue about an hour before Charlie was going to start June's autopsy. Plus, a couple of suspicious deaths came in around the same time. Most likely drug overdoses, but we need him to confirm before we can close those. Anyway, it sounds like they're slammed over there right now, but Charlie says he's going to try to get to June on Monday or Tuesday."

"But that doesn't slow anything down on our end, right?" Brett said.

"Not really." Irving began to gather his papers. "We know enough to keep pushing this investigation forward."

The conference door opened again and a pair of officers entered. They nodded at Irving, Brett, and Eli, and then found seats. More officers trickled in over the next few minutes until the room was full. There was no cross-chatter, no one telling dirty jokes. They were nearing the thirty-six hour mark since June Newmark's body was found and they had no suspects in custody. The mood was grim. The more time passed without an arrest, the more likely this case would go cold. A result no one wanted.

Irving stood and walked to the front of the room. "Okay, listen up. Here's what we know so far."

CHAPTER 13

Daniel Yoon's cousin didn't know a damn thing.

Brett spent two hours interviewing him, but his story never changed. He told her that Daniel had called a few weeks ago asking if he and some friends could stay at his apartment until they found a more permanent place of their own. The cousin's roommate had recently and unexpectedly moved out, and so the cousin said yes to Daniel because he needed help with the rent. He offered Daniel the second bedroom for half of what the last guy paid.

"I moved out when I was about his age," the cousin told Brett. "And it would have been a lot easier if someone had helped me the way I was going to help him. I wanted to give him a safe place to stay in the city. I see kids his age out here, sixteen, seventeen, younger even, living on the streets, turning to drugs, prostitution, getting into really bad shit. I didn't want him ending up like that. I wanted him to have a chance to figure out his life before he flushed it down the toilet, you know?"

When no one showed up on Thursday night, the cousin assumed Daniel had changed his mind. It wasn't until he got home from work late Friday afternoon and heard his Auntie Patricia's panic-stricken voice on the answering machine that he realized something was wrong. The cousin swore up and down and sideways that he hadn't seen or spoken to Daniel since he'd gone missing.

Brett took a quick look around the apartment, but found no signs of Daniel or anyone but the cousin living there. She left her business card and instructions to call if he heard anything from the missing boy, then hurried back to the car where she'd left Amma waiting with Pistol.

Today was one of Amma's good days—no confusion and not a single memory slip so far. These were the kind of days the neurologist had warned Brett about. Good days that would trick her into thinking there would never again be bad days, even though soon enough, bad days would be all they had left.

"I finished my book." Amma tossed the novel into the backseat. "It was garbage."

Brett twisted to look at the cover, but didn't recognize the title or author. It looked like a thriller with bold, blood-red font and cop car silhouetted against an LA skyline.

Amma tapped the dashboard impatiently. "Hurry up. We're going to be late."

Twenty minutes later, Brett and Amma walked into the downtown bookstore where Jimmy's event was being held. The place was packed. They tried squeezing their way through the crowd of excited customers to get closer to the small, raised stage set up near the back of the store, but only managed to make it as far as the last row of folding chairs.

A man stood and offered his chair to Amma. No one offered a chair to Brett. She got Amma settled into her seat, leaving Pistol with her so he could have a warm lap to snuggle with, and then pushed her way to the edge of the crowd. With her back against a bookshelf, she could see most of the room, and more importantly, Jimmy, who sat in a plush purple chair on a small stage.

A wooden cane tipped in steel leaned against one side of the chair. Trixie rested at his feet like a sphinx, with her leash loosely draped over Jimmy's leg. Her mouth was spread in a mischievous grin, her tongue lolling as she panted and gazed out over the gathered crowd with glittering, dark brown eyes. Jimmy's eyes glinted, too, though his were a deep blue, the color of a bottomless sea, swirled through with shadows and darting silver flecks. It was obvious from their expressions how much both man and dog loved being the center of attention.

Jimmy spoke without a microphone. His warm baritone filled the cozy space, expanding into the far corners of the bookstore and echoing off the wooden crossbeams overhead. Faintly beneath that, Brett could hear the murmur of rain on the roof and the soft rise and fall of voices near the front registers, but it was Jimmy who captured the audience's full attention. He was a natural storyteller, drawing in the crowd with his easy cadence.

As Jimmy told them about his hunt for notorious serial murderer Archer French, a man who had confessed to and was serving time for killing eleven women across the state of Oregon in the 1970s, his eyes scanned the room. He lingered on each face for a few seconds before moving on to the next, and it was this, Brett thought, that kept the crowd engaged. He wasn't telling them a story, he was inviting them to live it alongside him.

His gaze skimmed past her, then snapped back and stayed fixed. The corners of his mouth lifted in a surprised smile.

Jimmy looked good up there, comfortable in a black wool jacket over a light gray sweater and loose, darker gray slacks. A pen and the spiral binding of a small notebook stuck out from the pocket of his jacket. He never went anywhere without something to write on.

He was clean-shaven, as he always was, but his maple-brown

hair had grown longer since she last saw him. It was swept to one side, but kept slipping, falling over his eyes, which made him look younger and approachable. He was thirty-six this year, and fine lines were beginning to form, but somehow these made him more attractive. And apparently Brett wasn't the only one who thought so. There were plenty of young women in the audience staring at him with doe-eyes and wanting, but Jimmy didn't seem to notice them. His gaze stayed on Brett, as if she were the only other person in the room.

Growing uncomfortable with Jimmy's focused attention, Brett shifted her gaze away from him. Everyone listening clutched at least one copy of Jimmy's book in their hands. Raincoats were draped over arms and the backs of chairs. A few people carried umbrellas.

Brett's gaze swept over a woman standing on the other side of the room near a bookshelf filled with cookbooks. There was something about how the woman stood that looked familiar, an intensity to her posture that drew Brett's eyes back to her. She was the right height and body type with the same dirty-blond hair that fell in loose waves around her shoulders. Brett's skin prickled with warning. It couldn't be Clara Trudeau. Clara Trudeau was dead. Brett had watched her go under the waves and never resurface. She shifted to try and get a better look at the woman's face which was turned at an angle, but a man stepped in front of her, blocking her view completely.

Before Brett could decide if she wanted to try and get closer, Jimmy said her name.

Every single person in the crowd turned to stare.

"Wave, Brett, so everyone knows who you are." He flashed a wide smile. "Brett was instrumental in helping me track the Ophelia Killer."

Heat rushed to Brett's cheeks. She lifted her hand stiffly, offering an even stiffer smile.

"Even though Archer French turned out not to be Margot Buchanan's murderer, he did have a connection, and it was that connection that ultimately led us straight to his door. If I hadn't met Brett, if she hadn't been brave enough to share her sister's story with me, who knows how long French would have gone on killing."

Brett wouldn't call it bravery so much as desperation. But she didn't correct him. The audience shifted their attention back to Jimmy as he continued to talk. "Now, I know you all have plenty of questions for me. Who wants to get the ball rolling?"

Hands shot into the air.

Brett glanced at the cookbook shelf again, but the strange woman was gone. She found herself scanning the crowd. A faint pressure settled against her ribs as she remembered the dark night, the cold water, the hiss of the ocean pulling her under, almost drowning. The long search that came after. They never found Clara Trudeau's body, but that didn't mean she'd survived the frigid waters of Sculpin Bay. Even if by some small miracle she was still alive, she'd be a fool to show herself tonight, to come anywhere close to Jimmy. But it wasn't her. It couldn't possibly be her.

With loud applause, the event ended, and the store began to fill with friendly chatter. Chairs squealed as people rose from their seats and moved toward the signing line. Brett nudged her way through the mass of bodies to get to Amma and Pistol.

Amma smiled at Brett and motioned her to sit in a recently vacated chair. "Quite the turnout. Not that I'm surprised. It's hard not to be drawn to a man like that."

Her gaze shifted to Jimmy who was chatting with a woman about Brett's age as he signed her book. He laughed at something the woman said, and Brett felt a hot spark of jealousy ignite in her chest, but she quickly smothered it. She had no claim on Jimmy. She'd had her chance, and she turned him down.

As the woman moved away from the signing table, Jimmy looked over at Brett and winked. She smiled and tapped her watch. He held up his hand, spread his fingers, and mouthed, *Five minutes.* But from the way length of the line waiting to talk with him, she knew it would be longer than that. Amma didn't seem to mind. She sat content, humming to herself and scratching Pistol's ears.

Out of the corner of her eye, Brett saw a flash of burgundy, the same color jacket the woman near the cookbooks had been wearing earlier. Brett turned her head to see the very same woman, the one who couldn't possibly be Clara Trudeau, dart down one of the aisles in the fiction section.

"I'll be right back," Brett said to Amma. "Don't leave the store, okay?"

Amma nodded and patted Pistol's head. "We're not going anywhere."

Brett wove through the clusters of people still crowding the store. She rounded the corner where she'd seen the woman, but the aisle was empty. She walked to the end, looked left and then right, but the woman had disappeared again.

Brett searched every aisle in the store. She felt like she was chasing a ghost. When she was about to give up she saw another flash of burgundy near the front register. The woman paid for a book, then she was gone again, out the front door, before Brett had a chance to see her face.

Brett hurried outside. Rain dribbled from overflowing gutters. Cars drove past, their tires churning through deep puddles and splashing the sidewalk. Headlights sliced the darkness. The woman in the burgundy coat was nowhere to be seen.

As Brett walked back into the bookstore, she collided with Jimmy. He put a hand out, steadying her. "I thought you were leaving without saying goodbye."

"No, I thought I saw..." She glanced at the street, then shook her head. "Never mind. It was nothing." She smiled at him. "Long time no see. Do you always get this good of a turnout?"

She gestured to the stage where a handful of people from the earlier mob still lingered. They were gathered around Trixie now, feeding her treats and scratching her ears. Trixie basked in their attention, rolling onto her belly and kicking her feet playfully.

"I don't think they're here for me," Jimmy said with a laugh. Then he stepped forward and folded Brett into a hug.

"It's good to see you, Bretty." Only Jimmy could call her that and get away with it.

She relaxed against him, breathing in the damp wool and slightly bookish scent of him, like a library filled with leather-bound classics and comfy chairs. After a beat, she stepped out of his arms and smoothed her fingers over her hair. "Are you almost done here?"

"Yeah. A few more minutes, then do you want to grab dinner? I know this great Thai place down the street."

Brett checked her watch. It was almost seven, and they still had a long drive back to Crestwood.

"I already asked Amma," Jimmy said with a grin. "She said it was fine. Actually, she said, 'That sounds great, I'm starving.' So yes, even though you have a long drive back home, she's going to make you stop for food at some point anyway, so you might as well eat now, with me."

"Okay, enough," Brett said. "Twist my arm already. You finish talking with your adoring fans. I'll go get Amma."

But Amma wasn't in the chair where Brett had left her moments ago. Neither was Pistol.

CHAPTER 14

"Excuse me?" Brett approached an employee who was dismantling the rows of folding chairs and stacking them onto a cart. Her eyes never stopped scanning the store for Amma.

"Have you seen an older woman? Grandmotherly type. She has short, silver hair? About this tall?" Brett held her hand at shoulder level. "She was sitting right over there with a little brown dog, a Chihuahua with a white mark on his nose and ears that don't quite stand up straight? Did you see them leave?"

The employee shook his head and shrugged apologetically.

Brett spun in a circle, scanning the area, hoping Amma was browsing the shelves or checking out the calendar section on the far wall. The store was emptying out quickly, which made it easier to search, but Amma was nowhere to be seen. Brett's chest tightened as panic rose. She moved toward the front door again, grabbing the elbow of a different employee who was walking past and asking if she'd seen Amma. The woman shook her head.

"Is there another exit? A back door or something?" Brett asked.

"Not really," the employee said. "There's a loading dock at the back, and there's a door there, but it's only for employees."

"Is it locked?"

"Not during the day."

"Can you check for me?"

The woman nodded and left Brett. While she waited, Brett circled the store again, hoping she'd simply overlooked Amma, or that her grandmother had ducked out of sight at the perfect moment. Still not finding her, Brett began to call out. "Amma? Anita, are you here?"

People turned to stare.

The woman who'd gone to check the loading dock returned with a disappointed look on her face. Amma wasn't wandering somewhere in the back. According to a man working back there, she hadn't wandered out through the loading dock door either. The employee asked if Brett wanted her to make an announcement over the store's loudspeakers.

"Yes, thank you," said Brett. "Her name is Anita Wilson."

By this time, Jimmy, who had gone back to talking with fans near the stage before Brett realized Amma was missing, noticed something was wrong. He excused himself from the small cluster of people wanting their books signed and approached Brett. "What's going on?"

"Amma's gone. I left her right there." She pointed to the space where the chair used to be.

An employee was now pushing an end-cap filled with books into its spot.

"Maybe she took Pistol outside?" Jimmy suggested in a voice that was trying to be reassuring, but stirred Brett's panic hotter.

"I told her not to leave the store," Brett said.

"She couldn't have gone far." Jimmy released Brett and started to search down an aisle Brett had already gone down twice. "I'm sure we'll find her."

The music stopped, and a woman's voice cut in. "Mrs. Anita Wilson please come to the front desk. Mrs. Anita Wilson, your party will meet you at the front desk."

Brett swung her gaze toward the front of the store. She held her breath. A few seconds passed. She began to plan out what she would do next. Call Seattle Police. Drive through nearby neighborhoods, shouting her grandmother's name. Jimmy was right that she couldn't have gotten far on foot. Brett had been outside the store for a minute, maybe two. And Amma had been out of her sight for no more than ten. Brett began to drift toward the front doors.

She was almost to the registers when Amma appeared at the end of an aisle. She carried a book under one arm, Pistol under the other. Her mouth was pinched in a frown as she hurried in the direction of the registers. She stopped when she saw Brett, and her mouth pinched tighter.

Brett crossed the short distance to get to her. "There you are!"

"You didn't have to embarrass me like that," Amma scolded her.

"You could have told me you were going to walk around."

"I was looking for something new to read." She held the book out to Brett. The author of this book was the same as the book Amma had left in the backseat of the car earlier.

"Is this the sequel to the one you finished today?" Brett asked. Amma nodded.

"I thought you said it was garbage," said Brett.

"Yes, well, I still want to know what happens." She tilted her chin defiantly and marched to the register to pay.

Jimmy appeared beside Brett. She waited for him to say, *I told you she'd be fine*, but he didn't say a word, just stood beside her, studying Amma with worry folding his brow.

He had Trixie with him this time, and his cane, too. He leaned on it when he walked, the steel tip clicking on the floor, though it seemed more accessory now than necessity. The limp he'd had in the days after his surgery was barely noticeable anymore.

When Amma stepped away from the counter, Jimmy offered his elbow. "Shall we dine, madam?"

Amma slipped her arm through Jimmy's as he walked them out of the store.

Outside, everyone pulled up their rain hoods. Jimmy shook out an umbrella and held it over Amma's head. Pistol wiggled to be set down. Brett took the leash. He sniffed a post and lifted his leg, then spent a few minutes sniffing and wagging tails with Trixie. Jimmy unlocked his car and they left the dogs inside while they walked two blocks to the restaurant.

Dinner was uneventful. Jimmy ordered chicken curry and fried rice for the table. Amma ordered a bottle of white wine. They toasted to Jimmy's success. As they ate, he told them stories of his time on the road. The fans who wanted to buy him drinks, the missed flights, the interviews with movie producers, the time Trixie got stuck in an elevator without him and rode it all the way to the penthouse.

Brett sipped her glass of wine and tried to focus on his voice. She wanted to relax and enjoy herself, enjoy this time with her friend—the first time they'd really been together in almost a year—but her mind kept drifting to how twice in as many days, she'd had to go looking for Amma. She couldn't stop herself from spiraling into what ifs.

What if Amma had left the store and stepped into the street?

What if she'd been hit by a car?

What if she'd fallen and broken a hip?

What if she had gotten into a stranger's car, thinking she knew them?

When Brett tried to shove these unhelpful thoughts away, thoughts of June Newmark and Daniel Yoon slipped in instead. Where was Daniel hiding? Was he the one who killed June? Or was he dead, too?

Brett picked at her food, her appetite gone. She was anxious to get back to Crestwood and talk to Irving about what to do next since the cousin was a dead-end. Maybe Daniel had turned himself in during the time she'd been gone. Maybe they'd talked to somebody who'd seen something. But Amma wasn't in any hurry. She poured more wine and offered some to Brett, but Brett waved the bottle away.

"I'm driving, remember," she said, then added, "Actually, I think it's about time for us to head home."

Both Amma and Jimmy looked disappointed. Brett tapped her watch. "It's already nine."

"I can sleep in the car," Amma said with a flap of her hand.

"I can't."

"Alright, alright, party-pooper."

They boxed up the extra food and gathered their coats and purses. Jimmy paid the check, refusing to accept even the tip from Brett or Amma.

"Technically, my publisher's paying," he said in a conspiratorial whisper.

Outside again, the rain had turned to a light mist. Jimmy still held the umbrella for Amma as they walked back to his car to get the dogs.

"Where are you parked?" Jimmy asked.

"Down that way." Brett pointed.

He and Trixie walked with them. Brett got Amma settled in the passenger seat and Pistol in the back before coming around to say goodbye to Jimmy.

His expression was serious when he asked, "When will I see you again?"

She answered honestly, "I don't know."

"I could drive up right now." A smile toyed on his lips. "I could follow you in my car. I'm sure there are vacancies at one of the hotels as long as there are no festivals this weekend."

"There aren't," she said.

"Surprising."

"But Jimmy—"

"I don't have to be in Boise until next week," he interrupted her. "We could go up to the mountains and play in the snow."

"I wish, but like I told you over the phone, I've got this case." She hated that she couldn't say yes to him. "And I can't really take time away from it. Not right now."

"You're here, though aren't you?" That smile flashed across his face again, the one that made Brett's pulse speed up. The same smile that made her want to turn away so she didn't have to see it disappear.

"We're looking for this kid who we think saw our victim last," she explained. "His cousin lives in Seattle."

She didn't have to say more than that. Jimmy was smart enough to put the pieces together.

"Right. That makes more sense." His smile was bitter now. His laugh, shattered. "Obviously you didn't come all the way down here just to see me."

"I wanted to come to your event, too." She tried to backpedal, even though she knew it was too late. "It worked out that I could do both. Kill two birds with one stone, you know?"

He squinted at the street lamp. Orange ribbons of fog twisted in the light. He sighed when he said, "I'm not a bird, Bretty."

"You know what I mean."

"Okay, well." He stuffed his hands in his pockets and hunched his shoulders to his ears. "Thanks for coming. Lucky me, I guess."

"Jimmy, come on, don't sulk."

She wanted him to look at her the way he had inside the bookstore—with delight and surprise, like she was the one person in the room worth noticing—but he refused to lift his gaze from the sidewalk.

"I don't think I can do this anymore," he said.

"What? Stand in the rain?" She made her voice light, trying to steer the conversation away from more dangerous territory, but Jimmy wouldn't go for it.

He shook his head, hunching himself smaller. "No, Bretty, you know that's not what I'm talking about. I can't do this. With you." Finally, he lifted his head to look at her. "Last year, I put my heart on the line for you. I put my body on the line, too." He laughed again, anger visible in the twist of his lips and the way his hand reflexively drifted to his leg where the bullet had hit. "And you told me you wanted to be friends. So fine, I said, fine, let's be friends. It's better than nothing. But honestly, it doesn't feel like you even want to be friends, either."

"Jimmy, that's not fair."

"It's not? Tell me, Brett, tell me what being friends means to you. Because to me, it means talking every once in a while, supporting one another, being there for each other. I talk to Amma more these days than I talk to you."

"We live in different states."

"That didn't seem to matter before I told you I had feelings for you. You called me all the time. You were happy to have me visit."

"You're right," Brett admitted. "It's not the same."

Jimmy turned his gaze toward the street. His jaw was tense, as was his grip on the top of his cane. At his feet, Trixie, who had been quiet up to this point, whined and tugged on her leash. He gave her a little slack so she could go sniff a crack in the concrete.

"But it's not because of what you said," Brett continued, trying to spare his feelings. "I mean, maybe it is, I don't know, but also there's a lot more going on right now. With Amma. With work. I'm trying to figure out where I fit in with this department. Which means I'm trying not to stick out so much, which means running around buddy-buddy with a reporter probably isn't the best idea."

"Since when have you ever cared about shit like that?"

Jimmy hardly ever cursed. He always said swearing was for sailors and special occasions. This didn't feel like a special occasion to her, but there it was anyway.

"People change, Jimmy," she said, as tension threaded down her spine.

"I know that, Brett."

She was done fighting in the rain and done feeling bad for not giving him what he wanted.

"I have to go." She twisted away from him to open the driver's door.

He grabbed her hand. There was no violence to it, only a desperate hope. His voice was low, his breath grazing the back of her neck, when he said, "I still love you, Bretty. I don't think I'll ever stop."

He released her and stepped back. With a gentle tug on Trixie's leash, he vanished into the fog.

CHAPTER 15

On Monday morning, as Lizzie walked through the living room to the kitchen to grab some cereal before heading to school, she saw something on television that stopped her in her tracks. Daniel's mother faced a small crowd and a cluster of microphones outside the police station. She looked so small sandwiched between two men in uniform. Like a child, not somebody's mother.

The younger man on Mrs. Yoon's right was Lizzie's Uncle Eli. He wasn't really her uncle, just her father's best friend. Or ex-best friend. He hadn't come around much since last year, which she understood considering what her parents had done. It wouldn't look good for a cop to be friends with criminals. But even though she hadn't talked to him in months, she still thought of him as her uncle. He looked serious and stiff today in his plain blue uniform.

The stick-skinny man standing on Mrs. Yoon's left side was Crestwood's new police chief. Lizzie's grandmother had pointed him out at the diner a few weeks ago, telling her that she didn't have to worry anymore because Chief Harcourt was going to make their town safe again, the way it used to be. Lizzie hadn't liked him in the diner, and she didn't like him any better now, with his sideways smirk and flinty gaze.

He opened the press conference with a brief statement about needing the public's help to locate a witness who might have critical information about the ongoing investigation into June's death. Then he stepped aside and gestured for Mrs. Yoon to get closer to the microphones. Her voice trembled as she spoke.

"I don't care what you've done, Daniel. You're not in trouble. I just want you to come home. I need you to come home. Please. If you're listening to this. If you're watching. Please, come home. These police, these men, they want to help us. They can help you. But you have to come home. I love you, Daniel. Your mother loves you."

Her voice cracked like she was going to start crying, but she didn't. She tilted up her chin stoically and stepped back from the microphones, allowing the chief to step forward again.

With no sympathy for the broken-hearted woman beside him, the chief said, "Daniel Yoon is wanted for questioning in the death of June Newmark. Anyone who may have information about his whereabouts is encouraged to contact the Crestwood Police Department immediately. Now, if you have questions—"

He didn't get a chance to finish before reporters started yelling at him.

Lizzie's attention was so fixed on the press conference, she didn't hear Grandpa come up behind her until he cleared his throat.

She startled, spinning to face him.

"Easy, Lizbug," he said, talking in the voice he used with spooked horses. "It's just me."

He listened for a moment as the chief answered a reporter's question. The lines in his face deepened with concern. "I think it's time we sat down and had a long talk about all of this."

"About what?" Her throat was dry.

Grandpa gestured to the television. "About June. About that boy who's missing. About the fact that you think you have to keep secrets from me."

He walked over to the television and turned it off. He motioned for Lizzie to sit down, but if she sat, she'd have to talk to him, and if she talked to him, she'd have to admit that this was all her fault, and if she admitted this was all her fault, then she'd have to figure out a way to fix it. But the only way to fix it was to go back in time, and she couldn't do that, so what was the point of talking?

Lizzie spun away from her grandfather and ran through the house and out the back door. She sprinted across the neatly cut lawn toward the barns. Rain slashed across her face. She slipped on the muddy grass, caught herself on a fence, and kept running. She glanced over her shoulder once, but Grandpa wasn't coming after her.

Inside the barn was warm and sweet with fresh-cut hay. Just stepping through the doors calmed Lizzie's racing heart. It was quiet here, and there was a feeling that she had stepped into a place apart from the rest of the world—a sanctuary where nothing bad could ever happen.

Dim, golden light slipped through skylights in the ceiling. The horses in their stables huffed a greeting when she walked down the aisle to the stall at the far end where a shimmering black mare whinnied and tossed her head in anticipation. Lizzie grabbed a bag of oats from the tack room and went to greet the horse.

Of the six horses belonging to Lizzie's grandmother, Magpie was her favorite. And though Magpie had never said as much, Lizzie thought the feeling was mutual. The black mare nuzzled Lizzie's shoulder, then worked her velvet lips down her arm to her outstretched hand, snorting and huffing as she ate the offered oats.

Lizzie had no idea where Daniel was, but if she did, she'd tell him to not to come back here, not now that the police were looking for him. She didn't trust the police—not even her Uncle Eli—and she worried they would take one look at Daniel and decide what kind of person he was before he even had a chance to explain himself. It's what everyone did to Daniel, even Lizzie.

Daniel Yoon was a quiet kid, an awkward kid, the kind of kid who wore all black and ate lunch by himself and was always hunched over a notebook, scribbling. The kids at school picked on him, tripping him in the hallway and calling him mean names. Before last summer, Lizzie must have passed him in the hallways at school a hundred times and hadn't said a single word to him. She'd looked right through him, like he wasn't even there. Though it wasn't like he tried hard to get her attention either.

All that changed last summer in the parking lot outside the prison where Lizzie's father was serving his two-year sentence. She'd been upset about having to visit her father in prison in the first place, and then got even more upset when he spent the whole visit blubbering like a baby and blathering on about all the things in his life he regretted. Cry all he wanted, his guilty tears would never be enough to fix everything he'd broken. She'd fled the visiting room, out the front doors and into the parking lot, and that's where she found Daniel. He was leaning against the bumper of a beat-up old silver Chevy, a cigarette dangling from his lips like he was some kind of wanna-be-James-Dean-rebel-without-a-cause.

His eyes caught hers, and he jerked his head in silent acknowledgment. Ash from the cigarette fell to the pavement.

"Hey," he said.

Hey. Like it was no big deal that the two of them were running into each other hundreds of miles from Crestwood in the parking lot of a fortress made of impenetrable concrete walls and barbed wire fences. *Hey.* Like this wasn't the first time they'd ever spoken, the first time he'd even noticed her. *Hey.* Like they were already best friends.

He offered his cigarette, and though she'd never smoked before in her life, she took it and inhaled deeply, then immediately started coughing. He didn't laugh. He said, "Small sips," and she tried again and didn't cough.

"What are you in for?" He smiled at her when he said it because he knew, didn't he? Everyone knew about her mother and her father and the complete disaster of her life.

When she didn't answer, he tilted his head back and blew a perfect smoke ring.

"Can you teach me how to do that?" she asked.

"I can teach you a lot of things," he said, smiling at her again, and it was at that moment she realized she'd been wrong about him.

He wasn't someone to fear; he was the friend she needed.

She introduced him to June the very next day.

Lizzie swallowed down the bitter taste of grief rising in her throat. Magpie leaned over the stall door and nuzzled her hair, but it didn't make her feel any better.

With one simple word—*Hey*—Daniel had pulled Lizzie from the brink of her own expanding loneliness. She wasn't the only kid spending Saturdays visiting her dad in prison. She and Daniel connected over their shared losses and their hatred of the place that had ruined their lives. For as much as Lizzie wanted to escape Crestwood and her parents' long and twisted shadows, Daniel seemed to want it more. It was Daniel who planted the idea of leaving, but it was Lizzie who nurtured it and made it grow.

Guilt warmed her cheeks. It was her fault they were at the ruins that night. If she had never left the visitor's room, if she hadn't walked into that parking lot, if she had pretended not to see Daniel standing there, if she had done what she'd always done before and looked right through him, June would still be alive. She was sure of it.

The barn door creaked open. Grandpa came inside, shook out an umbrella, leaned it against the wall, and walked to where Lizzie stood near Magpie's stall. He pulled two carrots from his pocket and handed them both to Lizzie.

"I know you don't want to talk about this, Lizbug." His voice was gentle. "But I need you to tell me the truth."

"I told you," she insisted. "You were sitting right there when I told Detective Buchanan everything I know. I didn't kill her."

"I know you didn't." He put one hand on her back.

It took all her effort to pretend she didn't care.

"I believe you told Detective Buchanan the truth about not being there when June was killed," he said.

How, she wondered, how could he say those words so calmly? But when she glanced at him, she saw how the words aged him, breaking his hard outer shell. Tears glistened on his thin eyelashes. She fixed her gaze on Magpie, focusing all her attention on the dark strands of the forelock sweeping across her black marble eyes.

"What I need to know," Grandpa said. "What I need you to be completely honest with me about is that boy they're looking for. Daniel Yoon."

She tensed when Grandpa said his name.

"Do you know where he is?" Grandpa asked.

She reached and pushed Magpie's forelock to one side. "No."

Magpie nuzzled her hand. The horse could smell the carrots Lizzie was holding.

"He hasn't tried to contact you?" Grandpa's hand still rested between her shoulder blades as if his skeleton fingers would be enough to keep her from running again.

"I haven't talked to him since Halloween," Lizzie said. "I swear on my mother's watery grave."

She felt him stiffen behind her. He cleared his throat.

Lizzie offered Magpie one of the carrots. The horse chomped down on it, filling the barn with the sound of crunching. In another stall, a roan mare whinnied her jealousy.

"If you do hear from him, I want you to come tell me right away," Grandpa said.

When Lizzie didn't respond, he grabbed her elbow and turned her so they were face-to-face. "Do you understand me, Lizzie? I don't care if you think he's innocent or not, if he tries to get in contact with you, you will tell me or your grandmother or Detective Buchanan immediately."

His gray-blue eyes were clouded with fear.

She wished she could say something true to reassure him, something that would make him stop looking at her like that, but the truth was too painful to say out loud. June was dead because of her. Even though Lizzie hadn't pulled any trigger, she was as guilty as whoever had. But she nodded and softened her mouth into what she hoped would pass as a smile and said the words Grandpa needed to hear.

"No more secrets. I promise."

She shook off his tight grip and walked away. If she hurried, she could still make it to school on time.

CHAPTER 16

"No one wants to say it." Eli Miller ripped open a sugar packet and dumped it into the cup of black coffee sitting on the diner table in front of him. "But ten-to-one says that Yoon kid crossed the border before we even started looking for him."

Brett poured cream and sugar into her cup and stirred slowly. Normally, she liked her coffee bitter and dark, but today she craved sugar, hoping the sweetness would balance out the sourness leftover from her fight with Jimmy last night and the lack of progress they were making with the Newmark case.

"Daniel doesn't have a car," she pointed out.

"Maybe he stole one," Eli suggested.

It wasn't out of the realm of possibility. The Canadian border was less than an hour's drive from Crestwood, and if he got his hands on a vehicle, he could have been halfway through British Columbia before dawn.

"Any reports of stolen cars come in over the weekend?" she asked.

"No, but some guy did report a stolen fishing boat."

"So Daniel drove a boat to Canada? In the middle of the night?"

Eli shrugged and sipped his coffee. "Stranger things have happened. Besides, he wouldn't even have to make it all the way to Canada. There are plenty of islands between here and there he could be hiding out on."

"So he's a survivalist now, too?" Most of the islands Eli was referring to were uninhabited.

"People live out there," he defended himself. "Hippies, tribes, men who want a little peace and quiet." He lifted his hands like she was pointing a gun at him under the table. A grin spread over his face, his dimples creasing playfully. "Look, you're the one who asked me what I thought."

Even in the dim light of the Blue Whale Diner, his copper eyes managed to sparkle. Under the table, his foot found hers. She moved it away and shifted her gaze out the window.

The street outside was gray and damp. Over the weekend, the Halloween decorations had come down, replaced by twinkle lights, holly wreaths, plastic snowflakes, and Christmas cheer, though they hadn't even made it through Thanksgiving yet.

The section of Sculpin Bay visible from the diner churned with small white caps. Waves slapped against the sandy stretch of beach and rocked the newly built boardwalk that edged Egret's Park. A flock of seagulls huddled together in the grass near a playground where puddles were forming in the dirt. Every few seconds, one of the birds would stretch its wings and shake off the rain, which seemed pointless considering it was still coming down in buckets. It had been raining like this for three days straight. Brett didn't remember last year being so stormy and wet. She was starting to forget what the sun looked like and what it felt like to have dry socks.

She returned her attention to Eli, who was still watching her, that cool smile toying his lips. Lips that had been on hers last week, lips she knew tasted like the salt breeze and summer. She lifted her cup to take a drink of coffee and refocused her thoughts on the only thing she should be thinking about right now: Who killed June Newmark?

"Okay, let's go over this again," she said.

"Do we have to?" But the way Eli asked, gave Brett the impression that he would sit in this booth with her all day and go over the case a hundred times if that's what she wanted.

After the chief's press conference ended, the team working the investigation filed into one of the larger precinct conference rooms. The briefing was short. Brett updated everyone on her dead-end in Seattle. Irving updated them on his dead-end with Daniel's mother. Eli updated them on his dead-end at the school. The team emptied from the conference room with new assignments and follow-up interviews to schedule, but even though they had plenty to keep them busy, it felt like they were slipping into a quagmire. Three days had passed since June's body had been discovered, and their best suspect was in the wind.

Brett had come into the precinct this morning to attend the briefing. Normally, when they weren't working a big case like this one, she had Mondays off, in addition to Sundays. She planned to head straight home after the briefing and spend time with Amma, but Eli had slipped behind her as she was putting on her jacket and asked if she wanted to grab lunch.

They'd gone across the street to the Blue Whale Diner and grabbed a cozy booth near the front where they could look out over the bay. It was clear from the moment they sat down that Eli wanted to talk about things other than the Newmark case, but Brett had deflected him, asking him about Daniel Yoon instead. She thought if she went over everything they knew one more time, maybe things would start making sense.

"So these four kids are meeting up at Deadman's Point on Halloween," Brett said, stirring her coffee as she talked. "They're going to drive to Seattle in Adam's car and stay with Daniel's cousin, but Adam doesn't show up."

"Lizzie leaves when June's still alive," Eli added.

"That's what she says."

"You don't believe her?" His thick eyebrows arched in surprise.

"I'm keeping all options on the table," Brett said. "Option one, Lizzie leaves and June's still alive. That leaves June alone with Daniel. So either Daniel killed her and ran. Or someone else showed up that night after Lizzie was gone."

"And option two?" Eli tapped his finger against the side of his coffee cup.

"Lizzie is there when June is killed."

"I've known Lizzie since she was a baby," Eli said, his voice shifting to one of concern. "I know after everything happened with Clara last year—I know that surprised everyone. But I'm telling you right here and now that Lizzie is nothing like her mother. I don't think she'd be capable of hurting anyone like that, but especially not her best friend. She and June were inseparable. After the losses she's already suffered, I don't see her doing this. Not this."

"Okay, let's work under the assumption that Lizzie was there but didn't kill June. If she was there, then she knows what happened."

"And she's not telling us." Eli scowled at his nearly empty coffee cup, then scanned the restaurant for the server.

"We should talk to her again," Brett said. "Really push her this time. See if she'll give us something more to work with than 'I wasn't there, I didn't see anything.'"

A heavy-set woman with turquoise eyes and dark hair going gray at the roots approached the table with a coffee pot in one hand. She refilled Eli's cup, smiling as she did so. "The regular for you two today, or should I bring menus?"

Police were frequent customers to the Blue Whale since the diner was across from the precinct. Brett and Eli came in together at least once a week, sometimes more. Brett came in with Irving sometimes, too. It was convenient, and the coffee was better than the swill the precinct had, and their egg and English muffin sandwich was the perfect balance of grease, salt, cheese, and meat, and served all day.

Eli flashed the woman his million-dollar smile. "The usual is fine. Thanks, Dot."

Before she left to put their order in, Dot tipped her chin toward the picture window. "The way this rain keeps coming, won't be much longer before this whole town goes under."

But not everyone seemed to be so bothered by the downpour.

A mother and daughter walked along the Egret Park boardwalk, holding hands. They were both decked out in rain gear. The woman wore a teal and pink jacket with black boots. The little girl was dressed in yellow galoshes and a bright red coat. She jumped and flapped her hands like a bird each time a wave hit the shore.

"It's too bad this storm rolled in when it did," Eli said. "Really got us off on the wrong foot with this case. I don't know if we would have found more evidence than what we did, but it certainly didn't help us any." He took a sip of coffee. When he set his cup down again, he said, "The most obvious solution is Daniel Yoon killed her. His footprint was found next to the body."

Irving had confirmed Daniel's shoe size yesterday when he'd gone to the house to interview Patricia one more time. He wore a size ten sneaker, the exact size of one of the prints left at the scene.

"We already know Daniel was there," Brett said. "Lizzie told us as much. It makes sense we'd find his print near June. Whether he killed her or not is the question."

"He has motive," said Eli. "Those letters Irving found in his room prove there was something more than friendship going on between those two."

They were innocent letters, kids' stuff. *Meet you behind the soccer field. You look cute today. Can't wait to see you tonight.* The most salacious one said, *I miss your lips on mine.* All of them were signed, *Yours Forever and Always, Junie.*

The edges were decorated in childish, bubble hearts. Irving had also found a Polaroid picture of June and Daniel cuddled up together. Daniel had his arm around her, drawing her close. June pressed her lips to his cheek. They looked happy.

"You think they got in a fight?" Brett asked.

"Maybe she wanted to break up."

"Or he did."

"We still can't rule out the possibility that they agreed to some sort of Romeo and Juliet lover's death pact," Eli said.

"But why? If they were happy…"

The diner was filling up quickly now that it was almost noon. Brett found the low chatter and clink of dishes soothing. She let her mind wander, drifting along with the background noise until she struck on a new idea.

"Maybe Lizzie got jealous?" she suggested.

"She didn't seem to know about them, did she?"

Brett shook her head. "She said June didn't have a boyfriend. But think about it. If Daniel and June were keeping their relationship a secret, and Lizzie found out about it that night? Maybe she didn't like the idea of her two friends dating. Or maybe she had a crush on Daniel, and thought June was butting in where she didn't belong. As far as motives go, it's not outside the realm of possibility that Lizzie might have gotten angry when she learned the truth."

"Angry enough to kill?" Eli sounded reluctant to move Lizzie's name up to the top of the suspect list.

He'd been close to the family before last year, like an uncle to Clara and Marshall's only child. Since learning the truth about Clara, he'd put distance between himself and the Trudeau family, but it was obvious there was some loyalty still simmering beneath the surface.

"If we could find the weapon with Daniel's fingerprints on it, that would help," he said, shifting the focus back on the boy.

"If we could find a weapon at all." Brett rolled her eyes.

They didn't even know what kind of gun they were looking for yet. They were still waiting for the autopsy report. Charlie promised to have it done today or tomorrow, but unless he dug a bullet from June's chest, they wouldn't have much to go on. It wasn't a shotgun, Brett knew that much. There was a single entry wound, so most likely they were looking for a pistol or revolver, a handgun of some kind. Something shot at close range. She knew better than to make a guess before Charlie wrote up his report, but it was hard not to. She wanted to move forward on this case; she wanted some damn answers.

"We have that other footprint to consider, too," Eli said.

A men's size twelve had also been found beneath the trees, close to where June's body was dragged. They'd gotten lucky with the location of that print. It was well-preserved, protected from the rain by a thick, evergreen canopy. Heavy boots pressed deep in the mud formed a near-perfect waffle pattern that would otherwise have been washed away. The print was too big to belong to any of the teenagers.

"It fits with the theory that someone else was there that night," Brett said. "Have we looked at Ed Shoal's shoes yet? Maybe the print is his?"

"I've been by his house at least four times." Eli spread his hands in a shrug. "He's always there. I see him moving behind the curtain, but he refuses to answer the door."

"Keep trying. We need to know how much he saw out there, and if that print is his."

"He'd make a terrible witness in court," Eli pointed out.

"We still need talk to him, ask him to start from the beginning, tell us exactly what happened, what he heard, who he saw..." Brett drifted off as another idea caught her attention. "What about this teacher? This Mr. Cadden? What kind of feeling did you get talking to him?"

"Like I said at the briefing, he seems like a normal guy. Nothing seemed off about him. He's young, handsome, and people seem to like him. And he has good rapport with the girls on the soccer team. We're still interviewing the team, but Coach Lansing had only good things to say about him. Plus, he let me see his shoes, and he's a size nine men's. Not even close."

"What about the roses?" Brett thought of the single flower she'd found resting on June's chest, left as a token, perhaps an apology. The white pedals edged in blood red and glistening from the mist that had fallen overnight. "According to Lizzie, he gave flowers out to the girls after games?"

"He didn't seem to understand what the big deal was. Said he was trying to do something nice. Wanted to encourage them or something. Coach Lansing gave him the go ahead. No complaints from the parents or anything like that. Not that I've heard yet. We'll ask the girls as we go through their interviews, but it seems like it was something that only bothered Lizzie."

"And maybe June," Brett pointed out. "She quit the team, too."

"Yeah, Cadden seemed pretty upset about that," Eli said. "But he said he didn't know why she quit. One day she stopped coming to practice. And now, we're back to Daniel again."

Benjamin Cadden had told Eli in his interview that at the beginning of October, a few days after June quit soccer, Daniel Yoon had approached his desk after class and, out of nowhere, tried to punch him. Cadden was able to sidestep in time, and Daniel's fist glanced harmlessly off his shoulder.

"You really believe there was no provocation for that?" Brett asked.

"Daniel was a student in Cadden's charcoal drawing class for almost two months without a single problem. And he took classes from him last year, too. I checked with the front desk receptionist to confirm what Cadden said about Daniel never being late and never getting in trouble during his class. There was no detention, no arguments that Cadden could remember. He said he likes Daniel. The kid has talent. They got along well before. He was even setting up a show for him down at the community center next month. So he was completely baffled by Daniel's sudden outburst."

Brett tapped her finger on the saucer holding her coffee cup. "But it could make sense if what Lizzie told us is true. Maybe Benjamin Cadden was paying special attention to June, and Daniel didn't like that? Has anyone talked to Principal London yet?"

The question hadn't come up in this morning's briefing for some reason.

"Briefly, to confirm Cadden's story," Eli said. "And she told me she was as surprised as Cadden by Daniel's attack. She said Daniel didn't tell her why he did it. He sat in her office staring at his hands, refusing to say a word. Cadden wanted her to go easy on him since it was his first offense and considering his father's in jail. I guess the kids pick on him a lot at school." He shrugged one shoulder. "They gave him detention, and that was it."

"And he'd never shown any sign of violence before that," Brett mused.

"Or after," Eli added.

How did a kid who seemed as quiet and sensitive as Daniel did, a kid who liked to draw, who was smart and ambitious enough to try and get into Harvard, who brought a slice of pie home to his mother after every shift, who according to the people they'd spoken with so far had never even raised his voice to anyone—except for the incident with Mr. Cadden—how likely was it for that kind of kid to suddenly snap and shoot a girl straight through the heart?

But the way June's body was arranged suggested that whoever killed her had a personal connection, perhaps even felt guilty for what they'd done. They'd been careful with her body when they moved it, covered her face with a scarf, and left a rose in her hands. A stranger wouldn't go to all that trouble.

Dot appeared at their table with two plates. She set the egg and sausage sandwich down in front of Brett and the club sandwich with fruit instead of fries in front of Eli.

"Getcha anything else?" she asked, one drawn-on eyebrow lifted.

"This looks great, Dot," Eli said, reaching for hot sauce to sprinkle on his sandwich.

Dot hesitated like she was thinking about saying something else, then she offered them both a polite smile, spun on her heels, and went to help another table.

Brett watched her a moment before asking Eli, "Who do we have assigned to talk to Daniel's co-workers again?"

"I don't remember. Ennis, maybe." He took a bite of his sandwich.

"We should talk to the Newmarks again, too." Brett put ketchup on her home fries. "We need to find out if Peter's handled any particularly difficult cases recently. If there are any clients who aren't happy with him right now, or if they've been getting any threats."

Eli started in on the second half of his sandwich, without offering any feedback, so Brett continued talking. "Irving's going to swing by Patricia's house again today to check if there are any other relatives Daniel might have reached out to. But I think it would also be a good idea to get in touch with his father. Maybe Randall Yoon pissed someone off and that someone killed June and is now trying to frame his son."

"That seems a bit of a stretch." Eli sipped his water.

"Just seeing what sticks."

"Daniel," he said. "Daniel is what sticks."

"What about Danny Cyrus?" Brett asked.

Eli's eyebrows shot up. "What about him?"

"Danny knows every criminal in this town. He knows who's running, who's hiding, who's doing illegal shit. If this whole thing involves Randall Yoon, or whoever Randall was running drugs for, Danny will know. Maybe Daniel even went to Danny for help."

"We can't talk to Danny." There was a warning in his voice. "Stan won't let us anywhere near him."

Brett rolled her eyes. Danny Cyrus was an informant for some mysterious undercover operation that only Chief Stan Harcourt seemed to know anything about. Sometimes the chief would walk up to a detective's desk, slap down a piece of paper like he was giving out a Christmas bonus, and say something about how Danny says so-and-so's your man, he'll be at such-and-such place at such-and-such time, so don't be late. They closed a lot of cases because of information Danny Cyrus brought them, but Stan was the only person he was allowed to talk to. Brett had never been able to figure out if that was Stan's rule or Danny's.

"We can have Stan talk to him, then," she said. "We need answers, and if Danny has them, Stan shouldn't have a problem asking. He wants this case closed as much as the rest of us do. He's got the mayor breathing down his neck about it, right?"

Eli sighed loudly and shook his head. He popped a piece of cantaloupe into his mouth.

"What?" she asked.

His eyes were burnished brass, kind and shining, when he said, "I know it helps you to go over all this stuff twice, think out loud and all that, but can we please talk about something else now?"

"Sure." She smiled at him as she pushed her home fries around her plate. "What do you want to talk about instead?"

He leaned slightly forward. His knee bumped hers again under the table. This time she didn't move away. "How about when I get to be alone with you again?"

His hand slid up her thigh. She reached under the table and caught his fingers in hers, tangling them together.

"What are you doing tonight?" he asked.

She thought for a moment. He would probably have a small fire going in the fireplace, the lights turned low. He would cook her dinner, pour her a glass of expensive wine, play soft music. She could lose herself in the bass rumble of his voice as he told her about the boat he was building in his garage. A wooden kayak, nothing fancy, he would try to play it off like it was no big deal, but there would be pride in his voice, too, and she would ask him to show her the progress he'd made since last time. He'd take her hand and lead her down the hall. It would be a nice distraction.

Brett pulled her hand away and straightened in the booth, shifting her knee so they weren't touching anymore. "Amma and I are having dinner together tonight."

He nodded, smiling like he understood, like he didn't care that she was giving him the cold shoulder.

It wasn't that she didn't like Eli. She did. That was the problem. She worried she liked him too much. And for the wrong reasons.

When she looked at Eli, she saw herself at fourteen. She saw her summers spent in Crestwood, the summers when her big sister was still alive. Every Fourth of July through Labor Day, she and her sister would stay with their grandparents in the big house on Bayshore Drive. They would swim in the bay and at the community pool where the local boys like Eli would have diving contests and eat french fries and watch the girls sunbathe in their bikinis. They would go to the movie theater, and the boys would be there, too, throwing popcorn and laughing at the kissing scenes.

The summer Margot died, Eli hung around with the Buchanan sisters more than usual because his best friend Marshall Trudeau had fallen for Margot. Brett remembered feeling shy around Eli. He strutted confidence, and flashed his dimpled smile to get whatever he wanted. She remembered that summer wanting nothing more than to have Eli's hand around her waist, and now, when it happened, when he reached for her, she felt a spark of her nearly-forgotten youth. When she was with Eli, it felt like an alternate reality, like she might one day turn the corner and run into golden-haired Margot, head tilted back, laughing and alive.

Eli and Margot had never dated, but Brett remembered their playful flirting—Margot flirted with everyone. She remembered once at the pool, Eli scooped Margot up from the lounge chair and threw her in the deep end. He had touched her skin, breathed her air, heard her voice, seen the glint of mischief in her eyes. Eli had known Margot as a person, not just as a murder victim, a name in a file, a black and white photograph.

To him, Margot was more than another story to tell.

There was a moment last year, after Brett learned the truth about Margot's murder, when she blamed Eli in part for what had happened to her sister, believing he should have done something to stop it, believing he, like Marshall, had known more than he was admitting. But it hadn't taken her long to realize her anger was misdirected. There were dark currents swirling that summer, things she never saw coming, things she barely understood even now after so much had been revealed. One thing she was certain of, though, was this: Eli couldn't have saved Margot that summer any more than Brett could have, but given the chance, he would have tried.

Last August, Eli and Brett had hiked into the woods near Lake Chastain together. Brett didn't know the exact spot where her sister's body was found in the summer of 1964, but it didn't matter. They walked quietly through blue-green shadows until they found a sunny glade next to a babbling stream. Eli stood beside her as she knelt and placed a smooth black stone on the ground. She had thought about bringing flowers, but flowers reminded her too much of Archer French and heartbreak. So she found a river stone shaped vaguely like a heart and carried it around in her pocket for weeks, until finally she decided to go and pay tribute to her sister. It was her way of saying goodbye, but it felt like a beginning, too.

A few weeks after that, things between her and Eli went from just friends to complicated. They'd been drinking beers at a local bar after a long shift. They were flirting, she as much as him. She touched his arm, his leg. He brushed hair from her face. She laughed too hard at his jokes. They were both treading close to that invisible line between professional relationship and trouble, but neither were willing to take a step back.

When he had walked her to her car later, his arm slipped around her waist and then he was pressing her against the side of her VW Beetle and his lips found hers in the dark, and she melted into him. Her grief, the pressure of her job, her worries over her grandmother, her guilt over Jimmy—all of it disappeared in that moment.

It was hard to keep saying no to him, but it was for the best. Their being together couldn't possibly end well for either one of them.

"How about Wednesday?" he asked. "That's my day off. After your shift ends, you could come over."

She fumbled in her pocket for her wallet. "It's not a good idea, Eli."

"Dinner is always a good idea."

"You know that's not what I'm talking about." She dropped a five dollar bill on the table to pay for her lunch.

"I can get it." He waved her money away.

"I'm trying to keep things professional."

His eyebrows lifted.

"Come on, Eli, don't be stupid about this."

He stiffened, making no attempt to hide the hurt on his face. "I like you. I want to spend time with you. How is that stupid?"

Brett rubbed her temples. "If the other guys find out what we're doing, they won't shut up about it. And trust me when I say, you won't be the one they shovel all their shit onto."

"We can talk to the chief," Eli suggested. "I'm sure once he understands the situation—"

"The chief doesn't like me," she interrupted. "He'll use whatever this is—" She waved her hand between them. "—against me. He'll figure out a way to make my life in the department as miserable as he possibly can. He's been looking for a reason to fire me since the day I started, and I'd rather not hand him one on a silver platter."

"And what is this, exactly?" He mimicked her wave. "What is it we're doing here? Because I thought you had feelings for me, too? Was I imagining all of that?"

"No, Eli." She stretched her hand across the table, laying her palm flat. "It's just, it's complicated, okay? There's work. There's Amma."

She sounded like a broken record.

"I like being with you," she said. "You make things...easier." Realizing how belittling that sounded, she rushed to add, "You make things better. I'm happier when I get to spend time with you. It's just..." She trailed off.

"It's complicated." He took her hand and squeezed it once before letting go. He smiled as he reached for his own wallet. "Well, you know where to find me if it ever gets uncomplicated."

He wasn't rushing her to leave, but it felt like the conversation was over anyway. Brett slid out of the booth.

"Hey," he said, his tone easy again, relaxed. "What are you doing for Thanksgiving?"

She thought he was going to ask her over to his parents' house, and she was trying to think of a good excuse to say no, when he said, "You know how every year one of the detectives hosts Thanksgiving?"

She gave him a puzzled look.

"You know," he prompted. "The guys who aren't on shift, we all get together to watch football, drink beers, eat food, the usual.

And the schmucks who do have to work swing by when they can and grab some grub before they head out again. Ennis hosted last year. It's always a good time. Boosts morale, that kind of thing."

"My invitation must have gotten lost in the mail," she said, trying to sound light-hearted about it to cover her disappointment at not being included.

Eli studied her for a moment, then said, "Would you have come?"

She started to say yes, then stopped.

Last Thanksgiving, she'd wanted to do nothing more than what she did: hunker down with Amma in the house on Bayshore Drive, eat Chinese take-out, and watch Christmas movies. They were both grieving Margot's death all over again, the wounds reopened after learning the truth about that summer. Celebrating the holiday with a bunch of people she barely knew was not her idea of a good time.

"Probably not," she said with a shrug.

He smiled kindly at her. "You might want to consider stepping up this year and volunteering to host. Let the guys get to know you outside of the office, without the badge on. Let them get to know you the way I know you." His smile turned mischievous. "Well, not exactly the way I know you. What do you think? It could be a step in the right direction anyway."

With Amma's health deteriorating, plus the fact that Brett could barely cook a grilled cheese sandwich without burning the house down, it would be a tough dinner to pull off; but if it helped the squad see her as an equal instead of an adversary, it could be worth the extra hassle.

"Yeah, okay," she said. "Let me think about it."

The front door of the diner swung open at that moment, letting in a cold gust of wind. The woman in the teal and pink jacket, who had been walking along the boardwalk with the little girl in the red raincoat, now stood in front of the cash register, her eyes wide with panic. She clutched the little girl in her arms, balancing her on one hip. Rain dripped from their coats, making puddles on the floor.

"Someone call the police!" The woman's eyes were wild, scanning the room as heads turned to look at her.

She didn't appear hurt. The little girl didn't seem hurt either. She leaned her head against her mother's shoulder and sucked her thumb.

Brett took a step toward them.

Eli rose from the booth.

The server rushed out from the kitchen. "What is it? What's happened?"

"Police. We need the police." The woman shifted her child from one hip to the other.

Her gaze snapped to Eli, noticing for the first time his uniform and badge, the authoritative way he stood with his back straight and his feet slightly apart. She flapped her hand in the air, waving him over to her.

"Hurry! There's a...a foot." She gestured to the park across the street.

A wall of steel-colored clouds bunched against the horizon, a sign of yet more rain marching in their direction. It had been the same pattern since Halloween night: as one storm passed, another hit.

The woman was a shrieking gale when she said, "Someone's foot washed up on the beach!"

CHAPTER 17

The foot lay in the sand at the end of the boardwalk a few inches from the water. From a distance, it looked like nothing—an empty shoe, a piece of garbage washed up with the tide—but as Brett got closer, she could clearly see chunks of bone and flesh poking above the sneaker. Eli called it in, then worked to push the small group of onlookers back onto the grass where they wouldn't be in the way or disturb the scene more than they already had.

"Did you touch it? Did you move it at all?" Brett asked the woman who'd found the foot.

She stood a few steps behind Brett, gripping her daughter's hand tightly so the little girl wouldn't run off. Horrified, she shook her head and said, "No, we didn't touch it."

"I touch it." The little girl squirmed to break free of her mother's tight grip, failed, and slid to a heap on the ground.

"She didn't," the mother insisted. "We were walking along the boardwalk and she saw it. She thought it was a dolly or a toy, something to play with, I don't know. She took off running before I could stop her. I caught up with her though, before she could get too close."

Brett's eyes traced the boot prints in the sand. The larger ones ran over top of the smaller ones until they both came to an abrupt stop within arm's reach of the foot.

"I saw what it was and pulled her away. And then we went straight to the diner to get help. Neither of us touched it." The woman's gaze kept sliding over the foot, as if she couldn't stand to look at it for more than a few seconds at a time. "We moved to this town because we thought it would be safe."

She bent, lifted her daughter on her hip again, and walked in the direction of the diner. Brett let her go. She had the woman's name and phone number if she had any follow up questions.

The medical examiner's van pulled into the parking lot, and a young man in an oversized rain poncho stepped out. Kevin Park had been Whatcom County's assistant medical examiner for over a year now. He'd been hired on with the idea that he would take over when Charlie finally retired—if Charlie ever retired.

Over the past year, Brett and Kevin's paths had occasionally crossed, sometimes for work, more often at the grocery store. While he was always professional and courteous, Brett wouldn't exactly call him friendly. Not in the way Charlie was friendly, chatting up anyone who would listen, telling them things about his personal life that no one ever asked about. Kevin was the opposite. He was quiet and kept to himself. He came in, did his job, and left.

The poncho hood was pulled over his head but did little to protect his glasses from the lashing rain. He pulled the glasses off when he reached Brett and attempted to wipe them dry with a handkerchief, but as soon as he returned them to his face, rain spattered the lenses again. He sighed and held his hand above his eyes like the brim of a hat.

"Is this it?" Kevin asked. "No other limbs?"

"None that we've found," Brett said.

Kevin snapped on a pair of gloves and knelt beside the foot. He was gentle with it, turning the shoe to examine the bones, then turning it again to look at the shoe itself, a black canvas sneaker with white shoelaces and trim. He pulled a folded body bag from somewhere under his poncho and said, "If you don't have any objections, I'd like to go ahead and take it straight to the morgue where I can do a more thorough inspection. Out of the rain."

Brett's jacket was only waterproof to an extent and already she was starting to feel the dampness soaking through her shirt underneath. She didn't want to be out here anymore than he did. She nodded. "I'll follow you there."

He slipped the foot into the bag, tucked it under his arm, and hurried back to the county van with his empty hand lifted to protect his face from the rain.

Before heading to the morgue, Brett swung by the house on Bayshore Drive to change into dry clothes. Sculpin Bay raged. Waves rose like bucking horses before slamming down again, rushing quickly along the shoreline before being sucked back out with a deafening hiss.

Brett found her grandmother in the sitting room in front of her painting easel, streaking bold colors across a large canvas, bright contrast to the gloom outside. Pistol slept on the couch nearby. He lifted his head when Brett appeared in the doorway, thumped his tail once, then went back to sleep. Painting was usually a sign that Amma was having a good day. Based on the state of the canvas, she was just getting started and would be distracted for hours.

"I've got to stop in at the morgue for a bit," Brett told her. "Are you going to be okay here?"

"Isn't today usually your day off?" Amma added a splash of orange to a yellow sun.

Brett bent and kissed the top of her head. "I'll be home for dinner."

Crestwood General Hospital sat on a hill overlooking historic downtown. The building sprawled flat and beige. It looked like a place where people went to die. The interior was as run down as the exterior, the air chilled and bitter with antiseptic. Brett took the elevator to the basement, her least favorite part of the hospital because there were no windows and the artificial light scraped her eyes raw. Plus, it's where they kept the bodies.

The doors dinged open. Kevin stood in the hallway, as if he was waiting to take the elevator up. His expression brightened when he saw it was her. "Oh good, you're here. I was about to call you."

He turned away from the elevator and hurried toward the morgue at the end of the hall, calling over his shoulder, "I have reason to believe the foot belongs to Daniel Yoon."

Brett chased after him, her shoes squeaking over the linoleum. "Wait, what did you say?"

The foot and shoe were separated now, sitting side by side on a metal autopsy table next to a black sock that was drying stiff from salt and sand.

Charlie worked at a different table on the other side of the room. Sergeant Harris stood close by, his hands folded behind his back, his grim expression causing his mustache to droop. Both men looked up when Brett entered. Wes Harris nodded at her but said nothing. Charlie waved a scalpel in the air and said, "Not every day you get body parts washing up on the beach. Like I told Kevin, these storms churn up the bay pretty good. Never know what's going to float to the surface."

June Newmark's body looked small beneath the autopsy sheet. Her white-blond hair spilled over the silver table. One hand dangled over the edge of the slab, hanging limp in the air. Brett resisted the urge to go and tuck her hand safe beneath the sheet again. She pulled her eyes from June and focused on the foot.

Kevin snapped on a pair of gloves, handed a pair to Brett, and picked up the shoe first. He pointed to the midsole at some markings she hadn't noticed before. Someone had taken a pen to the rubber and drawn spirals and shapes and what looked like snakes and three-horned devils.

"I've seen Daniel wear these exact sneakers," Kevin said.

Brett straightened, surprised that Kevin would recognize shoes worn by a teenager. He had similar facial features: high cheekbones and a long, straight nose, but the shape of his chin was different, sharper and more prominent.

"Are you related?" Brett asked, then immediately regretted it.

"Why?" Kevin didn't sound at all amused. "Because we both have slanted eyes?"

She started to say no, but then realized that was exactly why she'd asked. Embarrassment flooded through her. "Sorry, that was stupid."

"We go to the same church," he said, his voice thin with impatience. "The Korean community in Crestwood is small. As you can imagine." He arched his eyebrows like he found her suddenly intolerable. "We try to look out for one another. Now, if you're done discussing the nuances of my social life, maybe we can talk about some of the other things I found that could be of use to your investigation."

He set the shoe down on the table. "For starters, the sneaker is a size ten."

The same size as one of the prints found near June's body. Brett picked it up and studied the pattern on the sole. It looked like a match, but she'd need to compare it to the pictures they'd taken to be certain.

"Now, at first I thought this was a simple case of disarticulation." Kevin gestured to the foot, and Brett set the shoe down to take a closer look.

"Human bodies fall apart quite easily, quite naturally, in fact,"

Kevin explained. "Especially in water. The flesh decays more quickly. Animals like fish or crabs eat away at it. Without tissue to hold them together, the joints come apart. But it usually takes several weeks, months even, for a body to fall apart in that manner. And if you look here…" He pointed to a pair of sharp bones no more than one-inch in height, jutting up from the ankle joint. "You can see that indeed the foot did not separate naturally at the joint. Parts of the tibia and fibula are still attached, which makes it more likely that something severed this part of the foot from the rest of the leg."

"Can you tell what?" Brett asked, bending for a closer look.

"Not with any certainty, but I can make a guess."

She straightened and motioned for him to go ahead.

"It's not a clean cut, not like a bone saw or ax might make. There are chips here and here." He pointed to two different spots. "Which indicates to me a chopping motion, a hesitancy by whoever was holding the blade. Another possibility, and one that seems more likely to me, is that the leg came into contact with a propeller."

"A propeller like the one on a boat motor?"

Kevin nodded. "The foot was in the water, so it's not much of a stretch to theorize that the rest of the body was near a boat at some point. Maybe he fell overboard or was pushed or… I don't want to speculate too much on that part of it, but contact with a propeller could explain how the foot became separated from the body."

His voice took on an instructional and detached tone, a clear sign he was trying to separate his personal feelings from the work that needed to be done. Brett recognized the shift because she did the same thing every time a case hit close to home.

"Is that what killed him?" She hoped not, considering what a painful and slow way that would be to die.

Kevin shook his head. "It's hard to say for sure with just the foot to examine. If I had the rest of the body I'd be able to tell you with more certainty. All I know for certain right now is that it's the right foot, something severed it above the ankle, and decomposition indicates it was in the water a few days. Which puts us in the right timeline for when Daniel Yoon disappeared."

"If we think the rest of him is floating around out there somewhere, then why did only the foot wash up?" Brett asked

"Because of the buoyancy provided by the shoe itself," Kevin explained. "It was light enough to float to the surface. The rest of the body probably sank. But with these storms, we might get lucky. He might wash up eventually."

On the other side of the morgue, Charlie started up a small bone saw, the high-pitched whirring sent jolts of pain through Brett's teeth. Normally, being in the morgue didn't bother her very much. It was never fun and it smelled terrible, but it was part of the job. Something about the bone saw, though, and knowing it was cutting into a girl who hadn't even made it out of high school yet, raised the hairs on her arms. She clamped down on her discomfort, trying to ignore the sound of splintering bone, and lowered her gaze back to the foot on the table in front of her. This was what she needed to focus on right now. Get through this part and then she could go home.

"Anything else you can tell me?" she asked.

Kevin reached for a vial and a scalpel, scraping some skin into the small glass jar, labeling it, and setting it aside. "I can run a few more tests, tox screens and that kind of thing, but I doubt they'll bring back anything very useful. A foot doesn't give me much to work with. Find the rest of him, and I'll be able to tell you everything you want to know. How he died, if he was sick or injured, what he ate for breakfast—"

A loud, metallic clink echoed through the morgue. Brett and Kevin both turned to look at the other autopsy table. Wes frowned at the contents of a small, steel bowl, shaking it gently. Whatever was inside rattled.

Charlie was bent over the body, elbow deep inside June's cracked-open chest. Brett's stomach leaped into her throat. She turned away before her egg and sausage sandwich made a reappearance.

"Bullet went straight through her heart and lodged in her spine," Charlie said, speaking slowly into a small tape recorder that hung from the ceiling. "Most likely her death was instantaneous, so at least she didn't suffer, at least there's that kindness."

Inside the steel bowl, the bullet rattled, rattled, became an echo so loud in Brett's head she could hardly focus. Kevin was talking to her, saying something about bringing Patricia Yoon down here to identify the foot.

He pointed at the heel. "There's a unique birthmark here."

It was light brown and shaped like a bean. Brett remembered from the picture Patricia had given her that Daniel had a similar looking mole on his left temple.

"There are tests we can run to look for familial markers, similar blood types," Kevin said. "But they're time consuming and expensive and not always accurate. I'll still send samples out to the state lab, of course, but it seems to me that Patricia's confirmation should be enough to get the ball rolling on a more thorough investigation."

Brett nodded, agreeing. She wasn't looking forward to telling Patricia the news that her son was no longer missing, but Kevin was right, it had to be done.

CHAPTER 18

"Third time's a charm," Eli said as he hauled himself out of Brett's car and tugged a rain poncho over his head.

Several other officers mingled in the parking lot at Deadman's Point. They sipped steaming coffee from paper cups and complained about the rain. No one wanted to be out here again, not early on a Tuesday, with the gray sky just now beginning to lighten and a wicked northern squall lashing them sideways. But no one wanted to admit defeat either. So they were all here, suffering together in a last ditch effort to find the gun that killed June Newmark.

Late on Monday, Patricia Yoon had identified the shoe as belonging to her son Daniel. She'd asked about the possibility of someone else wearing the shoe, then wept openly when Kevin showed her the foot and the small mark on the heel that she said she'd always seen as a sign of a long life, a blessing, she'd called it and then clawed at her chest like she was having trouble breathing. Kevin helped her into a chair and made her breathe slowly into a paper bag.

What am I supposed to do now? I cannot bury only part of my son. Where is he? Where is the rest of him?

Brett stared at the ocean through the windshield of her car, the haunting echo of Patricia's voice still ringing in her ears. He was out there somewhere, in the crush and flow of the current, trapped in the secret dark depths. Maybe the ocean would spit the rest of him out, or maybe it would prove to be his forever grave. Either way, they could no longer rely on him for answers. Whatever he knew about June's death, and his own, was lost to the waves now, too.

Brett grabbed her poncho and got out of the car to join the others.

Irving was leading this search. He broke the group into teams and assigned them to different sections of the park.

"No stone unturned," he shouted as the teams broke off and began searching. "Look in every nook and cranny. I want every square inch of this land combed over at least once by the end of the day."

"It's pretty obvious, isn't it?" Brett overheard one of the younger officers on her team say as they walked through the brush toward the ruins. "They tossed the gun into the ocean. They'd be stupid not to. We're wasting our time out here."

But even though every single one of them was thinking something similar, they still searched. Slowly, methodically, spread out in evenly spaced lines, they worked over the entire peninsula and the woodlands surrounding it. One team searched along the beach at Deadman's Point. Another searched the dock. Another picked over a rocky outcrop until the tide came in too far and threatened to sweep them out to sea.

Brett worked her way through a dense wall of trees near the ruins. She pushed aside branches and looked under rotting logs, swinging her flashlight to search the dark pockets of moss and shadows, hoping to find something useful hidden beneath the leaves.

For most of the day, the mood matched the weather—dreary, damp, and despondent. Despite wearing multiple thick layers, Brett was chilled to the bone. Her fingers ached and then went numb. She couldn't feel her feet inside her boots.

She imagined everyone else was feeling the same drop in morale, and her thoughts returned to what the young officer had said when they started. The gun wasn't out here. They were wasting time.

Then, and suddenly, someone started singing. The lilting tenor caught on the wind and another voice joined in, then another, until the entire peninsula echoed music. There was a rhythm to the song, a swelling and falling like the waves crashing to shore, a haunting melody that lifted the hairs on the back of Brett's neck. She didn't know the words, but it was a call and response, and at some point she found herself humming along with the melody, so lost in the notes she no longer noticed the rain or the ice in her blood.

The singing kept on, the voices moving from one song to another, but always with the same steady beat that drove Brett forward, deeper into the woods.

A branch snapped somewhere behind her. She glanced over her shoulder, expecting to see one of the officer's on her team, but she was alone. The singing was growing faint now, moving away from her. She'd walked too far, had perhaps even left the peninsula entirely. She turned to retrace her steps to the parking lot. Another branch snapped. This time when she scanned the brush, her eyes caught on a smudge of gray. A faceless ghost watched from the shadows.

She swallowed a startled scream. Her hand automatically reached for the gun holstered at her waist. The gray apparition shifted and stepped forward. Brett relaxed her grip on her firearm.

"Mr. Shoal?" she called out to the man dressed head-to-toe in gray rain gear. "What are you doing out here?"

"I heard the voices of old." Ed closed his eyes and began to hum the same shanty the men had been singing earlier.

When he opened his eyes again, there was a clarity to them that hadn't been there when Brett talked to him four days ago. He looked over her shoulder in the direction of the ruins.

"You're here because of that girl, aren't you?" he asked. "You're looking for the ones who killed her. Poor thing. They left her for the scavengers."

"You saw who did it?" Brett asked.

"I saw the ones who came after, the ones who ran through the dark."

Brett took a deep breath, pushing down her rising anger at the addled old man who spoke in riddles and nonsense.

"Mr. Shoal, we'd really like to get a formal statement from you about what you saw that night," she said. "Would it be okay if I took you home and asked you a few more questions there?"

"You have to be careful out here," Ed said, ignoring her request. "Evil lurks in the shadows."

"Mr. Shoal, it's important that you—"

"I saw them carry one body away," he spoke over top of her. "They came back for the other but it was too late."

"What do you mean it was too late?"

"You were already here." He twirled his finger in the air above his shoulder. "They didn't like the lights and sirens."

"Did you see what these people looked like?" Brett pressed. "The ones who carried the body away? Were you close enough to see their faces? Could you describe what they were wearing?"

His eyes drifted over her shoulder to stare at something in the trees. "How does one describe a ghost?"

A shrill whistle cut through the patter of falling rain. Brett twisted her head toward the sound. Either someone had found something, or Irving was calling off the search empty-handed.

When she turned around to talk to Ed Shoal again, the old man was gone.

————————————

The search turned up nothing but mud, mushrooms, cigarette butts, empty beer bottles, and a family of startled rabbits. Sopping wet and defeated, the officers piled into their cars and headed back to the precinct. No one spoke as they shuffled into the locker room to change into dry clothes.

Brett changed in the women's restroom. Henry had promised to turn one of the interview rooms into a proper locker room for her and the other female officer who worked Parking and Code Enforcement for the department, but he hadn't gotten around to it before he was forced to retire, and every time Brett brought it up with Stan, he laughed and told her she could use the men's locker room, same as the rest of them. This was always followed by something crass. *Don't worry, Princess, no one wants to look at your saggy tits.*

The coffee in the break room was stale. Brett poured out the old stuff and started a fresh pot. She kept going over Ed Shoal's cryptic words, trying to make sense of them, to see if any of it could be real or if it was nothing more than the ramblings of a confused old man.

A sharp rapping on the break room door interrupted her thoughts. Eli stood half in the room and half in the hallway. He smiled and tipped his head to one side. "A bunch of us are headed over to the Pickled Onion. Want to come?"

The Pickled Onion was a greasy bar a few blocks down the street from the precinct, and a favorite for the squad because the first pint was always free if you showed your badge. Brett had gone on her own a few times, but never been invited to tag along with any of the guys.

"Yeah," she said. "I could use a drink."

Everyone who had searched Deadman's Point today went, including Irving, who looked the most run down of them all. They crowded into the small space, shoving three tables together in the center of the bar. Eli pounded his hands on the table and shouted over their loud conversations, "First round's on me."

The men rolled their eyes and snorted with laughter. Their voices were thick with sarcasm when they thanked him for his generosity.

Eli grinned and said, "Fine. Second round's on me, too." The cheers were genuine this time, as he went to the bar to get their beers, and everyone else found seats.

Brett pulled up a chair beside Irving. "I ran into Ed Shoal out there today," she started to say, but Irving held up his hand, stopping her.

"I'm here to drink away my disappointment," he said. "We can talk about all the rest of it during tomorrow's briefing."

Eli returned, setting beers down in front of them. He held his glass in the air and said, "To finding the bastard and making him pay."

The men cheered again and clinked glasses. Brett sipped hers slowly, but the rest of them chugged and in minutes, someone else went to get the next round.

"You want a glass of chardonnay instead?" One of the officers teased her, jabbing his finger at the beer sitting in front of her that was still nearly full to the brim. It looked like she hadn't even taken a drink, though she had.

"Get her a shot of tequila!" another man shouted.

Irving leaned close to her elbow. "Don't pay attention to these idiots."

Someone set a shot glass filled with gold liquid in front of her. She picked it up, studying it a moment before tipping the glass to her mouth.

More cheers and table pounding. Fire raced down her throat, but she welcomed the heat, the way the tequila fuzzed the edges of her thoughts and loosened the knots in her neck. She slammed the empty glass onto the table with a defiant thunk. Another shot glass appeared in front of her. She grabbed it but instead of shooting it right away, she scanned the table, glaring at each and every one of them. "You assholes gonna make me drink alone?"

The group laughed. Eli leaped from his chair and within minutes everyone had a shot in their hands. Someone counted backward from three. A brief beat of silence as they drank, then clunking as the shot glasses hit the table again and a roar of victory shook the rafters.

Beside her, Irving coughed into his fist. His eyes watered from the alcohol, and he shook his head, making a sputtering sound, before breaking into soft laughter. "My wife's going to kill me."

"Make sure you get her to sign a confession first," one of the officers said.

Laughter exploded. More beers appeared. The orange lights of the bar blurred in a dreamy way. The country music playing over the loudspeaker sounded distant, like it was coming through a long tunnel. When a song came on that she knew, Brett swayed in rhythm with the guitar and twanging banjo.

"This is my song," she said to no one.

Someone pulled her to her feet and dragged her into an empty part of the bar. He swung her in a quick step, the lights turning to shooting stars as he spun her faster and faster. He let go of her hand, and she stumbled back to the table, laughing.

At some point, Wes came through the front door, which set off another round of cheers and beers. One of the officers gave up his seat for the sergeant, who sat down and grabbed the pint of the man sitting next to him. He tipped it to his mouth and drank the entire thing without taking a breath. When he finished, he wiped his hand across his mouth and said, "Now that we've gotten that out of the way... Who's hosting Thanksgiving this year?"

A groan rippled around the table.

Eli elbowed Brett in the ribs. She pushed back her chair and stood to her feet, feeling a little unsteady, but hoping no one would notice.

"I'll do it," she said. "I don't know the first thing about roasting a fucking turkey, but how hard can it be?"

The group lifted their glasses again, shouting in unison, "Gobble-gobble!"

She sat back down, pleased with herself, and with the smiles and pats on the back she was getting now.

The officer across from her leaned over the table and said, "My wife's allergic to nuts."

"You've got to leave the giblets inside the bird when you cook it," another said.

"No, you shove a whole green apple up in there. Leave the giblets for the gravy."

The conversation broke into smaller groups as the men began to discuss the best kind of stuffing and whether yams were best with marshmallows or without.

Irving lowered his head close to her, his words slurred as he said, "Diane and I have hosted several times over the years. If you need help, don't hesitate to ask."

Brett knew she wouldn't. Tradition was tradition, and if cooking a full Thanksgiving meal for these men and their families was what it took to prove herself a vital part of this team, then that's exactly what she would do.

Thinking about Thanksgiving made her think about Amma. She slipped away from the group and ducked into the small hallway outside the bathrooms where a payphone hung on the wall. The coin clattered into the slot. Amma answered after the third ring and reassured Brett that everything was fine. Pistol had eaten his dinner, and they were about to go on their evening walk. Brett promised she'd be home soon and hung up.

She turned to find Eli standing behind her, watching her with a look that spread heat through her veins. He slid his arm around her waist and pulled her close, rocking her gently with the music. "Want to get out of here?"

She started to nod, but then she saw movement in the shadows at the end of the hall. She stiffened and pulled away from Eli as Wes Harris appeared. His gaze skimmed over the two of them as he pushed his way into the bathroom.

"Shit," Brett said, smoothing her hand over her hair and straightening her shirt. "Shit, shit, shit."

"It's not a big deal," Eli tried to calm her. "He probably didn't even see anything."

The spot where they stood by the phone was dimly lit, but Brett was certain Wes had noticed them.

Eli reached for her again, but she pushed him away. "I have to go. Amma's waiting for me."

"Let me walk you out."

"No," she said too sharply.

He flinched like she'd slapped him.

"Let's just, let's not make a big deal out of this. Let's go back to the table, and I'll buy us another round." She grabbed his hand, giving it a hard squeeze before letting go and returning to the main part of the bar to order more beers. She ordered a coffee for herself.

After another thirty minutes, the group was growing even louder and more raucous, but Brett was feeling sober enough now to get herself home safely. Wes had returned from the bathroom, but said nothing about what he'd seen in the hallway. If he'd seen anything at all. One of the other patrol officers convinced Eli to play a round of darts, and Brett took the opportunity to sneak out without him noticing.

She was fumbling in her pockets for her car keys when she heard the crunch of gravel and the jingle of someone else's keys. Wes was getting into his car in the next spot over from hers. He unlocked the door of his Jeep, but didn't open it right away. Instead, he tilted his head back to catch the rain on his face.

"There's something about the rain at night, isn't there?" he said. "Like a lover's gentle caress."

She was glad for the darkness, that he couldn't see her embarrassment.

"Listen, if you saw anything back in there." She jerked her thumb over her shoulder at the bar. "It was nothing. It isn't what you're thinking."

"Don't worry." He popped open the door. The dome light flared, illuminating his knowing smile. "Your secret's safe with me."

CHAPTER 19

By Friday, everyone knew about the foot that had washed up on the beach. And everyone knew it was Daniel's.

Lizzie moved numbly through her classes, doing everything she could to blend in to the beige lockers and avoid the whispers and gossips, the people who said Daniel killed June, then threw himself into the ocean. She kept her hood up and her head down, but she still felt them watching her. She heard their whispers, how they were blaming her for June's death, too, because her mother's blood ran through her like a curse.

Just get through the day, she told herself, and then get through tomorrow and then the day after that and then she didn't know what but it had to be better than this.

"Watch where you're going." Someone elbowed her in the ribs.

She looked up and realized she was standing in front of the art classroom. It was a habit for her to come here looking for Daniel.

She peered through the open door. Mr. Cadden was hunched over his desk, scribbling on something. He stopped and jerked up his head as if he sensed her watching. Lizzie held his gaze for a moment. He pushed back in his chair as if he was going to get up and come talk to her. Lizzie bolted in the opposite direction, hurrying around the corner before he had a chance to catch up to her.

Later that night, as she was getting ready for bed, a tap sounded on her bedroom door. Grandpa popped his head in. "Hey, Lizbug, Grandma wanted me to remind you to wear something nice tomorrow."

He closed the door without waiting for her response.

That night she dreamed about a prison filled with severed feet and an ocean that spat up bones.

Saturday morning dawned gray and soggy, and all Lizzie wanted to do was sit on the couch and watch cartoons, but instead, she was stuck in the backseat of her grandparents' station wagon driving east toward the prison to pick up a father she wanted nothing to do with. Grandma's sweet perfume choked the air, but she wouldn't let Lizzie roll down the window. A boring news program played on the radio. Grandpa whistled a happy tune which clashed with Lizzie's looming dread.

She thought she was going to have more time to prepare for her father's release. If someone had told her he would be getting out ten months after he went in, she would have laughed. She would have said, without any irony, *Over my dead body.* But apparently no one cared what Lizzie thought. Ready or not, Marshall Trudeau was coming home.

She couldn't do this.

She couldn't drive two hours there and two hours back. She couldn't sit that close to her ex-con father and listen to him asking about her life, about school, about what she'd been doing since she wasn't playing soccer anymore, didn't she miss it? She couldn't look him in the eyes and pretend everything was normal and they could all go back to how things were before. She couldn't pretend she'd forgiven him.

Because she hadn't. She didn't know if she ever would.

The thought of his eyes taking in all the ways she was different now, his hand reaching across the center of the seat to offer his idea of reassurance, a squeeze of her hand, the very idea of being that close to him again, breathing the same air, made Lizzie feel like she was suffocating, like if she didn't get out of the car and right this second, she was going to die.

What Lizzie did next wasn't planned.

When the last light out of town turned red and Grandpa stopped, Lizzie unbuckled her seat belt, popped open the car door, and got out.

"Elizabeth?" Grandma stretched her hand across the empty backseat to try and grab hold of her before she slipped away. "Elizabeth? Where are you going? Get back here right this instant, young lady!"

Lizzie jogged away from the car. They didn't come after her. Not that she really expected them to. They couldn't leave their only son standing outside a prison with nothing but the clothes on his back.

A fine mist drifted from low-hanging clouds. Half-rain and half-fog, and Lizzie disappeared inside it. She walked aimlessly for a while until she found herself at the edge of Sculpin Bay. Near the horizon, a fishing boat bobbed in the heaving waves. Farther out, she could see the shadowed humps of islands curling around the mouth of the bay. She couldn't remember their names.

Motion drew her gaze back to shore. Lizzie walked toward a crouched figure digging in the sand. When she got close enough, she realized it was Adam Harris, and he wasn't crouching, but sitting with his knees drawn to his chest. One hand dragged a piece of driftwood through the damp sand, not digging, but writing something. When he saw her coming, he swiped the stick over the sand in a single, destructive motion before she could read what he'd written. He tossed the stick into the water, pulled a bottle from his jacket, and drank from it.

She sank down next to him. Cold damp seeped through the skirt her grandmother forced her to wear today.

"This is where they found Daniel's foot," Adam said, taking another drink from the bottle.

Lizzie looked up and down the beach. "I thought it was closer to Egret's Park."

"Sure." He shrugged. "Here, there, wherever. Does it fucking matter? They found his foot." He took another drink and mumbled, "That could have easily been you."

"Why would you even say that?" She started to scoot away from him.

"Or me." Another shrug. "We're all just trash bobbing on the sea of life, waiting to be washed ashore."

Lizzie might have found the words poetic, if they weren't so gruesome.

She studied Adam's profile. He was cute if you could look past the thick acne covering his chin and the annoying way he was always chewing his lips, shredding the delicate skin to a raw pulp. But he had nice eyes, dark brown and intense. And when he smiled, he made you feel like you were in on a secret. He wasn't smiling now, though, his scowl a cruel slash across his face.

She leaned over and yanked the bottle from his hand. "Can I? Thanks."

She drank deeply, tasting nothing, not sure if it was beer or something stronger, not caring, wanting only the obliteration. Heat expanded in her chest as fire raced to her belly. She kept drinking until the fire raced to her brain, too, numbing all thoughts of the foot on the beach, her two dead best friends, her father who would be so disappointed when he opened the car door and didn't find her there in the backseat.

When she handed the bottle back to Adam, he looked impressed.

His gaze roamed over her. "What are you wearing? You look like you're going to church."

A long plaid skirt with lavender and daffodil stripes, a Peter Pan collar blouse, a sky blue cable knit sweater, dainty brown loafers—her grandma bought the outfit special for her to wear today.

"My dad's getting out of prison. Or he's out. I don't know. My grandparents went to pick him up. I was supposed to go with them." She scooped a pile of sand and let the grains sift through her fingers.

"How come you didn't?" he asked.

She shrugged and slapped her hands together to get the sand off. Then she tilted her face to the rain and gave herself over to the tingling booze flaming through her veins. It was burning hotter now, making her blaze and spin. "I'm not sure what I'm supposed to say to him, you know? I haven't talked to him in months."

"You didn't go visit him when he was in there?"

She did only the one time, and it had been awful and humiliating. The visiting room smelled like piss and there was a baby screaming and guards standing against the wall to enforce the no touching policy. She had barely recognized her father who had grown a beard and lost twenty pounds. He looked like a stick man, gaunt and sickly, with dark circles under his eyes and a cut on his lip.

He had stared at her from across the table, stared like he was trying to drink in her soul, and then he'd started to cry. Not just cry—weep. He bent over the table and sobbed into his hands, and Lizzie was disgusted by his outburst, embarrassed that her father was the only adult in the room blubbering like this.

It wasn't like he was innocent. He may not have killed anyone the way her mother had, but he kept a man locked up in a hunting cabin for two days. He'd looked the other way. And though he swore over and over that he hadn't known what Clara had done, Lizzie didn't believe him. And she didn't feel sorry for him either. Not one bit. He'd gotten himself into this mess. He didn't have any reason to cry about it. That's when she'd gotten up and walked out. That's when she'd talked to Daniel for the first time.

"It was too far away." It was a truthful enough reason, and Adam seemed to believe it.

He nodded like he understood and took another drink.

"I haven't seen you at school," she said.

"I've been there." He shrugged one shoulder.

"So you've been avoiding me?"

"It's hard, Liz," he said. "Not having June there."

"And what? You think it's easy for me?"

"No, but it's different."

"Yeah, because she's my best friend." Lizzie grabbed the bottle from him, drinking to drown the sobs that were threatening to spill over. When she'd had enough, she shoved the bottle back into his hands. "Did you know she quit soccer?"

Adam nodded.

"She didn't tell me. Why didn't she tell me?"

"Maybe she thought you'd try and talk her out of it."

"I wouldn't have. Mr. Cadden's a creep. I would have cheered her on, taken her out for a milkshake to celebrate or something."

They sat a moment saying nothing, listening to the waves hiss and the wind moan and three seagulls scream about the unfairness of it all.

Then Lizzie asked, "What was she doing? If she wasn't at practice, what was she doing instead?"

Adam's eyes darted to her, then back to the ocean. "You don't know?"

"I didn't even know she'd quit so, no, I have no idea what she was doing." Lizzie scooped a handful of sand and flung it away from her. It was damp and heavy and fell straight back to earth. "I thought she was at practice."

"She was hanging out with Daniel. They were dating or hooking up or whatever." He lifted the bottle to his mouth again.

Lizzie choked on her surprise. She shook her head, trying to dislodge the high-pitched ringing that had started in her ears, a thousand seagulls shrieking, except it was all in her head. She shouldn't have had so much to drink.

"I don't believe you." She forced the words past lips that felt made of stone.

"It's true. I saw them."

"You saw them? What does that mean?"

"Lizzie. I saw them kissing, okay? His tongue was crammed down her throat, his hands were up her shirt. They were hot and heavy, okay? Acting like they were the only two people who existed in the whole goddamn world."

She tried to grab the bottle from him again, but he pulled it away.

Giving it a shake, he said, "It's empty."

He hopped to his feet, dusted sand off his pants, and extended his hand to help her up. "But I know where we can get some more."

Red lights strobed through the windows of Adam's pickup truck.

He cursed and pulled the steering wheel hard to the right. The wheels skidded in gravel. Lizzie grabbed hold of the handlebar on the door to keep herself from flying into the dashboard. Adam pulled the steering wheel the other way, and the truck lurched back onto the road.

Lizzie's screams were mixed up in giggles. She couldn't help it. Nothing was funny and everything was.

The neon sign of the quickie mart had made her skin glow pink while she waited in Adam's truck. Somehow he'd gone in and come back out a few minutes later with more booze. Even though he wasn't old enough to buy it, there it was in his hands, and this time whatever he'd bought them went down quicker and burned through her hotter than the booze on the beach. And now Lizzie was too drunk to think straight, too drunk to do anything but go along for the ride.

Red light, red light.

"Red light!" Lizzie screamed and pounded the dashboard trying to get Adam to stop, but he blew through the intersection like stoplights didn't exist.

Maybe they didn't. Maybe nothing in this world did. Not even her. Somewhere in the distance a horn blared and tires screeched. She rolled down the window and stuck her arm in the air, floating it in the currents, scratching her fingers against the night.

Lizzie heard sirens coming up fast, and then the truck went off the road again. She imagined herself flying through the windshield. She jerked forward, jerked back. Her head struck the seat hard, and suddenly she was watching stars spin overhead and one was getting closer, brighter, piercing through the window, and a woman was yelling at them to get out of the car and put their hands on their heads.

Lizzie shoved the truck door open and fell out onto the gravel shoulder. Her stomach quivered. The booze burned worse coming up. Liquid splattered onto the rocks in front of her, splashed on her hands which were spread over the ground, holding her still to keep her from flying into oblivion.

Someone grabbed her arm and jerked her to her feet. "Are you okay?"

The face in front of her was blurry. Lizzie blinked, and the details sharpened. It was the lady cop, the woman who'd ruined her whole life. She threw up again.

"Shit." Detective Buchanan let go of Lizzie and leaped away from her, but not fast enough. Vomit splashed down the front of her shirt.

Lizzie's face was damp. Was she crying? No, it was just the rain, this damn rain that refused to stop pouring down and down. She belched and said, "Sorry," and shifted her gaze to the puddles on the ground. Headlights and brake lights reflected in the surface, speckled and torn, red and white, a warning that came too late.

"Do you know who I am?" Adam shouted. "Do you know who my father is?"

"Your father could be the President of the United States, there's no way in hell I'm letting you back on the road."

Adam sang *99 Bottles of Beer on the Wall* all the way to the precinct and all the way down to the basement where the jail cells were and after the detective locked them in separate cells and told them to cool off, he was still singing.

Lizzie told him to shut up, but he didn't hear her. She sank onto the metal cot sticking out from the wall and covered her ears.

She didn't know how much time passed. At some point, Adam stopped singing. He didn't say anything to her, and she thought maybe he was asleep.

Detective Buchanan came down to check on them once. She stuck a bottle of water between the cell bars.

"What's going to happen to me?" Lizzie asked.

"I called your grandparents. They'll be here to pick you up soon."

Lizzie groaned and rolled so her face was to the wall.

How much time passed after that? She still didn't know. There were no windows down here, only a fluorescent light that was always on and the *drip-drip* sound of a leaky faucet.

She heard footsteps hurrying down the hallway. The heavy *clump-whump* of boots. She braced herself, but the footsteps didn't stop at her cell. They moved past her to Adam's cell at the end of the row. A clink, a rattle, then came the loud sound of a slap, skin connecting with skin.

"After everything that's happened, now you go and pull this shit?" Whoever the man was, he was pissed.

"I'm sorry, Dad! It's not my fault!" Adam's voice pitched into a whine that made Lizzie cringe.

"Nothing is ever your fault, is it? Look at yourself. You're a fucking mess. How many times am I going to have to come rescue you like this?"

It was quiet for a long time after that, so long Lizzie started to drift to sleep. In her drunken, half-asleep state, she thought she heard someone crying.

When she woke, she was alone and her head was pounding a heavy hammer of regret. She sat up, gripping the sides of the cot until the spinning lessened. Footsteps pounded down the hall again, but it wasn't her grandfather coming to save her. Nor her grandmother in a whirlwind of disappointment. When the footsteps reached her cell, when the door clattered and slid open, when she finally looked up, it was her father staring back at her.

Funny that she was inside now and he outside, but still there were bars between them.

She couldn't help it. She started to giggle.

"For fuck's sake, Elizabeth." He breathed the words out in one long sigh.

"I go by Lizzie now." She rose swaying to her feet.

Her father cursed again, shaking his head, then grabbed her arm and dragged her out to the car. As they were driving home, Lizzie realized the jail cell door had been unlocked the entire time she'd been inside.

CHAPTER 20

Brett scrubbed the vomit on her sweater with a damp paper towel. The paper shredded against the wool, turning it into an even bigger mess. She tossed the wadded up towel into the trash and stomped out of the bathroom.

Idiot teenagers. Someone could have been killed.

She hadn't technically arrested them, but Adam had been driving so erratically, so dangerously, there was no way in hell she could let him drive himself home. She'd shoved both Adam and Lizzie into the back of her car and driven them to the station where she'd called their parents.

She supposed she could have dropped them off at their respective homes, and maybe that would have been the kinder thing to do, but she was off-duty, on her way home from a quick trip to the grocery store and didn't want the hassle. Plus, seeing their panicked faces when she tossed them into the cells gave her some small amount of satisfaction.

A few hours in the clink might be all they needed to never do something this stupid again in their lifetimes. And anyway, her favorite sweater now reeked of vomit thanks to Lizzie, and she'd probably never be able to get the smell out, so it seemed fair to toss the girl in a jail cell for a few hours so she could think about her poor choices and how not to repeat them.

Eli was filling out some paperwork at his desk when Brett entered the squad room. He looked up, surprised to see her. It was almost 9:00 PM. Her normal shift ended three hours ago. His expression turned to one of concern as he said, "Please tell me we don't have another dead kid to add to the list."

She shook her head and told him about Adam and Lizzie. "They made it out alive this time."

"It sounds like you put the fear of God into them," he said with a quiet laugh. "The first time I got pulled over as a kid, the cop made me do all these sobriety tests. I'm pretty sure half of them were ones he made up on the spot. Like stand on one leg, flap your arms, bawk like a chicken."

"Yeah, I don't think that's standard material." She hovered near his desk, glancing at the report he was filing for a drunk and disorderly arrest. "Looks like you've had your own exciting night."

"Same old, same old."

Tension crackled between them, but it was different from the tension that had crackled between them last week. Last week was excitement and possibility. Tonight, the conversation felt stiff and uncomfortable, like they were talking around what really needed to be said. Brett found herself fidgeting—reaching for a pen on his desk, straightening a folder so it lined up with the edge.

"Are you covering for someone tonight?" she asked, forcing casualness into her voice.

Eli usually worked the day shift, but there was a shortage of patrol officers and so they often ended up taking on extra shifts. Overtime paid well.

"Yeah, Billy called in sick," Eli said. "I'm not sleeping much these days anyway, so I volunteered."

"Something in particular keeping you awake?"

"The usual. Too much coffee. Worried about the state of the world. This Newmark case isn't helping much." He shrugged one shoulder and kept writing.

Ever since the unproductive search at Deadman's Point on Tuesday, Brett's mind had been spinning circles, trying to come up with some new theory to move the Newmark case to a close.

The bullet Charlie had removed from June was a 9mm, which was all they knew about the murder weapon right now. They were hoping ballistics would be able to provide more specifics about the actual gun used to kill June, but it could be weeks before that report arrived. They were waiting on toxicology, too, for both June and the foot they believed to be Daniel's. They were interviewing teachers and students, but so far no one had anything very interesting to say. June got along with everyone and no one had a bad word to say about her. Daniel was a weird, loner artist who everyone avoided. Everyone wanted to talk about the punch that happened at the beginning of October, but no one knew what Daniel had against the art teacher, or what might have caused him to snap like that.

Daniel's unexpected aggressive behavior toward his teacher seemed to fit with the latest working theory that he had killed June and then killed himself. It was a theory that weighed heavy on Brett's mind, so she understood how Eli could be losing sleep because of it. Because of his relationship with Lizzie and her family, he knew June better than anyone else on the team. June had been Lizzie's best friend. Eli's path had probably crossed hers more than once over the years, at Super Bowl parties and family barbecues and camping trips to the mountains.

"You want to talk about it?" Brett reached for a chair.

Eli shook his head and tapped his pen on the report. "I really need to get this paperwork finished up and head back out there."

His tone was curt and dismissive. He wouldn't look her in the eye.

"Yeah, of course." Brett lingered, unsure if she should leave or press the issue.

Maybe Eli was upset with her about what happened the other night at the Pickled Onion, how she'd pushed him away. They hadn't talked about it, or about how Wes had seen them. She hadn't told him what Wes had said to her in the parking lot either.

Eli cleared his throat. He shifted his body in his chair so he was blocking her out, giving clear signals he didn't want to talk to her about anything right now.

"Right," Brett said. "I'll see you tomorrow."

Eli gave no response, his whole focus on the work in front of him.

She started to leave. As she reached the front door, orange lights flickered through the window, strobing across the ceiling. Eli's chair scraped against the floor as he stood.

"Tow truck?" He joined her by the front door.

"I sent one out right after I brought Adam and Lizzie in. I didn't think the kid would want his pickup truck sitting on the side of the highway all night."

The tow truck circled to the back of the station where they kept impounded cars. There weren't many. Most of them had expired tags or were vehicles too wrecked to drive. Adam's single-cab pickup rattled and clanked behind the tow truck.

"Should we call Wes back in here?" Brett asked.

"Don't bother," Eli said. "He can come get it in the morning. Adam's not going to be driving it anytime soon anyway, right?"

They walked outside and around to the back of the station where the tow truck driver was unhooking the small pickup. He was a burly man with a dark beard and sweat stains under his armpits. He waved some paperwork in the air. "Which one of you is going to sign this for me?"

Eli took the paperwork and scratched his name on the bottom.

Brett walked around the pickup, her eyes skimming over the bed and the bumper, the tires and panels. It didn't appear to be in any worse shape than before Adam dropped it into the ditch. She opened the passenger door and peered into the cab.

The dome light illuminated the interior—the tear in the faux leather seat, a scattering of fast food wrappers littering the passenger footwell, a pine-scented air freshener dangling from the rearview mirror. Dirty clothes and empty cassette tape boxes had been stuffed into the small space behind the bench seat. Two bottles of malt liquor lay empty on their sides on the driver's seat. One, still in a brown paper sack, poked out from under the passenger side.

Brett grabbed it and, realizing it was still full, tried to wiggle it free, but it seemed to be snagged on something under the seat. She felt around with her hand. Her fingers brushed against hard plastic and square edges. She worked it loose, pulling it out with the liquor bottle.

She set the liquor bottle on the seat and stared at the squat box in her hands.

The Polaroid camera was light gray with black trim and a black hand strap. Brett turned it over, inspecting every inch of it, remembering the dozens of Polaroids hanging in June Newmark's bedroom, her whole world captured in a three-by-five, white-framed square. Moments that would otherwise have been lost, preserved in an instant with the click of a button.

Brett found what she was looking for on the bottom of the camera. Scratched carefully into the paint with something sharp were the initials J.C.N.

June Carol Newmark.

Smeared onto the smooth gray plastic near the film compartment was what appeared to be a bloody thumbprint.

"I need evidence bags." Brett set the camera down on the seat next to the liquor bottle and stepped away from the vehicle. "And gloves."

"What did you find?" Eli leaned his head inside the truck.

"I think that's June Newmark's camera. There's blood on it."

Eli winced. "Shit."

He backed away from the vehicle like he wanted nothing to do with it, then spun on his heels and trotted into the precinct to get the gear she'd asked for.

When he returned, they worked through the car together, putting each piece of clothing into separate bags, marking down the date and time and other details. The clothes appeared to belong to Adam, mostly soccer jerseys, running shorts, basketball gear, and other sports items that were long overdue for a wash.

Under the same seat where the camera had been shoved, Brett found a wadded up shirt. It was light gray with long black sleeves, like a baseball jersey, but there were no numbers or letters printed on it. A large rust-colored stain spread over the front of the shirt. Brett showed it to Eli before carefully placing it into a bag.

"It's probably from a nosebleed," Eli said, and Brett wanted nothing more than to believe this was true.

"Lizzie said they were all supposed to be meeting at Deadman's Point that night," she said, bending and shining a flashlight beneath the seat to see if she'd missed anything.

The truck was clean now. Everything bagged and labeled and waiting in the parking lot to be carried to the evidence room.

"But she said Adam didn't show," Eli reminded her.

"Maybe he came after she left?"

"Wes said Adam was home all night, that he never left the house."

Eli sounded confident, but Brett thought about how many times she had snuck out of her own house when she was Adam's age, how her mother never even suspected. But she wanted to believe Wes Harris was a better father than that. She wanted to believe her detective sergeant would know where his son was at night. But something kept catching in the back of her mind, making it hard for her to dismiss the camera as nothing.

"There's a good reason why this stuff was in here," Eli said, forcing confidence into his voice. "He probably gave June a ride home from school at some point, and June left her camera here, or it fell out of her bag or something. We just have to ask him."

"And the blood?"

"A cut. A bloody nose. Maybe it's not even blood." He flashed her a nervous smile.

"We need to get this shirt and the camera to the lab as soon as possible. We need to find out if this is June's blood." Brett started gathering the evidence bags.

Eli stepped in and took them from her. "I'll do the rest of it."

"No, it's fine, I can help."

"You're not on shift, I am." Eli stacked the bags in a heap in his arms. "I'll log all of this and get a report written up, and in the morning, we can talk to Wes and get some answers from Adam. I'm sure it's not what we're thinking. In fact, ten bucks says this goes nowhere and we end up looking like asses when it's all said and done."

"I hope so," Brett said.

She helped him carry the bags to the evidence room at the back of the station and left him there to finish the paperwork.

Thirty minutes later, Brett was home, unpacking groceries in the kitchen, when Amma and Pistol came in from the backyard. Amma fussed with her jacket and dusted rain out of her silver hair. Pistol, too, shook rain from his fur, twisting his hips so hard, he almost toppled over.

When Amma finally noticed Brett, she seemed startled to see her. "What are you doing here?"

Pistol trotted to his empty bowl, sniffed it, then sat down with a huff and tilted his head, staring up at Brett with dewy black, begging eyes.

Brett smiled at him and then at Amma, but kept unpacking the groceries. "Sorry, I'm late. I wasn't expecting to be gone that long, but I had to make an emergency stop at the precinct. These kids were driving drunk. They could have gotten themselves or someone else killed."

She opened the fridge and put a carton of milk on the shelf, then a box of baking soda and a block of cheddar cheese. She put fruit and lettuce in the crisper. Chicken and bacon in the other drawer. Mayonnaise, mustard, ketchup, and Worcestershire sauce went in the door. She knew she'd forgotten a lot, but at least they had enough to last them until her next day off when she'd have a chance to go to the store again, properly this time, with a list. And hopefully, Amma wouldn't empty it a second time for absolutely no good reason.

That afternoon, while Brett had been at work, Amma had gone through the entire kitchen throwing away every single food item she could find. Brett came home to bare cupboards, a cleared out fridge, and a trashcan filled with half-rotten food, torn open boxes, and dented cans.

Luckily, Brett hadn't done any of the Thanksgiving shopping yet, since the party wasn't for another three weeks. But after a long day, with no progress on her cases, eating nothing but a granola bar, and drinking one too many cups of coffee, she had been looking forward to changing into comfy sweats and cozying up in front of the television with a hearty bowl of soup. Instead, she had to turn around and go right back out into the rain to get groceries so they wouldn't starve.

It had taken all her self-control not to reprimand Amma and try and shake some sense into her, especially when Amma called out to her when she was halfway out the front door, *Make sure you and your sister are home in time for dinner!*

Brett knew it wasn't a great day for Amma when she left three hours ago, knew it wasn't even a very good day, and she should have been prepared to come home and find her still unsettled. Nights were often worse than days. But in the rush of adrenaline from bringing Adam and Lizzie down to the station, plus the anxiety she felt about what she'd found stuffed under Adam's seat and how she was going to have to ask her boss about it, she'd all but forgotten about Amma's earlier loose grip on reality. Which was why it took her by surprise when Amma didn't come all the way inside the house, when she stood with one hand clutching the brass french door handle like her life depended on it, when she said through clenched teeth, "Please, leave."

Brett continued pulling cans and boxes out of the grocery bags and putting them away in the pantry. She kept her voice light, hoping that Amma would relax a little bit and come inside out of the sideways rain and gusting wind without turning the whole thing into a big fight. "I was thinking of heating up some chicken noodle soup. I know it's late, but unless you pulled some of that food out of the trash, I don't think you've eaten anything. Have you eaten anything?"

"You want money? Is that it?" Amma's voice was a tense thread about to snap. "I can give you money. Everything that's in my wallet in my purse by the front door—take it. Take whatever you find in there and get the hell out of my house."

Brett stopped putting away the groceries and turned to look at Amma, really look at her for the first time since she'd gotten home. Her eyes were wide with panic. Her mouth was set in a firm line. Her hands clenched at her side, the smallest and most fragile of fists. She stared at Brett, but it was clear she had no idea who Brett was.

"Amma, it's okay. It's me. It's Brett. You know me. I live here with you, remember?"

Something flickered across Amma's face, not recognition exactly, but something close to it. As quickly as it appeared, it slipped away again, and Amma's fists tightened. She shook her head, then took a step toward Brett. "You have until I count to three, then I'm calling the police."

Brett admired her grandmother's bravery, that she would face down a perceived intruder so boldly. But then, perhaps some of her old memories still churned beneath the surface of her confusion, and somewhere deep in her mind, she knew Brett was not a threat.

"There's no need to call the police, Anita." Brett hoped that hearing her name would break Amma out of her delusional state. "I'm going to finish putting away the groceries and make us some soup. Why don't you take Pistol into the living room and see what's on television?"

Amma's eyes flicked to the little dog who seemed to sense the tension building in the room and was pacing back and forth between them. Amma's frown deepened as she searched for some memory of herself with a dog. Apparently finding none, she bent over and started shooing poor Pistol toward the back door.

"Get out of here you mongrel. Shoo! Scram!"

Pistol was quick, darting out of her way easily and spinning to cower between Brett's legs, but the look of betrayal on his face was heartbreaking. Brett scooped the dog into her arms before Amma did something worse than simply flutter her hands and shout. Pistol leaned hard against Brett's chest. She could feel his tiny heart pounding.

Brett swallowed down her rising frustration, knowing that raising her voice would escalate the situation and cause her grandmother to become more agitated.

"Amma, please, take a breath, okay?" Brett spoke softly, but this did nothing to ease her grandmother's concerns.

Now she was flapping her hands at both Brett and Pistol, charging at them as she shouted, "Get out! Get out of my house! I don't want you here! Get out!"

Brett stood her ground, even as Amma's fists connected with Brett's shoulders. Her grandmother was surprisingly strong for someone who looked so frail.

"Amma, please, listen to me." Brett set Pistol on the floor, then grabbed hold of her grandmother's wrist as gently as she could.

She didn't want to hurt her; she just needed her to listen. Amma lifted her other hand to start hitting, but Brett grabbed hold of that, too, and Amma, sensing it was over, stopped struggling—whoever this stranger was, they'd won. Amma's head slumped forward and she started to weep, her shoulders shaking, her whole body trembling so hard, Brett worried she'd shake herself to pieces. She released her grandmother's wrists and grabbed her hands instead, squeezing them tightly, hoping this simple act of touch would bring her back to reality.

"Amma, it's me, it's Brett," she whispered the words. "Brett Buchanan. I'm your granddaughter."

Amma searched Brett's face with desperation, wanting this strange woman's words to be true, but then she shook her head and her entire body seemed to crumple under the weight of forgetting. "No, no, I don't have a granddaughter. I don't know who you are, but I want you out. Please, go. Please—"

Brett let go of Amma's hands and took a step toward the kitchen door.

She could withstand all her grandmother's small forgettings, how she had to daily remind Amma to wear a sweater, brush her teeth, close the door. She didn't even mind answering the same questions over and over—*Is Jeopardy on yet? When is Frank getting home? Can we take the boat out today?* The slips in time, the angry outbursts, the disorganization and middle-of-the-night wanderings—Brett could handle all of these things. They were difficult moments, certainly, and sometimes painful, too, but they were nothing compared to this: Amma looking her straight in the eyes and not recognizing her, looking and seeing not a beloved granddaughter, but a stranger she couldn't trust.

This was a loss for which Brett had not been fully prepared, despite the neurologist's warnings. Brett thought they would have more time, but she'd been wrong because here it was, without warning, and she realized even if she had listened, if she'd recognized the signs, she still wouldn't have been ready for the complete sucker punch of being forgotten by the only real family she had left in this world.

"It's okay, Amma." Brett spoke to her grandmother in a soothing rhythm as she backed out of the kitchen and into the living room. "You're safe. I'm going. I'm leaving. You're safe."

Amma stayed in the kitchen. Brett could hear her rummaging through drawers, perhaps finding a knife or something sharp with which to protect herself. Pistol trotted behind Brett, but cast worried glances over his shoulder at the banging, clattering sounds coming from the kitchen.

"It's alright, Pistol," she murmured to the dog, picking him up again and scratching under his chin.

As she passed the front door, Brett opened it and then slammed it shut. The sounds in the kitchen stopped briefly, then Amma's hurried footsteps pounded into the living room. Brett crept upstairs, watching from the landing as Amma peered through the sidelight curtains beside the front door. She snapped the dead bolt shut and double checked the latch, then retreated into the kitchen, her shoulders sagged with relief that her intruder was at last, gone.

Brett crept into her bedroom and waited there with Pistol until she was certain Amma was asleep. After the house had fallen into the comfortable silence of late evening, Brett left her room and went back downstairs to the kitchen to finally eat dinner.

She poured herself a bowl of cold cereal and milk, slowly opening and closing the cupboards so they wouldn't make any noise and avoiding the squeaking floorboard next to the sink. She kept one ear turned to the second floor, listening for the sounds of her grandmother stirring awake, but Amma either couldn't hear Brett's movements, or she had already slipped into some other delusion or perhaps reality, where the noises she heard were coming from someone she knew not to fear.

When Brett finished eating, she left her dishes unwashed in the sink and searched for a pen and scratch piece of paper. She found both in a drawer that also contained a box of tin foil, a yo-yo, and some old batteries.

She sat down at the table with a glass of whiskey. Pistol curled into a ball on her lap and fell right to sleep. His rhythmic snores kept Brett focused and calm as she wrote some of the hardest words she'd ever had to write in her entire life. She took her time, careful to make each letter neat so there would be no mistaking later what it said. Finished, she rose from the table with Pistol under one arm and taped the note to the refrigerator—right in the very center of all the other notes, in a prominent place so Amma would be able to see it every day.

The woman living with you is named Brett. Brett is your granddaughter. She is your family. You do not have to be afraid of her. She is here to help.

CHAPTER 21

It happened again today. During the Veteran's Day Parade on Monday morning, Lizzie thought she saw her mother moving through the crowded sidewalk on the other side of the street. It was the swing of her dirty-blond hair, the long coat that swished around her pudgy calves, burgundy like the one her mother pulled out of her closet when the weather turned cold and damp. It was the way she hesitated when she saw a uniformed police officer standing on the corner, how she tucked a loose bit of hair behind her ear, then turned and walked in the opposite direction, her shoulders rolled forward to hide her face.

Lizzie broke away from her grandparents and dad, giving them some lame excuse about needing to pee. Her dad called her name, but she didn't look back.

Despite the persistent drizzle, the streets were packed with people. A little rain couldn't keep them from their annual parade and the chance to gossip about June and Daniel and the increase in crime, the way their once perfect little town seemed to be coming apart at the seams.

Lizzie shoved her way through the crowd, ignoring their judgmental stares. She chased after the woman who couldn't possibly be her mother, but looked so much like her that the words *Mother, Mommy, Mom* floated to the tip of her tongue and stuck there behind clenched teeth. She darted into the street, dodging a Girl Scout troop and a trio of prancing ponies, their manes decorated with ribbons and flowers.

The cheers of the crowd pulsed in her ears. A car honked. Someone shouted at her to get out of the way. The woman in the burgundy coat turned to look over her shoulder at the commotion, and the spell was broken. Not her mother, not even close, but an older woman with sagging cheeks and a pinched-sour mouth and deep lines carved around her eyes and hair that was gray not blond. And now Lizzie didn't know how she'd seen any resemblance at all, how she could have been so mistaken.

She spun and ran in the opposite direction, away from the parade and her family and the woman who was not her mother.

The psychologist Lizzie was forced to talk to last year said that the ghosts she saw were a completely normal part of the grieving process. It had something to do with the fact that Lizzie had been given no closure when it came to her mother, whose body was never recovered. There had been a funeral, but Lizzie hadn't gone. A funeral was to say goodbye to the person you loved, and Lizzie didn't see the point when there was no one to say goodbye to and anyway, what she felt for her mother was far more complicated than love.

Lizzie didn't need a funeral to confirm the fact of her mother's death. She didn't have to see the body to recognize that Clara Trudeau was gone forever. So then why—if Lizzie understood logically that her mother was never coming back—was she still seeing the woman everywhere?

She saw her on Halloween night walking through the ruins. She heard her voice in the wind. That's why Lizzie had run away in the first place, leaving June and Daniel alone in the dark woods.

She'd been too afraid to face her ghosts, and now her two best friends were dead.

At some point Lizzie looked up from the puddles in the street and realized she'd walked over a mile since leaving the parade route on Main Street and was almost at the Newmark's mansion. June hated when Lizzie called it that. She claimed it wasn't that big of a house, but it was bigger than Lizzie's grandparents' house, which was big, and any house with separate wings, a ballroom, two kitchens, and a guest house by the pool was definitely a mansion.

She stood at the end of the driveway and stared up at the house. The dark windows stared back at her, and she couldn't shake the feeling that someone was in there, standing on the other side of the glass watching. She waited for the front door to swing open, for Mrs. Newmark to come running out, screaming at her to get lost. Mrs. Newmark used to like her, until last year. When she was Elizabeth, Mrs. Newmark hugged her and bought her and June matching clothes and kept a spare room made up for her, in case she ever popped over unannounced. She treated Elizabeth like another daughter. Not anymore. Mrs. Newmark didn't like Lizzie. She didn't like the girl with the short hair and scowling face who quit soccer and wore black lipstick, the girl without a mother. Mrs. Newmark had spent the past year moving around Lizzie like she was cursed, like a single touch would destroy their perfect family.

It turned out Mrs. Newmark was right.

Lizzie had destroyed them.

She trotted to the back of the house, staying close to the rhododendrons that grew in a prehistoric hedgerow against the brick wall.

June's room was accessible by climbing up a wooden trellis to a second floor window. June had started keeping the window unlocked for Lizzie after a fight with her mother last month when Mrs. Newmark said Lizzie was no longer welcome inside their house.

Lizzie was surprised to find the window unlocked today. It was the kind that swung open on hinges and was big and easy to crawl through. She slipped inside, her footsteps muffled by the thick carpet covering June's bedroom floor. She stood in the center of her best friend's room, breathing in the scent of her that already seemed to be fading. A tangy citrus, the faint smell of laundry detergent. Her bed was made. The canopy fluttered in the light breeze coming in through the window. Everything looked the same as the last time Lizzie was here. Except for the picture of the four of them that had been pinned over June's desk, which Detective Buchanan had now, nothing else looked disturbed.

Best friends were supposed to tell each other everything; they weren't supposed to keep secrets. Lizzie thought she'd known everything there was to know about June.

I saw them kissing, Adam had said.

Lizzie's thoughts leaped back and forth as she tried to resolve what she knew about her friend with what Adam had told her on the beach.

June told Lizzie everything, and Lizzie told June everything, too. That's the way things had been between them since the beginning—no secrets. If June had started dating Daniel, she would have said something to Lizzie about it, so they couldn't have been dating, and Adam was either lying, or he was confused about what he thought he saw. Then again, June hadn't told Lizzie about quitting soccer. Maybe she was afraid of what Lizzie might say, afraid she'd be upset. About what, Lizzie wasn't sure, but it was the only explanation she could think of for why June hadn't said anything about Daniel.

What other secrets had June been keeping, Lizzie wondered?

She went straight to June's closet, moving aside dresses and blouses and skirts and shoe boxes to get to the old dollhouse June's grandfather had built for her sixth birthday.

The doors in the dollhouse opened and closed. The furniture could be moved around. There were secret passageways and hidden cupboards. June had shown Lizzie once how it was the perfect place to hide things she didn't want her parents to find. She'd lifted a corner of the carpet in the ballroom to reveal a small cubby cut out of the floor where she was keeping a love note from a boy in their class.

Lizzie moved the miniature furniture out of the ballroom now and picked at the loose carpeting in the corner. She wasn't sure what she was hoping to find—evidence to prove Adam wrong, that June hadn't been keeping Daniel a secret. Or the opposite—undeniable proof that June and Daniel were meant to be together, the happiest they'd ever been. If they were happy in the weeks leading up to their death, maybe this would help ease the ache expanding in Lizzie's chest. If she knew they'd been happy, maybe all of this would hurt less.

What she found instead were three Polaroid pictures.

It took her a few seconds to figure out exactly what she was looking at, and when she finally did she almost shoved them back into their hiding spot under the carpet.

They were bad. Really, really bad.

There were three of them, apparently taken on three different days, in three different places, with three different people. The only thing that was the same in all three photos was the assistant soccer coach, Mr. Cadden.

In the first picture, Mr. Cadden and a girl from the soccer team named Rebecca were kissing in the front seat of his car. His fingers were tangled in her long brown hair. In the second picture, Mr. Cadden was leaning against the wall of the gymnasium beside another girl from the soccer team, Amanda. They stood too close. His hand cupped her face which was tilted down, her cheeks flushed a bashful pink.

The third one was the worst one: Mr. Cadden with his pants around his ankles having sex with a student on the desk in the art room. It looked like June had taken the photo through the small window cut out of the locked classroom door. It wasn't clear who the student was, but her gray skirt was pushed up, her bare legs wrapped around Mr. Cadden's waist, her turquoise tennis shoes a bright pop of color in the dingy classroom.

Lizzie flipped through the photographs slowly, a knot tightening in her chest. She knew the girls on the team complained a lot about Mr. Cadden's unwanted attentions, the way he stared, the way his hand lingered a few seconds too long as he patted them on the back, the way he hovered outside the locker room, but she hadn't known it was this bad.

But she did know, didn't she? Wasn't that the reason she'd quit soccer in the first place? Because barely one week into the new season, Mr. Cadden had approached her in the locker room and pressed his hand to the small of her back and his lips close to her neck and said, "You should always wear your hair like that. You look cute." They were in twin pigtails, tied low behind her ears. He reached up and tugged one gently.

Lizzie quit the team the next day, then cut and dyed her hair a few days after that.

She hadn't told anyone what had happened in the locker room that day in September or that this was the real reason she'd quit soccer; she let everyone assume whatever they wanted about her. But now, looking at these pictures, she wished she'd spoken up. She wished, at least, that she'd told June.

Maybe she and Daniel would both be still alive.

If Mr. Cadden knew these photographs existed, if June had shown them to him or threatened him in any way, Lizzie could easily imagine what would happen next. Mr. Cadden could have followed June after school, waited in the shadows near the ruins until Lizzie left and June and Daniel were alone. Maybe he wanted to wait to confront June until Daniel left, too, but Daniel wouldn't leave, and so he'd had no choice but to kill them both.

Somewhere in the house a door slammed, an echo of the gunshot Lizzie was imagining in her mind.

She jumped, and her elbow bumped against the dollhouse. A miniature oak door in the miniature kitchen swung open. Something glittered on the faux marble floor inside.

Lizzie wiggled her fingers through the opening and drew out a necklace. A heart pendant dangled from a slender gold chain. Inside the pendant was a single, small diamond. She held the necklace up to the closet light, letting the pendant swing and sparkle. She'd never seen June wearing this piece of jewelry, never heard her talk about it before. Maybe it was from Daniel, and that's why she'd never seen it—another part of her best friend's life hidden away.

Lizzie stuffed the photographs and the necklace in the pocket of her jeans, shuffled backward out of the closet, turned off the light, and crossed to the open window.

Footsteps pounded up the stairs.

Lizzie was swinging her leg over the casing and grabbing hold of the trellis when June's bedroom door flew open and her older sister Marcie stepped inside. Marcie froze when she saw Lizzie, and her mouth dropped in surprise. She swung her gaze over her shoulder, then back to Lizzie like she was trying to decide whether or not to call for help.

Lizzie didn't wait to see what she would do. She clambered down the trellis, leaping the last few feet. She hit the ground with a soft thump and ran.

CHAPTER 22

Tuesday morning was the first opportunity Brett had to talk to Wes Harris since Saturday night when she dragged his drunk son down to the station. Neither of them worked on Sundays, and they were both too busy helping out with the Veteran's Day Parade on Monday to do anything but wave at each other in passing.

As soon as Brett dropped off her jacket and purse at her desk, she stopped by his office. She rapped her knuckles on his half-open door.

He waved her to come inside. "Just the person I wanted to see."

She entered, shut the door behind her, and sat in one of the wooden chairs positioned in front of his desk. Wes lowered himself into his squeaking leather swivel chair and folded his hands on top of a stack of papers.

"I never got a chance to thank you," he said.

"For what?"

"For the other night. The way you handled my son."

Wes had stormed into the station late Saturday night red-faced and cursing. He'd gone straight to the cell where Adam was waiting and dragged the boy home without saying a single word to Brett. She'd happily stayed out of their way because at the time it was nothing more than a family affair. That was before the tow truck brought Adam's pickup to the impound lot, before they found the bloody clothes and camera stuffed under the front seat.

"He's a good kid most of the time," Wes was saying. "What happened on Saturday, that's not normal behavior. He knows better than to drink and drive. Hell, he knows better than to drink, period. I think it's this stuff with the Newmark girl. He knew her. They were friends, I guess, and it seems he's taking it pretty hard. He's missed some school. He's not sleeping very well. Nightmares, you know, that kind of thing. His mother and I, we're trying to get him to talk to his school counselor, but he refuses." Wes sighed and leaned back in his chair, running a finger over his mustache. "Anyway, none of that is your problem, is it? What I'm trying to say is that I appreciate you not coming down too hard on him the other night, what with everything that's been going on lately. I appreciate you calling me rather than filing an official report and turning it into a whole thing. You could have made his life a real nightmare, and you didn't. And I want you to know I appreciate you doing that for us."

Brett held her hands in her lap, feeling her heartbeat in the tight clasp of her palms. Nervous wasn't the right word for what she was feeling—embarrassed, maybe, horrified in advance over what she was about to say to her new boss.

She scooted forward on the edge of the chair. "After you took Adam home, the tow truck dropped off his pickup at the impound lot."

A thin wrinkle formed on Wes' brow as he frowned and said, "Yes, Eli told me."

Before Wes had taken the position as detective sergeant, he'd been the day patrol sergeant, in charge of the largest unit in the department, which was composed of more than thirty uniformed officers including Eli. The two men had been working together for years, and so it made sense that Eli would give his old boss a heads up if he thought there might be some kind of trouble. He could have at least kept Brett in the loop about it, too, so she didn't make an ass of herself like she was doing now.

"He told you that we found some suspicious items in the cab of Adam's truck?" she asked. Her voice sounded stiff and too formal. She told herself to relax; she was chatting with her boss, not interrogating a suspect.

Wes matched her formality, straightening his shoulders and growing taller in his chair. "I understand that you're just doing your job here, Buchanan, and while this is exactly the kind of thoroughness I expect from everyone on my team, I can assure you, the things you found in Adam's truck have nothing to do with the Newmark case."

"He had June's camera," she reminded him.

"She gave it to him to try and fix. Apparently, the shutter button was sticky. He's been taking an electronics class or something at the community college. He was trying to help her out, that's all. It's a shame he couldn't get it back to her before she was killed. I think that's part of the reason he's struggling so much right now." The stiffness melted from his shoulders again as he talked about his son. "He feels guilty, I think, for not fixing the camera sooner. And for not being there that night, too. Like if he'd been there, she might still be alive."

"I'm sorry, sir, but I have to ask…"

His eyebrows shot up, and he answered before she even started the question. "The bloody clothes, that's what you want to know about, right? Adam had a nosebleed after football practice a few weeks ago. Dumb kids were messing around in the locker room, rough-housing, and things got a little out of hand. He tripped into a locker door that was hanging open and started bleeding like a stuck pig. We thought for sure his nose would be broken with the amount of blood spurting out of him, but the ER doctor said he was fine. His eyes bruised up pretty good though. I guess he forgot about the clothes in his gym bag. I don't know. His mother and I, we're trying to teach him responsibility, you know? Raise him up to be an independent young man. I don't want him going away to college not knowing how to wash his own clothes. Looks like he could do with another lesson."

He chuckled and spread his hands across his desk. "I appreciate you coming to me with this. I would have questions, too, if our roles were reversed. I know we're just starting to get to know one another, but I want you to be able to come to me with stuff like this in the future. My door's always open, okay?"

Brett nodded and started to stand up, but Wes wasn't finished.

"Since we're talking about the Newmark case," he said, and she sat back down. "I think now's a good time to tell you that we're going to start scaling back the investigation."

"What does that mean?"

"Unfortunately, we can't keep throwing all our time and resources into one case. The world keeps turning, and assholes are still out there being assholes to other assholes. If our other open cases don't get worked, the mayor's going to come in here breathing fire about why we're letting his nice, quiet little seaside town descend into total anarchy and then we're all going to find ourselves heaped in an avalanche of shit."

Brett sensed what was coming and braced herself for it.

"Starting tomorrow, all detectives except Winters are back in the rotation. You'll pick up where you left off with your older cases and start cracking into the newer ones. Winters will continue as lead on the Newmark case. He'll have plenty of uniformed officers to help with phone calls and paperwork, and if he needs more help, he knows how to ask."

"There's a lot left to be done on the case," Brett said, thinking they weren't even close to finding answers, and instead of ramping down, they should be ramping up, re-interviewing people, this time with a focus on Daniel rather than June.

Because maybe June wasn't the intended victim, maybe she was simply in the wrong place at the wrong time. Finding out who wanted Daniel dead? That should be everyone's new priority.

"So there are a few loose ends." Wes waved his fingers in the air. "But Irving's been around a long time. I don't need to tell you that. He's more than capable of juggling the workload, especially if he's not taking on new cases. Which he won't be, thanks to you."

Wes leaned back in his chair, smiling, and cracked his knuckles. "Besides, I'm keeping Eli on the Newmark case, and I really don't think it would be a good idea for the two of you to be working that closely together, do you?"

Brett's cheeks flushed hot. Her gaze dropped to the floor. There was a yellowish-brown stain on the linoleum near a potted plant where water had leaked. She wasn't going to lie to her sergeant and say she and Eli hadn't been getting cozy together at the bar, but neither would she confirm his suspicions.

Wes seemed satisfied with her silence. He rocked out of his chair and came around the desk, perching on the front edge with his legs crossed at the ankles. "You know, Buchanan, I really do appreciate you being willing to support the case, and the team, this way. You and I both know the real work is in the day to day, the grunt and grind. That's how you rise to the top, that's how we all did. By starting at the bottom, working the boring cases no one else wants, proving you can show up day in and day out and get shit done. You can do that, can't you?"

"Yes, sir."

"Good." Wes clapped her on the shoulder amicably. "I knew we weren't going to have a problem. When I took over this position, Stan warned me about you. He said you were stubborn and liked to do things your own way, but between you and me, Stan can be a bit of a prick. I think you and I are going to get along just fine."

He straightened and went to open the door for her.

"You'll let me know if you need any help with that Thanksgiving dinner, okay?"

Brett returned to her desk in the middle of the squad room and sat down. She stared at the pencils sitting in a plastic red cup next to the phone, then grabbed the phone receiver, pressed it to her ear, and started to dial. She hung up before the first ring.

It had been over a week since her fight with Jimmy in Seattle, and they hadn't spoken since. Calling him now to complain about the way the department was handling a case seemed like a pretty shitty thing to do considering one of the last things she said to him was that being friends with a reporter was going to get her in trouble at work. She needed to rely on him less; she needed to figure this out for herself.

She got up from her desk and went downstairs to the evidence room. The clerk handed over the log without question. Brett flipped through it but found no entries for Friday night, or Saturday morning, nothing that had Adam Harris' or Eli Miller's names attached. The last entry from Eli was on Wednesday when he arrested someone for possession of marijuana.

Brett closed the book, handed it back to the clerk, and stepped around his desk to search the shelves. Maybe Eli had been planning to fill out the log later, but forgot. She looked for a box with the correct date and Harris' name marked on the label. When she didn't find one, she began opening boxes and bags at random, thinking maybe the clothes and camera had gotten put in the wrong place.

"Can I help you find something, Detective?" the clerk asked, clearly annoyed with her.

Brett shoved the box she was holding back on the shelf and left the evidence room. She marched upstairs to the dispatcher's desk. The radio was quiet. The man working it lounged in his chair, dipping a donut into a cup of hot coffee.

"I need you to tell me where Eli Miller is right now," she said, not bothering with niceties.

The man nodded at her, but kept chewing. One finger scrolled down the sheet of paper sitting in front of him, then he swallowed and said, "He's out at the marina following up with the owner of a stolen fishing boat. Need me to call him in?"

"No, that's okay," she said. "I'll head out there myself, see if I can catch him before he leaves."

It would be harder for Eli to lie to her if they were talking face-to-face.

"Honestly, Brett, I have no idea what you're talking about," Eli said. "You were there with me. We bagged the evidence together."

They sat in his patrol car in the parking lot of the marina. She'd had to wait only a few minutes after pulling into the lot before Eli came out of the glass-fronted building with a man dressed in overalls and heavy-duty rubber boots. The two parted ways at the end of the sidewalk, with the man hurrying toward a pickup truck and Eli trotting toward his cruiser. He'd looked surprised to see Brett, happy at first, but then worried when she said, "That stuff we took out of Adam Harris' truck the other night? Where did it end up?"

He didn't answer right away. He opened the passenger door for her, telling her to get in so at least they could talk out of the rain.

They'd been going in circles for almost ten minutes with Brett asking him about the missing evidence and Eli swearing up and down that the last time he checked, the evidence was exactly where he'd left it: safely locked up in the evidence room.

"Well, it's not there anymore," Brett insisted. "Your name's not even in the log."

"So, what are you suggesting?"

"You told me to go home. You told me you could handle it."

"And I did. I carried it down to the evidence room and boxed it up and—you know what? No. I'm not going over this with you again. I know how to do my fucking job." He stared out the windshield.

The soft patter of rain on the car roof filled the silence that pressed thick between them. Brett shifted her focus out the window, too, because staring at Eli's profile made her angrier.

He was lying.

She could see it in the hard jut of his jaw, the way he chewed on the corner of his lip, how he refused to look at her even as he grew more and more defensive. He knew where the evidence had disappeared to, but he was firmly committed to the lie that he didn't, and Brett could tell there was no way in hell she was going to get him to change his mind and come clean. What she couldn't figure out was if Eli was lying to cover his own ass or someone else's.

The dock was lined with large fishing trawlers and smaller, personal boats. They rocked and tugged against their ropes as the swells rose higher. There were a few boats out on the bay, larger, commercial trawlers that depended on the day's catch to pay their crew and didn't have the luxury of hunkering down on shore with every small storm that blew through. In the billowing fog, their lights shined bright.

The car radio squawked, and the dispatcher's voice crackled over the receiver. "Eli, are you still out at the marina?"

Eli let out a rush of air, like he'd prayed for this interruption and the great gods of the sea had listened. He grabbed the speaker and pressed down hard on the button. "I'm here. Just wrapping up the interview now."

"Stay put. There's a fishing boat coming in, says they dragged a body up in one of their nets."

Brett didn't wait to hear anymore. She pulled her hood over her head, got out of the car, and ran to the end of the dock.

At first she didn't see it; the fog was too thick. But then the dark hull appeared a mile or so off shore—a wavering ghost cutting through the white. The crew stood in a line along the railing waiting to throw down the ropes.

When they reached the dock, there was a flurry of motion as the crew secured the fishing vessel to the cleats and started to unload. Then everything slowed down again as the men stopped working to watch four crew members, including the captain carry a securely wrapped oilcloth off the main deck onto the dock where Brett and Eli waited. The men laid the body carefully on the damp boards at their feet and stepped back.

Eli looked at Brett like he was waiting for her to make the first move. She knelt and pulled the cloth back from the head. He was still tangled in netting, his bloated flesh pushing through the holes. Eli turned away first, sucking in his breath, but Brett soon followed, rising to her feet again and greedily gulping up the cool, salt air. She turned her gaze to the sky where seagulls drifted above the boat masts.

"It's bad luck finding a body in the water," one of the fishermen standing nearby said. He took a cigar from his pocket and lit the end, blowing smoke toward the ocean. "I don't care what the captain says, I'm not going back out there today. Fire me if he wants."

A few of the other fishermen grumbled and nodded. The storm was bad enough without having to haul in this kind of ghoulish catch.

"It's him, isn't it?" Eli asked.

Brett unwrapped the rest of the oil cloth and let her gaze trail down the length of the body, taking in the discoloration and places where his body had started to fall to pieces. The skin on his face and hands was puckered and peeling away in paper-thin layers.

Sea creatures had picked and nibbled at the soft parts around his eyes, nose, and mouth. Something with sharp teeth had taken a chunk from the side of his neck.

This body was in one of the worst states Brett had ever seen.

Her eyes moved to his legs where they were sticking out of the netting. The right foot was missing, the jagged end of the shin bones visible where muscle had been nibbled down to white bone by fish or crabs or some other sea animals. The left foot was still tucked inside a shoe that matched the one she and Eli had found washed up on the beach at Egret's Park a week ago.

It had taken two weeks, but finally Daniel Yoon had come home.

CHAPTER 23

"There's someone waiting to talk to you in interview room two," the front desk officer said when Brett arrived back at the station several hours later.

While she and Eli waited for Charlie to arrive at the docks, they'd taken statements from the captain and his crew. The fishermen didn't have much to add to what they'd already told the dispatcher: they'd been trawling near the mouth of the bay when they pulled Daniel Yoon's body up in their net. When Charlie finally got to the scene, he'd done a brief visual examination of the body before wrapping it up to take to the morgue for the official autopsy.

Fourteen days in the water wrecked a body in a lot of ways, but at least they could be certain about one thing now: Daniel Yoon hadn't thrown himself over any cliffs.

There was a jagged hole the size of a walnut torn through the back of his shirt a few inches below his left scapula. The skin and muscles underneath were ripped and raw, the short time in the water having done a number on the soft tissue surrounding the area. But even with the damage, it was obvious someone had shot the kid in the back.

Charlie and Eli didn't say a word to her or to each other. They silently lifted the body and carried it to the medical examiner's van together, then Eli got in his patrol car and drove away.

After the afternoon she'd had, Brett wanted nothing more than to go home, scrub off the stink and filth of the docks, and settle in front of the television with a stiff drink.

She grimaced at her own callousness. A boy was dead. He'd been drifting in the bay for two weeks, picked apart by sea creatures to the point he was barely recognizable. The news was going to devastate his mother. And all Brett could think about was citrus-scented shower steam and toasty pajamas and the first burning sip of whiskey that would loosen the knots in her neck.

She wasn't a heartless monster—it was a matter of survival. If she pressed every case close to her heart, carried it around with her everywhere, eventually she'd shatter. She'd lost plenty of sleep over this one already, and now with finding Daniel's body, everything was about to become that much more complicated.

The last thing she had energy for tonight was cracking open a new case. Whoever wanted to talk to her, and whatever they wanted to talk to her about, could certainly wait until tomorrow after she'd had a hot shower and a good night's rest, but the front desk officer was adamant that she deal with it now.

"She's been waiting for you for over an hour," he said. "Refused to talk to anyone else. Said it had to be you or no one."

"What?" Brett started to unzip her rain jacket, but one arm got stuck. She struggled with it a minute before breaking free. "Who's waiting?"

The officer checked a pad of paper sitting in front of him. "Marcie Newmark."

Brett bunched her jacket into a ball. Water dripped onto the mustard yellow carpet of the lobby. Her boots were sopping wet, too, and left faint damp marks wherever she stepped. "Did she at least tell you what she wants?"

"Sure, she said something about filing a breaking and entering complaint," the front desk officer said. "Which I started to do, but when she told me her name and who she thought had broken into her house, well, I thought it best if I get her set up in an interview room and have one of the detectives take a statement."

"But she wouldn't talk to anyone else?"

The officer shook his head and shuffled some papers. "I tried, but she said she'd only talk to you."

"And she's been waiting for how long?" Brett asked.

The officer's eyes flicked to the clock hanging on the wall behind her. "About an hour."

"You didn't think to call me?"

"Tried." He shrugged. "You weren't answering."

She moved her hand to her belt. Sure enough, her radio wasn't there. She must have left it on her desk or it fell out somewhere in her car.

The front desk officer gave her a judgmental look. "So, are you going to talk to her, or do I need to get someone else in here?"

"No, I've got it. Thank you." She walked through the door separating the public lobby from the main station.

She braced herself as she walked past Wes Harris' office. She didn't want to talk to him right now, not before she figured out what happened to the missing evidence, not with Daniel Yoon's body lying cold on the table and the investigation hitting another dead-end. An investigation she wasn't even technically a part of anymore. But Wes' office was empty, the door closed, the lights turned off. He'd probably heard about Daniel's body and rushed to meet Charlie at the morgue. They'd probably passed each other on the highway. Brett exhaled her relief.

Then she sniffed her armpits and made a face. The stink from the docks was worse than she thought. She stopped by the restroom to splash her face with water, wash the worst of the stench from her armpits with paper towels, and fix her ponytail. She didn't look great, but at least she no longer looked like a piece of flotsam battered by waves. Whatever it was Marcie needed to say, it was important enough she'd waited around for an hour. Brett could at least do her the courtesy of not showing up to the interview looking and smelling like rotten seaweed.

She took a deep breath and fixed a polite smile on her face, then went to talk to Marcie.

The young woman had been given the nicest of the three interview rooms to wait. Interview Room Two was where they talked to grieving family members or interviewed sensitive witnesses. Sometimes they even used it to celebrate officer birthdays, serving sheet cake and coffee from the very same honey-oak table where Marcie sat now.

Despite this being the most comfortable room with the most comfortable furniture, Marcie looked distressed. She sat stiffly in the chair, picking at the skin around her fingers. One leg bounced uncontrollably. She kept flicking her eyes around the room like she was chasing the motion of a fly. When Brett entered, Marcie swiveled around with a startled look on her face.

"Sorry to keep you waiting." Brett pulled another chair over to the same side of the table as her and sat down. "Did anyone offer you anything to drink?"

Marcie shook her head.

"Can I get you anything? Coffee? Water?"

"No, I want to get this over with. I told my mom I wouldn't be gone very long and it's…" She looked around the room, but there were no clocks in here. Her eyes flicked back to the window. "I need to get back home."

"And how are things at home?"

Marcie shrugged. "We're managing. Mom sleeps all the time. When she's not sleeping, she's wandering around the house like a zombie. Dad's back at work, obviously. When he's not working on his cases, he's calling in favors to everyone he knows, trying to find out what happened to June. He hired a private investigator." Marcie tugged on a dark strand of her hair. "He doesn't trust you guys to do what needs to be done. He says if you were going to solve this case, you would have solved it by now."

The girl was trying to push her buttons, and while some detectives might have been offended by Marcie's words, Brett wasn't one of them. If June's parents wanted to pay for a private investigator, she wasn't about to stop them. Her own father had hired a private investigator after Margot's death, and though for a while it had served the purpose of making her father feel slightly less helpless in the face of it all, ultimately the man hadn't been able to uncover any answers. The whole endeavor had been a waste of money, ending with her father even more frustrated and heartbroken than before. But maybe the private investigator Peter hired would have better luck with June's case. Sometimes a PI found things the cops missed; sometimes people were more willing to talk to someone without a badge.

"What about you? You're not back at school yet," Brett pointed out, making a mental note to get the investigator's name from Peter later.

"I need to take care of my family right now." A pained look flashed over Marcie's face. "I'll go back next semester."

She didn't sound very confident about that.

Brett leaned her elbows on the table. "Are there other people helping out at home? Aunts? Grandparents? You shouldn't be the one taking care of everything, you know."

Anger crackled in her brown eyes. "I didn't come here to talk about me, okay? I came here to report a burglary. I want her arrested."

"Who?" Brett asked.

"Elizabeth Trudeau." Marcie stiffened her shoulders when she said the name, and her chin tilted slightly higher. "When I got home from the parade yesterday, I heard someone moving around upstairs. I thought it was the maid, but then I remembered she had the day off. Dad was at work. Mom was conked out on the couch, dead to the world. I went upstairs and the sounds were coming from June's room. When I opened the door, I saw Elizabeth climbing through my sister's window. She was leaving, but she'd been in our house for who knows how long. In June's room. Messing around with her things. She saw me and she didn't say anything or stop. She just took off running."

"Did she take anything?" Brett asked.

"I don't know." Marcie shook her head in frustration. "I don't have an inventory of all my sister's things, but from what I could tell nothing valuable was taken. All my sister's jewelry was still where she kept it in her jewelry box. I think Elizabeth was messing around in the closet so maybe she took a shirt or something? Does it matter? She was trespassing. She shouldn't have been there. She needs to be arrested. I want her arrested."

Marcie's voice grew louder with each word.

"Did she cause any damage?" Brett understood the violation of finding someone in your house who wasn't supposed to be there, but it seemed excessive to arrest a teenager for climbing into her friend's bedroom, but taking nothing of value and harming no one.

"Did she cause any damage?" Marcie repeated the words with a shrill laugh. "She killed my sister."

"Did she tell you that?" Brett shifted forward in her chair.

Marcie let out a deep sigh and darted her gaze toward the small window. "She didn't tell me anything, but I know she did it. Who else could it be?"

She pushed back in the chair, clutched her purse to her side, and moved toward the door where she paused a moment, her eyes sparking dangerously when she said, "You need to do something about her. You need to lock her up and throw away the key before someone else gets hurt."

CHAPTER 24

Lizzie pulled the blankets over her head as morning light began to seep through her bedroom window. She was never leaving this house. Never leaving this room. Someone would bring her food. She would grow old pacing the plush carpet. Through the large window overlooking the pasture, she'd watch the seasons turn and the landscape change and maybe every so often she would crack the window for a breath of fresh air and think about leaving. But she wouldn't leave, not ever. There was nothing good for her waiting outside this room.

Someone knocked on the bedroom door, and her father, in a timid and watery voice, said, "Elizabeth? Are you awake? You're going to be late for school if you don't hurry."

She tugged the blankets tighter, vanishing the last sliver of light that was creeping through the fabric. She was shrouded in darkness, tucked away where no one could find her, safe in the heat and stink of her own breath. The bedroom door clicked open, then someone yanked the blanket from her. She shrank from the light, and from her father, too, who was patting her hip, saying, "Up, up, get up. I'm making pancakes."

Lizzie grumbled and rolled away from him. She tried to pull

the blankets over her shoulders again, but he still had a hold of them. The bed shifted as he sat down beside her.

"What's wrong?"

"I'm sick," she mumbled. "I think I have a fever."

He pressed his hand to her forehead. It felt like a stranger's hand. And wasn't he? Ten months away from her—ten months was long enough for both of them to become very different people than they used to be. His skin was rougher than she remembered. His hands smelled like sawdust and hay from the hours he spent helping out in the barn, when before they smelled like the Old Spice aftershave he used every day before he went to work in his fancy downtown real estate office.

"You don't feel warm," he said.

"My stomach hurts."

"Probably because you haven't had breakfast yet. It's the most important meal of the day, you know. Come on, up and at 'em." He patted her hip again, with a little more force this time, as if wanting to remind her that he still held some authority as her father.

She groaned into the pillow.

"Is this about that teacher you told Detective Buchanan about last night?" he asked. "You don't have any classes with him, do you?"

She shook her head. She didn't, but the high school was small and it seemed all the hallways fed into each other. She'd see Mr. Cadden eventually, even if she did everything she could to avoid him. She'd see him, and if he didn't already know what she'd done, he'd see it in her eyes. The betrayal. The fear. The disgust.

When Detective Buchanan came to the house last night, Lizzie knew even before she opened her mouth that she was going to ask about the Newmark house.

The Newmarks want to press charges. They want me to arrest you. You can't go into other people's houses without their permission. What were you doing there? Did you take anything?

Her grandparents and her father had stared at her like she'd grown two heads. Lizzie didn't bother pointing out that she had climbed through that very same window over a hundred times when June was alive and no one had complained about it before.

What did you do? Her father's voice trembled with fear or rage, Lizzie couldn't tell.

He was still mad at her for the whole drinking incident last week, for having to come and break her out of jail. The morning after, her father and both grandparents had stood over her bed with stern faces and empty threats. *No one's mad,* her grandfather had said, *we're worried, that's all. We know you can do better than this.*

The problem was, she didn't know if she could. Not in this town anyway—the rotted dock boards breaking beneath her feet, a barnacle she couldn't scrape off—this place that wouldn't let her be anybody but her mother's daughter.

She didn't tell them why she'd originally climbed up June's trellis. She missed her friend. She was lonely. She wanted to know why June had been keeping secrets from her. She didn't tell them any of that. She just said, *I gave June one of my sweatshirts a few weeks ago at school, and I wanted it back.*

And that's when Detective Buchanan told her about Daniel's body. A fishing boat had pulled him in. She tried not to think about the net tangled around his face, the rope cutting into his skin, about what a person would look like after that many days in the ocean. She excused herself, went to the bathroom and splashed cold water on her face. When she came back, Detective Buchanan studied her carefully.

I need you to be honest with us, Lizzie. I need you to tell me what really happened on Halloween night. I know you're scared, but you need to tell the truth.

But she had told the truth.

Don't be scared. I can help you.

She'd heard those words before, trusted them once, but she knew better now. She chewed on the corner of her lip and studied the ridges of her fingernails.

Do we need a lawyer? Her grandmother sputtered, rising from her chair and moving toward the phone sitting on the credenza.

Dad and Grandpa flashed her a hard look, and she sat back down.

You were with them that night, Detective Buchanan said. *You admitted you were there.*

Lizzie wasn't going to defend herself again. She'd done nothing wrong.

Except break her promises.

Except leave them alone in the dark.

It doesn't look good, Detective Buchanan said. *You breaking into June's room like this. Not after everything that's happened. Not after you admitted to being there that night. Were you jealous of them? Were you upset they were dating?*

Lizzie's heart leaped. Did everyone know but her? Had she been so oblivious to not see what was happening right in front of her?

She thought back to that night. How close June stood to Daniel, the way her white-blond hair brushed his black leather jacket. She couldn't be sure, but maybe their hands had brushed, too.

She understood now why the detective was here. This wasn't about her being in June's room. This was about June being dead, and Lizzie being the most likely person to have done it, even though she would never—not in a million years. She shot up from the couch and pounded upstairs. Her father called after her, and then she heard his footsteps on the stairs, but she was already coming back down, passing him on the landing.

I found these in June's room. She shoved the Polaroids into the detective's face.

Then she'd told them about the time in the locker room when Mr. Cadden was inappropriate. From the corner of her eye, she saw her father's fists clench. Her grandmother's lips pinched like she'd bitten down on something sour. Her grandfather, who had been standing near the window, stepped closer to Lizzie even though it was too late now to protect her.

Detective Buchanan's expression softened, and Lizzie knew she was thinking of a similar conversation they'd had last year at the police station. June had been by Lizzie's side during that awful experience, and she wished more than anything that her friend was here now, too. But she wasn't; Lizzie had to do this part herself.

She rushed to reassure them, *Nothing happened. I didn't let anything happen.*

Though she knew better than anyone how sometimes it didn't matter how hard you fought or if you said no, sometimes it happened anyway, even when you didn't mean for it to happen. And just because it happened, didn't mean you'd let it happen. She hugged her arms around herself, shoving aside the hazy memories of last Halloween at the Whitmore Mansion.

Everyone was staring at her, waiting for her to say more. She pointed to the pictures. *This is who you should be interrogating, not me.*

Detective Buchanan took the Polaroids with her when she left, but she hadn't said what would happen next. Lizzie had a feeling it wasn't going to end well. For Mr. Cadden or for her.

For better or worse, the kids at school liked Mr. Cadden. Maybe they didn't know his secrets, or maybe they did and they didn't care, but the truth was, if he was arrested, and people found out that Lizzie was the reason why, she'd become even more of a pariah than she already was.

So, no, she couldn't go to school. Not today. Not ever again. And no amount of pancakes could change her mind.

Her father rose from the bed and tugged her ankle. "This is the last time I'm going to ask you nicely."

And then what? She wanted to ask. *Will you lock me in a shed in the middle of the woods? Tie me up and leave me for dead?*

She wasn't being fair. He was trying to do something nice. He just wanted to make her pancakes. It wasn't his fault everything in her life was falling apart, but it felt nice to have someone besides herself to blame.

Lizzie didn't recognize the woman rummaging through the cubbies of art supplies next to Mr. Cadden's desk. She was young with a turned-up nose and thick, black hair piled in a loose bun on top of her head. When she saw Lizzie watching her from the open classroom doorway, she lowered her glasses and smiled. "Please tell me you're one of my watercolor students, because I cannot, for the life of me, figure out where they keep the paintbrushes around here."

Lizzie mumbled something and backed out of the classroom. The woman's smile turned to confusion, but Lizzie didn't stick around to answer any more of her questions.

Head lowered, she stumbled through the hallways, shoving and being shoved. She caught snippets of conversation, the rumor mill churning hard this morning.

"Did you hear? They arrested Mr. Cadden for June's murder."

"He was having sex with some of his students."

"Rebecca told me they were dating."

They'd go silent again when Lizzie passed them in the hall, but she felt their burning stares, their hatred of her stirring the air, making it nearly impossible to breathe.

When the bell rang, Lizzie found herself sitting at the back of her first period class without any real idea of how she'd gotten there. The teacher droned on about something, but Lizzie wasn't paying attention, and neither was anyone else. Notes were passed.

Whispers spread from one corner of the room to the other. Rain pelted the windows, sounding as if it, too, had something important to say. The whole world seemed to be talking about June and Daniel and Mr. Cadden.

A ping came over the intercom. The cross-chatter stopped as everyone turned to stare at the small speaker box hanging over the door. Principal London's voice crackled into the silence.

"Attention students and faculty. We'll be having a special assembly this morning. Attendance is mandatory. After you are released from first period, please make your way to the gymnasium in an orderly fashion."

The bell clattered, and the noise inside the classroom was deafening, as students scraped chairs and gathered their things, hurrying to get to the gymnasium. They talked over one another, offering theories as to what the special assembly was going to be about, and they all agreed it had to be because of Mr. Cadden's arrest, the murder of two students, the police who had been a near constant presence in their hallways for going on three weeks now.

Lizzie waited until everyone else had left the room before making her way to the gym. A few steps from the entrance, someone grabbed her elbow. She flinched, but relaxed again when she saw it was Adam. A worried look furrowed his brow.

"You're going in there?" he asked.

She shrugged. Where else did she have to go?

He tugged her out of the stream of students and backed her up against a nearby locker. His eyes darted. He kept his hand gripped tight around her bicep even as she tried to shrug him off.

"They're going to be talking about Daniel and June." His breath was hot and smelled a little like old milk.

"So what?"

"So, I can't sit there and listen to them pretend to care."

People liked June. Teachers, students, parents. Everyone. But

Lizzie understood Adam's reluctance. She, too, didn't want to grieve in public. She thought about what might happen if they went into that gym with their peers. She thought about how everyone would turn and stare at her when they said June's name. How people would whisper when they talked about Daniel—freak, weirdo. She imagined Principal London asking her to stand up and say a few words, tell the entire school what June was like when she was alive—*You were her best friend, weren't you?* She imagined Principal London pointing her out and saying, *If it wasn't for Lizzie Trudeau, we would have never discovered Mr. Cadden's sins. Thank you, Lizzie. Everyone clap for Lizzie.*

The buzz in her head that had been present all morning, turned to a roar. And there it was again—the feeling that the walls were going to collapse around her and she'd be buried alive.

She grabbed Adam's hand, and they hurried away from the gym, ducking through the doors at the end of the hall as the bell rang. They darted through the rain toward the football stadium and took shelter under the metal bleachers.

Lizzie hadn't talked to Adam since they got drunk and then arrested together.

"How much trouble did you get into on Saturday night?" she asked him now.

He shifted so his body was facing her. Inches separated them, and Lizzie could smell the sweat under his armpits and see raindrops wicking off his wool shirt. "If I show you something, will you promise not to tell anyone else?"

She mimed zipping her lip and throwing away the key.

Adam grabbed the bottom of his shirt and inched it up to his chest, revealing a wine-colored bruise the size of a saucer plate along his ribcage.

"Your dad did that?" Lizzie reached as if to touch him, then quickly pulled her hand back. "He hit you?"

He craned his neck to see the bruise better and pressed his fingers around its scarlet edges, wincing in pain before letting the shirt drop again. "I deserved it."

"Does he do that a lot?" Lizzie asked.

Adam ran his fingers through his hair and squinted across the football field. "Only when I do something dumb."

"He shouldn't hit you."

"Spare the rod, spoil the child." His voice dropped low when he said it, like he was trying to mimic his father.

"Have you told anyone else? Your mom? A teacher?"

His laugh echoed sharply against the metal bleachers. "He'd tell them I tripped or something. That I ran into a doorknob. I've always been clumsy that way."

"That's why you wanted to leave with us," she said, finally putting the pieces together.

Lizzie couldn't remember whose idea it was to leave Crestwood: hers or Daniel's. Daniel mentioned a cousin in Seattle. Lizzie said they should go visit him. And then never come back. Daniel said they'd have to go in the middle of the night so by the time anyone realized they were gone, it would be too late to come after them. He was worried about his father's old crew, dangerous criminals who wanted Daniel to pick up the business where his father had left off. Daniel wanted nothing to do with that life. He wanted a clean break, a fresh start, the same as Lizzie did.

June played along when they talked about leaving, but Lizzie could see the fear in her eyes, how she didn't really want to go anywhere. But if Lizzie was set on going, then June was going, too, and she'd do whatever she could to help turn their daydream plans to practical reality. June was the one who introduced them to Adam. Adam had a pickup truck. That truck was going to be their ride out of town. But Lizzie had never thought to ask Adam what was in it for him, or what he was running from.

Adam stuffed his hands into his pockets and scraped his toe against the soggy grass that grew patchy under the bleachers. "June didn't know," he said. "No one does. I mean, except you now, I guess, but yeah. He's part of the reason I wanted to go."

"And the other part?"

Adam's hand lifted to the bruise again and hovered a few seconds before sinking back into his pocket. He looked at Lizzie out of the corner of his eye, and it was like he was trying to decide if he could trust her. Then his gaze traveled to the hollow of her neck where the heart-shaped pendant she'd found in June's dollhouse rested. Lizzie had been wearing it since Monday; she had even kept it on when she showered and slept. She thought wearing it would help her feel close to June again, but it didn't; the metal was cool and unfamiliar against her skin. Her fingers rose now, brushing the gold chain.

Adam's eyes narrowed. "Where did you get that?"

His hand darted up as he tried to grab the necklace.

She stepped out of reach. "It's June's."

"I know it is. I gave it to her. I'm asking why you have it?" He devoured the space between them, looming over her, anger turning his whole body rigid.

Backed up against the bleachers with no escape route, Lizzie cowered, covering the necklace with one hand and holding up the other to protect her face. If Adam wanted to hurt her, there was nothing she could do to stop him.

Adam unclenched his fists and took a step back, rushing to apologize for lunging at her the way he had. "Sorry. I didn't mean to scare you. It surprised me to see you wearing it, that's all."

"You gave this to her?" Lizzie touched the pendant.

He nodded and shoved his hands in his pockets. "Last year. When I asked her to be my girlfriend. She turned me down. She told me her parents wouldn't let her date anyone. I told her to keep it anyway. Like a friendship thing."

Now it was Lizzie's turn to be surprised. June had never mentioned Adam or the necklace.

In middle school, and during freshman year, when they'd talk about boys, it was always with a youthful innocence. They talked about passing notes during class—*Do you like me? Check yes or no.* They talked about first kisses and which boy they wanted to hold hands with on the bus. But something changed last year, and Lizzie had barely noticed.

It must have been after what happened with Zach at that party. After June found out what Zach had done to Lizzie, she'd stopped talking about boys, stopped asking Lizzie to play Truth or Dare, stopped pointing out her crushes in the cafeteria. Lizzie never asked her to do that, but she could admit now what a relief it was to not have to pretend. Though, now she could see, too, how much of her friend's life she'd missed.

She had been so focused on herself and on getting out of this town, that she hadn't seen the mess unfolding right in front of her. Adam loved June but June loved Daniel, and Daniel had come close to punching out a teacher for June, and all Lizzie had been able to see was the crushing wreckage of her own life, all she'd been able to focus on was how to escape. If she'd looked away from her own pain for even a single moment, if she'd been half the friend to June that June was to her, maybe Lizzie could have seen what was coming. Maybe she could have helped. And maybe June would still be alive right now.

Lizzie reached around and unhooked the necklace. The gold chain pooled in the palm of her hand as she held it out to Adam.

But he frowned at it, backing away like the chain was going to leap up and bite him. "Throw it out. Or keep it. Or whatever. I don't want it. I gave it to her. I wanted her to wear it."

He spun around and trotted back toward the school with his shoulders hunched against the rain.

CHAPTER 25

Brett watched through the one-way mirror and listened over the crackling intercom as Irving asked Benjamin Cadden about the Polaroids. "This is you, right?"

She hated to admit it, but Benjamin Cadden was a good-looking man, with broad shoulders and defined muscles visible in the flex of his arms. His jet-black hair was smoothed to one side, every hair in perfect place. He had a square jaw and emerald eyes flecked with mischief. He was younger than Brett by a few years, in his late twenties according to his driver's license, and she could see how a vulnerable, young female student might be drawn to a man like Cadden, a man old enough to be interesting but young enough to be accessible, with both an air of authority and a playful dimple in his chin. What she didn't understand was how Benjamin Cadden had allowed himself to cross the line from teacher to abuser, from harmless flirtations to sexual deviance.

He barely glanced at the photographs and studied his nails instead. "Those girls are eighteen. Ask them."

"Oh, I can assure you, we will be asking them. We will be asking them a lot of things."

Irving stuffed the Polaroids back into the folder he'd carried with him into the room along with his tape recorder, a notepad, and a brown paper bag. He folded his hands over top of the folder and glared at the man sitting in the wobbly chair on the other side of the table. "You want to tell me where you were on Halloween night?"

The teacher's eyes narrowed to hard slits, but he said nothing.

Irving tapped one thumb against the other, trying to wait him out. Benjamin raised a single eyebrow and crossed his arms over his chest, defiant.

After a few more seconds, Irving slid the paper bag between them. He grabbed the bottom of the bag and tipped out its contents. A black handgun with a wooden grip dropped onto the table between them. Benjamin frowned. So did Brett.

"How about you tell me about this gun instead?" Irving gestured to it. "When did you buy it?"

"I've never seen that before," Benjamin said, his words coming in a rush. "I don't own a gun. I'm a pacifist."

"Did you buy it that night?"

"What?"

"Did you buy it before or after June Newmark showed you these pictures?" One-by-one, Irving took the Polaroids out of the folder again, sliding each one across the table and arranging them in a line in front of Benjamin Cadden.

This time the younger man couldn't help himself. His eyes grazed over the photographs, almost lovingly, and a smile tugged on his mouth. Then he seemed to remember where he was. His eyes snapped back to Irving's, and he shook his head. "I want to talk to a lawyer."

Irving didn't get up right away. He took his time putting the pictures back into the folder and the gun back into the paper bag.

"Guilty men ask for lawyers," he said. "You know that, right? You know you're only going to make this whole thing harder for yourself."

Benjamin fixed his gaze on a point in the corner of the room and said nothing.

Irving sighed. He pushed back his chair in no rush, giving Benjamin Cadden time to change his mind about that lawyer, but Irving made it all the way to the door, opened it, stepped through, and Cadden didn't blink, didn't cough, didn't even lose his balance in the wobbly chair.

When Brett met Irving in the hall outside the interview room, he shook his head. "I couldn't get a damn thing out of him."

"Where the hell did that come from?" She jabbed her hand at the paper bag.

"What do you mean where did it come from?" His brow furrowed.

"It's not a hard question, Irv."

"You were the one who served the search warrant this morning, weren't you?" Irving adjusted his tie, a navy blue one with seagulls in flight, and stepped around her, taking the paper bag and everything else with him to his desk.

Brett followed him.

After speaking to Lizzie yesterday and seeing the Polaroids, Brett had driven straight to the station and called the district attorney's office who had called a judge to issue an emergency warrant. Brett hadn't wanted to waste any more time than they already had, nor risk losing track of Benjamin Cadden before they had a chance to bring him in and ask him a few questions.

He'd been home alone, about to leave for work, when she, Eli, and two other officers showed up on his doorstep early this morning. She handed him the search warrant, and he hesitated a second before letting them inside. She arrested him right there in the front hallway for statutory rape.

"I think you have the wrong man," he protested without much enthusiasm as she read his rights.

Brett allowed Benjamin Cadden to call the school and arrange a substitute to take over his classes for the day. Then she and the other two officers searched the house for further proof of his improper behavior toward his students. And if they happened to find any evidence linking him to June and Daniel's deaths, so much the better. They hadn't found much of anything, or at least Brett thought they hadn't. A box of condoms. A single rolled joint. A receipt from the florist for a dozen roses. The Polaroids were still enough to bring him to the station for further questioning, but there hadn't been any guns.

Brett would have remembered a gun.

When Irving set the paper bag down on his desk, Brett picked it up, opened it, and peered inside. It was a Smith & Wesson, a gun of the same caliber as the bullet that killed June.

"What's the problem here, Brett?" Irving leaned back in his chair, watching as she shifted the gun in the bag so she could see the tag looped around the handle.

The problem was that even though the pistol used the same rimless, tapered cartridges like the one Charlie had pulled from June's chest, Brett had never seen this one before. It was her first time even hearing that they'd found a possible murder weapon, and she'd been the person in charge of searching Cadden's house.

Even though the gun had already been processed, she was careful not to touch it. She didn't want to give a defense attorney any reason to accuse them of mishandling evidence.

She recognized Eli's signature on the evidence label and noted that in the space where it asked for location, he'd written, *bedroom dresser, top drawer.*

"Where are the photographs we took?" Brett set the gun, still in the bag, back on Irving's desk.

He sighed, opened his desk drawer, pulled out a binder, and dropped it onto his desk with a loud thump. He took out a plastic canister that had been stuffed into a small envelope and waved it at her. "They haven't been developed yet."

It was entirely possible Brett had made a mistake. Things like that happened, no matter how careful you were in a search. It's the reason why she'd brought three other officers with her to Cadden's house. To double-check and make sure no one missed anything. To cover her own ass. Eli must have gone back through the bedroom at some point after her because all she remembered finding when she went through the dresser were socks, underwear, shirts, and pants. Maybe the drawer had a false bottom or a secret compartment, which would at least be a good explanation for why she hadn't found the gun, something besides human error and her own incompetence.

She glanced toward the back of the precinct where Benjamin Cadden waited in the worst of the three interview rooms—the one with the broken heater and flickering lights. "How long do you think we can hold him for?"

Irving scratched at the five o'clock shadow forming on his cheeks and said, "I suppose it depends on how good his lawyer is."

A few hours later, Benjamin Cadden walked out of the Crestwood Police Station a free man.

No one was more upset about losing their best suspect than Irving. Over the next two days, Brett watched him from across the room as he moped around the precinct, shuffling papers and slamming drawers. By Friday, she couldn't stand it anymore. She grabbed her jacket and keys, walked over to his desk, and rapped her knuckles lightly on the wood.

He blinked up at her with a dazed look on his face. The skin under his eyes was puffy from lack of sleep. His shirt sleeves were rolled up, the fabric wrinkled. There was a grease stain on his tie, which was royal purple with a single peacock feather down the middle. Irving was usually so careful about his appearance and especially careful about his ties. He tucked napkins into his collar when he ate. Or he took his tie off completely. Brett knew things were bad when he let himself get this disheveled.

"You look like you could use a drink," she said. "I'm buying."

The Pickled Onion was crowded. Not surprising considering it was Friday evening.

Brett and Irving weren't the only officers drinking away the disappointment of Cadden's release. Room was made at the table. Fresh beers were poured. A Merle Haggard song started playing over the speakers and someone shouted, "Turn it up!"

"I don't get it," Irving said. "We had the weapon. We had the motive."

"It's hard to explain how a man can be in two places at once," a detective sitting on the opposite end of the table said, reminding them of how the case fell apart so quickly.

Benjamin Cadden's lawyer had shown up within minutes of getting the phone call, in a bluster of cheap suit fabric, overpriced cologne, and legalese. He tossed around words like harassment, entrapment, defamation. After ten minutes alone with his client, he came out of the interview room with a haughty look on his face and a slip of paper on which he'd written the name and address of a motel on the outskirts of town.

Perhaps if you'd done a proper investigation before you arrested my client, we wouldn't have wasted all this time. He shoved the paper at them and went back into the interview room to wait with Cadden.

It took less than an hour to confirm with the manager of the motel that the teacher had checked in around seven o'clock on the night of the murders and checked out again early the next morning. Not only did the manager recognize the picture Irving showed him, but Cadden had also paid for his stay using a credit card. After viewing the grainy, black and white footage from the motel's security camera, it was clear that Cadden's car hadn't moved from the parking lot the entire night. The camera was set up above the front lobby and angled to capture the entire parking lot and most of the motel rooms, which were lined up in a long strip with a covered walkway and poor lighting.

It was the kind of motel where you stayed when you were down on your luck or trying to hide from something. Based on the manager's description of events—that Cadden had checked in with a female companion wearing a slinky dress, high heels, and bright red lipstick—it was assumed the latter. Benjamin Cadden wasn't married, but he was a well-known teacher and coach and inviting a prostitute to his house would have definitely stirred up the town gossips.

The security footage showed Cadden coming out of his room once to get ice from the machine around midnight. Otherwise, his door stayed closed, his curtain drawn, until 6:00 AM Friday morning, when he left the motel room, got in his car and drove away. The blond woman came out of the room a half hour later and walked in the direction of the nearest bus stop.

The motel was on the opposite end of Crestwood as Deadman's Point with over ten miles separating the two. Perhaps it was possible that Cadden had snuck out the back window of the motel, out of sight of the security camera, then walked or hitchhiked to Deadman's Point, killed June and Daniel, dumped Daniel's body, and walked back to the motel before dawn—possible but not likely.

"Maybe he had a partner helping him out," a uniformed officer said, tracing his finger through the condensation gathering on the outside of his pint glass.

"If he had a partner, good luck finding him," another officer said.

They'd rushed the ballistics tests for the gun found in Cadden's house after he asked for his lawyer, but it had still taken a whole day to get the report back, and ultimately, it wouldn't have made any difference since the report was inconclusive. To make matters worse, the grip and barrel had been wiped clean. There were no fingerprints, no blood evidence, no indication the gun had been anywhere near the crime scene, or even recently fired. They were still waiting on the autopsy report for Daniel Yoon and hoping for a bullet. Two bullets matching one gun would certainly make the investigation easier, but it wouldn't bring them closer to pinning the murder on Cadden. Not with his airtight alibi.

"Even if he didn't kill those kids, he's still a creep," said Eli, who was sitting across the table from Brett, but pretending like she didn't exist. "And he should still be rotting in jail for what he did to those girls."

"They were eighteen," someone said. "Age of consent."

"They were still his students." Eli curled his lip in disgust. "At the very least, he should be fired and never allowed to step foot inside a school again."

They ordered another round. Irving continued to mope, slouched in his chair nursing his beer. He'd done what he could—it wasn't his fault the pieces of this case weren't falling into place.

Brett leaned over to tell him that, but he shook his head. "I know what you're going to say, and I don't want to hear it."

Brett was three beers in and trying to decide if she should get a fourth or go home, when Benjamin Cadden walked through the front door. A hush fell over the table as every officer turned to stare at him. Cadden seemed unbothered by the attention. He flashed them a smirk and wiggled his fingers in their direction, then bellied up to the bar and ordered a beer.

The noise rose again as the officers grumbled and muttered under their breath. Two officers got up and went to the bar, placing themselves one on either side of Cadden's elbow. They weren't in uniform tonight, but still managed to be intimidating simply by their larger physical presence and unflinching posture.

They bumped Cadden deliberately as they leaned forward to get the bartender's attention to order more drinks. One of them turned and said something to Cadden in a sharp voice. Cadden shook his head, grabbed his beer, slid off the barstool, and walked to the back of the room where four young women were playing pool at one of the billiard tables. He started talking with them, flirting. The girls flipped their long hair and batted their dark eyelashes. The women all had beers so they had to be at least twenty-one, but they looked younger than that, young enough for Cadden to be interested. Brett looked away, echoing Eli's earlier disgust for the man.

Twenty minutes later, Cadden passed their table again on the way out. He was fumbling in his pockets for something. As he stepped outside, he pulled out a lighter and a pack of cigarettes.

Not a word was said; it was as if they'd talked about it before-hand, as if they could read each other's minds. Chairs scraped against the wooden floor as several officers, including Eli, rose in unison from the table and followed Cadden outside.

Brett glanced at Irving. He shook his head. "I can't stop you from going out there, but I can tell you that if you do, they won't just let you watch."

"What do you mean?"

The front door swung open briefly, letting in the sound of feet scuffling in gravel, the grunts and hollers of a fight.

Brett rose from her chair and rushed to the entrance. She held the door open, staring out into the damp mist. The bar sign cast a pale orange glow across half of the parking lot. In the dense shadows between two large pickup trucks, bodies scuffled and shoved. She couldn't see faces, only the shapes of heads and shoulders, a writhing mass of arms swinging and boots kicking. They had Cadden surrounded. The teacher did his best to stay on his feet, shoving back and spitting in their faces, but it was five against one. It was obvious who was winning tonight and who was going to go home with broken ribs and a black eye.

Brett stepped back inside the bar, letting the door swing shut again. She wavered another second over whether or not to intervene. She didn't think she could stop what was happening even if she wanted to, and she wasn't sure she wanted to. She kept thinking of the Polaroids Lizzie had shown her, the ones now marked as evidence, though they were useless in terms of making any kind of case against Cadden. So the girls were eighteen—that didn't absolve Cadden of guilt. Not in Brett's mind anyway.

She returned to the table and sat down next to Irving. "We should probably go out there and stop them."

Irving sipped his beer and said, "Probably."

"They could lose their badges."

"They won't," Irving said, in a way that made it seem like this wasn't the first time the police had kicked around a scumbag that got off on a technicality.

He seemed to sense her discomfort because he turned to look at her and said, "We all have to get it out of our system somehow. If you hold on to the darkness for too long, if you don't find a way to let some of it escape, you'll drown in it. Some people hunt. Some people fish. Some people drink. Some people fight. I have birds. What about you, Brett? What do you have?"

When the officers came back in, they were rubbing bruised knuckles and smiling. Eli had a fleck of blood on his cheek. He wiped it off with the back of his hand. They laughed and ordered another round. Brett watched the door, but Benjamin Cadden never came back inside.

Brett drove home that night with the radio turned off, the quiet swish of the windshield wipers keeping her company. She was still thinking about what Irving had said, about people needing a release. For a while, hers had been Jimmy. Their weekly phone calls had been her lighthouse shining through the dark. No matter how frustrated or lost she felt with a case, no matter how much chaos she was experiencing in her personal or professional life, she could count on Jimmy's voice to steady her again. She missed that. She missed him. She wondered if it was too late for her to tell him all of this, if he was finished with her for good, or if he'd been telling the truth when he told her that he would never stop loving her.

She was almost to her grandmother's house on Bayshore Drive when she saw the red lights flickering, reflecting off the rain in a panicked way. She drove a little faster, hoping they were for someone else, that they would be parked in front of a different house, not hers. But there they were: an ambulance in the driveway and a fire truck angled at the curb, with lights swinging, the incessant strobing brightness forcing Brett to squint.

Their closest neighbor, Kenny, stood on the sidewalk with his arms folded across his chest, his brow creased with worry. The front door of the house stood open, and as Brett parked her car across the street, the paramedics came out, carefully rolling a stretcher down the front steps. Henry was there, too, pressed close to the stretcher, his hand holding tight to Amma's.

CHAPTER 26

"What happened?" Brett rushed up the driveway to meet Henry and the paramedics. No one paid her any attention. "I'm her granddaughter. I live here with her."

They continued to ignore her as they carried the stretcher toward the ambulance and lifted it into the back.

"Henry! Please, tell me what happened!"

"I'm fine, dear." Amma's voice chirped from beneath a blanket. She coughed and then said, "I had a little accident, that's all. Nothing serious."

Henry stepped away from the ambulance and gestured for Brett to take his place, but all he said to her was, "I'll meet you at the hospital."

One of the paramedics helped Brett climb into the back of the ambulance. The other slammed the doors shut. The sirens let out an impatient squawk and then they were whisked away.

At the hospital, the paramedics wheeled Amma straight through the double doors leading to the emergency room while Brett was shuffled into the waiting room to fill out paperwork. Henry was already there. He rose from the chair he'd been sitting in and asked, "How is she?"

"They gave her oxygen the whole way," Brett said. "She was conscious, alert. She seemed okay."

Except for the coughing, the thick stench of smoke wafting off of her, and the charred and blistering skin on her right arm.

"She was in good spirits," Brett said, then stopped filling out the forms and turned to look at Henry. "What the hell happened?"

"I was going to ask you the same thing."

"You were there," Brett pointed out.

"She called me around six-thirty, but she wasn't making any sense. She was screaming at me, something about the baby upstairs, how she had to get the baby but the smoke was too thick." Henry ran his hand over his bald spot. His fingers trembled. "I didn't know what was going on. I told her to get the hell out of the house and go outside and wait for me outside. Then I hung up and called the fire department. I drove straight over there, as fast as I could. The fire truck got there before I did. Luckily, the fire was still small, it was contained to the kitchen, and they put it out easily enough. They told me they found Amma huddled up in the corner, crying and rocking like a little kid. They said she's lucky to be alive. Lucky that I called when I did. That the whole house didn't go up in flames. Damn it, Brett." He pounded his fist on the arm of the chair. "Where the hell were you? No, don't tell me. Work."

He got up from the chair and started to pace and tug on the ends of his mustache.

She didn't correct him or mention that she'd already clocked out of her shift, but instead of going home, she'd gone out drinking instead.

She asked, "Do they know how it started?"

Henry stopped pacing and whipped around to stare at her. "Do you hear yourself right now?"

Brett pushed her shoulders back, but said nothing.

"Your grandmother's back there—" He flung his hand at the

double doors leading to the triage area of the hospital. "She almost died tonight and you sound so nonchalant, like you're filling out a damn report for an arson investigation. Goddamn it, Brett. She almost died."

He dropped into a chair and buried his face in his hands.

Brett set aside the paperwork she needed to fill out and rested her hand between Henry's shoulder blades. His breathing was ragged, his whole body trembling.

"Henry, I'm sorry. It's easier for me to separate myself from it. It's not that I don't care. I do. Of course, I do. She's the only family I have left." She didn't count her father, whom she hadn't spoken with in years. Her throat tightened as she thought about what her life would be like once Amma was gone. She shook the feelings away, clamping down on the overwhelming urge to cry or scream or kick something. "I'm sorry. I should have been there tonight."

"I told you something like this would happen." He stood again, moving away from her touch and walking toward a large bank of windows lining one side of the waiting room. Darkness pressed against the glass. Rain glittered in the glow of the street lamps.

A man wearing blue scrubs entered the waiting room. He smiled at Brett. "You're Anita Wilson's granddaughter, is that right?" He checked his paperwork. "Brett Buchanan? We have you down as her emergency contact."

Brett rose from the chair. Henry left the window and came to stand beside her.

"How is she?" Brett asked.

"I'm happy to tell you that your grandmother's going to be fine. She had some pretty bad burns on her arm and is suffering some mild smoke inhalation, so we'd like to keep her here overnight for monitoring, but she seems to be a pretty tough old bird, and I believe she'll make a full recovery." His smile faltered. "What I'm more concerned about is her mental state. She seems to be suffering from a rather advanced stage of dementia. Is she seeing anyone for that?"

Brett explained about her grandmother's recent diagnosis, how they had seen a neurologist in Seattle last year.

"But no regular therapy? And she's living on her own?" the doctor asked.

"I live with her," Brett said.

His bushy eyebrows rose as he opened the chart in his hands and made a note. "While I believe the injuries she received tonight will heal with time, I'm concerned that her dementia will make it impossible for her to be left alone for long periods of time unsupervised. But let's not worry too much about that tonight." His warm smile returned. "I'll have someone come and speak with you in the morning about options. But for now your grandmother's resting comfortably in her room, if you'd like to see her."

Brett nodded.

Henry touched her elbow. "I'm going to go. Call me tomorrow. And don't worry, Pistol can stay with us until you get home."

Guilt flamed through Brett as she realized she'd completely forgotten about the little dog. She grabbed Henry's hand and squeezed it. "Thank you. I owe you."

He shook his head. "You don't owe me anything, Brett. We're family. Families look out for each other. Tell Amma I'm glad she's okay and to get some rest. Oh, and tell her not to worry about the kitchen."

He tipped his head at the doctor in thanks and left.

Amma looked so small lying in the hospital bed. The machines she was attached to looked far more substantial than her delicate frame. Her right arm was bandaged and positioned in such a way to avoid being bumped or jostled.

Brett sat in a chair beside the bed and listened to the steady beep of the heart monitor, watched the gentle rise and fall of her grandmother's chest.

It wasn't long before Amma's eyes fluttered open. Seeing Brett, she tried to sit up, but a bout of coughing consumed her and she fell back against the pillows.

Brett settled her hand on Amma's uninjured arm. "Hey, you. Easy does it. You just went through hell. Literally."

The corners of Amma's mouth twitched in a half-smile. Her eyes rolled toward the ceiling, and a single tear slid down her cheek.

"I'm so sorry, Brett," she said, her voice muffled through the oxygen mask that covered her face. "This never should have happened."

"You don't have to apologize. I'm just glad you're going to be okay."

"After you told me we were having all those people over for Thanksgiving, I was worried about what we were going to serve everyone," she kept talking. "There was this stuffing recipe in Better Homes and Gardens that I wanted to test out. I guess I got a little distracted because the next thing I know, the kitchen's on fire. I tried to put it out, but the flames were so big."

She started to cough again.

A nurse entered the room and hovered over Amma, checking her IV, and adjusting the oxygen mask. When the nurse left again, Brett patted Amma's hand and said, "It's okay, Amma. You didn't do anything wrong. Just rest. Try to go back to sleep. We can talk about this later."

Brett stayed by Amma's bedside for over an hour, listening to the steady beeps and clicks of the machines, watching her grandmother's eyes twitch beneath closed lids.

It wasn't very late, barely 9:00 PM but something about the dark room, the curtains drawn over the window, the quiet hum of the machines, made it seem like it was much later. To keep herself from falling asleep in the chair, Brett stood and stretched.

She went to the window and pulled back the curtain. Beyond her faint reflection in the glass, she could see bursts of light she knew were street lamps lining downtown's Main Street.

Behind her, the blankets rustled. Then Amma cleared her throat. Brett looked over her shoulder at the fragile woman who had been more of a mother to her than the woman who'd given birth to her. Amma was awake, her head turned toward the window and Brett. Her face was draped in shadows, giving an eerie, ghostly impression.

In a quiet voice, Amma asked, "What would you be doing right now if you didn't have to take care of me?"

Brett returned to the bed and kneeled beside it. She held Amma's uninjured hand, rubbing her stiff joints warm again.

"I know you wouldn't be in Crestwood," Amma said, her voice scratchy and hoarse. "I know that much. You and Henry both, you deserve so much better than this."

"What are you talking about? I like it here. I get to spend time with you. And don't worry about Henry. He'd be bored out of his mind if he didn't have you to worry about."

"You lie the same way your mother did," Amma said with a sad smile twisting her lips. "I could always tell when she was lying to me because she'd get this wrinkle, right here."

She smoothed her finger between Brett's eyes. Then she sighed and leaned back on the pillows, her eyes sliding closed again. "I'm so tired, my sweet. I'm so very tired. I don't want people to worry about me anymore. I don't want you to stay when you want to go."

"I'm not going anywhere," Brett said. "I promise."

But Amma had already fallen back to sleep.

The kitchen was wrecked. The range was charred and covered in ash. The wall above it, once a buttery yellow, was now gray and peeling, revealing the plaster underneath. Smoke streaked the ceiling black. Sludge covered the tile floor.

Brett pulled on a pair of rubber gloves, grabbed her bucket and shovel, and got to work clearing the debris.

Though Saturday night had been uneventful for her, Amma was staying one more night in the hospital, just to be safe, which left Brett with an entire Sunday to clean up as much of this mess as possible before her grandmother came home.

Henry had already been by to drop off Pistol and take a look at the damage. He'd promised to come back later that afternoon with better tools and a new stove to replace the one that had gone up in flames. Their best guess was that Amma had left a towel or something else flammable on a hot burner, forgotten about it, and walked away. Henry seemed to think the kitchen was entirely salvageable—*Nothing a little elbow grease and spit shine can't fix.*

Brett hoped he was right. Thanksgiving was in ten days, and while she was pretty sure the squad would understand if she needed to back out of her hosting duties, she really didn't want to. If they didn't get the kitchen put back together by Thanksgiving, she could always order Chinese food, or they could grill out on the back patio if they got lucky and it stopped raining.

She scooped ashes into a garbage bag and scrubbed the smoke on the walls like she had something to prove—and maybe she did.

The doctor she'd spoken with at the hospital this morning seemed to think Amma needed twenty-four hour care, and suggested moving her into some kind of nursing facility. When Brett balked at that, the doctor told her that a live-in nurse was another option, if they could afford it. "If you're not able to be with her for the majority of the day," the doctor had said, "you need to hire someone who can."

For now, Amma was getting good care at the hospital, and tomorrow Brett had the day off, and a few days of sick time she could use after that until they figured out a more permanent solution.

Pistol sat in the kitchen doorway watching Brett clean. His gaze followed her every move, and she couldn't tell if he was hungry, had to go outside to pee, or was nervous after yesterday's commotion. She tried to feed him a piece of chicken, but he turned away. She opened the french doors leading to the backyard, but he didn't go out. She scratched his head, and he leaned into her touch.

"I'm sorry I forgot about you," she said.

He licked her thumb.

An hour later, except for burn marks near the stove where a pan had fallen, the floors were clean. The walls and ceiling needed a new coat of paint, and she was still waiting on Henry to replace the stove, but the cabinets and everything inside were still in good shape, and the fridge and microwave were perfectly fine. She'd have to figure out how to get rid of the smell of damp ashes and burned plastic, though. She left the windows open as she cleaned, but that didn't help much to clear the room.

It was a start anyway.

She grabbed a beer from the fridge, cracked it open, and carried it along with Pistol upstairs to her grandfather's office.

Jimmy's phone rang so long, Brett almost hung up. When he finally answered, he sounded out of breath. "Hello? Hello? I'm here. Hello?"

There was a lot of noise in the background, voices and music and clinking plates.

"Jimmy, it's me. It's Brett."

"Hold on a second. Hold on, let me—" The background noise stopped. "That's better. Yes, hello. I'm here. Brett? What's wrong?"

"Why would something be wrong?"

"You only call me when there is," Jimmy said, his voice strained with impatience.

"That's not true."

The beat of silence stretched on long enough to be uncomfortable.

"How are you?" Brett tried to sound chipper and relaxed. "Sounds like you're having a party."

"Just a few friends over for dinner. Listen, I can't talk long. Is there something you need? Is Amma okay?"

She felt a flicker of jealousy that he asked about Amma but not about her. She swigged back her beer before saying, "We had an accident last night."

"What kind of accident?"

Now that she had Jimmy's full attention, she regretted calling him. It wasn't fair; Amma wasn't his family, and he shouldn't have to worry about her like this.

"Never mind," she said. "Forget it. I'm sorry, I shouldn't have called."

"Brett, what the hell. What accident? Did something happen to Amma?"

"She's in the hospital."

"What?" His voice shifted to panic. "What hospital? I can be there in a few hours."

"No, Jimmy, don't. She's fine. We're both fine. It was nothing. There was a small kitchen fire. Amma has some burns on her arm, but she's fine. She's coming home tomorrow. I'm sorry I called. I wasn't thinking, I just, I wanted, I don't know what I wanted, but really, don't worry about it. Go back to your party."

He was quiet long enough, she thought the call had been disconnected, except she could still hear him breathing. When he spoke again, anger lanced his words. "What the hell is wrong with you?"

She sucked in a sharp breath.

"You call me out of the blue to tell me Amma's hurt, that she's in the hospital, and then you tell me not to worry about it? You tell me to go back to my party?"

"Jimmy—"

"You don't know me at all if you think that I don't care what happens to you and to Amma. And you really must not like me very much either."

"Come on, that's not—"

"Why did you call me, Brett?" He interrupted her again.

She hesitated and then said, "I don't know."

He released an exasperated sigh. "I think you do know, you just won't admit it to yourself."

In the background, a woman's voice called for Jimmy. A dog barked.

"She's okay, Brett?" he asked. "Amma's going to be okay?"

"She's coming home tomorrow," she repeated, not exactly answering his question.

"Okay, if anything changes, I want to know." He paused and then with more force added, "I care what happens to you, Brett. To both of you."

"Say hi to Trixie for me," Brett said, hating how pitiful her voice sounded, choked with all the words she couldn't bring herself to say.

CHAPTER 27

"Mind if I join you?" Evangeline London didn't wait for Brett to answer before sliding into the empty booth across from her.

The high school principal was dressed for a business lunch at an expensive steakhouse in Seattle, not a quick cup of coffee at a greasy spoon diner in Crestwood. The mauve blouse under her gray blazer shimmered when she moved. Every one of her dark hairs fell in perfect place around her ears. The gold and purple of her eyeshadow brought out the green in her hazel eyes. She set a leather clutch down on the seat beside her and folded her hands on the table.

"How's your grandmother doing?"

At first Brett thought Effy was talking about the fire. It had been a week since Amma tried to burn down the house, and while the burns on her arm were still healing, she'd finally stopped coughing and, thanks to Henry, the kitchen was almost up and running again. He was actually over at the house right now finishing up the stove installation. He'd promised everything would be back in working order in time for Thanksgiving.

Amma hadn't wanted to be at the house with Henry making all that noise, so she was attending church today for the first time in a long time. Brett had walked her into the building, which was a few blocks from the diner, and gotten her settled in the third row from the front with her country club friends. She thought about staying, but the pastor, who heard from Henry's wife about the fire, assured her that Amma would be fine in their care. *You're more than welcome to stay for the service, but if you need to go across the street and grab a cup of coffee, the Lord will understand,* he'd whispered with a knowing wink.

She had almost hugged him, that's how grateful she felt for the much needed break.

So when Effy asked how her grandmother was doing, Brett was impressed with how quickly gossip traveled in this town, but then the principal clarified, "When she showed up at my office unexpectedly the way she did, I'll admit I was pretty impressed with how far she had walked. Even though she does seem to be in pretty good shape."

"She'd be happy to hear you say that." Brett smiled and lifted her coffee cup to take a sip. "But yes, she was fine after that. A little muddy and tired, but nothing some soap and a nap couldn't fix. I'm sorry about that. I know you have better things to do than babysit lost, old women."

Brett had been taking care of Amma all week and was starting to realize how much Amma's mental and physical states had declined in the past few months. She'd been relying on her grandmother to tell her when she needed help, when the dementia became too much for her to bear alone, but after spending this past week with her, Brett understood that this was never going to happen. Amma was too stubborn, even if the dementia hadn't been working overtime to confuse her self-awareness and sense of reality.

Effy tilted her head to one side and, with an easy kindness, said, "I had an aunt who had dementia. My mother took care of her for a while, until she couldn't anymore. I helped out when I could, when I wasn't away at school or working. I know how much work it can be caring for someone when she can't care for herself anymore. There are people you can hire, you know. To come in once or twice a week, or more if you need it. It can be a good compromise between no supervision and a full-time nursing home."

The words flew from Effy's mouth so quickly Brett had trouble keeping up.

"I know it's probably not an ideal situation," Effy said. "No one wants to put a loved one in a home, of course not, but sometimes you run out of options. We put my aunt in a home after she drove off with my little sister in the backseat and crashed into a telephone pole a few blocks later. Don't worry. Everyone was fine. My aunt was barely going ten miles an hour. Of course, my sister was screaming her head off, like she'd lost a limb, but she walked away without even a bruise. My aunt broke her wrist. She needed surgery. After that, that's when we decided we needed more help."

Effy cut herself off with a quick shake of her head. "I'm sorry, I'm probably stepping over some boundaries here, aren't I? If you wanted my opinion, you would have asked, right?"

Her smile was prim like everything else about her. She waved down their server and ordered hot water with lemon and a piece of dry wheat toast. Dot, who always seemed to be on shift whenever Brett came in, raised a judgmental eyebrow at Effy's order, but said she'd bring it right away. She refilled Brett's coffee cup with a smile and said, "You know, I'm still waiting for my interview."

"What interview?" Brett had no idea what the other woman was talking about.

Dot popped her hip out to one side, holding the coffee pot high in the air beside her shoulder. "Well, about Daniel, of course. I thought for sure someone would have come by weeks ago. I mean, I know y'all are busy over there, but it seems to me like finding out what happened to him should be at the top of your list. He was such a sweet boy."

She tilted her head toward Effy, as if the two of them were in on a secret. Effy stared at her with visible discomfort.

"Have they talked to you yet?" Dot asked.

Effy nodded. "Several times."

"See, that's what I thought. I don't understand it—"

"Hold on a second, Dot," Brett interrupted, trying to get back control of the conversation and figure out what the hell was going on. "You're saying no one has been in here to talk with you about Daniel yet?"

"Nope." Then she squinted at the painting hanging above the table and said, "Well, I suppose someone could have talked to Jack. He's the owner, but he's never here. I don't know if he even knows Daniel's name. Whenever he does stop by, he's always waving his hand, saying, 'Hey kid, hey you, hey honey, sweetheart.' That kind of bullcrap." She shrugged one shoulder. "We put up with it because he signs our paychecks, but honestly, this place runs fine without him. So if they talked to Jack about Daniel, I'm not sure what they would have found out. I was here on Halloween night with him, you know."

Daniel's co-workers should have been the first people interviewed after his mother. A detective should have come down here the day they knew he was missing. Brett would have come herself, but Irving had kept her busy with other things. She had a vague recollection of Eli telling her another detective had been assigned to the diner, and she assumed the work had been done.

The investigation into June Newmark's death was nearing the one month mark. Daniel's body had been found twelve days ago. She wanted to assume that this was a simple mistake, an oversight because of how focused they'd been on Benjamin Cadden, but once Cadden had been eliminated as a suspect, Irving should have gone back to the drawing board with his team, and if they'd done that, eventually the team would have ended up here.

Brett had taken the entire week off from work to care for Amma, so it was entirely possible there'd been new developments with the case that would have made talking with Dot and Daniel's other co-workers a waste of time, but from the way Dot was looking at her, with an impatient twist in her lips, it was obvious there was something important she wanted to get off her chest. Something she'd been wanting to talk about for a while.

The right thing to do would have been to tell Dot to come down to the station and talk to Irving. Or Brett could have talked to Irving herself when she went back to work on Tuesday and made sure he followed up. But her curiosity got the better of her.

"Did something happen during his shift on Halloween?" Brett asked.

Effy cleared her throat and asked, "Should I be here for this?"

But Dot was eager to tell her story and started talking before Brett could answer Effy.

"We had a girl quit on us a few months back, and I've been covering until Jack gets around to hiring another waitress, which might be never the way he's going about it. So I've been pulling doubles lately, working the lunch and dinner shifts." Dot moved the coffee pot to her other hand and tugged on the string of her apron. "So Halloween night was pretty slow. The usual crowd. Tony Moren was sitting over there." She pointed to a table on the other side of the diner. "Dumb idiot thought it would be funny to pretend he'd stabbed himself with a knife while trying to cut his hamburger. Made a real mess with the ketchup that I wasn't too happy about. I had to get the mop and bucket out. Then the fool leaves me a quarter for a tip."

She snorted, shaking her head, and continued, "So like I said, it turned into a whole thing with the mop, and then I had to dump the mop water out, and we've got a drain in the back, that's where we dump all our dirty water. So I drag the bucket through the back door, out into the alley and dump the water, and then I think after all that work, I might as well take a minute to myself and have a quick smoke. We've got a few folding chairs and milk crates out there, too, like a little break room. It's not bad as long as it's not raining, which it wasn't, not that night, this nasty storm hadn't rolled in yet. So I was sitting out there smoking and thinking about this song I heard on the radio." She paused and released a puff of air that fluttered her bangs.

Dot seemed like the kind of person who liked to listen to herself talk, which in this case was a good thing. People like Dot made the best witnesses; Brett didn't need to work very hard to get the story from her, all she had to do was sit back and listen.

"I know, I know, none of that matters. Get to the point, Dottie." Dot flapped her hand. "So I was sitting out there enjoying my cigarette when I heard a couple people talking. Well, it sounded more like fighting, if you want God's honest truth. They were yelling at each other, and things were getting pretty heated. I thought it was maybe two drunks who'd stumbled from the Pickled Onion, but when I went to peek my head around the trash bin to have a look-see, I was surprised to see one of the guys yelling was Daniel. I've never seen him angry like that, not even the time one of the other busboys sprayed him with boiling hot dishwater. Kid said it was an accident, but who's to say. Anyway, Daniel's a good kid. Always eager to help out even if it's not technically his job. Like the other month, Jeremy, he's our line cook, he was having some trouble with his missus. There was a miscommunication about who was supposed to pick up their kid from daycare or something and Jeremy had to run out real quick. Daniel stepped in and kept the grill going. Got a lot of compliments on his grilled cheese sandwiches, too. So yeah, we've had problem kids in the past, but not Daniel. He is one of the good ones." She paused and corrected herself. "Was, I suppose. Damn shame."

She glanced over her shoulder as the bell above the door jangled, but instead of leaving to greet the new customers, she turned back to Brett and said, "So to see him getting so angry like that, shouting and flinging his arms around, shoving the other kid, it was definitely out of character."

"Do you know what the fight was about?" Brett asked.

"From what I could tell, they were arguing over a girl." Dot's lips twisted into a knowing smirk. "Isn't that always what boys are fighting about? Girls or money. Well, these two, it seemed like Daniel was trying to get the other kid to back off. 'She doesn't like you,' he kept saying. 'She thinks you're a creep,' 'Stay away from her,' 'She's with me now.' You know, all that kind of macho, peacock-strutting stuff."

Daniel and June had been dating, but if someone else liked June, if someone wasn't getting the attention they wanted or felt betrayed—Brett could imagine a scenario where things turned bad between the three of them quickly. She had worked plenty of cases where people had been murdered for far more trivial reasons than love.

"The other kid, did you recognize him?" Brett asked. She had her suspicions, but hoped she was wrong.

"Oh, sure," Dot said. "He sometimes comes in for lunch with his father. That's why I thought for sure y'all would want to talk to me. Because his dad's a cop. I can't remember his name. Will or Walter, something with a W, but he's the tall one with the mustache like Bert Reynolds. It was his boy out there fighting with Daniel."

"How sure are you?" Brett pressed her. "Because it was dark, wasn't it?"

"There's a street light out there," Dot said. "They were standing right under it."

The bells over the diner's front door jangled again as another set of customers entered. This time Dot waved at them to let them know she'd be right over, before turning back to Brett, "The lunch rush is about to start, and I've got to get these people seated. So, I'm sorry we're going to have to finish this up later."

She left, and Brett turned her attention to Effy, who was watching Dot lead a family of four to a booth on the other side of the restaurant. The principal frowned. "Do you think she'll remember to bring my hot water?"

Brett leaned her elbows on the table. "Effy? What can you tell me about Adam Harris?"

CHAPTER 28

Eli was the first to arrive on Thanksgiving Day. When Brett opened the door and saw him standing on her front porch in his snug forest green sweater and ass-hugging dark jeans, she almost forgot she was upset with him. He grabbed her around the waist to pull her in for a kiss, but she shoved him off and backed inside the house.

"Come on, Brett." He stepped through the doorway and reached for her again. "No one's here yet."

She grabbed the bottle of wine he was holding and spun it around to look at the label. She didn't know very much about wine, but it looked expensive. "Is this from your parents' collection?"

She carried it into the kitchen, calling out, "Shut the door behind you, please."

The front door thumped shut.

Eli trailed after her. "You're not still mad at me about that stuff we found in Adam's truck, are you?"

"You mean the evidence for our murder case that went missing?" She set the wine down on the counter next to a stack of beers and a slow cooker filled with hot apple cider.

"I told you I had nothing to do with that." He made no attempt to hide the frustration in his voice.

"And what about the gun you found at Benjamin Cadden's house?" she asked.

"What about it?"

"Convenient, isn't it?" She opened the oven to check the turkey. Henry had done a great job installing the appliance; it seemed to be cooking the food just fine. "When I looked in the dresser there was no gun, but when you looked, abracadabra, there it was."

"Evidence gets missed in searches all the time." Eli grabbed a beer and cracked it open. "You should be thanking me for saving your ass."

"And yet..." She closed the oven and turned to face him.

He was leaning against the counter, his arms crossed over his chest, beer in one hand. "What's your problem, Brett? If you have something to say, come out and say it. Stop with the bullshit."

The doorbell rang. Brett took off the oven mitts she was wearing and tossed them onto the counter. She smoothed her hands over her hair and tugged on the long, wool skirt she thought had been a good idea when she put it on this morning. Now, the fabric felt stifling and hot.

"Forget I said anything," she told Eli as she went to answer the front door.

Irving and Diane greeted her with warm smiles and a homemade pie.

Brett had met Irving's wife a few times over the past year, though with the exception of Irving's fiftieth birthday party in June, they'd never spent more than a few minutes together in the same room. She was a white woman with gold eyes and flaxen hair who spoke four languages and didn't own a television. According to Irving, they'd met their senior year in college, when they were both attending the University of Chicago, and fell in love when they both reached for the same book at the library. Diane had grown up in Crestwood and after several years living in the city, yearning for wide open spaces and the sea-salt breeze, she moved back. Irving came with her. She was an English professor at the community college now and also worked on translating books. They had two cats and a parakeet named Atticus, but no kids. Though Brett was curious whether this was by choice or by chance, she didn't feel it was her business to pry; she never liked when people asked her about why she didn't have kids yet.

"How's the turkey cooking?" Irving wiped his shoes on the mat and stepped inside. He sniffed the air, and his grin widened. "Smells good. Need any help? Diane's got the forearms for potato mashing."

Diane indulged him with a laugh and swatted playfully at him with the corner of a crimson shawl she was wearing around her shoulders. "Yes, if you want to end up with over-salted, under-cooked, or burned to a crisp, I'm your woman."

Irving kissed Diane's cheek, then took the pie from her and carried it toward the kitchen.

Diane pointed after him, speaking in a stage whisper. "Just so we're clear, he made the pie."

"Diane! You promised you wouldn't tell her!" Irving called back with a smile.

Brett took their coats and delivered them to the downstairs bed-room. When she came back out to the living room, Diane and Irving were standing beside the fireplace, talking with Eli. Each of them held a glass of wine. Brett didn't have time to listen in on what they were saying because the doorbell rang again. This time it was Henry and his wife. And then two more officers right behind them. The house began to fill quickly after that, the conversations getting louder and more raucous with each new guest and fresh pour of wine.

Brett moved through the rooms, offering drinks and platters of crackers and cheese. Amma came downstairs at some point wearing a swishing violet dress and a huge smile on her face. She greeted Henry and his wife with a kiss on each cheek. The party was going well so far, despite Brett's earlier reservations that it would be a disaster. She'd thought about canceling at the last minute, but they'd already bought the food, and Amma seemed excited about it, and so even though sitting down to dinner with a table full of cops was the last thing Brett wanted to do today, here they were.

Henry appeared at her side, smiling. "How's the oven? Working okay?"

"So far, so good. Thanks again, Henry. I would have had to serve these people cold cereal if you hadn't come through for me."

"Big turnout this year." Henry scanned the room. "I'm surprised Stan let you all take time off for this. Especially with such a high-profile murder investigation still open."

"Maybe Stan realized that if all of his detectives flame out, there won't be anyone left for him to boss around," Brett said. "Plus, this dinner is tradition, isn't it? Can't disappoint people, can we?"

He studied her for a moment and then asked, "Everything okay, Brett? You seem distracted."

She thought about telling him—about the bloody evidence found in Adam's car that went missing a few days later, the gun that appeared out of nowhere that Cadden claimed wasn't his, the story Dot told about Adam and Daniel getting into a fight mere hours before the murders, Brett's growing suspicions that Adam might have had something to do with June and Daniel's deaths, the knot in her stomach that wouldn't untwist when she thought about how Eli might be involved. She thought about telling Henry everything. But Henry had worked with the department his entire career, and even though they'd screwed him over in the end, it wouldn't surprise her if he still felt some loyalty to the men he'd worked with for over half his life.

"I want today to go well," she said to Henry. "That's all."

"It will." He patted her shoulder and gestured to the people drinking and laughing together. "Seems to me like it already is."

Wes and his family arrived late. So late, Brett was beginning to think they weren't coming. She was in the kitchen stirring the gravy when they arrived and heard Wes' voice first, his laughter booming through the house. She wiped her hands on a towel and walked out to greet them.

Wes grabbed her hand, pumping it with energy. "I don't think you've met my wife yet. This is Laurie."

She was a strikingly beautiful woman with sandy-colored skin and rich brown hair that fell around her shoulders in loose waves. Her lips were bow-shaped and full. Her make-up was shades of autumn, and matched perfectly with her slimming, burnt umber dress. She unwrapped a red scarf from her neck, examining Brett with a flinty, cool gaze before her mouth parted in a brittle smile. "Wes says you're one of the most promising detectives he's ever worked with."

"I said she was one of the hardest-working," Wes corrected, then flicked his hand to his son who was lurking behind his parents, a scowl tugging on his mouth. "You remember Adam. Adam, say hello."

The boy grunted something that sounded like a greeting and wandered off to the opposite side of the room where some of the other officers' kids were crowded around Pistol. The little dog seemed happy enough since the kids were feeding him biscuits. Brett wasn't worried about him. If he got tired of the attention, he could always escape to her room upstairs.

Wes lifted his nose, sniffed the air, and then patted his wife on the hip, gently shoving her toward the kitchen. "Why don't you two ladies go and check on that turkey. I'd hate for it to burn."

"The turkey's fine," Brett said. She'd checked it not even five minutes ago. The skin was starting to crisp, but it would still be another thirty minutes before it was ready to carve.

A muscle in Laurie's jaw twitched as she offered Brett a stiff smile, tilting her head to one side. "Have you started the gravy yet? I have the perfect recipe. Passed down from my grandmother."

Wes turned away from his wife and Brett to talk with three men standing near the potted ficus on the other side of the room.

"Forgive my husband," Laurie said as she laid her scarf on the entryway table and walked with Brett toward the kitchen. "He's got a big heart but a caveman's brain. Have you got anything stronger than wine?"

As Laurie passed by the fridge, she paused to frown at Amma's notes fluttering beneath their magnets.

Turn the stove off when you're not cooking something.

You're allergic to peanuts—DO NOT EAT PEANUTS.

Brett had meant to take them all off before anyone got here, but she'd been so busy chopping and basting and prepping for the party, while also making sure Amma didn't cut her hand off with a knife or wander away, she'd completely forgotten. Laurie's fingers brushed over the note Brett had written the other night after she came home and Amma didn't recognize her. *Brett is your grand-daughter.* They hadn't had another incident like that one since, but Brett didn't know if it was because of the note or not.

"I've got some whiskey." Brett dug under the sink until she found the bottle. She poured some for Laurie and for herself. They clinked glasses and drank.

"God, I hate these things," Laurie said. "Every year I try to convince Wes that we should stay home. It's not worth the chance of food poisoning. No offense." She lifted the lid of the slow-cooker and sniffed. "Half of his guys are bachelors and don't know their giblets from their stuffings and think hot dogs are a fine substitute for turkey. It smells good in here, though, and this house...it's a lovely house."

"Thank you." Brett grabbed a saucepan and set it on the stove. "My grandmother's lived here her whole life."

Laurie poured herself a cup of the hot cider. "I saw you at the Miller's Halloween party last year, didn't I?"

Every year Eli's parents threw an extravagant costume party

for their friends and other influential people in the community. Brett had gone last year, but only because a suspect she needed to talk to was going to be there.

"Yes, you were standing next to that boy Marshall Trudeau punched," Laurie said, smiling, and for the first time since entering the house it didn't look forced. "We didn't officially meet but, I remember your dress. I remember thinking to myself that I had to find a dress like that. Where did you get it from? I hope you don't mind me asking."

"I don't mind, but also I don't know where it came from," Brett said, taking butter from the fridge and starting to melt it in the pan. "I borrowed the dress."

"Oh, that's a shame." Laurie poured a generous portion of whiskey into her hot cider. "But you didn't go this year, did you? To the Millers' party?"

"No, I didn't." Eli had invited her but she'd turned him down, giving some excuse about needing to catch up on work and spend time with Amma. Though the real reason she hadn't gone was because she'd been afraid he would introduce her to his parents as his girlfriend.

"Well, you missed a great showing," Laurie said. "The theme this year was famous couples."

"You went?" Brett tried not to sound too surprised as she turned away from the gravy to give Laurie her full attention. "I thought I remember Wes saying you both stayed home on Halloween."

"What? I don't know why he'd tell you that. Like I said, caveman brain." Laurie laughed, looking bewildered and slightly drunk. "The Millers' parties are the best, and we wouldn't miss them for the world. This year we dressed up as Bonnie and Clyde. It was Wes' idea." She laughed again, then pointed her finger at the stove. "Careful with that butter. It's fixing to burn."

CHAPTER 29

Wes clinked a fork against the side of his wine glass. "I'd like to make a toast."

The conversations happening around the dining room table quieted down as everyone turned to look at him. Several of the officers who were technically on-duty today had to leave before the turkey was carved, and Brett had sent them away with hot rolls and a slice of pie. But there were still about twenty people crammed around the large oak table in her grandmother's dining room. Amma sat on one side of Brett, Irving on the other. Eli was across from her, shoving his mashed potatoes around on his plate. He hadn't eaten very much since they'd sat down, when most everyone else had already gone for seconds.

Wes clinked his wine glass one more time, then raised it above his head.

"To family." He looked first at his wife and son, then at the rest of the people sitting around the table. "To friends who become family. To being there for each other when the chips are down. And to our hostess, who can cook a turkey as well as she can cook a perp."

Laughter rolled through the room. Glasses clinked together. People drank. More wine was poured. More food was passed.

Amma leaned close to Brett and clutched her arm under the table. In a hushed voice, she asked, "Who are these people? And what are they doing in my house?"

"It's people from my work, remember?" Brett whispered into Amma's ear and patted her hand reassuringly. "We invited them over for Thanksgiving dinner. They're friends."

Amma nodded like she understood, but a look of suspicion still haunted her eyes. She frowned at Eli and then asked him to pass the green beans.

Conversation turned to Christmas plans and how whale migration season was starting up and they'd soon see an influx of tourists. They kept returning to the weather, too, how it seemed the rain was never going to stop. Even now it rattled the window glass, tap-danced against the roof.

"We've been cursed," someone said.

Amma shook her head as she heaped green beans onto her plate. "People keep dumping bodies into the ocean to cover up their sins. Of course, the ocean's going to have some thoughts about it."

Everyone stopped talking at once. A fork clattered against the edge of a plate. Wes cleared his throat, dabbing his mouth with a napkin.

"What?" Amma looked around, settling on Brett. "If there is a curse, we brought it on ourselves."

A chair scraped loudly across the floor, as Adam Harris shoved back from the table and left the room. A few seconds later, the front door opened, then slammed shut.

Laurie looked like she was about to get up and go after him but Wes laid his hand on her arm and gave a small shake of his head. "Let him be."

The awkward silence stretched for several seconds, until finally Brett stood and clapped her hands together. "Who wants pie?"

Everyone sitting around the table groaned, grateful for the

distraction. Their voices tumbled over top of one another as conversation resumed. Wes shot her a look of gratitude.

Brett went into the kitchen to collect the pies and plates and to start boiling some water for coffee and tea. Amma came into the kitchen a few seconds later, carrying some dirty dishes. She set them in the sink with a clatter.

"I'm sorry. About what I said out there. I didn't realize it would upset people so much." She turned on the faucet and began to rinse the dishes before loading them into the dishwasher. "There are so many rules. It's too easy to get myself in trouble these days."

"You're fine." Brett squeezed Amma's arm, feeling the thinness of her, the delicate bone beneath. She hadn't noticed when it happened, when her grandmother had become so fragile, when they had switched roles with Brett being the one to offer comfort and support.

Movement through the kitchen window drew Brett's attention. Adam Harris trudged across the back lawn toward the dock, his shoulders hunched against the wind and slashing rain. As he stepped onto the dock, paused to look back toward the house, then darted out of sight behind the small boathouse.

Henry and his wife entered the kitchen, each of them holding a stack of dirty plates.

"We came to help," Henry said.

Amma took the plates from him to rinse in the sink.

The kettle on the stove began to whistle.

"Just in time," Brett said. "Grab those plates for me, would you?"

She sent them off with pies, coffee, tea, and whipped cream, but instead of following them back into the dining room, she slipped into her raincoat and boots, and stepped outside. She pulled the hood over her head and trotted down the lawn to the dock. The boards creaked underfoot as she made her way to the end where she'd seen Adam disappear. He was still there, standing with his back against the wall of the boathouse, sheltered beneath the eaves.

His nostrils flared for an instant when she rounded the corner, and he looked around for somewhere to hide the beer can he was drinking from. Then he shrugged, and his expression shuttered to aloof boredom. He lifted the can to his mouth and took a long drink. He smacked his lips when he was done and crushed the empty can in his fist.

"I see a night in jail did nothing to change your mind about drinking," Brett said, her words dry and unimpressed.

"Don't tell my dad." He gave a lazy shrug like he didn't actually care what she did.

"I'm sorry about what happened to your friends," Brett said.

He twisted his head to look at her. "Do you like being a cop?"

She thought a moment, watching the whitecaps rise and fall beyond the edge of the dock. Water splashed against the pylons, out of sync with the drumming rain. "There are good days and bad days," she finally said. "Like any other job. Why? Do you think that's what you want to do when you graduate?"

He laughed, bitterness darkening the sound. "Yeah, right."

"What do you want to do then?"

"Anything but that." He stared at the empty beer can. "A truck driver, maybe. A pilot. Something that will get me the hell out of this fucking town."

He hurled the can into the waves. Brett shoved down the automatic response to scold him for littering. The can bobbed on the surface of the water, slowly making its way back to shore.

"You were supposed to leave with them, weren't you?" she asked instead. "On Halloween. With June and Daniel and Lizzie. You were supposed to be meeting them at the ruins, right?"

"Yeah, so?" He shoved his hands in his pockets and glared out at the ocean.

"What time did you get there?"

Adam chewed the corner of his lip, then said, "I don't think I should be talking to you."

"Why not?"

He shrugged.

"The other night," Brett said. "When I brought you and Lizzie down to the station, I found some things in your truck. Some things that belonged to June. What were you doing with June's camera, Adam? Why was there blood on it?"

He whipped his head around, his eyes narrow, his mouth set in a hard line. It was an expression she'd seen on him before, the night she'd arrested him for drunk driving. Adam Harris, she realized, was under the distinct impression that he was untouchable.

Before she could ask any more questions, the dock boards groaned.

"Adam?" Wes rounded the corner of the boathouse. "Everything okay out here?"

His gaze darted between Brett and Adam, and a shadow passed across his face as he took a step forward, positioning himself between Brett and his son. "What's going on?"

"We're just talking," Brett said.

"She's interrogating me," Adam said, his mouth twisting to a smirk.

"I'm not." But she stopped, realizing how guilty her defensiveness made her sound.

"Adam, go wait in the car," Wes said, keeping his gaze fixed on Brett.

Even Brett could tell by the tone in his voice that this wasn't a suggestion, but Adam didn't move. Wes twisted around to look at him, and there was a moment where father and son stared at each other, an entire argument playing out in their silence. Then Wes jabbed his finger in the air, pointing it toward the road. "I said, go wait in the car."

The teenager stormed off the dock and disappeared around the side of the house. Wes exhaled a loud sigh and rubbed the bridge of his nose.

"Wes—"

"What the hell are you doing out here with my son, Buchanan?"

"I told you, we were talking."

"Were you questioning him about the Newmark case?"

Brett decided the best way to handle this was to be honest with him. "Yes. I asked him about the camera we found in his truck. And I asked him if he was at the ruins on Halloween."

"He's a minor," Wes said. "You can't talk to him without an adult present. Nothing he said to you can be used in court."

"Is there a reason he needs to be in court?" she asked.

Wes' gaze drifted toward the bay. A muscle in his jaw twitched. He seemed to be staring at a specific spot on the water, but when Brett looked, she didn't see anything but blues and grays, the surface broken by small waves.

"I was talking to Laurie in the kitchen when you first got here today," Brett said. "She told me you went to the Millers' Halloween party this year, that you dressed up as Bonnie and Clyde."

He continued to stare out at the water, saying nothing.

Brett took a step toward him, her hand reaching for his elbow. "Wes? Did you hear what I said? Laurie says you were at the party, but you told Irving you were at home the whole night."

"I was home." He jerked his arm back and spun to face her. "We dropped by the party for a few minutes and then we went home. There, satisfied?"

"And Adam was home with you?"

"Of course he was."

"And he never left?"

"Now you're interrogating me?" He threw his hands in the air. "This is ridiculous. You have some nerve, Buchanan. Is there something about me specifically you don't like? Or do you have a problem with all men who hold higher rank than you? Stan told me you tried to get him fired last year, too."

""I don't have a problem with you or anyone," she said. "I'm just trying to understand what happened. I want to know who killed June and Daniel."

"Well, you're knocking on the wrong doors, I'll tell you that much."

"There's a witness," Brett said. "A waitress at the Blue Whale Diner. She saw Adam and Daniel fighting a few hours before they were supposed to meet at the ruins. So, okay, maybe you didn't know about it, but no, your son was not home all night. And if he knows something that can help us close this case, then you have a responsibility to convince him to talk to us. You've been sworn to serve and protect. You have a duty to the truth."

The words dropped between them. Brett felt her heart hammering in her throat as she waited for Wes' response.

At his side, his hands curled to fists. "You've been with this department for how long, Buchanan? Two years? Three?"

The sudden change in topic gave her whiplash. There was anger in his voice, a crackling heat that made Brett take a step back. She was no longer under the protection of the eaves now. The rain lashed her hair around her face.

She answered his question. "I've been here one year."

She moved to Crestwood last summer after spending ten years working for Marion County as a sheriff's deputy.

Wes looked surprised. "I could have sworn you'd been here longer." He shook his head, like it didn't matter and asked, "And you don't have kids, right?"

He glanced up at the house, then continued, not waiting for her answer, "Then you have no idea how hard it is. How much you sacrifice. Every day you try to do what's best for them. Your whole existence becomes about protecting them and keeping them safe. And every day you pray that today won't be the day you fail them."

He took a step toward her, crowding her toward the edge of the dock. Her shoes bumped against the low railing. Below her, waves splashed the barnacle-covered pylons.

"He's a kid, Buchanan. He's barely sixteen." In the dim light of the swiftly-approaching evening, Wes' gray-blue eyes looked black. "So, he fought with his friends. So what? Who hasn't said things they regret, thrown a few punches they wish they could take back. Adam was home with me on Halloween, and that's the last time I'm going to say it."

He took a step back and ran his hand down his face and mustache in a futile attempt to brush off the rain.

"You know what frustrates me most about finding you out here talking to my kid without my permission?" he asked, calmer now. "It's that Stan told me over and over to watch my back around you. He said you weren't much of a team player, and I should get rid of you the first chance I got. But I stood up for you. I told him you'd figure it out."

The wind tossed a piece of damp hair into Brett's mouth. She swiped it out again.

"Stan can be a real shit sometimes. But, hell, you know that better than I do. With all his good old boy, dicks on the streets, cunts in the kitchen crap. I'm not saying I agree with him. I mean, I've always thought of myself as an equal opportunity kind of guy. Let a chick run with the big dogs, if she wants, but only if she can keep up." Wes tugged on the sleeves of his brown suit jacket. "I thought you were keeping up, Buchanan. But now I'm not so sure. Now I'm starting to think maybe I should have listened to Stan."

He thumped her roughly on the shoulder before he walked away. His final words, edged with ice water and veiled threats. "Don't make me regret my decision to keep you on the team."

CHAPTER 30

Thanksgiving was a bust exactly like Lizzie knew it would be.

"Let's keep it simple this year," Grandpa had said, before suggesting Chinese takeout.

But Dad wanted to show-off and prove to them, to himself maybe, that after a year in prison he could still cook a turkey and mash potatoes. He wanted things to go back to how they were before. But Dad had never been the cook in their family, had only ever made cereal, grilled cheese sandwiches, and blueberry pancakes. He'd always let Mom handle the rest.

Ever since Lizzie had told Detective Buchanan about what Mr. Cadden had done to her in the locker room, and ever since she'd handed over the Polaroids, she hadn't been able to get a moment's peace. If she tried to go into another part of the house for even a few minutes, her grandmother would follow her. If she went down to the barn to pet the horses, Grandpa showed up with some excuse about needing to fill the water troughs or check that none of the blankets had fallen off the horses. If she stayed in her room, her dad would be there, tapping on the door every half hour to check if she needed anything.

They worried because they cared, Lizzie knew that. Still,

it would be nice to at least go to the bathroom without hearing someone breathing outside the door.

She cupped her hands under the faucet and splashed water on her face. She touched her fingers to her sharp cheekbones, staring at the ghoul in the mirror. Dark circles bruised her eyes—part of it came from smeared mascara, part of it from not getting enough sleep. Skin flaked from her lips, shredded from her anxious gnawing. The black dye she'd used on her hair was starting to fade, her chestnut brown roots showing through, reminding her that she couldn't hide away forever.

Maybe everyone had a right to be worried about her. Maybe she wasn't worried enough.

The police had let Mr. Cadden go, and even though Lizzie hadn't seen him back at school yet, it seemed like only a matter of time before he came looking for her. Tattle-tale. Snitches get stitches. Dirty rat. She thought the pictures would have been enough for the police to lock him up and throw away the key. If she'd known there was even the smallest chance of him walking free, she would have kept her mouth shut.

A light tapping sounded at the door and her grandmother's voice drifted into the bathroom. "Everything okay in there, Elizabeth? Dinner's almost ready."

As if this stupid day couldn't get any worse, the smoke alarm went off. Grandma cursed, and Lizzie listened to her footsteps pounding down the hall toward the kitchen. The alarm shrieked for several minutes as her grandparents shouted in the background while they tried to figure out how to turn it off.

Once the alarm went silent again, Lizzie came out of the bathroom. The smell of smoke lingered in the air. In the kitchen, her grandmother was shouting, "I told you not to use that pan, Marshall! You never listen to me. If you'd listened—"

"Enough, Ma." Her father's stern voice cut her off. A fake smile spread over his face when he saw Lizzie standing in the doorway. "Ready to eat?"

The turkey was so overcooked, it was like chewing rubber. The stuffing was too dry and flaked like sawdust in her mouth. The mashed potatoes were glue that held everything together. Dad accidentally used salt instead of sugar in the cranberry sauce. The dinner rolls were hockey pucks with charred black bottoms.

Grandpa knocked one of them against the table and, with a grin and in a pirate's accent, said, "I always did love a good hard tack, yar."

Lizzie started to laugh, but both Grandma and Dad shot her angry looks. She slouched low in her chair and stabbed her fork into the potatoes, swirling them with the green beans that were more mush than bean.

Even the pumpkin pie was gross, and Lizzie loved pumpkin pie. She didn't know how Dad messed it up so badly, but the custard was soup and the crust was soggy and tasted like the inside of a shoe. The only thing that didn't make her want to throw up were the tiny butter pickles that came from a jar.

"Can I be excused?" Lizzie asked, pretending she was too full to eat even one more bite.

Grandma waved her hand, dismissing her, but Dad called her back. "We never said what we're thankful for."

Lizzie pulled her sweater sleeves around her knuckles. She waited for someone else to go first, but they were all looking at her. She exhaled a sigh and said, "I'm thankful dinner is over."

"Lizbug," her grandpa said in a low voice.

"He asked," she said. "I'm just being honest."

Grandma shook her head and reached for her glass of wine. "We can't have one nice dinner together without it turning into a fight?"

Dad's chair scraped across the floor. He grabbed his dirty plate and silverware and carried them into the kitchen. The noise he made as he rinsed and put them in the dishwasher was obviously meant to draw attention. Her grandparents were looking at her again.

"What?"

"You should apologize to your father," Grandma said.

"Isn't he the one who should be apologizing to me?" Lizzie stormed out of the dining room.

She started to go up to her bedroom, but then decided it wasn't fair. She'd done nothing wrong—why should she be banished? She turned on the television and flipped through the three stations that came in clear, but it was all football, football, and more football. She picked a game at random and flopped down on the couch.

After dinner, Grandma switched from wine to gin and tonics and fighting with Dad again about finding a job. Dad drank too many martinis and started fighting with Grandpa about who was going to win the football game no one actually cared about. Grandpa drank beer until he fell asleep in his recliner.

For the first time in over a week, no one was watching Lizzie.

She kicked off the blanket that had been covering her legs, slipped out of the room, grabbed a rain poncho off the hook in the front hall, pulled it over her head, and walked out of the house. The door slammed shut behind her. She hesitated on the front porch, waiting for one of the adults to come running after her. No one did.

She hauled her bike out of the garage and rode in the direction of town. Dark clouds raced along with her. Mist dampened her face and turned her fingers to ice. She pedaled fast to stay warm.

All of the stores on Main Street were closed, their windows dark. Lizzie biked through downtown and all the way to Deadman's Point and didn't see a single car or other living being. Everyone must have been at home having a nice Thanksgiving with their families.

Lizzie hadn't been back to the ruins since Halloween. Now, she stood staring at the crumbled piles of stone, the shadows deepening with the last gasp of daylight, feeling uncertain about whether she should stay or go back home where at least she'd be dry. She tugged on the heart pendant she still wore around her neck. Even though she knew now that the necklace had come from Adam, she couldn't take it off. It was the only thing she had left of June's, even if June had never wanted it in the first place.

June.

She'd been killed here, her body left to the scavengers and rain. Lizzie spun a slow circle, trying to figure out where it had happened. There were no bits of fluttering police tape, no chalk outlines, no bloodstains, no neon signs flashing: Here, Here, Over Here.

June could have been killed anywhere, even in the very spot where Lizzie was standing now. She hopped to another patch of damp grass, a shudder rolling through her. A cool breeze raised the hairs on the back of her neck. A rustling sound in the trees drew her gaze, but she saw nothing except swaying branches.

Get it together, Lizzie, she thought, closing her eyes and taking a deep breath.

She hadn't come here to scare herself. She'd come here hoping for something, some kind of sign, a voice in the wind, someone to tell her who killed her friends.

"Are you there?" Lizzie whispered.

In the corner of her eye, a shadow flickered. She skimmed her gaze over the ruins and there, again, another shadow, crossing in front of one of the windows. She couldn't be sure, but she thought she saw a hint of burgundy with ribbons of dirty-blond hair streaming behind.

"Hello? Is someone here?" Lizzie took a step toward the ruins.

She wasn't brave enough for this, but she kept moving closer.

The inside of the ruins smelled of campfire smoke and rotting wood. She walked slowly as she moved deeper into the building, feeling her hand along the stone walls for the simple comfort of something solid beneath her fingertips. Something clattered across the floor in front of her. It sounded like a glass bottle being kicked. She paused and tilted her head toward the sound as something too big to be a rat and not big enough to be human scurried in the opposite direction.

"Hello?" Her voice echoed against the damp stone and came back to her with a deeper timber.

"Hello."

She startled at the man's voice and took a step back. Her foot caught on an uneven part of the floor. She tripped and fell onto her butt. In front of her, the shadows wavered, and a shape splintered from the dark. A hunched figure shuffled toward her. She scrambled backward like a crab. Her fingers scuttled through dead leaves and bottle caps.

The apparition drifted closer, making a strange clicking sound. The figure stepped into a shaft of faint light streaming through a window, and Lizzie realized the clicking sound was a cane, and the shadow was no ghost at all, but an old man made of flesh and bone, with wrinkled skin and a chipped-tooth grin.

"You should be more careful." He extended a gnarled hand. "There's broken glass everywhere."

He helped her to her feet. She dusted off her pants, studying him more closely. He was probably as old as her grandpa, but he could have been older. Puffs of gray hair sprang from his scalp in patches, as though they were cotton balls stuck on with rubber cement. His eyes were watery, a bright blue color that reminded her of summer. He wouldn't stop smiling at her.

"Do you live here?" She looked around at the crumbling building with half a roof, broken windows, and no heating, unable to imagine someone calling this place home.

The man laughed and rocked on his cane, clutching one hand to his chest. He started to wheeze, then he coughed, caught his breath, and said, "No one lives here. Unless you believe in ghosts. You do, don't you? I can tell."

He pushed his face so close, she could smell cough drops on his breath and the pungent scent of urine wafting from his clothes.

"I saw you." His voice turned serious.

She shuffled a step back, wanting to put distance between her and the man, wishing now that she'd brought someone with her. Grandpa would have come, if she'd asked, but that would mean telling him about her ghosts that didn't exist, and that she was still unhappy and worried she would never be happy again. She didn't want to break his heart any more than it already was.

"I saw you," the old man repeated, wagging a finger in Lizzie's face. "You were with that angel girl. The fairy with the glowing hair."

Lizzie shook her head.

"You were here." Then his voice shifted to a higher pitch. He sounded like a squeaky door hinge. "'Give him a few more minutes.'" His voice dropped low again, but still different than his normal voice, this time deeper, smoother, like his mouth was melted chocolate. "'If she wants to go, let her go.'"

With a sickening twist of her stomach, Lizzie realized she'd heard those words before, that the man was imitating June and Daniel on the night they were killed.

"You were here." He continued to wag his finger in her face, even as she walked backward away from him. "But you left them."

She shook her head, and her mouth popped open to defend herself against his accusations, but then she stopped. Because he'd been here, too. This man with his cane and his weathered face, he'd been at the ruins on Halloween. He'd seen her and her friends. He'd heard them talking.

She stopped backing away from him. "What happened after I left? What else did you hear?"

The man's lips moved around silent words and then he repeated himself, "You left them."

"Did you see what happened?" Lizzie asked. "Did you see who killed my friends?"

The man's arm lashed out. He grabbed Lizzie, his grip surprisingly strong for someone who looked so frail. "You should leave this place. Nothing good happens here. There are unsettled spirits around every corner, and they are very angry. Angry at you. Angry that you left. Listen, you can hear them scream."

The wind whistled through cracks in the walls.

Lizzie wrenched free of him, turned, and ran.

The man's voice trailed after her, pitching high again and echoing through the corridors, June's last words chasing Lizzie through the ruins. "'It's not what you think. Wait, what are you doing? Put that down. Don't hurt him! Please!'"

A name Lizzie recognized ricocheted off the cold stones as the old man's cane struck the floor with a deafening crack.

CHAPTER 31

Brett should have seen it coming.

Stan Harcourt called her into his office first thing Monday morning after the long holiday weekend. He unwrapped a stick of mint gum, folded it into his mouth, and said, "We have too many detectives."

Brett stood dumbfounded in front of the chief's desk. She'd been planning to talk to Stan about her concerns with the New-mark case and Adam's possible involvement as soon as he got back from his Thanksgiving vacation, but now, standing here with her metaphorical pants around her ankles, she realized Wes had gotten to Stan first. And whatever he'd said had finally given Stan a reason to get rid of Brett, something he'd been trying to do ever since her first day on the job.

"What we really need is more bodies out on patrol," Stan said with a smirk twisting his lips. "We've got to get our crime stats down, and to do that we need to be one—" He held up a finger. "—arresting more people. And two—" He lifted a second finger. "—having more eyes on the streets. We want to make sure the criminals know we're out there watching and ready to respond at a moment's notice. The more they see us, the less crimes they'll commit."

Brett had never heard so much bullshit come out of one person's mouth in such rapid succession.

"Henry hired me as a detective," she reminded him, stalling the inevitable.

"Do I look like Henry to you?" Stan propped his bony elbows on his desk. He was a thin man with a bad comb over who kept a pair of reading glasses hanging from his neck but refused to use them, squinting at every document he was given instead.

Brett wasn't going to humor him with an answer.

Stan rolled his wad of chewing gum over his teeth as he flashed a cruel smile. "No, I didn't think so. Look, I know Henry gave you special treatment around here. You were his little princess and all that bullshit, but Henry's not driving this ship anymore. I am. And boy, did he leave me quite a mess to clean up. That's all I'm trying to do. We've got one too many detectives and a budget that's bloated fatter than a whale washed up at high tide. So I've got to make some cuts somewhere, now don't I? Last one in is the first one out, as they say. And I know it sucks, but it's where this department's at right now. And don't bother crying to your union rep, either because I've already run this past them, and they're on board. They agree that we all have to play our part. So what I need from you is to show a little team spirit. I know you have it in you."

He pumped his fist in the air half-heartedly. His grin was wolfish. The smell of his minty breath turned Brett's stomach.

A small voice in her head that sounded vaguely like Jimmy, told her to keep her mouth shut. Say *Yes, sir, thank you, sir,* and leave the office before making things worse. She had never been very good at keeping her mouth shut.

"Is this about Wes? About what happened on Thanksgiving?"

"Thanksgiving? What happened on Thanksgiving? Did you give everyone food poisoning?" Stan laughed like he'd told the funniest joke in the world. Then he folded his hands on his desk and said, "Has Detective Sergeant Harris expressed some concerns about having someone like you on his team? Yes. He says you're unpredictable. And that you've been taking a lot of time off recently to take care of personal issues. But my decision to put you back on patrol is based on the needs of the department. There are things around here that need to get done, paperwork that's piling up, quotas that need to be met. And the fact is, our patrol squad needs more bodies than our detective squad does. You haven't been away from patrol so long you've forgotten how it works, have you? I can set you up with another officer for a ride-along if you need a refresher."

"That won't be necessary," Brett said. "But, sir, I've been working closely with Irving on this Newmark case, and I have some concerns."

She laced her hands behind her back and braced herself for Stan's response.

He sighed, but waved her to continue. "Care to elaborate?"

She told him about the evidence found in Adam's truck, and how it went missing. Then she told him about Wes' story changing and the information she'd gotten from Dot about Adam and Daniel fighting outside the diner. Knowing she would probably be fired on the spot if she directly accused a sergeant's son, she said with caution, "I think Adam might have information about the murders, and I think his father knows this and may be actively obstructing the investigation."

Stan stopped chewing his gum. Red blossomed high on his cheeks.

Brett knew she was walking a thin line here by accusing her superior, but she pressed on, determined to say everything she needed to say while she had the chance. "There were some things Sergeant Harris said to me on Thanksgiving that make me think we might want to consider bringing in someone from the county or state to conduct an independent investigation."

Stan slapped his hands on the desk before she could say anything more. "Oh you are a piece of work, aren't you? A real fucking piece of work. I tell you to step down, and then you start blathering on, accusing your superior officer of conspiracy? How convenient is that?"

"Bring him in here." Now that she'd started, she couldn't shut up. "Ask him where he was on Halloween? Ask him about the fight at the diner."

Stan snorted a laugh. "I don't need to ask Wes a goddamn thing, Princess. You know why? Because we've been working together for a long time now. I know who he is and what he stands for. I'd trust him with my life. He trusts me the same. And who are you? A little miss priss who thinks she can come in here and change how we've been doing things for decades? You think we'll roll over because you tell us to? That just because you're a woman, you're smarter than the rest of us?"

"I never said any of that."

"You didn't have to say it. It's how you act." He rose and leaned over his desk, pressing all ten fingers down onto the wooden top. "I tried with you. I did my damn best to make you a part of this team, but do you know what good teams are built on? Trust. That's how the best teams work. No one's rogue. No one's running off doing their own thing. This squad, my squad—" He pointed at his chest. "—needs to work as a well-oiled machine. And you're a cog that doesn't fit. The men on this team understand about loyalty, but that's always been your problem, hasn't it? You've only ever looked out for yourself."

He pulled back, shaking his head, ever the disappointed father. "I'm tired of you stirring up trouble. I'm tired of everyone always having to watch their backs around you. I would fire you if I could, but I can't. Because vengeful bitches like you would sue the pants off of honest, hardworking men like me, and because your union rep says I can't. But by all means, if you don't want to be here, if you don't want to follow orders and do the work that's assigned to you, then please, do us all a favor, turn in your badge and show yourself out."

He gestured to the door, daring her to go.

Brett almost walked out right then and there. She did. But her mind kept returning to the Polaroid of June and Daniel, the two teenagers so young and full of life and hope for the future. A future that was erased in the time it took to pull a trigger. Those two kids and their families deserved answers. They deserved justice. And if Brett had to keep putting up with Stan's bullshit to get it, she would. She crossed her arms over her chest and stared him down.

Stan shrugged. "Suit yourself. I'll need you to move your things to your new desk by the end of the day."

"My new desk? Can't I stay where I am?"

"You don't need that much space, do you? You'll be working out of your car for most of your shift anyway. I'd really like to free up that desk for a new computer coming in next week. You can share with Nancy."

Nancy Fellowes was the only other female officer in the entire department. She'd worked Parking Enforcement since she'd started with the department over a decade ago, and in spite of her loyalty to the job and willingness to play by the rules, her desk was still half the size of the other desks and crammed into the corner by the bathrooms.

"That desk is too small to accommodate both of us working there at the same time," Brett pointed out, keeping her voice calm, even though on the inside she felt like grabbing the paperweight off Stan's desk and smashing it to the floor.

"Oh, don't worry about that." He marked something down on a piece of paper. "I'm switching you over to the night shift, too."

Brett could handle a demotion. Stan dismissing her concerns

about a case being mishandled didn't surprise her in the least. Being forced to share a desk with lilac-scented Nancy Fellowes made her grind her teeth, but whatever, she'd deal with it. But she needed to be home at night. Amma needed her to be home.

"Sir, I can't do that."

He jerked up his head, grinning. "I'd be more than happy to sign your resignation forms. Bring them by my office whenever you're ready."

Brett squeezed her hands together behind her back, trying to calm her trembling rage, and forced the words from her mouth, "Night shift is fine. When do I start?"

"Today." His smile was edged sharp. "There's a spare uniform waiting for you in the locker room. It'll probably be a bit big on you, but I'm afraid it's the best we can do for now. Next month, we'll see about ordering you something from the women's catalog. That's if we have anything left over in the budget, of course."

With that, Brett was dismissed.

The switch from days to nights was harder than Brett anticipated it to be, and she struggled to find a new routine that didn't make her feel like a zombie.

She clocked in now at 9:00 PM and clocked out around 5:00 AM unless the shift turned out to be especially busy and she needed to catch up on paperwork. Her new patrol lieutenant was less than thrilled to have her joining his team and looked the other way when the other officers came up with excuse after excuse as to why they weren't responding to call-outs. Routinely, Brett was the first officer on scene. Most of the calls turned out to be nothing more than bumps in the night, but every time she responded to a location, a report had to be written, which meant she rarely got home before 8:00 AM.

The twenty-something girl Brett hired to stay at the house overnight charged extra for every hour she was late. And Brett forked over the cash because what other choice did she have?

"I still don't understand why she's here," Amma said, after the second morning coming downstairs to find a strange young woman rummaging through her kitchen.

"Just in case you need something and you can't get a hold of me," Brett reminded her.

Brett didn't have access to her desk phone anymore. And if Amma called the station, there was no guarantee the front desk officer would answer, and no guarantee that if he did, he'd pass the message along to Brett.

The girl who stayed over didn't have to do much. Amma put herself to bed and mostly slept through the night. All the girl had to do was be here to make sure Amma didn't accidentally burn the house to the ground or trip and fall on her way to the bathroom. It was an easy gig and easy money, and Brett felt better leaving Amma, knowing she wasn't completely alone.

After Brett got home from the precinct, she would spend another hour, sometimes two, trying to unwind. She took a shower, made herself a cup of tea with a splash of whiskey, ate a bowl of cereal or an entire bag of potato chips, watched a morning news program where the hosts were talking about what to do with Thanksgiving leftovers, and tried to fall asleep. But something always jerked her awake before her eyes were fully closed. Amma needed her to reach something on the top shelf in the kitchen. Pistol barked at the mailman. Their neighbor Kenny came by with banana bread and a new stack of cozy mysteries for Amma to read. Pistol barked at Kenny. Pistol barked at everything.

She was lucky if she got a solid two hours before she had to wake up and get ready for her next shift, and the lack of sleep was starting to wear on her.

Her head felt too heavy to carry around, yet at the same time light enough to float away. She couldn't seem to get used to seeing in the dark, but when the morning came, it was all too bright. She was hungry when she should be sleepy, sleepy when she should be wide awake, eating Frosty Queen fries and a burger at two in the morning and pancakes with bacon at two in the afternoon.

At this rate, Stan and the rest of the department might get their wish. Not even four days on the night shift, and she was reaching her breaking point. She needed to sleep. To sleep, she'd have to quit, which didn't sound so bad when she was sitting in her patrol car in the dark, in a scratchy-wool uniform that draped over her shoulders like a potato sack and smelled like old french fries no matter how many times she washed it.

The radio crackled. The night dispatcher's voice was a welcome break from the past two hours of silence. Friday nights were usually busier than this, but the rain seemed to be keeping everyone inside. Well, not everyone. "We've got a report of a single car rollover accident out on Red Fox Road," the dispatcher said. "Fire and medical are en route. Car 32 please respond."

There were six cars out on patrol tonight in addition to Brett's, but the unspoken rule was that unless she was already attending to another call, Car 32 responded to everything.

Brett grabbed the microphone and pressed the button. "On my way."

The Jeep was flipped onto its roof in a ditch. The front end was crumpled against a large oak tree. Smoke trickled from the engine compartment.

Brett slammed her car door shut and walked over to a group of firemen and paramedics who didn't seem to be in any hurry to do their jobs. One of the men stepped from the group to meet her, saying, "Driver didn't make it." Which explained why they were all standing around in the cherry red strobe lights doing nothing. "We're ready to cut him out whenever you are. Medical examiner's on the way."

She followed the fireman over to the car and squatted down to peer through the shattered driver's side window. The driver was an older, white male, with a deep gash in his forehead and a steering wheel in his lap. She didn't recognize him. The windshield was cracked and smeared with something sticky that looked vaguely like brain matter. Poor bastard hadn't stood a chance.

Brett rose to her feet and signaled for the firemen to start pulling apart the car.

As they worked, Brett walked along the road, searching with her flashlight. There was no evidence any other cars had been involved. About a hundred yards from the tree, the road veered sharply to the right, and it was here she found rubber tire marks streaked across the asphalt, where the man had tried to slow, but lost control and careened into the ditch. He'd probably been drinking, definitely speeding.

Metal screeched as the firefighters cut the body free.

Brett rubbed her temples. The headache she woke up with this afternoon was getting worse. With the medical examiner's van just now arriving and the tow truck taking its sweet time, Brett had a feeling she would be working well past the end of her shift. She still had to break the bad news to the man's family, too. She sighed. One thing at a time.

She approached the van as it parked behind her patrol car. Kevin Park stepped out of the driver's side. He looked surprised to see Brett waiting for him in the rain.

"Since when do you work patrol?" he asked.

"Since four days ago," she said.

He glanced over her shoulder and grimaced. "Looks bad."

They walked to where the firefighters worked to pull the body from the car. The firefighters greeted Kevin with somber expressions, then stepped aside to let him have a look. Kevin scowled and shook his head. "Such a waste."

One of the firefighters found the man's wallet and handed it to Brett. She flipped it open and studied the address. The street where he lived was just a few miles up the road.

"He almost made it home," she said.

Once the body was safely loaded inside the van, the firefighters piled into their truck and drove away. Kevin shut the van doors, and Brett stepped aside, assuming he'd go, too, but he propped himself against the side of the van, shoved his hands in his pockets, and said, "I've been trying to get a hold of you all week. I've been calling. I've left several messages."

Brett thought of the blinking red light on her old desk phone, how many times she'd walked past it and ignored it partly out of spite and partly because Stan had made it perfectly clear it wasn't her desk anymore. Not her desk, not her business.

"Yeah, sorry about that. They moved me to a different desk," she said. "What's up?"

"The ballistic report came back on the bullet we pulled from Daniel Yoon."

"Took long enough," she said.

"Holidays," he pointed out. "Plus, I think they were dragging their feet because they wanted to make sure they got it right."

Brett raised her eyebrows. "Got what right?"

His frown deepened as if he was unsure about whether or not to tell her what was in the report. After a few seconds, he adjusted his glasses, cleared his throat, and said, "The bullet that killed June Newmark and the one that killed Daniel don't match."

It wasn't what Brett had expected him to say, but she kept her expression neutral as he explained June's bullet was a 9mm, most likely from some type of Luger, while Daniel's bullet was clearly a .38 Special. Two different bullets from two different handguns meant two different shooters.

There was a small probability of one shooter using two different guns, but as Kevin went into further detail about the trajectory of the bullets through each body and how gunpowder residue had been found on June but not on Daniel—meaning she'd been shot at close range while Daniel had been gunned down from a distance—the more convinced Brett became that there were two people out on that peninsula the night June and Daniel were shot. Two bullets, two guns, two dead kids, two killers who even now, nearly a month into the investigation, remained nameless, faceless enigmas. And there wasn't a damn thing Brett could do to change that. Not without deliberately disobeying orders and butting heads with the chief again. Not her case, not her problem—she could hear Chief Harcourt's stern voice in her head.

"You need to get that report faxed over to the station as soon as possible," she told Kevin. "The detective assigned to the case needs to see it right away."

"I can send it tonight, after I get this body tucked away." He took his hands out of his pockets and turned to watch a pair of headlights approach from a distance.

"That'll be the tow truck." Brett stepped away from Kevin and lifted her hand to wave down the driver.

CHAPTER 32

When Brett pulled her VW Beetle into the parking lot of the Edgewater Nature Reserve two days later on Sunday morning, Irving was already there, standing near the information board that offered maps and brochures about the various migrant and native birds likely to be visiting the wetland preserve. He was statue-still, holding a pair of binoculars to his face as he studied a clump of scraggly willows.

Brett got out of the car and grabbed her backpack, a pair of binoculars, and the coffees and pastries she'd purchased from her favorite bakery on the way here. Hearing her footsteps in the gravel, Irving lowered the binoculars and turned toward her. She handed him one of the two coffees.

"You missed a Lazuli bunting," he said, taking a careful sip. "But at least the coffee's hot this time."

"It was hot last time, too."

Irving grunted and jabbed a finger at the bag in her hand. "Those had better be fritters."

She handed him the bag. "Sorry I'm late. Slept through my alarm. Night shift is killing me."

"We could have canceled," Irving said and took another sip of coffee.

"And have you miss out on a Lazuli bunting? Never."

"Which reminds me..." Irving pulled out the spiral-bound notebook he carried with him everywhere. He made a note on one of the pages. "That bunting brings me up to one hundred and thirty-four."

Irving had shown her the notebook once. He called it his Life List, a record of every unique species of bird he'd sighted since he started birding ten years ago. Though he kept track of every bird he saw day-to-day, the Life List birds received a star beside their entry. The first time he saw a species of bird he had never seen before, a bird that was new to him, he wrote down what it was and where he saw it and then marked a star in the margin next to its name. There were contests he could enter, competitions between birders to see who could spot the most birds in a single year, but he wasn't interested in any of that. He was a birder because he loved birds. And he kept track because he liked to see where he'd been and who he'd been and how he'd changed from bird to bird.

"Ready?" He returned the notebook to his pocket and stepped onto the trail.

Brett nodded and followed him down the narrow footpath that would lead them deeper into the wetlands.

Their bi-monthly trips to the Edgewater Nature Reserve had started last spring. Brett and Irving were working together on a difficult case involving the death of a minor. The parents had left the child alone in the bedroom and gone to get high in the basement. When they came back upstairs, they found the toddler crushed under a large bookshelf. They hadn't even heard the crash.

Brett had been working on prepping her testimony for trial, and Irving was double-checking the file to make sure everything was in order. Their backs ached from sitting too long, their stomachs burned from drinking too much bad coffee, and they were sick with grief over the parents' terrible negligence. It was a heartbreaking and avoidable death. One neither of them wanted to deal with. Several hours into their shift, Irving had stood up from his desk so fast he'd knocked the chair over.

"I don't know about you, but I could use some fresh air."

Brett followed him out to the parking lot, thinking they would stretch their legs for a few minutes and go back inside, but Irving walked out of the parking lot and kept right on walking, ten blocks down to the bay.

Strolling along the beach with his hands laced behind his back, he pointed out birds to Brett as they appeared, listing the various gulls, terns, and sandpipers. Telling them apart by the different wing and beak markings, though to Brett they all looked pretty much the same. When there wasn't a bird to name, they walked in silence, listening to the hiss of waves against the sand and the clatter and squawk of gulls twisting circles overhead.

Maybe it was the walking, or the simple fact that they weren't suffocating in a cramped and dimly lit conference room anymore. But Brett liked to think it was the brown pelican. An endangered bird that visited the Washington coastline seasonally, according to Irving, its silhouette against the glassy blue was prehistoric and intimidating. They watched it glide and then suddenly swoop, diving its whole body into the water before bursting from the waves again in an elegant arc, its hamper-like beak filled with seawater and fish. As the bird flew out of sight, Irving had turned to Brett and said, "Even on the ugliest of days, beauty still exists. Though you might have to look harder to find it."

It became a habit for them after that, an unspoken arrangement where Irving would get up from his desk, grab two coffees from the break room, and walk outside, and Brett would follow. They would look for birds and talk about anything but their cases.

After a few weeks, Irving suggested they meet at Edgewater Nature Reserve where they were more likely to encounter far more interesting birds than the standard seagulls and crows that hung out near the precinct. Now every other Sunday, one of them brought coffee, and they walked and looked for birds and talked about anything but work.

"How's Diane?" Brett politely asked about his wife.

"She's planning our retirement trip," Irving said. "A literary tour of Europe."

"You still have a few years before that happens, don't you?"

He grunted, which wasn't much of an answer.

Brett studied Irving's profile as they walked. Rugged, high forehead, sharp chin, fine lines creasing the brown skin around his mouth. A rookie officer in Crestwood the year Brett's sister was murdered, Irving had been with the department for over twenty-one years. When Henry Bascom announced he would be stepping down as chief, Brett thought Irving should have been the one to take his spot. She asked him about it later, why he hadn't applied, and he told her that he had but they told him he wasn't qualified. He shrugged it off, saying he didn't want the extra re-sponsibility anyway. He said he got into this work to help people, not play politics. She hadn't pressed him further, but wondered if the reason he wasn't considered for the position was less about his qualifications and more about the color of his skin. Sometimes she thought the residents of Crestwood only put up with Irving because he refused to leave. They'd grown used to having him around, but they couldn't bear the idea of a Black man in power.

Brett wanted to believe she could trust him, that if she told him she thought their detective sergeant might be involved in covering up a crime, or something worse, that Irving would be on her side. But even though he didn't quite fit in with the rest of the squad and had taken a lot of shit from them over the years, he'd stuck with it—stuck with these men, men like Stan—for over two decades. And the one year she'd known him, even with the dozen birdwatching trips they'd been on together, felt like nothing in the face of that kind of commitment. Walking behind him on a foot-path that took them into the marsh, she realized she had no real idea where his loyalties would fall, if he was forced to decide.

The wetlands were a cacophony of bird songs. Honking geese. Tittering warblers. Laughing chickadees. The shrill triplets of redwing blackbirds. Brett lost herself in the sound for several minutes as they pushed deeper into the wetlands through bushes and tall marsh grass that scraped against her pants with a quiet swishing sound.

Irving paused at a bush covered in small, red berries to watch a group of birds with reddish-brown feathers dance and flit.

"Sparrows?" she asked.

He nodded. "Want to guess what kind?"

"House?"

"Swamp," he said with a grin, gesturing to the marshland through which the path cut.

"Makes sense."

They walked farther in, stopping every so often to scan the bushes and trees for birds. Irving lifted his binoculars to scan the sky once or twice.

"We got lucky with the rain," he said.

It was a small miracle. After over a month of non-stop storms and torrential downpours, the rain had suddenly stopped. The clouds still hung overhead, smudging the sky to a colorless void. But it was nice to be dry again. Relatively. A gentle breeze rustled the bare branches, shaking stray droplets onto their heads.

"It's supposed to start up again tonight," Irving added.

By the time they reached the wooden viewing dock at the end of the path, Brett's pants were soaked from the marsh grass, and her neck hurt from twisting to look for birds. Her headache was back, too, a throbbing pulse behind her eyes. The aspirin had worn and the coffee wasn't helping. She leaned her arms against the railing and stared out over the flat wetlands that stretched as far as the eye could see, edged on one side by a tangled mess of trees. The marsh was dotted with gray and white bodies of birds. Egrets and geese, mostly. Irving lifted his binoculars.

Brett exhaled a loud sigh.

Irving kept his binoculars lifted, but said, "If you've got something on your mind, Brett, you might as well say it."

"I have some concerns about how the Newmark case is being handled."

Now it was Irving's turn to sigh.

"I know, I know," she said. "We don't talk about work when we're out here. But I need to talk about this, and I can't talk about it at work because I'm walking a thin enough line there as it is and if anyone hears me say what I'm thinking..." She let the words trail off because she wasn't even sure she should say them to Irving.

"Go on." Irving lowered the binoculars and turned to face her. "I know I'm not going to get a moment's peace until you say what you have to say."

She started to talk but he held up a finger and added, "This is the one time I'm going to let you break our rule. I know Stan ruffled your feathers by putting you back out on patrol. I know that's not where you want to be, so maybe I'm feeling generous because of that. But don't think this is going to become a habit."

"One time only, got it." She scratched at the wood railing, flecking off bits of moss that had grown in the damp, shaded spots. She inhaled deeply and shoved all the words out at once before she lost her nerve. "I think Wes is lying about where his son was on Halloween night. I think Adam was at Deadman's Point, not at home. I think he showed up after Lizzie left. And I think he might know what happened to June and Daniel. I think he might even be the person responsible—"

"These are pretty serious accusations," Irving interrupted.

"You know that right? You'd be stepping into a minefield. Especially if you don't have evidence to back it up."

"I wouldn't bring it up if there wasn't evidence." She told him everything she'd already told Stan about Adam's strange behavior, June's camera, and the bloody clothes found stuffed behind the seat of his truck that were conveniently missing now; how Wes lied about his whereabouts on Halloween. "He wasn't at home, he was at the Miller's party with his wife. He claims they left early, but I'm not sure I believe him. All we have to do is talk to the other people who were at the party, find out if anyone remembers what time the Harris' left. It will be easy enough to find out if he lied to us. And if he lied about that, then what else is he lying about?"

"Stop." Irving sounded angry. "Just stop."

She waited for him to say something, but he stayed silent, staring across the marsh at a trio of ducks paddling slowly through the reeds. His fingers shifted around his binoculars as if trying to decide whether or not to use them. After a few minutes, he turned to look at her. Shadows moved across his face.

"Why am I just now hearing about all of this?" His voice was low, on the verge of cracking. "This is my case, remember? My name's on this damn thing, my reputation, and you go to Stan before coming to me?"

"I thought the chief would want to know what's going on with his team."

Irving's jaw tightened. "Or do you think I'm somehow involved, too? That I might be covering for Wes?"

She started to say no, but then stopped because she'd worried about that exact thing.

"You've known him longer than you've known me," she said.

"Look." He rubbed the bridge of his nose. "Maybe I shouldn't be telling you this. No, I know I shouldn't. Stan would shit a brick. But I'm going to tell you because you seem to have it in your mind that no one's working this case. Let me reassure you that we are. And no one wants this thing closed more than me. I'm working my ass off to get some answers for those two kids' families. And just so you know that I'm not trying to bury this, I can tell you we have a suspect and we're actively building a case."

"Who is it?"

At first it seemed like he wasn't going to tell her, then he said, "You didn't hear this from me, okay?"

She nodded.

"We're looking at Lizzie Trudeau again."

A laugh escaped Brett's mouth. Irving glared at her.

"You can't be serious," she protested.

"She admitted to being there, so she had the opportunity. Her grandfather has an entire cabinet full of guns in his study, so she had the means. Her two best friends were dating, and she didn't know about it, so jealousy could speak to motive."

"What kind of guns?" she asked.

"What?"

"What kind of guns does Robert own?" She didn't remember seeing a gun cabinet when she talked to Lizzie last month, but she'd walked through only one room; she hadn't searched the place.

"Hunting rifles, mostly," Irving said. "A few pistols."

"Anything that would fire a .38 Special or a 9mm?"

Irving's eyebrows shot up.

"Kevin Park faxed you the ballistics report, didn't he?" she asked.

"I haven't seen one yet." He ran his hand over his grizzled cheek. He never shaved on Sundays. "I've been calling over there trying to get an update, but no one's called me back yet."

"That's strange," she said, "I ran into Kevin out in the field Friday night. We were responding to an auto fatality. He'd been trying to get in touch with me about the ballistics report. He says the bullets don't match. That June was killed with a 9mm and Daniel with a .38 Special. I told him to talk to you, and he promised he'd fax over the report right away."

"If he did, I didn't get it." Irving looked like he didn't quite believe her.

After he got the report, it wouldn't matter if he believed her or not. The implications would be the same. "Two guns, two killers," she said. "Let's go with your theory that Lizzie is one. Then who's the other?"

He blinked at her, an annoyed look creeping onto his face.

"What about Benjamin Cadden?" Brett asked, reminding him of the teacher they'd questioned as a suspect before he produced an airtight alibi. "The gun we found in his dresser, that was a 9mm, right? If he had the 9mm, then Lizzie must have had the .38 Special. Was there a .38 Special in Robert's gun cabinet?"

Reluctantly, Irving shook his head.

"Were any of the guns missing?"

He shook his head a second time. "Robert said they were all accounted for, but you know better than anyone how that family likes to protect its own."

Irving gave her a knowing look.

"Lizzie is not Clara," Brett said.

"I know you want to stand up for her, I get that, but how well do you really know her, Brett? She's more than capable—"

"You really think a girl Lizzie's size, who can't be more than 90 pounds soaking wet, lifted Daniel's body all by herself and carried it out of there?"

"Adrenaline can make people do amazing things. Plus, didn't you say that Ed Shoal claimed to see more than one person in the woods that night? So, if he's not crazy, and you're right about the two guns, someone else was with her. Someone who could have carried the body."

"Like Cadden."

"Cadden's got an alibi we couldn't crack even if we spent weeks trying." Irving sounded disappointed.

Brett waited a minute, hoping he might come to it on his own. He stayed quiet, though, and it was up to her to point out the most obvious solution. "Adam is strong enough to carry a body."

As soon as the words were out of her mouth, Irving's demeanor changed. His shoulders tensed and his scowl intensified.

"Don't." His voice was a low growl.

"A .38 Special," she continued, ignoring his warning. "I carry one on my hip every night. So do you. So does everyone on the squad, including Sergeant Harris."

"Brett, I'm warning you. This is not a path you want to go down."

"The evidence that implicates his son in a murder investigation conveniently goes missing," Brett pressed him. "He lies about his whereabouts on the night of the murders. The gun we found in Cadden's house was clearly planted."

"We don't know that," Irving argued.

"Things aren't adding up here, Irving. There are too many discrepancies, too many pieces that don't fit. Can't you see that?"

"All I see is a recently demoted officer holding a grudge," he snapped at her.

"Don't be an idiot," she snapped back.

"You want to talk idiotic?" Irving grew taller, stretching himself to his full height and waving his hand in the air around his head. "You're accusing a sworn officer, a man who's served this community for over a decade, who's protected its citizens, you're accusing him of what? Of covering up a murder? Of getting the entire squad in on it, too?"

"I'm not accusing him of anything," Brett protested. "I'm merely giving you information and asking for further investigation. I'm asking for someone to talk to him again, and talk to Adam, too. I'm asking you to do your damn job."

"You're asking to get your ass kicked."

"Excuse me?"

"You're insubordinate, Brett. And you've been insubordinate since the first day you got here. Honestly, I'm surprised you lasted as a detective for as long as you did. Stan should have put you back on patrol weeks ago."

Her mouth dropped open, but no words came out. She had no idea what to say to that.

Irving filled her silence, "Come on, you can't tell me you didn't see this coming. You're arrogant. And your ego takes up more space than Ennis' mutton chops. You think every case will fall apart if you don't have your hands all over it."

"Tell me how you really feel," she muttered.

He glowered at her. "What can you do that the rest of us can't?"

She shook her head, too angry to give him a straight answer.

"I'm serious, Brett," Irving continued. "All of us have been investigating and closing cases for years before you showed up. Some of us years before you ever got your badge. You think you're special, but you're not. You're a grunt like the rest of us. You come in and you shovel shit then you go home and try to forget about how terrible the world is. The next day you come in and do it again. We're all doing that. We're all doing the best we can, you get that right? We're just trying to do our jobs. At least, that's what I'm out there doing every damn day. But you..." He laughed, turned to face the marsh again, and lifted his binoculars. "I don't know what the hell it is you're doing."

Brett stared at him, taken aback by his cynicism. This job wasn't easy. She wasn't going to stand here and try to argue otherwise. Day in and day out, they dealt with the worst of humanity, and some days it felt like no matter what they did, or how hard they worked, they would never be able to push back the darkness that threatened to overtake them. But she had always thought the work she did, even if it wasn't always satisfying, was good, and that she did it for the right reasons. To help lost people find their way home and hurt people find answers and broken people find healing. She wasn't trying to make Irving's life, or anyone else's, more difficult.

"I'm trying to help," she said in a rough voice. "A girl is dead. A boy was shot by a cop's gun."

"You have no proof of that," Irving's voice was quiet. He kept his eyes fixed on the treetops.

"Someone needs to be held responsible. Someone needs to ask the hard questions," she insisted. "If you can't, or won't, do it, then I will."

When he turned his gaze on her again, his face was drawn with worry. "You need to leave it alone. You're in enough trouble as it is. I can handle it. Let me handle it."

She stuck out her jaw defiantly and crossed her arms over her chest, not completely believing his half-hearted promise.

"I mean it, Brett." Irving glared at her as he tapped his fingers against his binoculars. "Stay away from this case. Stay away from Adam. And stay away from Wes. I've been here long enough to know these guys have your back until the day they don't." His tone softened as he reached to squeeze her shoulder. "Please, Brett. Listen to your elders for one goddamn time in your life. I heard you today, okay? I heard what you said, and I'll take another look, see if I can fill in some of the blanks and get us some answers that make sense. You're a good cop, but it's okay to let someone else take the reins every once in a while, do you hear me? You don't have to do everything."

He released her shoulder and turned to face the marsh again. On the horizon, dark clouds were starting to bunch up against the faded gray. The wind picked up, swaying the reeds.

Irving lifted his binoculars and pointed the lenses toward a small island rising from the middle of the water. He whistled through his teeth. "Now, there's a beauty."

Brett didn't follow his gaze. Birdwatching was the last thing in the world she cared about right now. Without a word, she turned and followed the path back to her car. Irving could keep his birds and bad advice. Brett had work to do.

CHAPTER 33

Brett parked her VW Beetle along the curb in front of Wes Harris' house. He and his family lived on the south side of town in a new construction, single-story bungalow with neatly-trimmed hedges and a white picket fence. It was a nice house for a cop's salary.

Brett opened her purse and ran her fingers over the silky red scarf she'd found buried beneath a pile of mail on the entry table yesterday. At first, she thought it was one of Amma's, but Amma said she'd never seen it before, and then Brett remembered seeing Laurie Harris wearing a scarf like this one on Thanksgiving. She must have left it behind in Wes' mad rush to escape Brett's pressing questions. Almost two weeks had passed and Laurie hadn't come around looking for it, so Brett decided she'd be doing the woman a favor bringing it back. It was a nice scarf, fine fabric and fringed edges, and it looked expensive.

Irving's warning to stay away from the Harris family echoed in her mind, but she shoved it away. She had a very good reason to be knocking on the Harris' front door this morning.

She ran the scarf through her hands as she waited on the porch for someone to answer. Wes was at the precinct. Brett saw him in his office as she was clocking out of her shift. But there was a sedan in the driveway, and though it was still early, not yet 8:00 AM on a Tuesday morning, she had a feeling Laurie Harris was the kind of woman who had all of her daily chores checked off her to-do list before breakfast.

As expected, an energetic, smiling Laurie yanked the front door open. Her hair was done up in a tight chignon, her make-up perfectly dewy. She wore a simple A-line dress that fell around her calves. In one hand, she held a dust rag. But her toothy smile twisted to a look of panic when she saw Brett standing on her porch.

She braced herself against the door and sucked in a sharp breath, her whole body tensing as her brain jumped to the worst conclusion. "Did something happen to Wes? Please, tell me. Don't drag it out."

It was every spouse's worst nightmare. An unexpected knock. A cop standing on your front porch with a sorrowful look on their face.

Brett quickly reassured the woman, waving the red scarf in the air. "Wes is fine. I'm returning this. You left it at my house on Thanksgiving, I think."

Laurie's hand flew to her neck, whether out of relief that she wouldn't have to plan a funeral or because she was grateful the scarf had been found, it wasn't clear. "Oh. Oh! God, you scared the living shit out of me. Please, come in out of the rain."

She stepped back from the door, and Brett followed her inside. It would have been rude not to.

Laurie chattered nervously as she led Brett into the kitchen. "He became sergeant for me, you know, because I was so afraid of getting the call, of one of you coming to my door and telling me he was dead. I told him he had two options: find a desk job or quit. So when you showed up here, standing there looking like a drowned puppy, Christ, I didn't know what to think. Pardon my swearing, too. Wes doesn't like that. He says I sound uneducated, but some-times a woman needs to let it fly, you know what I'm saying? Of course you do. Working day in and day out with those brutes. You know how good a properly timed 'goddammit motherfucker' feels, don't you? I'm sorry, I'm talking too much. It's the nerves. The adrenaline rushing right out of me. Coffee?"

She was pouring two cups before Brett could answer. She pushed one of the cups toward Brett, who sipped the bitter brew, letting the taste of it jolt her back to the reason she'd come over here in the first place.

She said, "I'm sorry I didn't get to say a proper goodbye on Thanksgiving and to thank you for helping me with the gravy."

"Oh, you don't have to worry about that, but thank you for bringing back my scarf." Laurie brushed her fingers over the scarf, a small furrow forming in her smooth brow. "It's the second one I've lost this year. I don't know where my head's been lately, but this one..." She hugged the scarf close to her chest for a brief second before laying it back on the counter and folding it into a neat square. "This one belonged to my grandmother. She got it in Paris when she was a nurse during the Second World War. I probably shouldn't wear it anywhere, but it's so lovely, isn't it?"

Brett nodded, then asked, "Was the other scarf your grandmother's, too?"

"Oh, that old thing," Laurie said with a flip of her hand. "No. That was one I got at a Christmas bazaar a few years ago. Simple black, but elegant. The kind of scarf that goes with everything."

Brett set her half-empty coffee cup on the counter with a loud clatter. The scarf covering June's face had been black, simple, elegant. But of course, there could be hundreds of scarves matching that description hanging in coat closets and crumpled in hat boxes all over Crestwood.

Before Brett could ask Laurie for more details, the other woman was refilling Brett's cup and saying, "I'm absolutely sure it's around here somewhere. Wes says we'll probably find it during the move." She smiled. "Things like that always have a habit of turning up again, don't they?"

For the first time, Brett noticed the boxes scattered throughout the house. "You're moving? Wes hasn't said anything."

"No, he wouldn't. It's not a sure thing yet." She lowered her voice even though no one else was home. "We're waiting to hear about a transfer. If he gets it, we'll be off to Greenville, South Carolina. That's where my family's originally from. But don't tell him I said anything. He doesn't like me talking about our personal business. And probably he'd bust a kidney if he found out I was telling you." She laughed and shook her head. "I've got the woman who's been trying to steal my man away from me standing in my own kitchen and I'm talking her ear off like we've been friends for years. Come on, Lore. Get a grip."

"Wait," Brett interrupted, trying to keep up with Laurie's quick speech patterns. "Stealing your man? Wes? You think Wes and I are...?" She fumbled for the right words. "You think Wes is cheating on you?"

Laurie laughed again, a bright sound. "No, Wes would never. He's as loyal as they come. But I saw how you looked at him on Thanksgiving, and I get it. He's a handsome man, smart, kind, and Lord, that mustache. I get why you'd try to sneak in there and steal him out from under me, but honestly, I'm not worried." Her eyes moved over Brett's body in an appraising way. A smug smile twitched the corners of her mouth. "Wes has always liked a more feminine type."

Brett ignored the other woman's jab. "I'm not sure I understand. Did Wes tell you that I came on to him?"

"Well, not exactly. He said you were trouble. I suppose I just assumed..." She shrugged.

"I didn't," Brett said forcefully. "I wouldn't. We work together."

"And when has that stopped anyone?" she asked with a playful wink, which made Brett wonder if Wes had told his wife about seeing Brett and Eli together at the Pickled Onion.

She hadn't spoken to Eli since Thanksgiving. Now that she worked the night shift, she barely saw him at the station. Sometimes they'd pass each other in the hall, but he always seemed to be in too much of a hurry to stop and talk, and she was fine with that. Whatever had been building between them the past few months, shattered the second he refused to take responsibility for the missing evidence.

Brett shook her head. She hadn't come over to Laurie's to talk about her love life or who she was and wasn't flirting with at the office. She'd come to find out what she could about Adam.

"So, South Carolina, huh?" Brett shifted the conversation away from her non-existent love life. "How does your son feel about that?"

"Oh, he's excited," Laurie said. "Well, excited might be the wrong word. He hasn't complained about it yet anyway. He'll be closer to his grandparents, for one thing. And I think with the death of those two kids last month, that hit him pretty hard, and it will be good to put that behind us and be somewhere without all those bad memories."

"He was friends with June and Daniel, wasn't he?" Brett already knew the answer, but was hoping Laurie would have more insight into her son's relationships.

"He and June have known each other since kindergarten." Laurie clutched both hands around her coffee cup, holding it close so the steam rolled over her face. She stared across the room with a distant look in her eyes. "Poor Shirley. I can't even imagine." A shudder rolled through her. "I keep thinking how easily it could have been Adam out there that night. If we'd stayed at the party longer, it could have been him out there on those cliffs, his body you found, his funeral to plan." She shook her head as if trying to rid herself of the awful images she'd conjured. "Honestly, I can't wait to get out of this town. There's something not right about this place. I've felt it ever since Wes moved us here after Adam was born. We should have left a long time ago."

Brett agreed with her about that, but she was more interested in the timeline of the Miller's Halloween party.

"You said if you'd stayed at the party, Adam would have been out at the cliffs?" Brett tried not to sound too interested, even though her pulse was racing the way it did when she knew she was getting close to uncovering some scrap of truth. "Why do you think that?"

"He was leaving when we got home," Laurie said. "His truck was halfway out the driveway, the little shit. Don't get me wrong, I love the boy, but he tries my patience sometimes. He wasn't supposed to be going anywhere. He was grounded, but you know how kids are at this age. He thought we'd be gone for a while and he wanted to go out trick-or-treating with his friends."

"Why did you come home early?" Brett asked.

"Bad scallops." Laurie clutched her stomach and grimaced with the memory. "Once I started throwing up, I couldn't stop. Wes got me inside, put me to bed with a barf bucket and a glass of water, and then went out to bring Adam home. If he hadn't done that, who knows what might have happened to our precious boy. So thank God for bad scallops, I suppose."

Brett laughed along with Laurie, but it was a forced sound, her mind racing, trying to connect the dots. Sweat dampened her armpits. "What time did Wes and Adam come home that night?"

"Oh, midnight? Later than that? I don't know. I was too sick to pay much attention." Her cheeks flushed red and her fingers fluttered around her neck. "I remember hearing their voices, and it was still dark. A door slammed. Then I woke up, and it was morning and someone was cooking bacon in the kitchen and I had to use the bucket again. What a nightmare. I told the Millers about it a few days later, and told them they might want to think about getting another caterer for next year's party. They said I was the only one who got sick though, so maybe the scallops had it in for me. I've never been a big shellfish fan."

"Sounds awful," Brett said, trying to keep Laurie's guard down.

The woman had been surprisingly forthcoming, more than Brett had anticipated. Laurie's version of that night contradicted her husband's, and while it opened a door to ask more questions, it wasn't quite enough to build a case. It wasn't proof. She needed something irrefutable, something Irving couldn't shrug off as coincidence.

Brett swept her eyes around the kitchen, but nothing was out of place, and she was running out of reasons to stick around. She set her cup on the counter and smiled at Laurie. "I should get going. Thanks for the coffee. Stay away from the shellfish next time, okay?"

Laurie walked her to the front door. As they passed through the living room, Brett stopped in front of the fireplace, noticing for the first time what appeared to be a very old pair of flintlock muskets mounted above the mantel. The hardware shimmered. The wood had been polished to a sheen.

"Are you a collector, too?" Laurie asked, gesturing to the muskets.

"I can appreciate good craftsmanship," Brett said.

Laurie's face brightened. "Well, then, you can't leave without seeing the Luger Wes inherited from his grandfather. It's a true one of a kind. The story Pop told was that he took it off a dead Nazi during the war. I don't know if that's true, but Wes says the gun's worth a lot regardless of where it originally came from. A real collector's item, he likes to brag about it at parties."

Brett's thoughts immediately jumped to what Kevin had told her about the ballistics report, how June was killed with a 9mm handgun, most likely a Luger. Wes owning a similar type of gun was one too many coincidences for Brett to overlook.

She offered Laurie an eager smile. "A real Nazi Luger? Wow, yes, I'd love to see it!"

Laurie bounced from the room with a delighted clap of her hands.

While Brett waited for her to return with the gun, she circled the living room, scanning the shelves, flipping through a small stack of mail, finding nothing of interest until she came to an upright piano pushed into the corner. Sitting on top of the piano on a lace doily was a small crystal vase, and inside that vase was a clutch of roses, dewy with raindrops as if they'd been clipped from the garden this morning.

Brett ran her finger over the white petals trimmed blood red. It was the same color of rose that had been left on June's body.

A floorboard creaked and Laurie stepped into the living room with empty hands and a worried look on her face. She noticed Brett admiring the roses and said, "Aren't they lovely? That particular bush has always been a surprisingly robust bloomer. All the other roses finish and wither by early October. But this one clings on for another few weeks. It never fails—every year, I'll get out my pruning shears at the end of the month and head out in the garden only to find fresh blossoms. I call it my winter miracle."

Brett nodded, her mouth too dry to speak.

Laurie spread her empty hands with a half-hearted shrug. "I hate that I got your hopes up. The gun wasn't in the safe. Sometimes Wes takes it out to clean it. I could look in the garage. Maybe he left it there."

But she made no move toward the garage door, and Brett knew Laurie wouldn't find it there even if she did go looking. She swallowed the lump in her throat. "Laurie? Has Adam ever used the Luger before? Does he have access to the safe? Does he know the code?"

Laurie's cheeks flushed red, and her smile vanished. She clutched her hands tight against her stomach, and Brett could tell by the sudden hard glint in her eyes that Laurie Harris was finally starting to put the pieces together on her own, seeing the real reason why Brett had come by the house this morning, the real reason for all her probing questions.

Her voice trembled on a knife's edge when she said, "I think it's time for you to go."

"I can help you, Laurie." Brett kept her voice steady and soft. "I can help you and I can help Adam. But you need to tell me the truth."

"I'd like you to leave. Now." It seemed southern hospitality only went so far.

Brett slipped past Laurie and out the front door, which slammed shut behind her. The lock thudded into place. Brett trotted through the rain to her car. Her pulse was racing, but it had nothing to do with the short distance she'd traveled from porch to curb.

The missing scarf, the roses on the piano, the Luger that wasn't in the safe where it was supposed to be—Brett couldn't quite piece together the details of how it all unfolded, but she knew now, without a doubt in her mind, that Adam had been at Deadman's Point the night June and Daniel were killed. And that Wes was lying to protect his son.

CHAPTER 34

When Brett arrived at the station Wednesday night to clock in for her next shift, she found Irving waiting for her in the locker room.

"I'm glad you're here," she said. "We need to talk about the case. I went by Laurie's yesterday—"

"Shut up." He grabbed her arm and yanked her out into the hallway.

Irving was a big man and his grip was strong. Brett struggled a few seconds before giving up and allowing herself to be dragged into the last of the three interview rooms. Once inside, he released her.

She took a step back, rubbing her arm. "That's probably going to leave a mark."

"You made me look like a fool," he snapped.

She crossed her arms over her chest, waiting for him to explain.

"I talked to Wes like you wanted me to." Irving loosened his tie, a pale pink fabric with a long-legged white crane in mid-flight. A bead of sweat trickled down his forehead. "I asked him about the ballistic reports first, because what you told me the other day and the information I got was contradictory."

"How so?" she asked.

"The report that finally came through from the medical examiner's office said the bullets matched. A single 9mm was responsible for the deaths of June and Daniel. The bullets were fired from the same gun we found at Cadden's place."

"No, that's impossible. Kevin was very clear—"

"Did you get his signed statement?" Irving interrupted. He leaned forward, grabbing one of the metal chairs for support. "Did you see the report? Did he show you the bullets?"

"No," she said. "Like I told you, we were out at a scene."

"So you don't actually know if he was telling the truth, do you?"

"Why would he lie?"

"I don't know. Why does anyone lie?" Irving's fingers tightened on the back of the chair.

"There has to be some mistake. Maybe they faxed over the wrong report? That has to be it. I mean, Kevin was very clear with me about the bullets being from two separate guns, so if you got a report that says differently, then I don't have any idea what's going on."

"That much is obvious." He let out a sour laugh as he shoved away from the chair and started to pace the small room. "Wes called up Charlie while I was in his office. Kevin was on the call, too. It was all four of us there on speaker phone, and Kevin made it very clear that he'd never said anything to you about a ballistics report."

"What?" The room grew hot as the walls crowded closer. "He's lying."

"Then let me ask the same question you asked me. Why would he lie?"

"Wes must have told him to keep quiet about the real report." It was the only thing that made sense. "Someone threatened him."

"Do you know how crazy you sound right now?" Irving stared at her in disbelief.

"I'm not crazy," she said. "You know I'm not. Look, I was at

Wes' house yesterday. I talked to his wife. She confirmed that they left the Miller's party early. She got sick off some scallops or something. She said when they came home, Adam was driving away from the house, and Wes went after him. Think about it, Irving. What if Adam made it to Deadman's Point that night? What if something happened out there? What if something went wrong? Wes Harris owns a Luger, Irving. It's a family heirloom. Laurie was going to show it to me, but she said it wasn't in the safe. That can't be a coincidence."

Irving threw his hands up, exasperated. "You really are trying to get yourself fired, aren't you? Why don't you do us all a favor and quit already?"

She took a breath, about to argue with him more, but something kept her quiet. The fleeting thought that Irving knew more than he was saying, that someone had threatened him, too. He looked scared right now, not angry.

He sighed and shook his head. "Yeah, I suppose that's not going to happen anytime soon, is it?" He rubbed his eyes and when he looked at her again, the fear was gone, replaced by a steel-edged resolve. "Okay, fine. Here's how this is going to work from here on out. You're going to leave this case alone. Got it? You're going to come in and do your fucking job the way you're fucking told to do it, and you're going to leave me alone to do mine."

He flung open the interview room door so hard, it slammed against the outside wall.

Brett waited a few minutes, trying to slow her breathing and the rapid skip of her heart. She brushed her fingers over the place where Irving had grabbed her and winced at the flare of pain. What hurt more than the bruise forming on her arm, though, was the realization that Irving had finally picked a side, and it wasn't hers.

Dispatch sent Brett out on so many bullshit calls during her Wednesday night shift, she barely had time to stop for a pee break. If it weren't for the fact that she was crisscrossing the city so often she had to stop for gas twice, she would have had to piss in an empty bottle. The calls were varied: suspicious persons, blaring alarms, abandoned vehicles, bumps in the night. She responded to everything they sent her to, but no matter what the call was, whenever she got there she found empty buildings, deserted alleyways, no cars matching the description they gave over the radio, and no people waiting to speak to a uniformed officer.

By the seventh empty parking lot, she understood what was happening. They were treating her like a threat, hoping that if they sent her out on enough bullshit calls, she'd give up and roll over, turn in her badge and walk away.

They couldn't get rid of her that easily.

When dispatch called with another report of a suspicious persons in a neighborhood she'd driven through not even an hour earlier, she kept her voice bright and chipper when she radioed her response, "On my way. Keep 'em coming, boys."

By the end of her shift, Brett could barely hold her eyes open. The five cups of coffee she'd had during her shift had burned through her quickly, leaving her nerves frayed, and her mind anxious. So when she pulled into the driveway of her house and saw the front door standing wide open, it was natural for her thoughts to jump to a similar scene last month when she came home to find Amma being carted out on a stretcher, half the kitchen up in flames.

She parked the car crooked in the driveway and ran through the front door, shouting for Amma, not caring that it was still early enough for the neighbors to be asleep. Pistol raced from the kitchen and started jumping on her legs, yapping excitedly, matching her energy. There was no smell of smoke, no alarms going off, no paramedics in the house. But there was no sign of Amma either.

Brett found the young woman she paid to watch Amma in the kitchen, perched on the counter top with the phone pressed to her ear, twisting the cord around one finger, giggling and kicking her feet in the air. She made a face when she saw Brett and then spoke to the person on the phone, "Trevor? Yeah. I have to go."

Before she'd even hung up, Brett demanded, "Where's my grandmother?"

The twenty-something rolled her eyes and slid off the counter with a shrug. "She took Pistol for a walk on the beach."

"You didn't go with her?"

The girl looked incredulous. "It's raining."

"Pistol's right here." Brett lifted the little dog off the floor.

"Oh," the girl said.

"Oh? That's all you have to say?" Brett marched to the french doors and jerked them open.

Pistol wriggled to be put down. She set him on the porch, and he trotted back into the comfort of the warm house.

Brett didn't see Amma anywhere on the beach or the dock. She walked around the side of the house and even checked inside the boathouse, but Amma wasn't hiding in there either. The *Anita Horizon* was still moored in its dry dock. Brett rushed back inside and grabbed the phone to call Henry, but before she had a chance to finish dialing, someone was pounding on the front door.

Pistol started barking. Brett dropped the phone into its cradle and hurried into the living room. The pounding continued, insistent. Pistols' barks grew louder and more frantic. Brett scooped up the dog, told him to hush, and yanked open the door.

Wes Harris stood on the front porch with a tense smile on his face. "I found something of yours."

He stepped to the side and swept his hand theatrically toward his car parked in the driveway. Amma sat in the front passenger seat. Her silver hair flew in wisps around her face. She blinked up at the house, and Brett could tell from her expression that she was having an episode. How bad of one, Brett wouldn't know until she talked to her.

Brett set Pistol on the hall rug and ran to Wes' car. He trailed after her with his hands shoved in his pockets, whistling a bright tune.

The car was still running, the heater turned on full blast. Brett opened the passenger door.

"Amma? Are you alright? Are you hurt?"

The older woman blinked at Brett with a look that was becoming all too familiar. Amma didn't recognize her. Brett could see it in her eyes. The question mark, the fear. Brett swallowed down a sob. It would do neither of them any good for her to get upset. Amma needed her to be calm. Brett reached to help her out of the car. She was wearing pale blue capris pants and a light sweater set along with a pair of huarache sandals. Clothes that were better suited for the middle of summer than the middle of December. Her hair, her clothes, her skin, everything was damp from the spitting rain.

"I found her on my way in to work this morning." Wes leaned against the hood of his car. He flashed his teeth, a knowing glint in his eyes. "She was wandering near Egret's Park."

Egret's Park was almost five miles by car from the house on Bayshore Drive, closer to three if you kept to the shoreline. But it wasn't an easy walk. The stretch of beach between the house and Egret's Park was narrow and rocky, cluttered with driftwood and dangerous spots. Go at the wrong time and a person could easily be swept out to sea by a sneaker wave.

"I guess I got a little turned around, that's all," Amma said with an apologetic shrug.

Brett took Amma's elbow and started to walk her back to the house. Wes trailed after them.

"You're lucky I drove by when I did. We get a lot of unsavory characters moving through that part of town. Drifters and the like."

"Thank you for bringing her home." The words were sharp on her tongue as she reached the front door and pushed Amma inside.

"Oh, I was happy to. I know how important family is, and I hate to think what could have happened to her if I hadn't come along." There was a spark of violence in his eyes when he said it.

He shoved his hands into his pockets and walked back to his car, whistling the whole length of the driveway. He paused with one hand on the car's roof and called back to Brett who hadn't moved from the porch. "Oh, by the way, Laurie told me to tell you hello, and thanks again for returning her scarf."

Again, the flash of teeth. Again, a spark of something dangerous.

He touched his fingers to his forehead in a half-salute. "Have a good day, Buchanan."

He opened the car door, got in, and drove away.

Brett slammed the front door closed and leaned back against it. She could hear Amma upstairs, rustling around in her bedroom. She closed her eyes, taking one breath and then another, trying to figure out what the hell just happened.

Wes Harris hadn't brought Amma home as a favor to her. Plain and simple, he wanted Brett to know that he was watching, that he would always be watching. He was flexing, telling her to get in line, keep quiet, and do as she was told. Be a good girl and look the other way.

"Who was that?"

Brett had forgotten about the sitter. The girl was leaning in the doorway, her hip popped to one side, her jaw working over a wad of pink bubble gum.

"You can go home now," Brett said.

"You haven't paid me yet?"

Brett dug a twenty dollar bill out of her pocket, shoved it into the girl's hands, and pushed her out the door. She closed her eyes and leaned back against the door again, feeling the press of the solid wood beneath her fingertips, waiting for the buzzing in her head to subside. When it did, she went and looked for Amma.

Her grandmother was upstairs in her bedroom, curled into a tight ball beneath a heavy quilt, shivering from cold or fear. Brett wasn't sure which.

"Amma?" Brett laid her hand on the bed near her grandmother's foot, but not touching her for fear that she'd startle her or send her spiraling deeper into confusion. "Are you okay? Did that man hurt you? Did he do anything to you?"

"He brought me home," Amma said.

"You walked all the way to Egret's Park?"

"No," Amma said. "A nice man drove me there."

"Wes?"

"Who's Wes?"

"The man you were just with."

"Frank? No, he's at work, dear. We'll tell him when he gets home."

"Amma, please. Try and remember. Did that man drive you to the park today? Or did you walk there?" Brett moved her hand to cover Amma's foot. "It's important."

She needed to know what Wes was capable of, how far he was willing to go to protect his family and his own reputation.

"I'm tired." Amma rolled away from Brett's touch. "I think I'm going to close my eyes for a bit, if that's alright with you, dear."

Brett left Amma alone and went back downstairs. She stared out the back door, watching the ocean pummel the shore. She was in over her head and needed help, but she didn't know where to turn. The state police would laugh her right out on her ass if all she brought them were theories, suspicions, and anecdotal evidence. She needed proof. Something irrefutable. She needed to talk to Kevin Park again.

Brett's opportunity came three days later on a Saturday during Crestwood's annual Christmas Bazaar.

Downtown was a crush of people and cars. Main Street was blocked off and filled with booths and families doing last minute shopping. A carol group wandered through the crowd, their a cappella voices rising above the clamor of energetic conversations. The air smelled of fresh cut pine trees and gingerbread.

The luckier patrol officers were assigned to Main Street crowd control where they chatted with kids, passed out Junior Sheriffs badges, and made sure no one got too drunk off the eggnog Mary Andress was serving from her cafe, Crumbles and Cakes.

Brett was assigned to one of the parking lots. She sloshed through a muddy field, waving cars to empty spots, making sure traffic kept moving and no one got into a fender bender. It was bullshit work given to rookies or anyone who was in the dog house with the chief. A full day on your feet, sucking exhaust fumes, trying to teach idiots how to park, getting yelled at by people who thought they deserved to jump the line because their engine growled louder than everyone else's. Brett had been at it only an hour and already two cars had bumped into her leg. On accident, supposedly. She could feel a blister starting to form on her big toe. Her boots and slacks were sloppy with mud.

She'd thought the crowds would be kept away by the weatherman forecasting sleet, but the cars kept coming, filled with people perhaps panicked by the fact that they had ten days left to get their Christmas shopping done, or maybe after a month and a half of nothing but rain, they were simply sick of being stuck inside.

Brett waved another car down the aisle, pointing at the next empty spot. She scanned the lot. It was almost full. Another twenty cars and they'd have to start sending people to overflow.

On the other side of the lot, she saw Kevin Park getting out of a small sedan. He opened a pink umbrella and went around to the passenger side to help a young woman out of the vehicle. They were smiling at each other with the shine of new love. Kevin put his arm around the woman, holding her close under the shelter of the umbrella as they walked toward Main Street.

Over the past few days, Brett had left several messages at the morgue, asking Kevin to call her back, hoping she could get some answers from him about the differing ballistics reports. Yesterday, she'd stopped by the hospital during her shift, but the offices were locked and the lights turned off. She'd been planning to stop by his house on her next day off, but this would be faster.

Brett got the attention of the other officer working with her, a young kid who'd started a few months after her. He looked like he was barely out of high school, but seemed eager to find his footing in the department and rise in the ranks.

"I need to take a bathroom break," she told him, and the kid didn't question her because even though they were both out here doing this shit job in the mud, she'd worn her badge longer, and that still meant something.

She hurried after Kevin, catching him as he was about to step onto crowded Main Street.

When she touched his elbow and said his name, he flinched and spun around with his fists clenched, the umbrella lifted like he would use it to protect himself and the woman he was with, if that's what it came down to. The remnants of a nasty bruise were visible on Kevin's face below his left eye, a purple scuff in the center, fading green and yellow around the edges.

Brett dropped her hand and took a step back. "Who did that to you?"

Kevin relaxed slightly, brushing his fingers over the bruise. "No one. I fell."

The woman darted a panicked look in his direction.

"Kevin, you can tell me the truth," Brett said.

He spat out a laugh. "Yes, because that worked out so well for me the last time."

"Why did you change your story?" Brett asked. "About the ballistics report?"

He flinched again, then turned to the woman and gave her a reassuring smile. "Sarah, why don't you go find us some eggnog?"

He handed Sarah the umbrella and nudged her in the direction of the bustling bazaar, but she held her ground, setting her mouth in a thin, defiant line. He bent so their foreheads were touching and stroked her cheek with his thumb. "I'll be fine. Please. Mary's eggnog is my favorite, and she runs out every year. I'll catch up to you in a few minutes."

Kevin watched as the crowd folded around Sarah, then he turned to Brett with a scowl. "I was wrong, okay? I got it mixed up. The reports, I mean. The bullets came from the same gun, from a Luger, like Charlie's report says. I was looking at something else, at a different report from a different case. I got confused, that's all."

"I don't believe you," Brett challenged.

"You don't have to believe me," Kevin said. "It's the truth. Whatever report was faxed over to your office is the right one."

"Bullshit."

His hands curled to fists, and a muscle in his jaw clenched. "She's my wife, you know," he said, looking toward Main Street where the woman and the pink umbrella had disappeared from sight. "I still get a kick out of saying that. My wife. We've only been married six months."

"Congratulations," Brett said, but there was no enthusiasm in her voice.

"I didn't think I could love anyone as much as I love her," he said. "She's my whole world. I don't know what I would do if something happened to her."

"They threatened her?" Brett lowered her voice as a family of four passed nearby. "Is that what happened? Who was it? Was it Wes Harris? One of the other officers?"

Kevin continued to focus his gaze on the shifting crowd. "I didn't ask for this, you know. I was just trying to do my job."

"Tell me what happened," Brett said. "I can help."

"Can you?" His gaze shifted to the badge on her chest, the gun on her hip. "Just because you're one of them, doesn't mean they won't come after you, too."

"There are other people we can contact, other departments that can step in and help," she said. "If you can get me the bullets, I can send them to the state lab and have them run the tests again. I can get internal affairs involved."

"I can't." Kevin lowered his gaze to the ground.

"I can protect you." Even as she said it, she knew it was a hollow promise, that short of following him around all day and night, there would be nothing she could do to keep him safe.

"No, it's not that." He swiped his hand through his hair, shaking out raindrops "I don't have access to the evidence anymore."

It made sense. Once tested, the bullets would have been sent back to the station, logged, and stored in the evidence room until they brought a suspect to trial.

But Kevin wasn't done talking. "You know how it goes. All that moving around between labs, evidence changing hands...it's hard to keep track of everything."

"Are you saying what I think you're saying?" She stared at him, but he refused to look at her. Choosing instead to watch people shuffle past carrying packages and bags to their cars.

With a heavy sigh, he finally said, "I'm saying that if you went looking for those bullets, you wouldn't find them." He snapped his gaze to her, a warning in his eyes. "And I'm saying there's no use pushing this any further, unless you want to walk out to your car one morning on your way to work and find Danny Cyrus waiting for you."

The name sent a shock through Brett. "What does Danny have to do with this?"

Kevin raised his eyebrows and gestured to the bruise under his eye. Before Brett could ask for more details, his gaze shifted to where Sarah had reappeared at the edge of the crowd holding two cups of eggnog.

"If you'll excuse me." He slid past Brett. "I have some Christmas shopping to do."

When he reached his wife, he took one of the paper cups, then leaned over and kissed her cheek. Slipping his arm around her waist, he pulled her tight against him, as if afraid someone might come and steal her away.

CHAPTER 35

The Christmas Bazaar started to wrap up at 4:00 PM, but it took another two hours for Main Street to clear and the booths to pack up and go home. Then another hour to get the heavy traffic cleared out. By the time Brett got back to the station it was well past 7:00 PM and already dark as midnight. She didn't think she'd ever get used to how quickly night fell during this time of year, how slow the sun was to rise in the mornings. These long nights settled cold and dark in her bones, twisting every shadow to a monster, every whisper to a terrible secret.

As Brett changed out of her muddy uniform into black pants, a black hooded sweatshirt, and a dark blue rain jacket, she thought about what Kevin had told her about Danny Cyrus. He hadn't come right out and said it, but the implications were clear: the bruise on Kevin's face had come from Danny and was meant as a warning to Kevin to keep his mouth shut about the contradictory ballistics reports. What Brett wanted to know was if Danny was working on his own or if someone had paid him to rough Kevin up a bit. There was only one way to find out.

Brett readjusted her holster so it was hidden under her rain jacket. She smoothed her hair into a ponytail and pulled her hood over her head. Before she left the station, she called the house to check on Amma.

Henry and his wife had accompanied her to the bazaar today since Brett had to work, and now they were together at the house, enjoying a warm bowl of soup and fresh bread for dinner. Amma sounded happy, content.

"Let me talk to Henry?" Brett asked.

A few seconds later, Henry's deep voice came on the line. He told her they were keeping a bowl warm for her.

"That's why I'm calling," she said. "One of the guys called in sick. They want me to cover for him." The lie slipped from her mouth too easily. "Could you stay with her tonight?"

After last week, Brett had fired the twenty-something girl who clearly didn't want the job anyway. When questioned, the girl couldn't remember if Amma had gone for a walk alone, or if Wes had come to the house first and driven off with her. Two very different scenarios with two very different repercussions, but the sitter had simply shrugged and popped her gum and said, *I can't be expected to watch her all the time.*

Brett had shown her the door and told her don't bother coming back. She hadn't had time to find a replacement yet and had been calling in favors with Henry again.

"There are clean sheets in the linen closet," she said, even though he hadn't agreed to stay the night yet. "Please, Henry. Just this one time."

He sighed, but agreed. "I'm eating your soup, though."

"Deal."

The sleet the forecasters had promised was coming down in painful shards. Brett raced across the parking lot to her VW with her hand lifted to protect her face.

She stopped in at the Blue Whale Diner first, to refuel with a grilled cheese sandwich, tomato soup, and a hot cup of coffee. She had a feeling it was going to be a long night, and she needed all the extra energy she could get. An hour later, Brett was driving east toward Lake Chastain to see if she could get some answers out of Danny Cyrus.

She'd brought up the man's name as a person of interest early on in the investigation because of his criminal associations with Daniel Yoon's father, but both Eli and Irving had told her not to go poking around Cyrus' property and to let the chief handle it. She'd assumed that at some point Stan Harcourt had talked to Danny and come up empty-handed, which was why no one had mentioned him again. But maybe Stan never talked to him. Or maybe he had, and whatever Danny told him, he decided to keep to himself.

Brett didn't trust Danny Cyrus. And she didn't trust Stan Harcourt. Sadly, she wouldn't have been surprised to find out that Stan had called in a favor and sent Danny to threaten Kevin, though she could only speculate as to why Stan, Wes, and the rest of the squad would be so desperate to bury the ballistics report. It didn't look good—that's all she knew. God, she hoped she was wrong about all of this. She wanted there to be some other explanation besides corrupt cops and conspiracies.

It took Brett longer to find the road to Danny's trailer in the dark than it would have during the day. The rain had let up some, but now mist clung to the low spots, obscuring details. She found it eventually, and eased her VW onto the packed gravel, careful to avoid the biggest potholes and muddy spots. The last thing she wanted to do was get stuck out here and have to call for a tow.

Halfway up the road, she pulled the VW into a wide spot on the shoulder and parked. She tightened her rain hood and touched her gun, as if it were a talisman to protect her. She wasn't going to get the truth about what was going on with this case by asking politely. It was time she started playing by their rules.

She got out of the car and started walking toward the sound of voices clamoring in the distance. Above the pattering of raindrops against bare branches, a loud cry went up and then came the rumble of laughter and excited chatter.

Danny's weekend fight club was still up and running, which shouldn't have surprised Brett, but did. She thought it had been shut down last year. Danny's relationship with the chief clearly came with perks.

Brett pushed through tangled branches until she broke into a wide clearing where a large group of men gathered in a loose circle, churning the mud with their heavy boots. Some of the men wore rain gear. Others were bare-chested, their rain-damp skin pale and glistening in the wane light shining from a trio of propane gas lamps sitting on stumps outside the main circle. The men stood shoulder to shoulder, all facing a large space in the center where two fighters dodged and darted, swinging bare-knuckled punches at each other. The men's bodies were the ropes. The earth was the mat.

The spectators clamored and jeered and slipped money into the hands of a kid who barely looked old enough to sign a contract, let alone be a bookie for an illegal fight.

The fighters moved around each other warily, then lunged, becoming locked in a violent embrace. Their movements stuttered in the lamplight, like the flickering of an old movie reel. A few seconds later, the two men broke apart, and the crowd let out a roar as the taller of the two swung his fist over and down, connecting with the shorter man's temple and dropping him to his knees. More shouting echoed through the dark, along with some groans of disappointment as the taller man was deemed the winner.

The dim light from the lanterns twisted everything into a strange kaleidoscope, melting the men's faces into shadowy masks that made it impossible for Brett to tell if there was anyone here she knew. Danny had to be mixed up in that crowd somewhere, but she couldn't see him. The men were so busy watching the fight, no one had noticed her lurking in the shadows at the edge of the clearing. As a new set of fighters entered the ring, Brett took a small step forward, trying to get a better look at the men's faces.

Behind her a branch cracked, and Brett started to reach for her gun, but she didn't move fast enough. Someone clamped down on her arm and jerked her backward. Another arm slipped around her chest, holding her still. She felt the man's heartbeat against her shoulder blades, his heat pulsing through his clothes.

"Are you here to fight or bet?" Danny Cyrus' smoky breath poured over her. "Those are your two options. We don't allow lookie-loos."

She struggled against his choking embrace. He released her long enough to spin her around so they were standing face-to-face, but his hands clamped down on her arms so she couldn't buck away from him or grab for her gun. They were so close she couldn't focus on anything but his eyes. Hard, copper stones with onyx black centers. He smelled of rain and mud and bitter tobacco.

A smile creased the corners of his eyes. "You lost?"

"I need to talk to you." Her breath puffed white between them.

"You know where I live. Come around during the day like a normal person." He started to shove her back through the woods where she'd left her car.

She dug in her heels, fighting him. "If I came knocking, you wouldn't answer your door."

"Don't know until you try."

"Kevin Park," she blurted out, and the name was enough to make Danny pause.

"Who?"

"You know who. He's the assistant county medical examiner. Dark hair. Young. Wears glasses."

"What about him?"

With a hard wrench, Brett pulled herself from Danny's grasp.

She backed away from him and reached for her gun. His eyes tracked her hand, and he shook his head, tutting at her. "I wouldn't if I were you."

He flipped open his jacket, showing her a sawed-off shotgun hanging from what looked like a homemade holster strapped around his waist. The shells looked big enough to blow the head off a cougar. Or a human. He kept his hand on the grip, daring her to make the first move, as he said, "Funny. I thought after you found out what happened to Margot you'd burn rubber trying to get the hell out of this town."

Danny Cyrus had been the main suspect in Margot's murder for over a decade, and though he was ultimately taken off the suspect list, he'd spent the past twenty years building a reputation for himself as someone not to be messed with.

His eyes moved up and down the length of her, as his mouth twisted into a smirk. "If you're sticking around for good, then I think it's time you and I got a few things straight."

"I want to know why you hit Kevin, why you threatened him," she said. "Did he owe you money or were you doing a favor for someone in the department?"

Danny's smile grew wider. "Why? Did he file a complaint?"

"Would that make a difference?" She challenged him.

"I'm going to say this to you once, so listen good, because the next time I find you trespassing on my property, I'm not going to be feeling so patient as I am tonight." Danny devoured the distance between them. Flecks of spit landed on her cheeks as he talked. "Don't go swimming in the ocean if you don't want to get eaten by sharks. There's still time for you to get out of the water, Brett, and if I were you, that's exactly what I'd do. I'd swim as fast as I could back to shore. Or whatever shitty little swampland you crawled out of."

He shoved past her, moving out of the shadows and into the clearing.

The men were starting to circle up again, placing their bets on a new pair of fighters.

Brett stayed in the shadows a few more minutes, watching the fight. Danny Cyrus circled the edge of the crowd, slapping backs and giving high-fives, throwing his head back in a laugh, as if he were the king of these woods, as if nothing and no one could touch him. And maybe they couldn't, not if he was under Stan Harcourt's protection.

Brett didn't know how a man like Danny had enmeshed himself so deeply into the department that he now somehow got to exist outside the bounds of the law, but it didn't sit right with her. It never would. No matter how much power a person had or who he knew or what he felt he was owed, actions should have consequences.

She thought about this as she walked quickly back through the woods to her car. What she was thinking about doing next was definitely questionable in terms of ethics and legality and went against everything she'd been taught as a police officer, but if the ends justified the means, did that settle the matter? She wasn't sure, but right or wrong, if she were caught out here tonight, she would accept the consequences.

After digging a pair of wool gloves and a flashlight with questionable battery life from the glove box, Brett circled around the clearing, back through the woods, to a different, smaller meadow where a single-wide trailer rested on concrete blocks. None of the lights were on inside, but Brett still waited in the shadows of the old growth fir trees that grew around the meadow until she was certain no one else was here. After a few minutes, she pulled the gloves on and crept through the dark, past Danny's motorcycle and a stack of firewood. The steps creaked underneath her as she opened the trailer door and slipped inside.

She moved quickly, snapping on the flashlight and working her way from one end of the trailer to the other. For some reason, she thought Danny's living quarters would be a mess of cigarette ash and rotten food, but the place was immaculate and smelled of lemon cleaner. She looked in cupboards and under cushions, not really sure what it was she was hoping to find. Kevin wasn't going to file charges against Danny for assault. Even if Brett could talk him into it, Danny would probably wiggle out of the charges somehow. She needed something to connect Danny to this case—one small thing, some bit of physical proof that she could bring to the state police.

The flashlight flickered. Brett slapped it with her hand, and it brightened again. She stepped through the doorway of the last place she hadn't looked yet, Danny's bedroom, and let out a startled yelp. Her hand automatically reached for her gun, pulling it from the holster, as her heart leaped into her throat.

She aimed the barrel at the grizzly bear looming in the corner. It stood on its hind feet, claws raised to swipe. The mouth was open in a silent roar, fanged teeth as long as her forearm, sharp enough to tear her apart. It's marble eyes glinted in the beam of her flashlight, and that's when her rational brain finally caught up with her survival instincts. The bear made no sounds. It didn't move. It didn't even blink. The animal was stuffed.

Nervous laughter slipped from Brett's mouth before she could stop herself. She dropped her gun back into the holster and pressed her hand to her chest, trying to catch her breath and get her heart to slow to a reasonable pace. Leave it to Danny to fit a seven-foot taxidermy bear in this cramped room that was barely big enough for the king-sized mattress he slept on.

Even though the bear was harmless, Brett still couldn't get used to being in the room with it. She swept the flashlight over the taxidermy beast one more time and that's when the beam caught on something stuffed inside the bear's open mouth.

Brett took a step closer.

The gun had been shoved between the bear's sharp yellow teeth in a macabre display. It was a nice-looking gun with a slim barrel and an angled grip. Someone in a previous life had obviously cared for it, buffing the hardware, polishing the grip, but how it had ended up here in Danny's trailer, propped inside the gaping mouth of a taxidermy grizzly, Brett could only guess.

Carefully, she wiggled the gun free and turned it over in her hands. She'd seen a German Luger before and was certain that's what this gun was. Whether or not it was the same gun missing from Wes Harris' safe, a cherished heirloom passed down from grandfather to grandson, was another matter entirely. But if it was the same gun, how did Danny end up with it? More importantly, was she finally in possession of the weapon that killed June Newmark? She'd need to take it with her and ask the state lab to run some tests before she would know for sure. And somehow she had to do all that without Wes Harris and Stan Harcourt finding out about it.

She tucked the gun into her jacket pocket and turned to search the bed and the small nightstand beside it. A set of keys with a fishing bobbin attached to the ring rested on top of a stack of porn magazines on the nightstand. There was nothing in the drawer, nothing under the mattress, but if the gun she'd found was what she thought it was, she wouldn't need anything else.

As she exited the bedroom, the metal steps leading into the trailer popped loudly, and then the front door swung open.

CHAPTER 36

Brett looked around the trailer for somewhere to hide, but it was too late. A shadowy figure stepped through the front door. She unholstered her service weapon and widened her stance.

The man entering the trailer swung his head toward her and barked a question. "What the hell are you doing in here?"

"Eli?" Brett lowered her weapon so it was pointed at the floor instead of his chest, but kept it in her hand, uncertain if she could trust him.

"I saw you at the fight," he said. "I saw you talking to Danny. Are you trying to get yourself killed?"

Eli stepped closer to her and flung his hand at the gun still gripped at her side. "Put that thing away. Jesus, Brett. What are you going to do? Shoot me?"

He grabbed her arm and hustled her out of the trailer.

"If Danny knew you were snooping through his shit…" Eli didn't finish the threat.

Once they were in the safety of the trees, Eli let go of Brett's arm. He looked her up and down, then asked, "Aren't you supposed to be on duty right now?"

"I worked at the bazaar today," she said. "Fourteen hours straight."

"So what the hell are you doing here? You should be home in your pjs, drinking a glass of wine."

"I could ask you the same thing." She scowled at him and folded her arms across her chest. "I didn't know you were a gambler."

"I'm not," he said with a sheepish look on his face.

He was dressed in loose-fitting, black pants and a white tank top that looked gray in the dark. Mud splattered his chest and arms. At least, Brett thought it was mud. There was a smudge of something above his right eye, but when she reached to wipe it away, he flinched as if hurt. She realized the smudge was blood, that he'd been cut.

"You were fighting?" She stepped back from him. "Do you come out here a lot?"

His silence was all the answer she needed.

"Why didn't you tell me?" she asked.

"There's a lot you don't know about me." The way he said it felt like a threat.

She shook her head and took another step back, feeling anxious now to return to the safety of her car.

"Don't look at me like that," Eli said, matching her step for step. "Like what?"

"Like I'm the bad guy. I'm not going to hurt you. Brett—" He sighed and stopped moving toward her. He held out his hands, loose and non-threatening. "I know you're mad at me. I get it, but I'm not someone you have to be afraid of."

"He came to my house," Brett said. "Wes did. On Thursday morning. He said he found Amma walking alone in Egret's Park and he was doing me a favor bringing her home, but the way he said it, the way it happened...I don't trust him, Eli. I think he's covering up his son's involvement in June and Daniel's deaths. And I don't know how deep you're in with him, but I thought you should know that he threatened me. He threatened Amma. And I think he sent

Danny to beat up Kevin, too. So forgive me if I don't exactly trust you because if these are the kind of people you're loyal to—Wes and Danny—if this is what you're doing in your free time—" She waved her hand in the direction of the clearing where faint shouts could be heard drifting through the dark. "Then, yes, I think I have every reason to be scared."

The look Eli gave her was strange. Hurt, surprise, and anger shifted across his features until he settled on a decision.

"Come with me." He closed the distance between them and grabbed her arm again.

"I'm not going anywhere with you." She tried to shake him off, but his grip tightened.

"You want answers, don't you?"

She nodded.

"Then come with me. It's not safe to talk here." He looked around as if the trees surrounding them were listening to every word.

Brett and Eli drove in separate cars to Deadman's Point. It was the only way Brett felt comfortable following him anywhere.

They parked side by side near the old dock, under a weak street lamp. As soon as Brett climbed into the passenger side of Eli's car and shut the door, he started in on a lecture. "You really shouldn't have been out in those woods tonight."

"Neither should you," she snapped back.

"You got lucky."

"If you brought me out here to give me a dressing down, then I'm going home." She reached for the door handle.

"Wait." Eli's hands tightened around the steering wheel. He stared straight out the windshield when he said, "Daniel shot June."

The words rang in Brett's head. She stared into the inky-black night. It was impossible to tell where the ocean ended and the sky began. Six weeks ago, two kids had been shot not even a half-mile walk from where they sat now. Two kids were dead, and it felt even more senseless tonight than when Brett first found June's body.

"Daniel shot June," she repeated the words, testing them out. It was a theory they'd worked with early in the case, one they'd set aside after finding Daniel's body. "If Daniel shot June, then who shot Daniel?"

Eli's profile was a sharp silhouette against the orange glow of the street lamp.

He closed his eyes and lowered his head. "Try and understand. It was dark. Daniel had a gun. He'd shot someone, Brett." He lifted his head, swinging his gaze toward her. "A girl was dead, and he was afraid Adam would be next."

"Wes?" Brett spat the detective sergeant's name out like a bitter seed. "Wes shot Daniel?"

"What would you have done?" Eli's voice turned defensive. "If you'd walked into a situation like that? There's a girl bleeding out on the ground and your kid's being threatened by a man with a gun."

"I'd hardly describe Daniel as a man," Brett said. "He was seventeen. He was still a kid."

"He had a gun."

"And that justifies shooting him in the back?"

A furrow wrinkled Eli's brow as he shook his head. "No, Wes said Daniel was charging him. That he was attacking. He was very clear about that. It was self-defense."

"I saw the gunshot wound." Brett gripped the seat, digging her fingernails into the worn leather. "We both did. You were standing right there on that dock with me when they pulled his body from the water. And now you're going to sit here and tell me it was self-defense? How can shooting a kid in the back be self-defense? It can't. You know it can't. Daniel was running away."

Eli shook his head harder, refusing to agree with her assessment. "His body was mangled from being so long in the water. The decomp was significant. There's no way you would be able to tell what actually happened by looking at him the way we did."

"Kevin confirmed what I saw," she insisted. "He told me the bullet struck Daniel in the back, that it went through his heart before slamming into his breast bone. Kevin said Daniel was some distance away from the shooter before he was gunned down. You're really going to sit there and keep lying to me about all of this? You're going to sit there and try to convince me Daniel Yoon wasn't running away? When I saw with my own two eyes, when I know damn well what happened."

Eli's expression darkened. "I know Wes. He's been my supervisor since I signed on. At least he was until his promotion. So yes, I'm absolutely certain that he would not have shot someone who was running away."

"Okay," Brett said, willing to talk this through. "Let's say it happened like you said it happened. Let's say Wes walked into this terrible scenario where there's a kid wielding a gun, and another kid shot and bleeding, and Adam, what was Adam doing during all of this?"

"He was down on the ground with June, trying to keep her alive."

"Okay, so Daniel's what? Waving the gun around? Pointing it at someone?"

"He was pointing it at Adam. Wes said when he got out of his car, he could hear Daniel shouting, 'I'm going to kill you, I'm going to fucking kill you.' His survival instincts kicked in. He did what he's been trained to do. You know how quickly these things happen. Seconds, Brett, not even. That's how long he had to figure out what the hell was going on and decide. Life or death. His life, his son's life, or Daniel's? He did what was necessary to protect himself and to protect Adam."

She could picture it. The shadows strangling the night, making it hard to see who was threatening whom, who needed protecting. Adam down on the ground, trying to keep his friend from bleeding out. Daniel standing above him, waving a gun, threatening words spewing from his mouth, brimming violence. If that's the way it happened, if that was the truth, then yes, Brett could understand the choice to shoot. She could even see how a scenario like this could have led to Daniel being shot in the back. But what she didn't understand was everything that came after. If Daniel was the aggressor in this situation, if he was the one who shot first, why throw the body in the ocean after? Why work so hard to cover up the truth of Adam and Wes' involvement?

"I don't get it," she pressed. "When Daniel was down, when he was no longer a danger to anyone, why didn't Wes call it in? He should have called it in. He should have told the chief immediately, turned over his badge and gun and waited for an independent investigation to decide if he made the right choice. But he didn't. You can see how that makes it hard for me to believe a word you're saying?"

"He panicked," Eli said. "He wasn't thinking straight. The gun Daniel was holding, turns out it belongs to Wes. It's a family heirloom or something. Somehow Adam had gotten it out of the safe and brought it to the peninsula that night. He said that he was meeting his friends for a séance, but that he was scared of being out at the ruins after dark, so he brought the gun for protection. He said he got there late, that he wasn't expecting Daniel to be there. According to Adam, Daniel's a creep. He was stalking June, wouldn't leave the poor girl alone. When Adam got to the headland, he found Daniel attacking June, trying to rape her. He took the gun out and told Daniel to stop. Daniel went nuts. Charged him. They grappled, but Daniel's the bigger kid and he got his hand around the gun. I don't think anyone meant to shoot June. The gun went off and June was in the path of the bullet."

Eli pressed his lips together for a minute, his eyes closing again, heavy with the grief of an avoidable death. When he opened his eyes again, he shifted his gaze to the ocean. Brett moved her gaze in the same direction, unable to look at Eli any longer.

In the distance, a single pinpoint of light bobbed on the waves.

"Wes was afraid people would get the wrong idea because Adam was the one who brought the gun," Eli said, his voice quieter now. "He was worried they would blame Adam for what happened. He was trying to do what he thought was best for his son."

"By covering up a crime," Brett said. "By lying and destroying evidence."

She sat in the darkness next to Eli, going over the story he'd told. The pieces were all there, and she could see how they might fit, but something wasn't quite right. It was the way the four kids had looked in the Polaroid that Irving had found in June's bedroom. The way they were smiling, relaxed. If what Adam said about Daniel being a danger to June was true, that picture wouldn't exist. Then there was the picture of June and Daniel together—he wasn't stalking her; they were in love.

"They weren't meeting for a séance," she finally said.

"What?"

"You said Adam told Wes that they were meeting for a séance. They weren't. They were running away. They were planning to leave Crestwood and live in Seattle. All four of them."

"Who cares why they were meeting?"

"You knew that already." She twisted to face him again, her anger rising. "You worked this case with us. You read Lizzie's statements. I told you about my conversation with Daniel's cousin. You helped us come up with theories and collect evidence. You knew Daniel and June were dating, that they were all planning to run away together. And now you're sitting here telling me this bullshit story about Daniel attacking June, and Adam trying to protect her, and Wes stumbling upon the whole scene at the perfect moment and making a snap judgment because he believed his son's life to be in jeopardy? No. No way. It doesn't make sense. Besides, if Adam is as innocent as Wes says he is, why go to so much effort to keep people from finding out he was there that night?"

"I told you, he panicked," Eli insisted. "He wasn't thinking straight. He'd been at my parents' house for the Halloween party, so maybe he was a little drunk, too."

"That makes it worse, you know."

Eli traced one finger over the top of his steering wheel. "I don't know what you want me to say, Brett. I'm telling you the truth. I'm telling you what Wes told me."

"Yeah, and I'd love to know how you got involved in all of this in the first place." She flopped back against the seat, crossing her arms over her chest.

The light on the horizon, probably a fishing boat, moved slowly north.

"Wes called me into his office the day after it happened," Eli said. "He knew I'd responded to Deadman's Point for the disturbance call, and he wanted me to get rid of that report. He told me what happened, told me that I'd be doing him a huge favor by making the call disappear until he had a chance to take care of it."

"What does that mean?" Brett scoffed. "Was he planning on dumping June in the ocean, too? Pretending it never happened?"

"No. I don't know." He shook his head frustrated and confused. "I thought he was going to tell the chief, come clean, but he needed time. But by the time he called me into his office, you already had the report and were on your way to the ruins. The other guys, they thought sending you out to talk to Ed Shoal would be funny. They had no idea what was going on. That June's body was still out there. When you found her, we had to come up with another plan. Blaming Daniel, calling it a murder-suicide was our best option until that fishing boat dragged up his body. But then we got wind of what that teacher was doing."

"Cadden? The gun in his dresser." Vindication had never felt so disappointing. "I knew it wasn't there the first time I looked."

"No, you were right. You didn't make a mistake," Eli admitted. "The Smith & Wesson was from an old drug case I handled a few years ago. Some idiots dumped a duffel bag with cash and weed and guns in a kid's playground. I took the gun from evidence before our search knowing that no one would miss it. Slipped it in Cadden's dresser after you'd already gone through it."

"Why?"

"Wes asked me to."

"And you agreed? You were fine framing an innocent man?"

"He's not innocent." A darkness edged Eli's voice. "He's a pervert preying on vulnerable girls. Sure, he hasn't killed anyone yet, but he might. We've seen it before. A sexual predator escalating to murder. It's not unheard of. And even if he doesn't ever kill anyone, we'd still be doing the world a favor locking him up."

"That's not how this works, Eli. You can't punish people for crimes they might commit later."

He laughed. "Doesn't matter anyway, does it? Sicko's walking around free as a bird now, doing whatever the fuck he wants with whoever the fuck he wants. Don't come crying to me when someone gets hurt."

"So what's the plan now?" She tasted the bitterness on her tongue. "Last time I talked to Irving, he said Lizzie Trudeau was the prime suspect."

Eli clenched his jaw. "She admits to being there that night, doesn't she?"

"So that's it? You're going to throw a fifteen-year-old girl to the wolves to protect a man who's most likely lying to you. Who admits to shooting at least one kid that night, but probably shot two."

"I told you. It was self-defense."

"And don't even get me started on the laundry list of crimes he's committed trying to cover his own ass," Brett continued. "He won't protect you, you know. Once this gets out. He'll turn on you faster than you can say, 'Sir, yes sir.' And when the dust settles, I highly doubt Wes Harris is going to be the one headed to prison."

Eli slumped forward and rested his forehead on the steering wheel. "It got so fucked up so fast. We had a plan and then when that fell through, there was Cadden, which felt like a perfect sort of justice, but now, I don't know. I don't want anyone else getting hurt. Not you, not Amma. Not Lizzie. But Wes...I mean, what if he's telling the truth? What if he didn't do anything wrong? Does he deserve to have his life ruined because he chose to protect his son?"

"And if it didn't happen the way Wes says it did?" Brett's voice trembled. "If Daniel did nothing wrong? Those kids didn't deserve what happened to them. And what about their families, Eli? What kind of justice is this for them?"

"Brett, I don't know what I'm supposed to do."

"You have to talk to the state police." She rested her hand on his shoulder. "That's the only way you can fix this. You have to tell them everything you just told me. Tell them about Wes asking you to falsify a report, tell them about planting evidence at Benjamin Cadden's house, tell them about the physical evidence you conveniently lost that places Adam at the scene of the crime. Because I bet my entire year's pay that the blood we found on that shirt in Adam's truck would have been a match to June's. Tell them what you know, and they'll have to open an independent investigation. Wes won't be able to hide behind his badge or the chief's desk if the state police are involved. And you won't have to carry this around anymore either. You shouldn't have had to carry it around this long to begin with."

"You don't understand, Brett." Eli straightened again and ran his hand down his face. "Wes, he's like a brother to me. I look up to him. And he looks out for me. He always has. That's the way we do things. We look out for each other. I can't stab him in the back like this."

"Was he looking out for you when he dragged you into this mess?" she asked.

His sigh was rough and trembling. He reached for her hand. She let him take it, even though his touch made her sick to her stomach now that she knew what he'd done.

"You'll be there with me?" he asked.

She nodded. "I have to give them this."

She took the Luger from her jacket pocket and held it out for him to see.

Eli sucked in a sharp breath. "Where the hell did you get that?"

"I found it in Danny's trailer tonight."

"Danny was supposed to get rid of it when he got rid of the stolen boat he used to dump Daniel's body," Eli said.

"Apparently, he changed his mind about the gun," she said. *And maybe about the boat, too,* she thought, remembering the set of keys with the fishing bobbin attached that she'd seen on his nightstand.

Eli reached for the gun, but Brett pulled it away, shoving it back into her pocket. She wasn't going to make the same mistake as last time; she wasn't going to let evidence disappear again.

"We have enough for them to take us seriously," she said. "They won't be able to shove it under the rug once we tell them what we know. I think I can get Kevin to give testimony, too. Once he sees that he's not the only one willing to stand up to Wes, I think he'll feel safe coming forward."

"We're going to have a lot of people pissed at us." Eli rubbed his neck. "You know that, right?"

She nodded.

"You're sure you want to do this?" He looked like he was going to be sick.

"There's no other choice," she said. "And the sooner the better. Before any more evidence gets conveniently misplaced or witnesses move out of town."

Eli rested his head against the seat. After a few seconds, he said, "Are you free Monday?"

She nodded and reached for the door.

"If we leave by seven, we can miss some of the city traffic," he said. "I'll be at your place by six-thirty, okay?"

"If you're late, I'm leaving without you," she said and slammed his car door shut.

It was three long steps to go from Eli's car to her VW. The entire way, she held her breath, waiting for something bad to happen—for Eli to come after her, bash her head against the rocks, and shove her into the waves, or for the crack and smoke of a gunshot in the dark. Only when she was alone in her car, driving home on a darkened highway with no headlights in her rearview mirror, did she let herself breathe again.

CHAPTER 37

When Lizzie stopped by her locker Monday morning, between first and second periods, she found Adam standing with one foot propped against the metal doors, blocking her from getting her books.

"Hey, Lizzie." He smirked. "Long time, no see. If I didn't know any better, I'd think you were avoiding me."

"Are you trying to make me late for class?" She snarled at him, using anger to hide what she was really feeling: fear. "And yes, since you asked, I have been avoiding you."

"I see you're still wearing the necklace." His eyes drifted down to her collarbone where the gold heart dangled.

She'd been wearing it all month long, ever since Adam confronted her about it under the bleachers, confessing that he'd given the necklace to June as a token of his affection—affection that June had rejected.

Lizzie brushed her fingers over the chain. "It reminds me of her."

Adam sighed and dropped his head back against the locker door with a dull thud. "Skip class with me. If I have to listen to Mrs. Schweitzer prattle on about the Civil War for one more day, I'm going to shoot myself."

Lizzie flinched at his choice of words, then shoved him to one side, opened the locker, and grabbed the books she needed for her next class. "I'm avoiding you, remember?"

She slammed the locker shut and turned to go, but Adam snagged her arm and pulled her back. "We have fun together, don't we? Come on, Lizzie. Please?"

The voice of the old man she'd met wandering the ruins on Thanksgiving Day echoed through her head. *Don't hurt him! Please, Adam, don't—* The rest of the sentence was cut off by the cracking of his cane against the cold, stone floor.

The old man could have been lying or could have been crazy, but he'd also repeated verbatim what June and Daniel had said to Lizzie minutes before she left, and her gut was telling her the old man wasn't crazy or lying. He'd been at the ruins that night. And he saw Adam there, too. What she was less certain of, and the main reason she'd been avoiding Adam for the past two weeks, was his role in Daniel and June's deaths.

If the old man was to be believed, June was scared of Adam that night, pleading with him not to do something, not to hurt someone. The only other person who was at the ruins that night as far as Lizzie knew was Daniel. June was pleading with Adam not to hurt Daniel. The thought left Lizzie feeling sick to her stomach. The other idea twisting her thoughts to dark shadows was how much the crack of the old man's cane sounded like a gunshot. She could be letting her imagination get the best of her, filling in the blanks because even the most unlikely answer was better than none. Or Adam could be the person responsible for June and Daniel's deaths. He could be a murderer.

Speculation was spinning her dizzy. The only way to get the truth out of him was to ask.

"Okay, yeah, let's get out of here," Lizzie said as the bell rang signaling the start of class.

Thirty minutes later, they sat in his truck parked outside Crumbles and Cakes Cafe, eating buttermilk muffins and drinking hot chocolate.

"You lied to me," Lizzie said, blowing on her hot chocolate to cool it down.

"About what?" Adam peeled the sleeve from his muffin.

"You were at the ruins on Halloween," she said bluntly, hoping his reaction would help her know what to say next. "You showed up after I left."

He frowned as he picked off a chunk of muffin top and dropped it in his mouth with such nonchalance that she was certain she'd gotten it all wrong. The old man was crazy. Lizzie was crazy, too, for thinking Adam could possibly have anything to do with June's death. Of course he didn't. He would never. He loved June.

"Who told you I was there?" he asked.

"So, it's true?" She twisted in her seat to look at him. "Because if you saw something, if you know something, you should go to the police. I can come with you. We'll go together."

He stared through the windshield at the rain running swiftly into the gutters, saying nothing. After what seemed like an eternity of silence, Lizzie put her hand on his arm. "Adam, tell me what happened. I won't be mad. I promise. I want to help."

He tore off another chunk of muffin but instead of eating it, he pinched the crumb into a tightly packed ball. As his fingers worked over the pastry, he flicked a glance at Lizzie and said, "Tell me the worst thing you've ever done."

Lizzie narrowed her eyes at him. She hadn't left school to talk about her issues, but if it helped Adam open up to her, she'd tell him whatever he wanted to hear.

"I don't know." She shrugged. "I lie to my dad and my grandparents. I lie to everyone."

"Everyone lies about everything." He sounded annoyed at her answer. "What else?"

She thought for a moment, then touched the gold chain on her neck and said, "I broke into June's room and stole this necklace."

"Come on." He sounded mad now, and his muffin was completely ruined, squished inside his tight fist. He turned his cold gaze on her. "Stop fucking around, Lizzie. I want to know. The worst thing you've ever done. I can't tell you my secrets until you tell me yours."

"I don't have any secrets." She sipped some of her hot chocolate, but it was too sweet and turned her stomach. Unable to drink anymore, she placed the cup into the center console holder until she had a chance to throw it away.

"Everyone has secrets," he said quietly.

"What happened, Adam?" she asked. "I know you were there. Tell me what happened to June. Tell me what happened to Daniel."

She wanted to give him the benefit of the doubt that he was going to tell her the truth now, and that whatever he said would make a perfect sort of sense and absolve her and absolve him, too. He would tell her someone else was there that night, some monster with a rotten soul showed up out of nowhere and killed their friends. Or he would tell her it was an accident, that he hadn't meant for the gun to go off, and he was sorry, the sorriest he'd ever been, but he was ready to take responsibility now and make things right.

Instead Adam turned to her with a twisted grin and said, "Tell me what you think you know, and I'll tell you if you guessed right."

She tensed. If he wanted to turn this into some kind of sick game, fine, but she wasn't going to play. No matter how badly she wanted to know the truth.

She reached for the door handle. "I'm going back to school."

"Lizzie, wait." Adam grabbed her arm again, like he had earlier when they were standing in front of her locker.

"Adam, that hurts." She tried to twist free, but his grip tightened.

The look in his eyes reminded her of a possum Grandpa had found trapped in the barn last summer. Glinting panic, teeth bared, desperate and unpredictable. Grandpa had told her not to think too unkindly of the creature—he wasn't dangerous, just scared. *He's caught where he doesn't want to be, that's all.*

Lizzie stopped struggling against Adam. She sank back against the truck door. As she relaxed, so did he. Eventually, he let go of her arm.

"I thought I saw my mom's ghost at the ruins on Halloween, and that's why I took off," Lizzie confessed. "I was a coward. I ran away because of some stupid shadows and a little wind. I left my best friend standing there in the dark, even though I promised her we'd stick together, and now she's dead. It's my fault she's dead."

Her voice trembled, but the words hadn't been as difficult to say as she thought they would be. In fact, it had been a relief to let them out. Her chest didn't feel so crowded with emotion now; it was easier to breathe.

"So that's it. That's the worst thing I've ever done. That's my big secret. Now you tell me yours." She shoved her jaw forward, daring Adam to follow her lead.

It took him a minute, but when he finally spoke, the words tumbled from his mouth as if he had no control over them, as if his guilty conscience was in the driver's seat, ready to relieve itself of its heavy burden.

"I didn't lie about being grounded," he said. "I was grounded. But my parents went to this party, and I snuck out of the house. By the time I got to Deadman's Point, though, it was after midnight, and you were already gone. June and Daniel were still there. I could see them standing together near the ruins. They were holding hands."

When he finished, the tightness across his shoulders had vanished, his jaw unclenched, the worried furrow in his brow smoothed out, and he looked like a kid again, a scared kid who'd been carrying too many secrets for far too long and was glad to finally be rid of them.

"See, that wasn't so hard to say, was it?" Lizzie offered him a gentle smile and half of her muffin, but he shook his head at the muffin, his shoulders tensing again.

"What happened after you got there?" she asked, wanting to keep him talking. He'd admitted he was at Deadman's Point, which was a start, but she could tell by the look on his face, that there was so much more simmering beneath the surface. If she pushed him hard enough, maybe she'd finally have her answers. "You saw June and Daniel, and you did what? You went over and talked to them? Were they mad because you were late?"

He pinched his eyes shut and shook his head. "No, that's not—" A sigh exploded from his lips. "I shouldn't be telling you any of this."

He snapped his eyes open and turned in his seat so fast that Lizzie flinched, thinking he was going to grab hold of her again. A shadow eclipsed his face when he said, "But you can keep a secret, can't you, Lizzie? You never told anyone about your mom. You're not going to tell them about me."

"What are you talking about?" Pressure built in her chest.

"You knew your mom killed all those people, and you didn't rat her out."

"I didn't know," she insisted. "If I had known I would have gone to the police right away. I would have told somebody."

His mouth twisted into a cruel grimace again as he snorted a laugh. "You shared a roof, Lizzie. She made you dinner and drove you to school. You probably braided each other's hair and had little gossip sessions and mother-daughter sleepovers. You don't have to sit there and bullshit me. I'm not going to get you in trouble. I'll keep your secrets, you'll keep mine. That's how this works."

Lizzie swallowed down the lump in her throat, the bitter aftertaste of sludgy hot chocolate making her gag. She hadn't promised Adam anything. She hadn't agreed to keeping his secrets. She shook her head. "It's not the same thing. If you hurt June—"

She watched his face change, his grin fall away, as panic flooded over him.

"It was an accident," he blurted, then he grabbed her wrist, holding on like she was the one thing in the world that could save him. "Lizzie, you can't say anything. Please, you can't tell anyone. I didn't mean for it to happen."

"For what to happen, Adam?" She'd gone cold all over except for where his fingers touched her skin, five burning points searing to the bone. "What did you do?"

"It was Daniel's fault." Adam's lip curled into a snarl. "If he hadn't tried to take the gun from me, it wouldn't have gone off."

"A gun? Why did you have a gun?" Lizzie's heart slammed against her ribcage as her eyes darted over Adam's clothes, looking for an odd shape, a bulge in his pocket, any indication he might still have the gun with him right now.

"It was my granddad's," he muttered. "I wanted to make sure we had protection."

During all their talk about leaving, the four of them had never once discussed the possibility of needing protection. They were driving to Seattle, to Daniel's cousin's apartment, where they would get jobs at restaurants and coffee shops. They weren't trying to survive in a nuclear hellscape, fighting off packs of irradiated wolves. Lizzie would have never gone along with the plan if Adam had said he was bringing a gun; guns were dangerous.

Her hand was going numb from Adam holding on too tight. He stared at her like he was waiting for her to say something, waiting for her to tell him that she wasn't mad. But she was mad. No, she was furious.

"You shot June." The words left her feeling hollowed out and trembling.

Adam tightened his grip on her wrist, his voice cut through with rage. "I didn't shoot anyone. It was Daniel. He did it. He took the gun from me. He was mad that I'd brought it. He had to be in charge of everything, didn't he? He thought he was such tough shit, that everyone should do whatever he said. He took the gun and started waving it around. I told him it was old. I told him to be careful. But he never listened to anyone."

He trailed off, his voice choked with emotion.

Lizzie shook her head, struggling to piece together Adam's confession so it made sense. Adam brought the gun, but Daniel took it from him. Or he tried to take it. Or they were fighting over it when it went off, killing June. But whose finger was on the trigger? Why had the old man made it sound like June was pleading for her life? Adam said it was an accident, but could she believe him? And then there was the most glaring issue of all, the hole in his story she couldn't ignore.

"If Daniel shot June, if it was an accident..." Her voice was barely louder than a whisper. "Then who killed Daniel?"

His lips peeled back in a snarl. "If I told you that, then I wouldn't have any secrets left, now would I?"

"We have to tell the police." The words left her mouth before she realized what she was saying.

Adam loomed closer to her, his breath sugar sweet from the hot chocolate. "You're not going to say a damn word to anyone. You're going to pretend we never had this conversation."

She reared away from him, trying to put as much space between them as she could, but the cab of the truck was small and there was nowhere to go. She tried to reason with him. "If it was an accident like you said it was, then there's nothing you have to worry about. You just have to tell the truth and everything will be okay."

Outside, the rain was coming down harder, skittering across the windshield and knocking on the metal truck roof, filling the cab with noise.

Adam stared at her with a mix of desperation and disgust, like she was the final thread keeping him tied to a world in which he'd lost all faith and that thread was slowly unraveling.

"Please tell me you don't seriously believe in all that 'tell an adult and let them handle it' bullshit. Because the last time I told an adult anything, I got the shit kicked out of me."

Lizzie thought of the bruises he'd shown her, the purple marks his father had left across his ribs. But they didn't have to tell his father, they could tell someone she trusted.

She pushed her shoulders back and raised her voice, trying to be firm with him. "If I go with you, no one will hurt you."

He snorted a bitter laugh.

"You just have to tell the truth," she repeated because she didn't have any other good arguments. "You owe June that much at least."

At the mention of June's name, Adam seemed to soften. His lower lip trembled as he stared at Lizzie with a helpless expression. "And then what? What happens after I tell them the truth? I spend the rest of my life in jail. That's what happens."

His voice turned brittle again, his fingers twisting around her wrist, turning her skin red.

"If it was an accident—" She started to say, but he gave her a hard shake and her head cracked against the window.

"And what if it wasn't?" He spat the words at her. His eyes flashed rage. "What if *I* was the one holding the gun? What if I shot June on purpose? What if I shot her because she deserved it? And what if I shot Daniel, too? Does that change anything? Now that you know what I'm capable of?"

"Let go of me!" Lizzie grabbed his wrist with her free hand and dug her fingernails deep into his skin, so deep he yelped and let go, drawing his arm to his face to inspect the damage.

"Bitch," he muttered. "You made me bleed."

It was nothing compared to what she would do to him if he touched her a second time.

"I'm not afraid of you." She shoved the words through clenched teeth.

Before she had time to react, his hands were clamped around her throat. She didn't even have time to gasp in surprise.

"Are you afraid of me now?" His calm tone unnerved her.

Gone was his fear and any regret he may have been feeling about what happened to June. He seemed to be in survival mode now, willing to do anything to keep her from telling his secrets. Lizzie clawed at him and bucked, trying to get him to loosen his grip, but he was strong, and every attempt to break free made him squeeze tighter.

"I could kill you, too, you know." His face was pressed so close to hers, she could see every zit and dirty pore. His breath was stale. "I could kill you right now and no one could do a fucking thing about it."

Her eyes swung wildly from side to side, trying to see the street and the sidewalk, to get someone's attention, but the rain was keeping everyone inside and even if someone did walk by and see what was happening inside the truck, she wasn't sure they'd stop to help. There were plenty of people in this town who would be happy to see her gone.

Flashes of light burst in Lizzie's eyes as she started to run out of air. Was this how it had been for her mother? Drowning. The world folding into black. She opened her mouth, but no sound came out, not a whimper, not even a choked sputter. Just when the edges of her vision started to go black, Adam let go of her.

She sucked in a sharp breath, her throat stinging where his

hands had been. Air rushed into her lungs, and she'd never felt more happy to feel her ribs expand. She panted and fumbled for the door handle, trying to escape before he attacked her again. But he was slumped over the steering wheel now, his face buried in his arms, his shoulders shaking as his rage left him.

His voice was muffled. Lizzie had to lean in to hear what he was saying.

"He should have stayed away from her. He should have left June alone. I loved her. I loved her so much, it killed me to see her with him. I would have done anything for her. And I was fine being friends. I really was. She told me her parents wouldn't let her date anyone. I was fine with that. But then I saw her with Daniel. She kissed him. She let him do things to her, but when I would brush her hand, barely even touch her, she'd flinch like I was diseased. It was never supposed to be her. I was aiming for him. June just got in the way."

He sucked in a shaky breath and then lifted his head and turned to look at Lizzie, blinking in surprise, like he had forgotten she was in the truck with him, like he hadn't meant to say all that, realizing for the first time what kind of trouble he was in.

Adam lunged toward Lizzie again, and she raised her hands to protect her throat, but he didn't attack her this time. Instead, he reached around her and shoved open the truck door. Cold wind rushed in. Rain battered her face.

"Get out."

She didn't wait for him to ask a second time. She grabbed her backpack and slid out of the truck onto the sidewalk. Leaning over the now-empty seat, Adam narrowed his eyes on her. "I'll fucking kill you if you breathe a word of this to anyone. No one will believe you anyway, you know. Even if you do tell. You're the daughter of a murderer. I'm the son of a cop. Who do you think they'll listen to?"

He slammed the door shut and drove away, tires squealing.

Lizzie walked home with her hands shoved in her pockets and her shoulders hunched against the rain. Afraid to face her grandpa's disappointment and her father's questions about why she wasn't in school, she ducked into the barn. Maggie draped her head over her stall door and whinnied a cheerful hello. One of the other horses huffed and stamped a hoof.

Lizzie went into the feed room and scooped oats from the bucket, filling the horses' feed troughs one by one, leaving Maggie for last so she could stay in her stall, curled up in the warm hay near the horse's reassuring presence.

She tucked her knees into her chest and buried her face in her arms.

Lizzie thought she'd felt the worst pain in her life after she learned the truth about her mother, but what Adam had told her today was worse. This was grief that scorched and burned the world red. This was a loss she could never forgive. She lifted her head and brushed her fingers over her throat, flinching at the bruises Adam had left behind.

When he'd choked her, Lizzie had flashed back to last year, the falling-down mansion, the pitch-black room upstairs, Zach pinning her against the wall, his hand clamped over her mouth. She'd been lucky that night, too, lucky enough to walk away from her attacker. Not like June. June, who'd found Lizzie at the party last year, wandering around the house, dazed. June, who had taken her home and held her hand while she cried. June stuck beside her when Lizzie came forward and told the truth about Zach. June believed her story when no one else did. June had saved her. June was the very best part of Lizzie's stupid, miserable life and now she was dead, and it was all Adam's fault.

To keep herself from crying, Lizzie thought about killing.

She had never understood it before, how someone could so callously take another person's life, but now she got it. She would kill Adam if she had the chance. She would take a shovel to his head, crack his skull wide open, then use it to bury him behind the barn, drive his truck deep into the woods where no one would find it. If anyone deserved a death like that, it was Adam Harris. He'd stolen the star from her sky, the sun to her moon. He deserved nothing less than what he'd taken. And after it was done, Lizzie would live with her secret until she died, carrying on as if nothing had happened, feeling no regrets. Her mother had done it, so why shouldn't she?

Lizzie stayed in Maggie's stall for a long time imagining the many ways to kill a person and get away with it. Her eyes stayed dry as rain pounded the barn roof. At some point, the horse nudged her arm for attention, and Lizzie lifted her head, blinking against the light that had turned soft and gray.

She didn't know what time it was exactly, but she was getting cold, and she couldn't stay in the barn forever. Eventually, she'd have to go inside and face the consequences of ditching school, but when she tried to stand, the world spun out from under her feet, and she sank slowly back to the floor. A few more minutes hidden away couldn't hurt.

It could have been a few minutes or an entire hour—time had ceased to make sense the minute Adam shoved her out of his truck. Lizzie heard the barn door creak open, the horses whinnying a greeting. Footsteps shuffled into the barn and for a brief second, she thought Adam had found her, that he had come all this way to tie up loose ends and make sure she kept her mouth shut—permanently.

But then she heard her father's voice call out with uncertainty. "Lizzie? Are you in here?"

A whimper escaped from her mouth. The footsteps hurried to Maggie's stall. Her father peered over the door, his brow furrowed with worry. "Lizzie? What are you doing down there? Why are you on the floor?"

He slipped into Maggie's stall and dropped down onto the hay beside her, moving her damp hair back from her face, checking to see if she was hurt. His eyes narrowed on her neck, where she was certain Adam's fingers had left their mark because her skin still burned and it hurt to swallow, and when her father touched her, she flinched from the pain.

"Who did this to you?" His voice turned angry.

Lizzie shook her head. She opened her mouth, then closed it. Then, for the first time since hearing June was dead all those weeks ago in the principal's office, Lizzie cried.

Huge, gulping sobs. Her body wracked with grief. Her shoulders heaving. She hadn't cried this hard in years, and it felt like she was splitting open. It felt good. It hurt like hell. She couldn't stop even if she wanted to.

Her dad didn't know how to respond to her outburst at first. He stiffened, then looked around like he was expecting someone else to come and take care of her. Finally, he pulled her into his lap and wrapped his arms around her, rocking her gently, even though she was too big and everything about the hug was awkward. She didn't care. She pressed into him harder, letting his flannel shirt soak up her tears. She realized as she sat there crying in his arms, that it was the first time they'd been this close since his arrest last November, the first time she'd hugged him and let him hug her back.

"Tell me, Lizzie," he said. "Please, tell me what happened."

There was something about the solidness of her father's chest, the deep rumble of his voice, the steady thump of his heart, the sweet scent of hay, and the soft nickering of horses that made her feel, for the briefest moment, like her old self. Like Elizabeth—the girl from Before who didn't know a thing about grief and broken hearts, lying mothers and dead best friends.

She missed that girl.

That girl could have stayed in the barn, safe with her father for as long as she wanted. But Lizzie wasn't that girl anymore. She hadn't been that girl in a very long time.

She lifted her head and wiggled free of her father's embrace. Reaching behind her neck, she unclasped the heart-shaped pendant. She poured the chain into one palm and then the other, the cool metal pooling and turning warm in her hands as she told him everything that happened on Halloween night, everything Adam had confessed.

CHAPTER 38

The ruddy-faced state trooper Brett and Eli spoke to on Monday morning seemed unimpressed with their story, bored even, but he filed the report, bagged the Luger as evidence, and assured them an investigation would be opened into the Newmark/Yoon case. He also promised to speak with the deputy chief about sending their complaints about Wes Harris to internal affairs. He spat out the special department's name like the words tasted bitter.

The sun was shining when they stepped out of the squat concrete building in Marysville. Brett squinted against the brightness. She'd forgotten how blue the sky could be, how the sun could feel like a familiar hand brushing against your cheek.

"Well, that was easy." She looked back at the District 7 offices, the darkened windows like unblinking eyes casting down judgment.

"I don't know about you, but I could use a drink." Eli rubbed his neck.

"It's barely ten o'clock in the morning," Brett pointed out.

"It doesn't have to be right now." He opened the passenger door for her. "How about dinner?"

"You're kidding, right?" She slid into the car and buckled her seat belt.

"I'm trying to build a bridge here, Brett," he said. "I'm trying to apologize."

"You can just say the words."

He shut her inside the car, walked around to the other side, and slid in behind the steering wheel. He slammed the door shut, but instead of starting up the engine, he twisted in his seat to look at her. "I'm sorry, Brett. I fucked up. Okay? Is that what you want to hear? I fucked up, and I'm trying to make it right. And look, I understand if you never want to see me again after this, but at least let me take you out to dinner. To say thank you or goodbye or whatever."

He waited for her to say something. When she didn't, he faced forward again and started the car. As he pulled out of the state police parking lot, he said, "You know we're going to face the firing squad over this. We might as well have one last good meal."

"Not a date," Brett finally said.

"Not a date," Eli agreed, but he sounded disappointed.

Brett thought she would feel relief after leaving the state police offices. The trooper they'd spoken with had said and done all the right things. She should have been relaxed knowing she made the right choice, the only choice, and that a new investigation would be opened, and this time it would be thorough and fair. June and Daniel's families were going to finally get answers. That should have been enough. But the knots in her stomach twisted tighter the closer they got to Crestwood.

She couldn't stop thinking of the conversation she'd had with Henry late Saturday night after leaving Eli at Deadman's Point. When she'd come through the front door, she thought she'd find Henry asleep on the couch, but he was still awake. He had muted the television and offered to make her tea.

"Anita's been sleeping for a while now," he said. "I gave Pistol first watch."

As he made tea, Brett went upstairs to change out of her muddy clothes into dry ones. Returning to the living room, she curled up on the couch, watching the images move across the television screen, but not really following anything that was happening.

Henry handed her the tea and sat down next to her with a cup of his own. "You want to tell me what the hell is going on?"

"What do you mean?" The tea was too hot to drink. She blew across it, steam billowing around her face.

"You weren't covering anyone's shift tonight," he said, matter-of-factly.

She started to protest, but he held up one hand and shook his head. "Don't treat me like I'm stupid, Brett. Stan's got you working patrol and you tell me it's for budgetary reasons, but you forget, I set up this year's budget before I left. There was enough to keep you on as a detective. So clearly, he's punishing you for something. And then today Amma tells me a story about a man who came to the house and told her he'd kill you if she didn't get in his car."

Brett's grip tightened around her tea cup. "She told you that? Was she...did she know what year it was?"

"She sounded pretty lucid to me." His eyes narrowed. "How much trouble are you in, Brett?"

She told Henry everything then, repeating some things he already knew and sharing her doubts about Eli's version of events. He listened, quietly, staring into his tea. By the time she was finished, both of their cups had gone cold.

She waited for Henry to say something. Instead, he stood without a word, took her tea cup and carried it into the kitchen along with his. The microwave beeped and whirred and beeped again, and then Henry returned once more with hot tea.

"You're not surprised," she said when he handed her the re-heated cup.

"No, I'm not." He sat down again and let out a weighted sigh. "I was with that department a long time, remember?"

She tensed. "What's that supposed to mean?"

"Just, this isn't the first time a complaint about Wes has come up. I mean, the incidents I know about, they weren't this bad, but no, I'm not surprised by anything you told me." Henry set his untouched chamomile tea on the table in front of him and stayed leaning forward, resting his elbows on his knees. "Wes performed a traffic stop early on, when he was still a patrol officer. He shot and killed the driver. Said the man was making a move for a gun. Problem was, we searched the car after and didn't find any gun. Not even anything shaped like a gun. Then there was the kid he kicked the shit out of over a stolen candy bar. He said the kid had a knife, but again, we never found one."

"And nobody thought that was a problem?" She didn't hide the disgust in her voice over what Henry was telling her.

"He was reprimanded," Henry said. "Given more training, but at the end of the day, he was doing his job. If we fired every officer for making a few mistakes, there wouldn't be anyone left. The world would be run by criminals."

"Henry," she said, her voice low. "A simple mistake is filing the wrong paperwork. A simple mistake is arresting the wrong guy. A simple mistake is taking a left when you should have taken a right. Killing someone because you think their wallet is a gun— that's not a mistake. It's negligence. It's reckless. Wes Harris is dangerous, and the fact that half the squad is covering for him makes me think it's the culture of this department, not one bad officer."

Henry shook his head. "You don't understand. Sometimes you have to make decisions for the greater good, you have to do the wrong thing so the right thing can get done, too."

"That doesn't make any sense," she said.

"There were things I did as chief," he continued. "Things I'm not proud of. Things we had to do to keep the peace, but no matter what, I always tried to make decisions for the betterment of this town and the people who live here."

"Who gets to decide that?" she asked. "Who gets to decide what's better?"

"The world isn't good guys and bad guys, Brett. It's more complicated than a hero riding off into the sunset while the villain swings from the hangman's noose."

"You don't think I know that?"

He studied her face a moment, a deep sadness filling his eyes. "You could be chief one day, you know. If you wanted it, you could have it."

Brett laughed loud enough she worried about waking Amma.

"I'm not kidding," Henry said. "You're exactly what that department needs, and you've got the right temperament for it, too. I know enough people that I could pull some strings, and make it happen."

Becoming chief of a department had never even crossed her mind. It was a lot of responsibility she wasn't sure she could handle. Plus, she had joined the force to help people, not to play politics and plan budgets.

"If you were chief," Henry had said. "You wouldn't have to play by anyone else's rules because you'd be the one making them."

Over twenty-four hours had passed since that conversation. There was no way anyone would ever consider her for the position of chief now. Not after what she and Eli had done—going to the state police, accusing a superior officer of covering up a crime, effectively ruining whatever careers they might have had if they'd said nothing and looked the other way. It didn't matter if they were right about Wes; what mattered was that they could no longer be trusted.

There was no sun in Crestwood. The second they passed into the city limits, the clouds clamped down around them again. Fat rain drops splattered against the windshield. None of it helped with Brett's brooding mood.

As Eli pulled up to the house on Bayshore Drive, she couldn't stop ruminating over the idea that they'd done the wrong thing by talking to the state police. Maybe they should have handled it privately, the way the squad had handled Benjamin Cadden outside the Pickled Onion. Maybe Wes would have listened if they'd spoken his language of fists and threats, and maybe Brett was a coward for letting someone else do the dirty work.

———————————

After confirming her evening plans with Eli, Brett went inside to find Amma.

She was sitting in front of a blank canvas easel in the living room, scowling at the paintbrush in her hand. When Brett entered the room, her scowl deepened.

"You've been working too hard lately," she scolded. "Let me talk to Henry, see if he can do something. He shouldn't be working you this hard."

"Henry's not the chief anymore, Amma, remember?"

"Yes, of course I remember." She wagged the brush in the air. "But he still pulls weight over there, doesn't he? He can say something to that—to whoever that man is who's your boss now."

"Thanks, Amma, but I don't think it's a good idea."

Brett glanced at the clock above the fireplace, realizing that for the first time in several days, she had hours ahead of her with nowhere to be and nothing to do.

She sat down in a wing-backed chair near Amma's easel. Pistol jumped into her lap. Brett scratched the dog as she tried to get a conversation going with her grandmother. "How are you doing, Amma? How are you feeling?"

Amma dabbed red paint onto her brush, then frowned and dunked the brush into a mason jar filled with water sitting on a table nearby. "Oh, good days and bad days, dear. Good days and bad days."

"One more than the other?"

Amma lifted her gaze to meet Brett's. "One needs the other, you know. How can we tell what is good if we don't have something bad to compare it to?"

"Oh, I don't know," Brett said. "I worry that if there's too much bad, you'll forget there was ever anything good."

"Don't be a pessimist, Brett," Amma said, returning her attention to the blank canvas in front of her. "Be grateful for the good days, that's all I can tell you. Be grateful for the days when the ocean is calm and the sun is shining. Don't waste time worrying about when the next storm will roll in. Enjoy the blue skies while they're here."

She dabbed her paintbrush into a smear of aquamarine then changed her mind again and washed the paint off in the water.

"What are you painting today?" Brett asked.

"I haven't decided yet. Or I have, but it keeps escaping me. I hear blue and red and lettuce, but when I go to put the brush on the paint, I can't see what it is I'm supposed to feel."

Brett didn't completely understand her grandmother's nonsense-speak, but she didn't push for clarity. Sometimes logic wasn't what was needed; sometimes it was enough to let her exist inside the sparking creativity of her scattered thoughts. If she was happy, if she was calm.

Amma chuckled to herself, as if she realized that what she said hadn't made much sense. "I don't expect you to understand. You've always been more interested in sculptures than my silly watercolors."

Brett had never in her life expressed interest in sculptures, though her grandfather had been something of a collector.

"You miss him, don't you, Amma?" Brett asked quietly.

"Who's that, dear?" A furrow formed in her brow, and the brush in her hand trembled.

With an exasperated sigh, Amma tossed the brush into the jar with the others, set her painting palate on a small side table, and rushed into the kitchen like she'd forgotten to turn the stove off. But when Brett went after her, she found Amma standing at the sink, her hands gripping the counter top, her gaze fixed out the window toward the bay. The clouds had lifted enough to reveal a grouping of islands off in the distance, their rounded shapes dark mirages against the pale gray.

Amma's doctor had explained what would happen. The decline would be slow or it would be quick, but there would be a point of no return where Brett would need to make difficult choices. They'd held out as long as they could, but watching Amma now, seeing her struggle to paint, coupled with the frequency of which Amma was forgetting things and how often she was wandering off, made Brett realize they were getting very close to that point.

This would be easier if her mother was still alive. Or if she had siblings, cousins, anyone to share this burden. The idea of calling her father flitted through her mind, but her father lived on the East Coast now with his new family, his better family. She rarely spoke to him, and when she did, she always ended the call feeling worse than when it started. Besides, Amma was her maternal grandmother. Her father had no responsibility here. The time was drawing close, and Brett was the one who would have to make the decision for the both of them.

Amma turned her head and smiled at Brett. "One day I'd like to be out there again. One day I'd like to see how far I can go."

She pushed away from the counter, stepping close to Brett and brushing dry fingers over her cheek. "You should come with me. You and Pistol. We'll find a boat that's big enough for all three of us."

"That sounds like quite the adventure." Brett smiled at the

thought of the two of them with the wind at their backs, chasing the horizon, Pistol standing on the bow, a crooked-eared figurehead.

Amma walked to the french doors and pressed both of her hands flat on the glass. "I still know how to tie a bowline. And a square knot. And a sheepshank. I still know which way to turn the sails so the wind catches just right."

Her voice was quiet and wistful, as if she was talking more to herself than Brett, trying to convince herself she was still very much the woman she used to be.

"It wouldn't be such a bad way to go," Amma said. "Sailing into the sunset, never to return. It would make things a lot easier for both of us."

"Amma, don't say things like that." Brett took her elbow and guided her away from the back door. "I have a few hours before I'm meeting a friend for dinner. If you'd like, we can play a couple hands of gin rummy."

"That sounds quite nice, dear." Amma sighed and patted Brett's hand, allowing herself to be led back into the living room.

The restaurant Eli picked was a seafood and steakhouse on the outskirts of town that boasted a spectacular view of the bay. For a Monday night, the place was crowded, which Brett supposed had something to do with the holidays and family visits and people getting tired of cooking. Even with the increased business, she and Eli were seated quickly. He ordered without looking at the menu—a sixteen ounce T-bone, medium rare, a side of fries, and a draft beer. Brett ordered the salmon and a glass of chardonnay.

"I've been so nervous, I've barely eaten anything in the past two days," Eli said as they waited for their food. He studied her across the table. "How are you so calm?"

"Do you think I'd make a good chief?" she asked.

He started to laugh, then cut himself off. "Oh, that's a serious question."

"Henry said he thought I could do it."

"Sure, I could see that." Eli paused to thank the server for bringing their drinks and to take a large gulp of beer, then asked, "Wait, was this before or after our little field trip to the state police?"

"Does it make a difference?" Brett tasted her chardonnay then set it aside to drink with her food.

A look of pity crossed Eli's face. "No one's going to want to touch us when they find out what we did."

"We told the truth," she said.

"We threw our superior under the bus," he said. "We're traitors to the badge."

"That's a little extreme."

"You did think about this, didn't you? Before you went rolling in there with your moral high ground? Before you dragged me along with you?" He pushed his empty pint glass to the edge of the table. He'd gone through it fast. He waved to the server and asked for scotch on the rocks.

"Thought about what?" she asked when the server left.

"About the consequences of 'doing the right thing.'" He used air quotes when he said it. "I thought about it. I drove by your house five times this morning before I finally pulled into the driveway."

"So people are going to be pissed, so what?" she said. "They'll get over it."

He stared at her for a long time without talking. She shifted in her chair, darting her eyes around the restaurant. There were a few people she recognized from around town, but no one she knew by name, no one who would report back to Amma. She was glad for that, knowing how people liked to talk, knowing how it must look—her and one of Crestwood's most eligible bachelor's dining together at a table by the windows with a stunning view of the crimson sunset. A candle flickered between them. It could have been romantic.

"We're lucky if we don't get fired," Eli said. "We'll certainly have black marks next to our names. No one on the squad is going to want to work with us after this. They're going to treat us like lepers. And if you're thinking you can transfer, don't bother. Because no other department in the country will take us."

The server brought Eli's scotch and then their food, but before Brett could lift her fork to start eating, Eli lifted his drink.

"A toast," he said. "To the moral high ground."

He clinked his glass against hers.

An hour later, they paid the check and walked out to the car.

Eli reached to open the door for Brett and as he did so, he leaned in to kiss her. His breath reeked of scotch. She pushed him away.

"You're drunk," she said.

"Am not." His words were slurred, the grin on his face sloppy.

"How many of those scotches did you have? Two, three? Give me the keys." Brett held out her hand.

"No, I'm fine, really, I can drive." But he dug in his pocket and handed the keys over to her. His fingers lingered on hers. His gaze lingered, too.

"Brett," he whispered.

"Don't." Her fingers curled over the keys, and she stepped away from him.

He leaned against the roof of the car, watching her walk around to the driver's side. When she opened the door, he asked, "We did the right thing, didn't we? I need to know we did the right thing."

"Get in the car, Eli."

The road back to town from the restaurant was narrow and winding, a two-lane highway that hugged the coastline, rising to high cliffs that overlooked the ocean before descending again to the valley on the other side. Brett set the windshield wipers at top speed and turned the headlights to their brightest setting, but she still couldn't see more than a foot or two of the road ahead.

Eli sang along with the radio, getting every word of the song wrong. The ocean crashed in the distance. Brett caught dark glimpses of it through gaps in the trees. She tightened her grip on the steering wheel, knowing how easily it would be to lose control on a road like this, the asphalt slick with rain, the guardrail offering little more than a flimsy illusion of safety.

The bend in the road was hairpin sharp. Even if the other car had been using its high beams, Brett wasn't sure she would have seen them in time. Not that it would have mattered. The car was in the wrong lane, barreling straight toward them.

Eli shouted something.

Brett slammed her foot hard on the brake and jerked the wheel to the left. The night filled with the loud screech of metal on metal. The whole car shuddered. Brett was whipped violently against the door. The seat belt tightened across her neck. Sparks exploded in her eyes as she gasped for air and tried to bring the car back under control. But it was too late.

It sounded like the world was breaking apart around them, the roar of splintering metal and hissing trees was deafening. Brett's stomach rose into her throat, and for half a second they were weightless, flying. Then they were falling again, plunging into an abyss. With a loud crack, the car hit a tree and everything went dark.

CHAPTER 39

Brett opened her eyes but the world stayed pitch black. She tried to move, but pain forced her still. Someone was screaming.

"Brett?" The voice was nowhere and everywhere all at once.

At least the screaming had stopped.

"Brett, are you with us?"

I'm here, Eli, she said even though her lips didn't move, her jaw clenched against the throbbing pain in her right leg. She wanted to feel him, to make sure he was real, that he was still with her. She tried to reach out her hand, but grasped only air, and then more pain flashed through her like fire.

"Can you open your eyes for me? There you go. Easy does it."

Weren't her eyes already open? It was night. And she was glad for the dark, because there was nothing out there she wanted to see. But she tried anyway because Eli kept telling her to do it, "Open your eyes, Brett. I need you to open your eyes and look at me? Okay?"

The world was blinding white and unfamiliar. She clamped her eyes shut again, welcoming back the nothingness. But she could no longer pretend she was still in the car on the side of the cliff. And she could no longer pretend the man looming over her hospital bed was Eli.

She fluttered her eyes open again.

The man—glasses, gray hair, definitely not Eli—smiled at her. "Hello, Brett. Glad to have you back. You're at Crestwood General Hospital. You're in the emergency room. Do you remember what happened?"

She tried to sit up. Pain screamed through her. The doctor told her to lie still. He said her right leg was broken, a compound fracture stabilized for now until they could get her into surgery. She'd suffered bruises from the seat belt, cuts and abrasions, a gash on her head where she hit the car door. She probably had a concussion, but they needed to do some scans to make sure it wasn't something worse.

"You're going to be in a lot of pain for the next few weeks, but you're going to live," he said.

She listened with the kind of numb stupor only strong drugs could provide.

When he finished explaining her injuries and what would happen next, he asked if she had any questions.

Her throat was raw from screaming, and the bruise from the seat belt didn't help any with the pain, but she forced the words out, each one like splintered glass. "Eli? With me. How bad?"

The doctor looked down before he answered.

She knew what he was going to say before he said it. But she needed to hear the words out loud. She needed someone else to confirm that what she had experienced was real and not some lucid nightmare.

Brett knew they weren't going to survive when the car broke through the guardrail. She caught a glimpse of the horizon, of white waves breaking far from shore, before the car dropped and slammed into a row of trees. It was quiet then, and dark. She'd blacked out, for a few seconds or minutes. It couldn't have been very long because it was still night when she opened her eyes and the car was still hissing steam.

The panic came first, then confusion, then sheer and stabbing agony. She screamed Eli's name over and over, fumbling with the seat belt that was locked tight around her chest, pinning her in place. Even if she could get it off, it wouldn't matter—her right leg was crushed under the crumpled dashboard. There was no way she was getting out of this wreckage on her own.

She stopped screaming and listened for his voice, a groan, a sputter, a cough, a sigh. *Anything, please, anything.* All she heard was her own panicked breath, and the wild roar of the waves below them.

It hurt to scream, but it was all she could do at that moment. Instead of his name, she screamed for help. She didn't know how long they hung there stuck, how long she sat in the car with him dead beside her before she saw the flicker of lights, heard the distant wail of sirens, and someone calling out that help was on the way.

"I'll let you rest some more," the doctor said, interrupting her nightmare memories. "Someone should be in soon to take you for that head scan. And if that comes back normal, we'll start prepping your leg for surgery. Want to get you back on your feet as quickly as we can. If you need anything in the meantime, push that button for the nurse."

As the doctor left her room, she glimpsed a uniformed officer sitting in the hallway outside her door, flipping through the pages of a magazine.

He glanced up seconds before the door swung shut and their eyes met. His gaze was sharp and jagged with accusations.

Her fault, her fault, her fault.

The door clicked shut, and Brett was alone again.

The next time Brett opened her eyes, sunlight was streaming through the hospital room window, and Irving was standing in front of the glass watching two pigeons strut on the small, false balcony outside her room. His hands were laced behind his back, one thumb quietly tapping the other. The last time they'd spoken, they'd fought about the case and Wes. He'd told her to back off and leave him alone. So much had happened since then, it was hard to believe only a few days had passed. It felt like a lifetime.

"It's too bright," she said, pulling the blanket to block the light. "What time is it?"

"Almost three," he answered, then added, "You know, some historians think that pigeons were the first bird to be domesticated. During the Mesopotamian era, people used them to send messages. Of course, you probably already know that. But people also raised them as food. I'll have the roast pigeon with a side of dates." Irving stared at the pigeons another second, then pulled the curtains closed and walked over to the bed.

The tie he wore today was one she hadn't seen before. A teal background with two rosy-throated hummingbirds dipping their long beaks into cone-shaped flowers. There was something abstract and messy about it that didn't seem to fit with Irving's usual style.

"I like your tie," Brett said.

Irving frowned at the pattern. "Diane gave it to me."

"Well, it's nice."

He smoothed the tie flat again and fixed his gaze on her. There was a stretched-out moment where neither of them spoke, then they both started talking at the same time, their words running over top of each other.

"Irving, I'm sorry, I—"

"I'm sorry, Brett, I—"

It hurt to laugh, but she was unable to stop herself. She hissed in pain and clutched her side.

"Is it bad?" Irving pulled a chair closer and sat down. "The doctor who did the surgery this morning said you needed some screws or something."

"I'll live," she said, feeling her grief rise again, dark and churning. She shoved it away, focusing instead on the small threads in the blanket covering her body.

"Brett. What happened?" Irving asked the question gently, without any accusation in his voice.

She relaxed her head against the pillow. "I was hoping you could tell me."

"All I know is that last night, dispatch gets a call about a car through a barrier on Chuckanut Highway," he said. "First responders confirmed one dead on scene, another transported here via Life Flight."

Brett remembered the sirens, the screeching of metal as they cut her out of the car, her own screams as they tried to lift her onto a stretcher. She passed out again at some point, embracing oblivion.

"It took a few hours before we were told who was in the car," Irving continued. "I came straight the hospital when I found out, but it wasn't until late this morning when they finally told me you were going to be okay." He paused, a pained look moving over his face. "They waited to tell us about Eli until after they knew you were going to make it. Last night...where were you two going?"

"Home," Brett said. "We were out at that fancy steakhouse, you know the one with that great view, having dinner. We were celebrating." Her laugh was bitter and short, but this time she welcomed the pain. "We told the state police everything, Irv. About June and Daniel. About Adam. About Wes. Eli gave a formal statement about being asked by Wes to falsify reports and tamper with evidence. They're going to open an investigation. Eli asked me to dinner after it was all over. He wanted to apologize for what he'd done, but also, I think it was kind of us saying goodbye. I don't know. Does it matter now?"

"They tested your blood when they brought you in," Irving said. "It came back as .05. You were drinking."

"I had a glass of wine with dinner," she said. "And .05 is below the legal limit."

"The bartender from the restaurant said you ordered a lot more drinks than one glass of wine."

She didn't like his tone. "Is this an interrogation?"

"I'm trying to figure out what happened."

"I'll tell you what happened." She shoved herself into a sitting position, even though her ribs complained and sharp pain shot through her leg. "Eli and I went to Salty's Grill. He ordered steak, I ordered salmon. I had one glass of wine and Eli drank two beers and a half a bottle of scotch. I took his keys so I could drive us home. We were driving on Chuckanut Highway, listening to the radio when we came around the sharp bend and almost ran head-on into another car."

Irving's expression made it clear that this was the first he was hearing about another car being involved.

"It was in our lane, Irving." Her anger faded as quickly as it had sparked. "I don't know if it was broken down, or if it swerved at the last second, but it was just there. Without any warning. I had seconds to decide what to do. Not even. I barely had time to blink. I jerked the wheel. It was instinctive. If I'd had more time to react, to fucking think, I would have pulled the wheel the other way, to the right, instead of the left. We would have been fine if we'd gone to the right."

She pinched her eyes shut as the memories crashed over her again. Eli shouting, grabbing for her hand. The crunch of metal. The feeling of falling. Her stomach twisted now, thinking about it, and she groaned. "I'm going to throw up."

Irving grabbed the pink basin by her bed and held it under her mouth. She heaved hard enough to feel one of her ribs pop, but nothing came out. She gasped and fell back against the pillow, mumbling an apology, feeling humiliated to be so broken in front of this man who until recently she'd so admired.

He gave her a few minutes to catch her breath before asking, "Brett, are you sure there was another car involved?"

She nodded. "Examine Eli's car if you don't believe me. I think the front bumpers scraped, we got that close to it. I remember the initial impact, remember thinking that we'd gotten lucky, we'd escaped by the skin of our teeth. Then we broke through the guardrail. Look at the car. There has to be paint transfer or something."

She stopped talking. She didn't like the way he was looking at her. She couldn't decide what pissed her off more—his pity or his disbelief.

"You think I'm lying," she said.

He shook his head. "Looking at the car's not an option, Brett."

"What do you mean, it's 'not an option?'" She dug her fingers into the scratchy hospital sheets. "It should have gone straight to impound."

"It was too dangerous to try and recover it," he said. "They had a hell of a time getting you out safely as it was."

"So, where is it then?"

"Still out there, as far as I know. Maybe in a heap at the bottom of the cliff by now." He paused before continuing, "It was reported as a single car accident. There was a witness. A driver coming up Chuckanut Highway the same direction as you. He said he saw your brake lights go over the edge, that's what made him stop. We asked him about other cars. He said there was no one. He said the road was empty in both directions."

"And I'm telling you there was another car," she insisted. "You have to go back. You have to send a tow truck to recover it. Or at least send someone out to inspect the damage."

Irving sighed, clearly losing patience with her. "Even if the car was recoverable, the way you crashed through that guardrail, hitting all those trees on the way down—I doubt anyone would be able to tell one dent from another. Besides, it's not like finding evidence of a collision with another car will change how things turned out."

Now she was the one staring back at him in disbelief.

"What would it prove, Brett?" he asked.

"Intent," she answered. "That someone tried to run us off the road."

That it wasn't her fault. She pressed her head into the pillow and squeezed her eyes shut, but the tears fell anyway.

She didn't know why she had survived the crash, and Eli hadn't. Stupid, blind luck. Twisted fate. A butterfly flapped its wings, and God snapped his fingers. According to the doctor, the surgery on Brett's leg had gone well. They'd used two screws to hold the bones in place. She was staring down a long recovery time, but eventually she'd walk again. And Eli would still be dead.

She heard Irving get up from the chair. A few seconds later, the curtains clattered open, and light flooded the room. Brett opened her eyes and turned to look at him. He had his back to her, staring at the spot where the pigeons had been roosting a few minutes ago. The birds were gone now.

"Irving," she said, her voice cracking with emotion. "You have to believe me. I don't know if it was because of the rain or if the car had a flat or if the other driver was drunk or if it was waiting for us to come around the corner, but I swear to you, there was another car out on the road with us. Maybe it drove off before the witness showed up, but it was there. I know what I saw. And I have a bad feeling about it. I don't think it was a simple accident, wrong place, wrong time kind of situation. We had just talked to the state police. What if someone? What if Wes—"

"Don't." Irving jerked his head around to look at her. His eyes sparked with anger.

"Don't what, Irving?" she pressed him, her anger rising hot again. "Don't ask questions that need to be asked? Don't stick my nose where it doesn't belong? Don't try to find out why two innocent teenagers and a good man are dead while the entire police force seems content to look the other way and pretend everything is perfectly fine?"

"Brett, stop." He fixed his gaze on her. "I believe you."

She opened her mouth to argue, but snapped it shut when she realized what he'd said.

"You do?" The words squeaked from her mouth.

He returned to the bed and sat down, taking her hand and wrapping it up with both of his. "I should have believed you from the beginning, from the very first time you came to me with concerns about the case. You were right that there were things that didn't add up. I didn't want to see them. I didn't want to admit that we'd let things get so bad in the department. I mean, I know there were things going on. Favors, small bribes, things that got overlooked, reports that got lost, traffic tickets that disappeared. But it was never a big case, never anything that really mattered. I didn't want to believe that one of our own was trying to get away with murder. I'm sorry. I should have listened to you. If I'd listened, you wouldn't have had to go to the state police. You wouldn't have had a reason to be at that restaurant. Eli would be—" A sob broke loose before he could finish.

He dropped his head down.

"You can't let him get away with this, Irving," she whispered.

He took a single, deep breath, collecting his emotions before lifting his face to hers again. Determination flickered in his eyes when he said, "I'm going to talk to the prosecution's office. I've got an appointment with them tomorrow. And a call in to the state police, too. Stan has no idea. Though I'm sure when he finds out what I'm planning, he'll come after me with everything he's got. Hopefully by then, we'll be so far out ahead of this, he'll need a time machine to catch up."

"What can I do?" she asked.

"Nothing." He patted her hand. "Right now, your only job is to rest and watch to see if those pigeons come back."

He pointed at the window as he rose to his feet. It seemed like he was on his way out the door, but he lingered at the foot of her bed. He fussed with his tie and jacket. His teeth worked over his lips. His eyes moved around the room. It was clear he had more to say to her, but whatever it was scared him.

"Say it, Irv." Her heart caught in her throat.

"I don't want you to panic," he said. "Henry's got everything under control."

Brett readjusted herself in the bed. "Henry?"

It occurred to her that she hadn't seen or heard from Amma yet. She'd been so focused on Eli and trying to figure out how the accident even happened, so numb with grief and pain medication, she hadn't thought to worry until now. But of course her grandmother would have been at her bedside after a tragedy as big as this one. Unless— Brett tensed, grabbing hold of the blankets again to shove them off.

Her face must have said everything, because Irving stepped forward, shaking his head. "Brett, I told you not to panic."

"Tell me what happened to her. Did she fall? Is it bad?"

Irving laid his hand on her good leg. His touch was feather-light, but still reassuring.

"Your grandmother's missing," he said.

Brett shook her head against the pillow, struggling through the fog of morphine to understand exactly what Irving was telling her.

"Her sailboat is missing from the dry dock, too. We think she must have taken it out onto the water. We've got boats out there right now, searching the bay. Henry's getting a search and rescue command center set up at the community center near Egret's Park. He's got volunteers scouring the shore." He squeezed Brett's leg gently, then let go. "The whole town's out there looking for her, Brett, so I'm serious when I tell you not to worry. We're going to find her."

The only word Brett could croak out was, "When?"

"Sometime after you left for dinner last night," Irving said.

"When Henry heard about the accident this morning, he went straight to the house to check on Amma. Pistol was waiting by the front door, acting like he hadn't eaten in days. But Henry said that's how he always acts so he wasn't too worried at first. After he searched the house, he called some of Anita's friends, but no one had seen her. It was around noon, I think, when he realized the boat was missing, too. After that, he didn't waste any time calling for help and getting searchers out on the water."

Brett's grip tightened on her blankets. She'd thought the worst had already happened. Now she feared Eli was only the beginning.

"There are some squalls coming in later this evening," Irving continued. "But there are plenty of boats out there looking for her right now, and they'll stay out there for as long as they can. We'll find her, Brett. We have to. I promise you, we're doing everything we can, and the best thing you can do for her right now is rest. And don't worry about Pistol, either. Diane's taking good care of him."

He smiled, but she couldn't force a smile in return. She nodded, feeling dazed, her head spinning, the pain in her broken leg flaring hot, becoming almost unbearable. The medication was starting to wear off. She laid her head back on the pillow as Irving left her to rest with reassurances that as soon as he knew anything more about the search he'd call.

She had fired the sitter, fought with Henry, and left Amma completely alone, stupidly believing everything would be okay. Now her grandmother was missing, and there was nothing Brett could do about it because she was trapped in this hospital with a broken leg.

She pushed the call button. The nurse came in a few seconds later, smiling brightly, eying the pulse and oxygen monitor next to Brett's bed, making notes in her chart, then asking her about her pain levels and shining a penlight at her face to check her pupils.

Brett winced away from the bright light. "When can I get out of here?"

CHAPTER 40

Two days later, Brett was released from the hospital.

As the orderly maneuvered her wheelchair into the elevator and pushed the lobby button, he said, "Bet you'll be glad to get home."

Glad wasn't the word she would use. Relieved maybe, certainly anxious and impatient.

As of a few hours ago, when Irving called the hospital room to give her an update on the search for Amma, there'd been no news. Henry had spent every waking moment over the past forty-eight hours—and even some hours he should have been sleeping—looking for her. Boats still crisscrossed the bay, as people scoured the beaches and trails on foot. Border patrol had been alerted, as had the coast guard, but there was still no sign of Amma or her boat. Even though the odds of finding her were lessening with each passing hour, Brett wasn't ready to give up hope. Not yet.

The doctor had told Brett to take it easy over the next few months and let her body heal, but she was already making plans for how she could help with the search. She could use something to distract her from the physical pain she was in.

The elevator lurched, and Brett winced. Her right leg was in a brace, propped up on the footrest at a weird angle that made her hip hurt. No matter how many times she tried to shift her weight, she couldn't get comfortable. Her body hurt in other places, too. Her back from whiplash, her stomach from seat belt bruising, her head from the concussion, her wrists from gripping the steering wheel too tightly.

The doctor said it would all lessen with time, that she'd be out of the brace before she knew it, that as long as she rested and didn't push herself to get back to work too soon, she'd make a full recovery. *Let someone else take care of you for a while,* he'd said to her during his last visit. She'd had to bite down on her tongue to keep from laughing in his face. There was no one she could ask to drop everything and take care of her like that.

Her father was on a business trip in China, but even if he was available, she didn't want his help. Irving had his hands full as acting detective sergeant and interim chief since both Wes and Stan had been placed on leave pending an independent investigation into June and Daniel's deaths. Irving's wife Diane had brought Brett a change of clothes this morning and promised to come by tonight with a chicken casserole, but she had classes to teach all afternoon. Eli was dead, his body lying on a cold slab in the morgue of this very hospital, the very thought of it making Brett want to punch something, or someone.

And then there was Amma. Brett closed her eyes, trying not to think about what would happen if they never found her because they were going to find her. But even when they did, it's not like Amma was in any position to become Brett's caretaker.

Brett was going to have to figure out how to manage on her own with a broken leg and a raging headache and the guilt of Eli's death and Amma's disappearance weighing heavily on her shoulders. But at least she didn't have to worry about how she was getting home.

Irving said he'd take care of it, which Brett assumed to mean he was sneaking away from the chaos at the precinct to drive her and get her settled before he left her to fend for herself. She would ask him to make up the bed in the downstairs guest room. And leave a large bottle of ibuprofen and a glass of water on the nightstand. And a stack of those thrillers Amma loved to hate so much.

But when the elevator dinged and the doors opened into the lobby, it was Jimmy Eagan who stepped up to take the wheelchair handles from the orderly, not Irving. Jimmy who winced when he saw her and said, "You look like shit, Bretty."

Brett choked out something between a laugh and a sob, then said, "You think this *looks* bad? Imagine how much it hurts."

He put one hand on her shoulder and squeezed gently. She slid her hand over top of his, holding him there, feeling the heat and softness of his skin, bewildered, because she still wasn't sure he was real. It could just be the last of the good drugs making her hallucinate.

"What are you even doing here?" she asked, as he wheeled her out of the hospital to where his car waited by the curb.

"Irving said you needed a ride home." Jimmy pressed the wheelchair brake to keep her from rolling away.

He opened the car door, and Trixie and Pistol jumped out together, their bodies wagging in a frenzy as they rushed to greet Brett. Pistol rose on his hind legs and did a little spin. Trixie's tail knocked against Brett's broken leg and it hurt like hell, but also she was laughing because the dogs were energy and life, the happiest dogs she'd ever seen, and Jimmy was here. Jimmy was here to take her home.

As he helped her get settled in the front seat of the car, he told her how Irving had called him Tuesday from the hospital while Brett was in surgery, how he'd canceled all his upcoming book events, packed a bag with his and Trixie's things, and drove too fast over the speed limit to get to Crestwood.

"I got here late Tuesday night," he said.

"And I'm just now hearing about it?" It was Thursday. He'd been in town two whole days already and hadn't come to see her.

"There was a lot going on," he explained. "I was helping Henry get the search for Amma up and running, plus I needed to get the house ready for when you came home, and I promised my editor I'd cover this story so I've been sending him updates, trying to get some articles written when I'm not helping Henry."

She stared at him, confused. "Amma's disappearance is making headlines in Oregon?"

"No, but Wes Harris is. The murders. The cover-up. The fall of a corrupt police force. My editor lives for salacious headlines like those."

He was quiet for a minute before adding, "I also didn't come by the hospital sooner because I didn't know if you'd even want to see me."

"Don't be stupid, Jimmy." She grabbed his hand and smiled at him with stunned disbelief. "I still can't believe you're here."

"Now you're the one being stupid, Bretty." He smiled back at her. "This is what friends do for each other. They show up."

It took a second to figure out how to fit Brett's leg in the car and how to fold the wheelchair so it fit in the trunk and where to put the crutches so they didn't hit anyone in the head, but eventually Jimmy figured it out, and they were ready to go.

Even though he drove carefully, every bump on the road sent spikes of pain into Brett's bones, and every oncoming car or tight corner caused her to flinch.

"I'm sorry about your friend," Jimmy said when they were stopped at a light halfway between the hospital and home. "I know there's not a lot I can say to make this easier on you, but I'm here if you need to talk about it. If you need anything, just tell me."

People moved along the sidewalks through downtown Crestwood, their arms loaded down with last minute Christmas gifts. They laughed together, touched hands, arms, faces. They helped each other across the street. And there was a snow-globe surrealness to the whole scene, a fragility Brett had never fully grasped until now. How quickly life could be taken from you, how quickly your whole world could be tipped upside-down and shaken to chaos.

"Turn left at the end of the street," she said, as the light turned green and Jimmy pressed his foot on the gas. Right would take them home; left would take them out of town to the highway where the accident happened.

"Are you sure?" Jimmy asked.

"I need to see it," she said.

The only sign that anything terrible had happened on this stretch of Chuckanut Highway was the busted out guardrail. The metal was ripped in half, the two pieces hanging jagged over the edge of the cliff. Otherwise the road was completely clear of debris. There were no black marks on the road, even though Brett distinctly remembered braking when she came around the corner and saw the headlights. But everything happened so fast. Maybe there had been no time for her to brake, and she only wished she had.

In the daylight, the road looked so much wider, so much less dangerous. It wasn't raining anymore; the sun was even peeking from behind thin clouds. But the night of the accident, the road had been slick with puddles, and the windshield wipers were working overtime. Conditions that, even without a car forcing her off the road, would have been difficult to navigate.

Jimmy parked on a gravel turnoff a few feet back from the broken guardrail. He went to get the wheelchair from the trunk, but Brett grabbed the crutches instead, and somehow managed to push her way out of the car and hobble to where she had driven off the cliff.

Jimmy rushed to her side. "Easy does it. I really don't want to have to drive you back to the hospital."

"I'm fine," she said, but leaned into the hand he laid on the small of her back to steady her.

The gravel shoulder went about a half a foot past the guardrail before the land dropped off sharply, giving way to boulders and trees and eventually, the ocean. Sculpin Bay was visible through the dense pines. A long sliver of dark water stretched from one point of land to the other. The bluer, deeper ocean beyond was a whipped frenzy of white caps and rushing seagulls. Small boats bobbed in the distance and Brett wondered if they were all looking for Amma.

She shifted her gaze down. Eli's car was crunched between two spindly pine trees, and teetering precariously on the side of the cliff, a good fifty feet below where she and Jimmy stood now. Some part of her had hoped Irving was exaggerating the precariousness of the situation, but she could see for herself now how lucky she'd been. If it hadn't been for the trees, the car would have plunged another fifty feet straight into the ocean. There was no point putting anyone else's life at risk trying to salvage the car. Looking at it now in the light of day, she didn't know how they'd even managed to get her out alive.

She took a shuddering breath and turned away.

Jimmy's hand pressed firmly against her back, but he didn't say anything. She didn't need him to; his presence was comfort enough. She shuffled on her crutches until she was facing him.

"I'm sorry." Her voice cracked. "I've been a real shitty friend lately."

"You and me both." He laughed softly, keeping his arm around her waist as if he thought she might tip over in the wind. But she was glad for his strength in this moment, glad that she didn't have to try and bear the weight of everything alone.

He leaned his head close to hers and said, "When Irving called me and told me you'd been in an accident—God, Brett, I couldn't breathe. I thought I'd lost you and I couldn't breathe." He inhaled sharply now, his grip tightening around her as he drew her closer. "I'm not ready to lose you. If that means we're friends and nothing more, so be it. I can do that. I can be your friend. I can—"

"Shut up, Jimmy." She lifted her face to his and their lips met halfway.

He tasted like salt, like sorrow, but in this moment there was nothing more she wanted or needed.

When she pulled away, he was looking at her with a question in his eyes, and she knew he wanted to ask what the kiss meant—if it was just grief or if she was coming around to the idea of loving him.

"I don't know, Jimmy." She offered him a half-smile that she hoped held more kept promises than broken ones. "Ask me tomorrow after the good drugs wear off."

She turned away from the broken guardrail and shuffled back to the car.

CHAPTER 41

On Friday morning, Henry called the boats back to the dock again. Brett understood the reasoning, but she didn't have to like it. This was the second time since she'd been released from the hospital that the weather had turned from clear, blue skies to roiling thunderclouds without warning. One minute, the bay would be as still as glass, almost summer conditions. The next, huge swells thrashed and boiled, wind cracked sails, and clouds broke open, dumping buckets of cold rain.

"We don't need anyone else going missing," Henry grumbled as he reached for the radio to make the announcement.

It wasn't safe to search in those types of conditions, Brett knew that, but Amma was still out there, and if it wasn't for this damn broken leg and the fact that Jimmy refused to leave her side, Brett would be out there, too. Squall or no squall, if she could, she would be on a boat searching.

Not that Jimmy or Henry would let her anywhere near the docks in her condition.

Jimmy almost left her at home with the dogs today. He'd argued that she was still recovering, that she needed rest, that there was nothing she could do, that she'd be in the way. But Brett had spent the past two days lying useless in a hospital bed, and she couldn't do it anymore. Jimmy finally agreed to bring her along after she promised to do nothing more strenuous than pass out sandwiches.

The community center was close to the docks near Egret Park with facilities big enough to handle all of the searchers and volunteers coming in and out all day and night. According to Jimmy, there had been hundreds of people helping out the first two days, but they were moving into day four now. Between the weather and lack of progress, people were losing interest. And hope.

But there were at least fifty people still searching, and a dozen boats willing to go back out on the bay after this latest storm passed.

"What about these islands?" Brett tapped her finger on a small grouping located at the mouth of the bay.

Henry squinted at the map and shook his head. "We sent a boat out there on Wednesday. We thought if she was adrift, the tide might push her into one of those, but we didn't see any signs of her or the boat. There's an outcropping of rocks that makes it hard to get close to shore, but the searchers went around a couple of times and said they didn't see anything to indicate Amma had made it there."

Brett was still angry with Henry about his confession that during his time as chief of the Crestwood Police Department, he'd looked the other way when earlier complaints came in about Wes Harris' behavior on the job. Complaints that, if handled properly, could have ended with Wes Harris being fired. She didn't know if that would have changed anything for June and Daniel, but it could have meant a different ending for Eli. As hard as it was for Brett to forgive Henry for that, no one else had his kind of sway in the community and access to resources. No one else would look for Amma with the same kind of commitment and intensity. And since Amma was Brett's priority, that meant setting aside her feelings until her grandmother was home safe.

"Send someone out again after this storm passes." Brett studied the map so she wouldn't have to look Henry in the eyes. "We've got to double check everything. Have we called Skagit and Whatcom sheriffs yet? What about the marinas?"

"Brett," Henry said her name in the same tone he'd used with her when he was still chief and she was a detective working under him.

The authority in his voice made her look up from the map. She was seated in a folding chair. He stood beside her. She'd never felt so small next to him, never more like a child.

"I've done all that," he said. "I've called everyone there is to call. The boats are searching. People up and down the coast know to keep an eye out."

"There has to be something else," she said.

He shook his head, rubbing the bald spot. "I know it's hard, but we're doing the best we can, and there's really not much else we can do now but wait and hope she turns up."

But he turned his attention to the map again, as if she was right and there might be something they'd overlooked. Some people would have told her after this long that she needed to start considering the possibility that Amma's boat had capsized and Amma had gone under with it, but Henry didn't want to admit those truths any more than Brett did. So they both kept their mouths shut and tried to think of a place they hadn't searched yet.

Jimmy groaned as he got up from the chair he'd been sitting in next to Brett since they got here. He'd been hunched over a notebook, writing a rough draft to turn in to his editor, but now he closed the book, stretched his arms in the air, and twisted, working the kinks from his back. Trixie and Pistol, who had been curled at his feet, both hopped to attention, wagging their tails, eager to do something other than sleep.

"I'm going to take the dogs out and get some hot chocolate. Want anything?" He addressed both Henry and Brett.

Henry asked for a coffee. "The real kind from Mary's place, not that swill the department brought in."

Brett shook her head. "Nothing for me."

"One apple cinnamon muffin coming right up." Jimmy clipped on the dogs' leashes and walked toward the door.

"I like that man," Henry said, and even though Brett hadn't asked for his opinion and shouldn't care either way, she felt a flush of warmth and something that she refused to admit was pride.

Brett studied the map once more, her eyes running over the blues and greens, the lines that were useless in leading them to Amma. Ever since hearing about her grandmother's disappearance, Brett had been trying to figure out why Amma had left the house in the first place and why she'd taken the boat out with the weather so unfavorable.

She kept returning to the conversation they'd had in the kitchen before Brett left for her fateful dinner with Eli. How distant Amma had seemed as she gazed out on the ocean, her sighs sounding less like sadness and more like hope. Brett remembered her tilting toward the waves, like she was asking them to carry her away.

It was possible Amma had intended to disappear, to sit inside the boat she loved so dear, drift into the sunset, and never return. If that were the case, Brett doubted they would ever find any trace of her. Amma would make sure of that. But possible and likely were two different things, and Brett wanted to believe that Amma wouldn't have left her alone like this—not without saying goodbye, leaving her loved ones to worry and fret. Unless Amma forgot for a moment who she was and who she loved and where she was supposed to be. Maybe she'd wanted to take the *Anita Horizon* out for a quick jaunt, but forgot which direction to steer home or how to work the rudder and sails, and then the storms had come and done their worst.

There was one more scenario Brett didn't like thinking about because, like Eli's death, it laid the blame firmly at her feet. After

Brett left the house on Monday night with Eli, someone could have come to the door and either convinced Amma to leave willingly or physically forced her out. And there was only one person Brett could think of angry enough to come after her family in that way.

As if she conjured him with her thoughts, Wes Harris entered the community center on a gust of cold wind. A small group of people came in with him, everyone looking half-drowned, half-starved, and miserable. They trudged toward the refreshment table, shaking rain from their coats and murmuring softly to one another.

Wes wore a baseball cap with the Crestwood PD crest embroidered above the bill, as if he was trying to prove something. Sure, he was currently suspended and under investigation for obstructing a homicide investigation, but he was still one of the boys, ready and willing to play ball. Say the word and he was happy to step in again and do whatever needed doing. As he took the hat off to hang on a hook, his gaze caught Brett's from across the room. He smiled at her, his thick mustache lifting at the ends. Brett didn't smile back.

"What the hell is he doing here?" she snapped at Henry.

He followed her gaze to where Wes now peeled off his rain jacket. He was laughing with a middle-aged woman about something.

"He offered to help search," Henry said defiantly. "I'm not turning anyone away."

Wes tipped his head back, his laugh booming through the large room.

Amma was missing and this man was smiling, laughing, relaxed like nothing was wrong. Anger flamed through Brett, a sudden spark that burned hot and fast. Before she realized what she was doing, she grabbed her crutches that were leaning against the table, hauled herself to her feet, and hobbled over to Wes.

He stared at the brace on her leg for a beat too long. When he looked in her eyes again, all Brett saw was a man who would do anything to protect himself.

"Glad to see you up and about, Buchanan," he said, without much sincerity. "I heard about what happened. It's a miracle that anyone survived."

She shoved close to him, knocking him a step backward. "Don't you dare. Don't you fucking dare."

"Hey, now. What did I say?" He lifted his hands in feigned innocence, trying to placate her. "I'm glad you lived to fight another day, that's all."

"And Eli?"

"Can't say he didn't get what he deserved." Wes spoke so quietly, Brett thought she might have misheard him, but then his mouth curled into a cruel smile, and he added, "If you're not with us, you're against us. Miller knew what he was signing up for, though I'm not sure you did."

She shifted her weight so she was stable on one crutch, then used the other to shove Wes' shoulder. "Where is she?"

The smile dropped from his face as he took a step back, but Brett matched him step for step, jabbing with the crutch. "What did you do to her?"

"Knock it off, Buchanan."

"Where's Amma? Where's my grandmother? What the fuck did you do to her?"

"I have no idea what the hell you're talking about."

"When did you take her?" Brett had him backed up against a wall now and it felt good to see a spark of fear in his eyes. "After you heard about the accident? When you found out I was in the hospital, you saw your opportunity and you grabbed it?"

The room, which had been noisy with conversation, grew quiet now as people turned to watch the argument unfold.

"How much pain medication are you on right now, Buchanan?" he taunted her.

"I know what happened at Deadman's Point," she said, no

longer caring about the strangers in the room, the other people listening in. Let them hear, let them see the kind of monster Wes really was. "I know you were there that night. I know Adam was there, too. Eli told me everything. He told me you shot Daniel."

"If he told you everything, then you know I had no choice." He kept his voice low, trying to keep the conversation between the two of them, but it was too late for that. Most of the people in the room had their heads turned, listening with interest.

"I don't believe that," Brett pushed him. She had no proof, only a sick feeling in her gut, but she was tired. So damn tired. And done playing his twisted games.

"If your self-defense bullshit was true, you wouldn't have worked so hard to cover it up after. You want to know what I think happened?" She didn't wait for his response. "I think your son shot first. He brought the Luger with him, and, whether he meant to use it that night or not, the gun went off. He shot and killed June. Then you showed up or maybe you were already there, I don't know, but at some point, you realized what Adam had done, and you took it upon yourself to try and fix it so no one would find out. You couldn't have anyone coming forward and saying what really happened that night, could you? You couldn't risk Adam's future, and you couldn't risk your own. So you shot Daniel in the back. A kid, a scared kid, who was running away from something. From someone. From you. Why? Because he was afraid of you, not the other way around. Daniel was a witness. He was the only other person who knew the truth about what Adam did. If Daniel talked, Adam was a goner. So you killed him. You killed Daniel. And then you spent weeks trying to cover it up, manipulating people, destroying evidence, doing whatever you could to steer the investigation away from the truth. From the fact that your son is a murderer, and so are you."

"You have no idea what you're talking about." The haughty

smirk slid from Wes' face, replaced with a tense rage, but in his eyes flashed fear, and that's when Brett knew she was closer to the truth than she'd ever been.

"It's time to come clean, Wes," she said, gentling her voice, trying to appeal to his humanity. "Two kids are never going to have a chance to grow up. A good officer is dead. It's time for you to stop hiding and tell the truth about what happened. Tell the truth about everything. About June and Daniel and Adam. About Eli. About Amma. Because you did something to her, too, didn't you? You killed her like you killed Eli? Like you killed those kids? Like you tried to kill me? Who's next, Wes? Who else has to die before you finally tell the truth?"

Brett wasn't expecting what happened next. She thought Wes would duck away from her and flee the building like the humiliated coward he was. She thought he might laugh and carry on with the charade of innocence because he was that convinced no one and nothing could touch him. Instead, he stepped forward, rising to his full height and jabbed a finger into her chest. She swayed, unsteady on her crutches, but managed to stay standing.

"The truth is whatever I say it is." Spit flew from his mouth. "The truth is you're a bitter hag and an incompetent cop who's working under her own agenda. The truth is you'd say and do anything to get my job. The truth is you were drunk the night Eli died, but you got behind the wheel anyway. The truth is Daniel was a scumbag drug dealer like his scumbag excuse for a father. The truth is there have been a lot of accidents happening around here lately, and if you don't get the hell out of my face, we might end up with another."

She blinked at him in disbelief. "Did you just threaten me?"

"I'm saying you might want to watch your step. My suspension won't last forever." He knocked into her shoulder as he brushed past her, hard enough Brett lost her balance.

She fumbled with her crutches and started to fall. Strong hands grabbed her elbows, holding her up and helping her to a nearby chair. She turned her head to see who her Good Samaritan was and to thank them. Irving frowned back at her, deep creases forming canyons in his brow.

"Feel better now?" he asked.

She didn't. All she felt was crushing exhaustion and a flare of pain in her right leg and a dull ache in her temple and the sudden desire to crawl under a pile of warm blankets and not come out until spring.

Irving held out a cup of water that he seemingly pulled from nowhere.

"Drink this," he ordered.

She sucked it down, not realizing how thirsty she'd been until that moment, her mouth cotton-dry.

"Wes did something to Amma." She tried to sound convincing, even though she wasn't completely convinced herself. "At least, it's something I think we should look into—the possibility that she didn't leave the house on her own."

"Okay," Irving said, without any doubt in his voice. "I'll make sure they include that in their list of interview questions."

"What?" She blinked at him, confused.

He pointed his finger toward the front windows of the community center where people were starting to gather, clucking with interest at whatever was happening outside. Brett rose to her feet to see over their heads. In the parking lot, Wes Harris was talking to three men in black suits with slicked-back hair and serious expressions. Wes flung his hands in frustration while the man in the center of the group spoke to him. After a few minutes, the man who seemed to be in charge stepped forward. He grabbed Wes roughly by the arm and spun him around, pushing him against the hood of a dark SUV and slapping handcuffs over his wrists.

"State agents," Irving explained. "They're taking over the Newmark and Yoon cases."

The men in dark suits held Wes' head as they shoved him into the backseat of the SUV.

"I got permission from Eli's parents to check his apartment for the evidence you said went missing," Irving said. "We found most of it. Adam's bloody clothes and June's camera, everything you found in the back of the Harris' truck. It was all still bagged and labeled. I'm sure a good defense attorney will argue to get it thrown out, but it's something to get us started anyway. That, along with the gun you brought them the other day, was enough for the state to decide to take a closer look at Wes' involvement in the murders. I only wish Eli was still here to tell his side of the story."

There was a lump in Brett's throat, and she swallowed hard around it. Eli could have dumped the bags in the ocean, burned them in a campfire, buried them in the woods. But he'd held on to them. She didn't know if Eli would have come forward if she hadn't pushed him, but she felt better knowing he'd had doubts, that his loyalty toward Wes hadn't been completely blind.

"I also went back over the entire investigation," Irving said. "Every scrap and jotted note in both files. Remember those two footprints you found at the scene?"

"One was Daniel's," she said.

"Right. Well, Wes keeps a spare pair of boots in his office. I checked this morning and the size is a match at least. Beyond that, it's hard to say, but I'm sending the entire file over to the state this afternoon, so it's out of my hands now. They'll be the ones doing the official match, but it's a high probability that the prints will be enough to place Wes at the scene the night June and Daniel were murdered."

Brett stared at the dark SUV idling in the parking lot.

"The state police will want to talk to you again to take a more formal statement and ask some follow up questions," Irving said.

"I'll tell them whatever they want to know," she said.

"This is good, Brett," he said. "We're going to get the truth now."

"He won't be indicted," she said.

"We don't know that."

But she knew. There was too much at stake. No one wanted to put a cop like Wes on trial, no one wanted the media circus, the budget cuts, the potential lawsuits, the reforms that would certainly come after. The people in power would want this case and all the baggage that came with it to disappear as quickly as possible. So they'd try to cut a deal, or they'd bungle the paperwork so badly even a shitty defense attorney would be able to get the case thrown out. Two kids murdered, a good cop dead, and Wes and his son could still walk away unscathed.

Brett's whole body hurt now, the ibuprofen she took earlier that morning finally wearing off. Her headache turned from a dull thud to a sharp ringing. The air tasted like smoke and burned rubber. She felt like she was coming around that tight corner on Chuckanut Highway again, her stomach knotting as the flare of headlights blinded her and she realized their fates were in her hands. She'd had no good options that night, only a choice decided at the last second and a heart filled with fear.

The front door of the community center clicked open, and Jimmy walked in with the two dogs close on his heels. His hands were busy with leashes and coffee cups and brown bags filled with pastries. He stopped short in the middle of the room and looked from Brett and Irving to the small crowd by the window watching the dark SUV finally pull out of the parking lot.

He looked back at Brett, catching her gaze, and asked, "Someone want to tell me what the heck I missed?"

CHAPTER 42

Two days after Wes' arrest, Irving showed up on Brett's doorstep early in the morning with his hat in his hands. She'd been planning to attend June Newmark's funeral later that afternoon, but from the look on Irving's face, she had a feeling that she wasn't going to make it.

Delaying the inevitable, she hobbled a few steps back from the doorway, gesturing him to follow her inside. "Jimmy's got some coffee going."

But Irving stayed where he was on the porch, his stern expression never changing.

"Whatever it is, Irv, I can handle it," she said softly.

"I'm sorry, Brett." His voice was gruff and trembling.

At that moment, Trixie and Pistol came rushing to the door. They slipped around Brett's legs, and the crutches she was still getting used to, and sniffed Irving's muddy boots. Jimmy came up behind her to wrangle the dogs back inside. He took one look at Irving and slipped his arm around Brett's waist as if he could tell what was coming and wanted to keep her steady.

She leaned into the strength of him, grateful for the gentle squeeze he offered, the pressure a reminder that if she couldn't hold herself up this time, he would be there to keep her from falling.

Irving sighed, darted his eyes to the sky as if sending up a brief prayer, then dropped his gaze back to Brett and, using his serious cop voice, said, "The call came in about an hour ago. They may have found the *Anita Horizon*."

A lump formed in Brett's throat, but she didn't sway or lose focus.

Some part of her had always known this was coming. She'd been preparing for it ever since Irving first told her Amma was missing. Five days had passed since then. Five long days of scraping together enough people and boats and resources to scour the coastline with waning hope in their hearts. Even Brett had started to wonder if it was all a waste of time, but Henry—Henry refused to quit.

All week he'd been calling the hospitals and morgues in Whatcom and Skagit counties, and every time he heard the same thing: *There is no one here matching that woman's description.* But he kept calling and he kept searching and he kept rallying the residents of Crestwood to come out and look for Amma. *One more day,* he kept saying. *I know we'll find her, we just need one more day.* Jimmy took the dogs and walked the beaches as often as he could, searching for some sign, something to bring them closure—one way or the other. Sometimes, if her leg didn't hurt too bad, Brett walked with them. But every day that passed with no news, Brett felt Amma slip further from her grasp.

And now, finally, Irving was standing in front of her, working his hands around the brim of his hat, and she knew, even before the words left his mouth that it was over.

"There's a small island near the mouth of the bay," Irving said. "It's uninhabited, but a fisherman was motoring past there early this morning, and said it looked like a boat had been smashed up on some rocks. He saw some debris washed up on the beach, but the waves were too big for him to get in close enough for a good look."

Jimmy's grip tightened around Brett. "Can you take us out there?"

She was grateful to him for asking the question stuck in her throat.

Irving hesitated as if thinking through his options, then he nodded.

"When?" Jimmy asked, but Brett was already reaching for her raincoat hanging on the hook near the door.

"If we're going today, we need to go right now," Irving said, glancing nervously at Brett, whose bruises hadn't yet healed, her leg still in a brace. "Weatherman says another storm will be rolling in late this afternoon. But from the looks of the clouds, it could be sooner. We don't want to be out there when it hits."

Jimmy nodded. He helped Brett put on her raincoat, then reached to grab his own. "Let me get the dogs settled," he said to Irving. "We'll meet you at the dock."

A half hour later, they were on a boat, roaring toward the mouth of Sculpin Bay and a speck of dark land the captain called Desolation Island.

"Lots of boats find their way to the bottom of the ocean out here," the captain said. He was a grizzled-looking man with a thick red beard and a pipe clenched between his teeth, and Brett would have laughed at the cliché if she wasn't so nervous.

She could barely stand being out on the water on calm days. Diesel fumes mixed with salt air and the faint hint of rain. Wind whipped her hair and the scarf around her neck. With the waves rising almost to the prow of the boat, bucking them like wild broncos, it was all she could do not to scream at the captain to turn around and take them back to dry land.

Her fingers clawed at the boat railing as it bounced over wave after rough wave. Every time the hull slapped against the water, pain shot through Brett's leg. She clenched her teeth, trying not to think about how much it hurt. She would endure this if it meant finding Amma.

Jimmy glanced at her and shouted over the sound of the motor, "Are you okay? You look like you're going to—?"

She twisted away from him and threw up over the side of the boat.

The captain let out a braying laugh and muttered something about sea legs.

Irving said nothing, his eyes fixed on the horizon where purple clouds were starting to push closer to land.

Jimmy rubbed Brett's back and offered her a drink of water from a canteen he'd packed before they left. Brett sipped at it, her stomach feeling slightly better, though nothing could be done about the ache in her leg or the dread building in her chest.

Desolation Island was bigger than it looked from faraway. According to Irving, it was about three square miles of land, a jagged and wild place, covered in pine trees and sheer cliffs. There appeared to be a narrow beach on one end, but no good way to get to it. Toothy rocks jutted from churning white water, stone ramparts letting no one pass.

"Not very inviting," Jimmy said.

The captain flashed a grin. "Some folks say it's cursed. There's a strong current around the whole island. If you're not careful, you'll end up on those rocks."

Which was apparently what had happened to the *Anita Horizon*.

Brett saw the mast first, snapped in half, the sail dragging through the water on the other side of the jagged stone parapets. As they drew closer, she could see that the boat had broken clean in half and the bow had drifted to shore where waves rocked the hull gently, pulling it back into the ocean before shoving it higher onto the sand. The other half of the boat was completely gone, vanished somewhere beneath the waves. Small pieces of splintered wood were scattered across the inlet and narrow strip of beach.

Brett stood, trying to get a better look, but they were a good distance away, too far to see if there were any signs that Amma might have survived the wreck.

"We have to get closer!" she shouted to the captain, waving her hand at the beach. "We need to search the island!"

Amma could be hurt or sheltering from the elements somewhere in the trees. There would be no certainty, no knowing one way or the other unless they found a way to push ashore and take a look around. But the captain shook his head and pointed to where the purple clouds had turned as black as night, forming an intimidating wall of rain bearing down on them.

"That storm's about to hit!" the captain shouted back to her. "And I'm telling you, we don't want to be out here when it does!"

Brett turned to Irving, pleading with him. "She's a strong swimmer. She could have made it to land! Please, we have to see if she's there!"

Irving seemed about to order the captain to steer the boat through the churning water to the beach, but a flash of lightning drew his gaze skyward. Seabirds beat a frenzied path toward the mainland, racing the storm.

Irving gave Brett an apologetic look as he shook his head. "He's right! It's too dangerous!"

The wind howled. The trees on the island began to bend and sway. And maybe it was the motion of the branches, or the fog that was rolling in thick and fast, or a deer bending to pinch a delicate fern, but, high on the cliffs above the beach and the broken pieces of Amma's sailboat, Brett could have sworn she saw someone standing in the shadows. Before she could point out the strange figure to anyone else, the captain whipped the boat around to the mainland and opened the throttle.

Jimmy leaned in and put his mouth close to Brett's ear. "We'll come back," he promised. "When this storm passes, we'll come back and see what we can find."

All her life, Brett never had much use for tears. Her father, who had very much wanted a boy but got another girl instead, would say, *I'll give you something to cry about,* and pinch her arm when he heard even the quietest of sniffles. He was always telling her to toughen up. That whatever problem she was having, crying wouldn't solve a damn thing. *Think, Brett,* he'd say, tapping a hard finger against her forehead. *Stop crying and think of a way to fix it.*

He'd never told her what to do if something couldn't be fixed.

Blame it on her broken leg, or on the *Anita Horizon* scattered in pieces, tossed about on a relentless sea. Blame it on Amma who had gone out on the boat alone. Blame it on the unlucky luck of being at the wrong place at the wrong time. Blame it on monsters dressed as heroes. Blame it on this place, this town that some days seemed like nothing more than a yawning black hole of misery. Blame it on the raging ocean forever beating against a lonely shore. Blame it on everything falling down around her all at once, on the fact that she would be spending Christmas alone this year. All of these things were enough to push her over the edge, but it was the tender way Jimmy took her hand and folded it inside his own that did it—the knot that had been building in Brett's throat for weeks finally came loose.

She turned her head so no one would see her cry.

Her tears mingled with the spray coming off the sides of the boat and the rain starting to fall. Always after today, when she thought about grief, she would remember the taste of these storm-tossed waves.

CHAPTER 43

Lizzie brought daisies to June's funeral because they were June's favorite flower. She didn't know why it had taken so long for them to finally bury her friend. There were rumors of misplaced paperwork, the medical examiner dragging his feet, the police department refusing to release the body while the investigation was still open, a pending lawsuit to move the process along, but after Adam's dad was arrested, none of that stuff seemed to matter anymore.

Three days before Christmas, and seven weeks after her tragic death, June Newmark was finally being laid to rest.

More people came to say goodbye than Lizzie expected. There were a lot of kids from school, as well as June's extended family, and a bunch of strangers who were probably friends with June's parents. A few cops showed up, too, but none of them were Adam's dad. Adam didn't come, either. The paper this morning said both were being held for questioning in the deaths of June and Daniel. There was a picture on the front page of Mr. Harris being led away in handcuffs by men in fancy suits.

The state police were involved now, her father had told her as he made waffles this morning before the funeral. The FBI, too. *But that's good, that's what we want.* He'd patted her hand across the breakfast table. *Don't worry, I'll be with you the whole time.*

Lizzie sat at the back of the church with Dad on one side and Grandpa on the other. Grandma sniffled into a tissue beside him. The preacher rambled for a long time about June, in a way that made it clear he didn't know anything about her. Lizzie let her eyes drift from the white lilies draped over the closed coffin to the stained-glass windows letting in rays of tinted sunlight. Orange and blue and green and purple. A glowing Jesus surrounded by children, his arms wide open, his smile soft and kind. Lizzie felt a tear slip down her cheek, and when Grandma handed her a clean tissue, Lizzie took it.

Daniel's funeral, a quiet affair compared to this, was held a few days ago, on a Thursday in the middle of the school day. Lizzie was the only kid from Crestwood High to attend. The rest of the people scattered in the pews had been family and his mother's friends from church.

Lizzie had approached Mrs. Yoon after her son's service ended. She'd been standing in the church parking lot, small against the vast expanse of gray sky looming above her. Her eyes were closed and her hands were clasped in front of her like she was praying.

Lizzie cleared her throat, trying not to startle the woman. Mrs. Yoon's eyes fluttered open and she narrowed her gaze on Lizzie. "You were a friend of Daniel's?" she asked.

Lizzie nodded. She'd never met Mrs. Yoon, not officially. The way Daniel talked about her, she seemed like the kind of woman who was tough and hard to please, who wouldn't ever approve of any of his friends or choices. So Lizzie was surprised when Mrs. Yoon stepped forward and embraced her, when she whispered, "Thank you. It gives me great comfort to know that there are others who love him and who will miss him as I do."

"He didn't deserve what happened to him." Lizzie could barely choke out the words.

"No. He did not." Mrs. Yoon pulled away and smoothed her hands over her skirt. Her eyes were dry when she tilted her head to the sky again and said, "I think it might snow."

Like a gift, a flake fell softly into her dark hair, clinging white for a second before melting.

The snow that fell the day of Daniel's funeral was gone now. It barely lasted a day, a thin dusting that melted as soon as the sun touched it. And every day after that first icing, the sky had stretched blue overhead, a vibrant color that made Lizzie's eyes ache.

June's service ended in a prayer. People filed out of the church to their cars. The cemetery service was supposed to be private, for family only, but Lizzie wasn't about to let her best friend, her sister in all but blood, be lowered into the earth without her. Dad drove her, saying nothing as she got out of the car and walked to where she could watch from a distance beneath a bare-limbed oak tree growing on a small hill.

The Newmarks stood shoulder-to-shoulder in front of the open grave. Mrs. Newmark's sobs echoed across the sloped lawn.

June would have taken a picture of this scene if she were here. Her family's dark silhouettes contrasted against the brilliant blue of the winter sky. Sorrow and joy, despair and hope. She would have said they looked like crows, standing with their drooping feathers and hunched wings. She would have watched a few minutes, then dared Lizzie to climb into the tree, as high as she could. *Can you see the ocean from up there?*

Lizzie waited until the coffin was in the ground and the family was gone. She waited until the earthmover piled dirt in a rounded mound. Then she walked to the place where her best friend was buried and laid down her small bouquet of daisies. She crouched in the dirt, waiting to cry, but she'd done all the crying she was going to do for now, and all she had for June today was an apology.

"I shouldn't have left you alone that night," she said. "You would have never left me. And I'm sorry. If I could do it over again, I would have stayed."

She didn't know if it would have changed anything. For all she knew, Adam left his house with rage in his heart and intent to harm, and her presence would have meant one more dead body to bury. But maybe—maybe she could have said something or done something to keep that gun from going off. Maybe she could have pushed June out of harm's way or talked Adam out of pulling the trigger in the first place. Maybe everything would be different now if she had chosen to stay.

Lizzie walked back to where her father waited under the oak tree. When she reached him, he lifted his hand and tucked a stray piece of hair behind her ear. His thumb brushed across the line of her chin as he said, "I wanted better for you than this, Lizzie. I still do. If there was some way I could change what's happened—"

"We don't get do-overs." She interrupted him before he rattled off his list of regrets; she had enough of her own to carry around now. "We just have to live with our choices and do better the next time. Choose better."

He seemed surprised by her words, which were as close as she was going to get to forgiving him. When he smiled, there was sadness in it, but hope lived there, too.

"I know this past year has been hard on you," he said. "But I'm proud of you. If you didn't know it already, now I'm saying it. You've grown into a strong, young woman in spite of everything, and I feel like I have so much to learn from you. And, Lizzie, I'm saying sorry, too, okay? I'm so sorry, so very sorry. And I'm going to keep saying it until you believe it. I know I can't take back anything I did. I know we don't get do-overs, but if we did, I'd get it right this time. I'd choose you."

She hugged him. She wasn't sure she trusted him completely yet, but she was getting there. She understood better now how the right thing wasn't always the easy thing, how sometimes fear could twist the truth and make you think you had no choice. But there was always a choice, even if it took you a while to find it. There was always more than one way through the dark.

As they walked through the cemetery to the parking lot, Lizzie admitted something to her father that she'd never admitted to anyone. Not even June.

"I miss her," she said, and though she didn't say her mother's name, they both knew who she was talking about. "Does that make me a bad person?

"No, baby girl," he said. "It makes you human."

He drove them back into town where they sat in the car in front of the police station for a few minutes, watching a pair of seagulls fight over a paper bag. When the birds flew away, Dad grabbed her hand and gave it a reassuring squeeze. "You ready?"

She took a deep breath, holding it until she couldn't anymore, counting to thirty before unbuckling her seat belt. "Ready or not."

They got out of the car and went inside together.

Even after it was over, after Lizzie told the tall agent with the dark, curly hair everything she knew and everything Adam told her, after she answered all their questions, even then, it didn't feel like enough.

Tell them the truth, her dad had said right before they walked into the station. *That's all we can do now. That's all we have left.*

It felt like so little compared to what they'd lost.

She didn't care why Adam had done it. She didn't want to hear his explanations or excuses. What she wanted more than anything was for him to admit to what he'd done and accept the consequences. She wanted him to apologize. She wanted from Adam what she'd never gotten from her mother—the chance to forgive him and move on with her life.

Sometimes at night, when Lizzie closed her eyes and darkness swallowed up the world, she thought about what her mother would have done to Adam if she was still here. Sometimes it made her feel better thinking about revenge, but she never let herself wallow in that dark place for very long.

She was her mother's daughter, after all, but she was so much more than that, too.

They left three days after Christmas.

"I don't understand," Grandma said as they carried their suitcases to the car Dad had bought second-hand from a friend of Grandpa's. Technically, Grandpa bought the car, but he put the title in Dad's name so no one could claim he stole it.

"You don't even know where you're going." Grandma clutched a handkerchief to her chest. "Are you even supposed to leave? What about your probation?"

"We're not going far, Ma." Dad scooped Grandma into a gentle embrace. "I can't leave the state for at least another year. We need a change of scenery, that's all. We need a fresh start, and we're not going to get that here."

"I know you and I have our differences." Grandma's voice trembled. "But really, we're fine having you here. You can stay as long as you want, you know that. This is your home."

Dad lifted the final suitcase into the trunk of the car. "This town stopped feeling like a home for us a long time ago. Isn't that right, kiddo?"

His eyes were still a little red and puffy from Uncle Eli's funeral, where they'd stood side-by-side in the back of the overflowing the church, staying only long enough to say their silent goodbyes, leaving before anyone noticed them and came over to talk. On the drive back to the ranch, Dad had glanced in the rear view mirror and said, "I'm glad that's all behind us." And there was something about the way he said it that broke the tension and let Lizzie know that it was okay, she could laugh if she wanted—life was bigger than the sadness she felt right now.

"Ready to burn rubber?" Dad slammed the trunk shut and thumped his fist on it twice to make sure it was closed.

Lizzie ran to where Grandpa and Grandma stood on the front porch. She had already said goodbye, but she hugged them again now, Grandma first, and then Grandpa.

He held on to her tightly, pressed his mouth against the top of her head, then cleared his throat and pushed her away, holding her at arm's length, studying her face as if he was trying to memorize the shape of it.

"You know where to find us if the road gets too lonely." He smiled when he said it, but his eyes were damp with tears. "No matter what, we love you."

Those words were almost enough to make her change her mind. He seemed to sense her hesitation because he gave a quick shake of his head and pushed her toward the car. "Grow wings, Lizbug," he said so only she could hear.

"Call and let us know when you get settled!" Grandma shouted as they drove away.

In the side mirror, Lizzie saw Grandpa brush away tears.

"What's the plan, kid?" Dad asked, when they reached the last stop sign before leaving Crestwood city limits.

"Drive south," Lizzie said.

"And then what?" he asked.

She took a quarter from her pocket. "Whenever we reach a town we flip this coin. Heads we stay, tails we keep driving."

Dad turned south. They listened to the radio as they drove. Forests gave way to fields, but for a long time the ocean stayed visible to the west as a thin silver line, chasing alongside them, flashing in and out of sight.

Ten miles later, they came to the first town, but it smelled the same as the town they'd left, like briny, rotting fish. Dad idled in the intersection of a downtown that looked nearly identical to Crestwood, except the names of the stores were different.

"Well, kid?"

"Tails," she said, without bothering to flip the coin.

They drove another eighty miles south on the I-5 freeway like this. Lizzie calling tails and Marshall saying nothing about the fact she wasn't even flipping the quarter.

In Seattle, they stopped for lunch, and Lizzie did actually use the quarter then. It clattered on the table between them. Tails. And she breathed a sigh of relief because she didn't think she could stay in the place where, in another life, she might already be living with June and Daniel. If Halloween night had gone differently, the three of them would have been two months into their new lives, new apartment, new jobs. The echoes of what might have been were too loud for Lizzie here. So they kept driving.

They reached Vancouver, Washington as the sun was starting to set. Up ahead, Lizzie could see the green towers of the Interstate Bridge, Oregon on the other side, the flickering lights of Portland, the planes taking off and landing nearby. So many people moving, going, leaving, arriving, living lives that had nothing to do with hers.

There were two exits left before they crossed into Oregon, and Lizzie could see her dad getting antsy and wanting her to decide. He drummed the steering wheel, casting sidelong glances at her and clearing his throat a few times. They could take the last exit, go east on Highway 14, see how living that far from the ocean changed the shape of their souls. But the prison was east and since they were both trying to start over, Lizzie didn't think it would be fair to her father to drive closer to the past he wanted to leave behind.

She rolled down her window and inhaled deeply, smelling nothing but car exhaust, rain on pavement, and the bright, clear copper scent of winter. Then she flipped the quarter. She didn't need to. This city was where they would end up staying, where they had always been headed, as close to leaving as possible. But it felt wrong not to let fate have at least some say. The quarter spun in the air a few times then dropped into her palm. She clamped her fingers around it.

"Well, kiddo?" her dad asked. "What's it going to be?"

Lizzie opened her hand and held the quarter out so he could see.

CHAPTER 44

One week after Wes Harris' arrest, Jimmy's article appeared in the *Oregonian*. There'd been a print delay due to the Christmas holiday, the article being deemed too important to be buried in an avalanche of wrapping paper and glittery bows. But by Saturday, three days after Christmas, the news of the cover-up was finally making its way to people's front doorsteps.

Before joining Brett at the booth she'd managed to wrangle from a family of four at the busier-than-usual Blue Whale Diner, Jimmy stopped at the metal newspaper box by the entrance, dropped a quarter in the slot, and grabbed a copy of the thick newsprint, headline blaring: **CORRUPTION PLAGUES INVESTIGATION IN MURDER OF LOCAL TEENS.**

He dropped the paper on the table in front of Brett as he sat down.

Three photographs accompanied Jimmy's front page article. The most prominent one smack in the center was of Wes and Adam Harris walking into the Whatcom County courthouse flanked by their attorneys. The other two were smaller, school portraits of June and Daniel printed side-by-side along the bottom of the front page. The two teenagers looked impossibly, heartbreakingly young.

Brett regretted drinking the diner coffee on an empty stomach.

The acidic liquid roiled now, threatening to come back up. She shoved the paper away without reading the article. Technically she'd already read it, or a version of it anyway.

Last night, Jimmy had handed her a stack of typed pages and said, *I want to make sure I get it right.*

But he always got it right. Telling the stories of the victims, the ones who could no longer speak for themselves, that had always been Jimmy's strength. He presented the evidence, the facts as he knew them, in a way that was simple, yet powerful. No one could read his article and not be moved by the tragic deaths of June Newmark and Daniel Yoon, outraged and incited to demand justice.

The department is corrupt, Jimmy had written. *The apple is rotten at its core. The police are more dangerous than the criminals, and the public can no longer trust the people in power to do the right thing.*

Time would tell if his article made any bit of difference and if the power structure would be toppled, or if things would stay the same for men like Wes, men who believed themselves above the law because they owned the law, decided the law, enforced the law.

Jimmy pulled the newspaper close to him. His eyes skimmed over the typeset. Brett knew he was looking for typos, misprints, anything out of place. Satisfied, he pushed the paper away again and folded his hands on the table, fixing his gaze on her. "How are you feeling?"

"This wool is making me itch." Brett scratched at the collar of the high-neck, long-sleeved black dress she was wearing.

She had wanted to wear her uniform to Eli's funeral, but when she tried to put it on earlier that morning, she'd gotten as far as buttoning up the dress shirt before catching her reflection in the mirror. She stared, hardly recognizing the stranger looking back at her. The stress of her injuries, the ongoing investigation into Wes and his son, the search for Amma, then finding her boat in pieces and coming to terms with what that meant for Brett's future—all of it was starting to take a toll. Brett hadn't been sleeping well since the accident. The smallest noise woke her up, and the night-mares didn't help. She wasn't eating, either. At best, food tasted like dust, but more often it tasted rancid. She'd lost weight. The uniform hung sloppy on her shoulders. The pants wouldn't fit over the brace she still wore on her leg.

Suddenly unable to breathe, choked by the weight of heavy fabric, Brett had ripped the uniform off, kicked it into a pile on the floor, and sank down on her bed in her bra and underwear. She couldn't do it. She couldn't be the person she used to be. And she didn't know how she was going to come back from this, what her life was even supposed to be anymore.

Just when she was about to slip into her sweatpants, crawl back into bed, and stay there for the rest of her miserable life, she heard footsteps on the stairs and the click of dog toenails on the hardwood. Jimmy knocked on the door and asked her if she was ready to go.

"I need a minute." Her voice warbled.

"Can I come in?"

He didn't wait for her answer. He entered the room with Trixie and Pistol close behind him. He looked at the uniform on the floor, looked at her on the bed with her head in her hands, went to her closet, and pulled out three dresses all the same shade of black. He laid them on the bed beside her, then kneeled and pulled her hands from her face so he could grip them tightly in his.

It had been nine days since their kiss on Chuckanut Highway, but they hadn't talked about what it—why it happened, what it meant. Brett could tell Jimmy was waiting for her to start the conversation. Brett was waiting for something, too, she just wasn't sure what. For the ringing in her head to subside. For Amma to come home. For the nightmares to stop and the lump in her throat to vanish. For a day when she woke up and didn't feel like crying.

"You don't need to wear the uniform," Jimmy said gently. "But you need to be there. They need to see you there."

He had helped her to her feet and held her steady as she got dressed.

Jimmy stared at her now across the diner table.

"What?" She plucked at the nylon stockings that were itching her now too, wishing she had more time to go home and change before her meeting with Irving. But Eli's funeral had run longer than anticipated, and Brett wanted to get the rest of it over with as soon as possible.

Only twelve days had passed since the accident, but it felt like a lifetime. Twelve days since Eli was killed, twelve days since Amma went missing. One week since Wes was arrested. Six days since they found the *Anita Horizon* splintered in pieces, with no sign if Amma had survived or not. Henry had officially called off the search and rescue efforts on Christmas Eve. With the discovery of her wrecked boat, most of the volunteers had given up hope. It didn't make sense to keep searching for someone who was never going to be found.

Go home and hug your families, Henry had said to a small crowd of tear-stained faces as they packed up gear and broke down the folding tables in the community center. *Hug them tight and count your blessings.*

Henry promised Brett he'd keep searching on his own after the new year, and Brett wasn't going to stop him, if that's what he needed to do, but she knew in her heart that nothing would come of it.

She sighed and glanced at her watch. The piece of jewelry had been special to her from the day her grandparents gave it to her as a birthday present over twenty years ago, but it seemed to take on new meaning now that Amma was gone.

Jimmy had taken Brett to Desolation Island a second time like he'd promised, but they'd found no signs of survivors, of anyone being on the island at all. Without a body, without the certainty of knowing one way or the other, Brett was tempted to cling to the thinnest thread of hope that Amma was still alive somewhere, that someone else was taking care of her now. But what chance did hope stand in the face of cruel reality? A sunken boat, a barren island, a mocking ocean—Amma was never coming home, and Brett needed to try and move on if she could, for her own sanity. She needed to shut the door on 1985 and not look back, take a step in any direction, even if it ended up being the wrong one.

The door of the Blue Whale Diner swung open to let in another group of hungry customers. Dot flitted from table to table, rushing to get the orders in, the food out, the checks paid. Brett had never seen the diner so busy—funerals made for good business, she supposed.

Jimmy reached across the table and took Brett's hand, rubbing his thumb over her knuckles. "You don't have to do this right now if you don't feel up to it, you know. Irving won't care if you take a few more days to decide."

"A few days won't change my mind." She squeezed Jimmy's hand, then caught Dot's attention and gestured for a check.

Irving had stayed behind at the station as part of a skeleton crew so the other officers could attend Eli's funeral. When Brett laid her holstered gun and badge down on the desk in front of him, he laughed and shook his head. "What are you going to do all day, Brett? You can't just sit on your grandmother's back porch and watch the birds fly by."

"Why the hell not? Sounds like a good life to me."

"Don't bullshit me."

She flinched at the anger in his voice.

His expression softened as he rubbed his hand across his cheek.

"I'm sorry, you're right. It's your choice. If this is what you want to do, I can't stop you. But before you go, I want you to hear this. I want you to hear it, and I want you to believe it." He leaned his elbows on the desk, tilting his shoulders toward her. "You have good investigative skills and great intuition. You're an asset to this team, and there is still a place for you here as a detective. I can file the paperwork this afternoon. Say the words, and it's yours."

She couldn't help but feel a swell of pride, even as she knew that what he was saying wasn't entirely true.

Within the first hour of his arrest, Wes Harris had lawyered up. One week later, he was still refusing to cooperate with the investigation. In a statement given before Christmas, his attorney claimed Mr. Harris was innocent of all charges, and he was certain that, once the evidence was presented, a jury would agree. Jimmy had been watching the press conference in Amma's living room. Sickened by the thought of the case going to trial, Brett told him to turn it off.

The attorney was right about one thing: no jury was going convict Wes or Adam Harris for murder. The evidence just wasn't there. The bullets from both guns had conveniently gone missing, misplaced in the shuffle from one lab to another. The Luger had been wiped clean, and there was a reasonable explanation for why Wes' prints would be on the gun he carried every day to work. The boot print was hard to ignore, but all it proved was that Wes was at Deadman's Point at some point. Brett knew the defense would argue that the scene hadn't been secured properly, and Wes had been there in an official capacity, helping with the investigation. They would say that's when the print was made, not the night before.

As for witness testimony, Lizzie Trudeau had recently come forward with new information about Adam's part in June's death, information she claimed he told her during an emotional confession, but Adam denied all of it. He claimed Lizzie was lying and stuck with his story that he had never made it to Deadman's Point that night. His father had caught up with him before he reached the headland and dragged him home. His explanation for the camera and the bloody t-shirt found stuffed under the front seat of his truck was just as ridiculous as the excuse Wes had given in his office weeks ago—June had loaned Adam the camera; Adam had loaned June his shirt one day when she got a bloody nose at school. He was going to give the camera back to her, but never got the chance. What happened to June and Daniel was a tragedy, the lawyer insisted, but Adam Harris and his father weren't involved.

Crazy Old Ed Shoal's testimony wasn't much use, either. Even if he had seen what happened and who was there, he couldn't hold on to reality for more than a few minutes at a time. No attorney with any kind of humanity would ever put him in front of a jury. Laurie Harris wasn't talking anymore, and Danny Cyrus, the only other person who might have been able to shed light on the events of that night, had left town soon after Wes was taken into custody. State police were keeping an eye out for him, but Brett doubted they were looking very hard.

Kevin Park's testimony about being threatened by Danny Cyrus and asked to falsify reports and lie about the bullets, would go a long way to help the charges of conspiracy against Wes and others in the department stick, but unless Adam or Wes came clean with a confession, there was no way to know for certain what had happened to June and Daniel on Deadman's Point, who had pulled the trigger and why.

Brett had her theories, but theories were useless without evidence, even if they had the ring of truth. Not that the truth mattered to most of the men still working for the Crestwood Police Department.

What mattered to them was that Brett had turned her back on another officer, snitched when she should have kept her mouth shut. She'd told her story to the press, too, aired their dirty laundry, and it didn't matter that she had done the right thing, and that it was Wes who should be punished, not her. Their loyalty was to one another, not the law. Their code was brotherhood, not justice.

At the funeral today, Brett had approached the coffin to offer her condolences to Eli's parents and say a silent goodbye. After, as she hobbled along the path to where Jimmy was waiting for her at the edge of the lawn, she noticed movement in the stiff row of uniformed officers standing off to one side of the grave. One by one, as Brett passed by, each man following another's lead, they turned their backs to her.

Brett had broken their unspoken rules. Even if she wanted to stay, she wouldn't be welcome. No matter what Irving said, or how much he claimed to be on her side, there wasn't a place for her here. Not anymore.

Besides, his position as chief was temporary. By some fluke of paperwork and seniority, he had taken over for Stan who had been asked to step down while the allegations of corruption were investigated. Brett doubted Stan would ever return to this office, perhaps he'd never be allowed to wear a badge again, but she doubted it. He'd be back in one capacity or another. As for Irving, once the powers-that-be found a more suitable replacement—a man more like Stan who would do as he's told—Irving would be shuffled back into his position as detective. Maybe they'd give him the title of detective sergeant as a consolation prize, but as for chief? Brett guessed he had a month, maybe two before he was replaced. And she knew whoever they replaced him with would make her life a living hell.

Because the men who ran this squad would never be on her side. Even Henry, who had hired her, only ever saw her as temporary, a quota to fill, a lesser version of the men on his team who did the real work. She broke their rules simply by being a woman. And even if she tried to play their game, someone would always be there to shove her down again. She wanted to belong to this club, but now she saw clearly that she never would. Even if she did every single damn thing they told her to do, bent over backward and played by their the rules—it would never be enough.

She would never be enough. Not for them.

"I appreciate the opportunity, Irving," she said. "I really do, but you and I both know there's nothing left for me here."

"You've given eleven years of your life to this work," he said. "Are you really going to walk out of this office and leave all that behind?"

There was something in his eyes she recognized—regret, yearning, a desire to cut himself off from this broken system like she was doing and start over with something new. But he was also angry with her, hurt by her decision not to stay.

Brett thought then about who she might have become if Margot was still alive, if her sister hadn't been murdered when Brett was just fourteen, if she hadn't felt so lost in the years after. She might have become a professor like her father, or a nurse like her best friend's mother, or married a banker and ended up having two daughters of her own. She certainly wouldn't have pursued the path she was on now. She would have never even thought about being a cop.

Her uncle had been a detective for the Chicago PD for many years, and oh, the horror stories he'd told. Her parents would have never wanted this life for her, but what her parents wanted ceased to matter after Margot died, after her father moved across the country, after her mother abandoned her, too. Brett had wanted to do something great with her life. She wanted to do good. For a while, as a deputy with Marion County, she had done a lot of good. She used to think it was good anyway.

Not every part of police work was heroic. So much of it was mundane and repetitious, but there were moments. The time she helped a mother give birth on the side of the road, the baby screaming life into the dark rain. The times when she offered comfort to those who were so fresh in their grief, who had found their loved ones dead by natural or unnatural causes. The times when she sat in front of a jury and testified against murderers like Archer French, her testimony part of the reason violent criminals were taken off the streets for good. The times when her work helped people—those were the times she felt powerful. When the uniform turned her into a hero.

She thought by being here in Crestwood, she would find the same. She imagined herself as a detective working the hard cases, bringing closure to families who desperately needed them, families like her family had once been. She imagined herself fixing what was broken.

But now, standing in front of Irving's temporary desk, her scratchy wool dress still smelling of funeral flowers, the pain in her leg a familiar ache, she was finally coming to understand the truth of herself and the badge she'd worn so proudly for over a decade: the only difference between a hero and a villain was how the story got told.

She shook her head. "I'm sorry, Irv. You should have seen the guys at the funeral. They wouldn't even look me in the eye. I know you want things to be different, I hope they can be, but I won't be here to find out."

His face creased with disappointment, but she could see he was starting to accept her decision. He sighed as he said, "There are shitty people everywhere, Brett. In every job, not just this one. And if good people like you do nothing and walk away, the world will just keep on being shitty."

That might be true, but so was this: if she stayed, the good parts of her would wither until one day she would become un-recognizable even to herself.

Talking with Jimmy last night, she realized that all she'd been doing for the past eleven years was waiting for something bad to happen, every day expecting the worst. She was tired of that kind of life. She wanted to see what else was out there, if she could be a different kind of person, one who wasn't always twisting shadows into monsters and looking for the exits in every room she entered. She wanted to know how it felt to live without the dead haunting her dreams.

She thought about asking Irving to come with her, leave this rigged game behind and start over with something new, something that could stay good, but she knew he wouldn't. He was too invested, too close to retirement, too tangled up in the lives of the men he'd worked with for decades, men he still trusted in spite of himself. And he had Diane to think about, too. A wife who depended on him. Brett had only herself and nothing to lose.

Just another grunt, Irving had called her once, and at the time, she'd been hurt by his words. But she was grateful for them today because it made leaving easier. She didn't have to worry about what would happen to Irving or the department. They'd easily find someone to replace her, someone who was willing to do what she wasn't.

"I'm no one special, remember?" She smiled gently at him so he understood that even though she was leaving, she had forgiven him. "This department did just fine before I showed up. I'm sure it'll do just fine after I'm gone."

Irving laid his hand on top of her gun and badge. Not hers anymore. She rose to her feet, fumbling to get the crutches under her shoulders.

"So, I'll see you Sunday?" she asked when she reached the doorway.

They hadn't been out to the nature reserve together since the beginning of the month when they'd fought about how June Newmark's case was being handled. There'd been so much going on, and if Brett was honest, she hadn't trusted Irving completely. Part of her wondered how much he really knew about what was going on with Wes, and what role he might have played in the cover-up. But Irving claimed Wes never asked him for favors, and that if he'd had any proof about what was happening, he would have done his best to stop it. Brett wanted to give him the benefit of the doubt. Ever since Eli's death, Irving had done nothing but back her up and push the investigation in the right direction. She wanted to trust him again—returning to their old routine felt like the first step.

"You'll scare the birds off with those." Irving frowned at the metallic click the crutches made whenever she took a step.

She laughed and for the first time since the accident, didn't feel a sharp pain stabbing her ribs. "I'll bring the wheelchair," she said. "I can hold the binoculars while you push me around. Doctor's orders."

"That excuse isn't going to work forever, you know."

"Four more weeks. Oh, and don't forget. It's your turn to bring the coffee."

He grunted and asked her to close the door on the way out.

No one in the squad room spoke to her or asked if she needed help as she packed a small cardboard box of personal things and left the precinct for the last time.

Jimmy was waiting for her in the lobby.

"How did it go?" He took the box and held open the front door for her.

The sky above them was a blank slate. Not a single wisp of cloud tarnished the soft blue. Brett stared up at it, blinking against the brightness, waiting for something to happen, for relief to wash over her, or to feel that burden lifting, to feel that she had done the right thing. But all she felt was the soreness in her arms, a bad itch down her leg, and a gnawing in her stomach because she'd only had coffee at the diner when she should have ordered a sandwich. If this was supposed to be the moment her new life began, it felt curiously similar to her old one.

It wasn't until they were almost to the car that Brett realized she was still listening for the crackle of the radio, for a voice to cut in and tell her where she was headed next.

It would take time, she knew, to get used to the silence.

For now, she focused on all the sounds she'd been missing before: the cackle of gulls cartwheeling toward the beach, the *crick-crack* of crows perched on lamppost, the high-shriek of a hawk circling overhead, the distant growl of a motor boat, the gentle splash of waves against stones, and Jimmy's voice telling her to watch her head as he helped her into the car.

She waited for him to come around to the driver's side and get in before she twisted in her seat to face him. They had always been able to read each other's silences, so she wasn't surprised when, with a wary look, he said, "Spit it out, Bretty."

"I want you to stay."

His brow knitted in confusion. "Well, that's good, because I have to drive you home."

"No, Jimmy. You know that's not what I mean." She reached across the console to take his hand. "I want you to stay here in Crestwood. With me. For however long. I don't know, but we can figure that out later. There is plenty of room in the house and with my leg still healing, with Amma gone, it's been nice to have you here, I've missed you, and I think you should stay."

As she was talking, his confusion had turned into amusement. With each word, his smile grew wider, and a quiet laugh puffed from his mouth.

"I'm being serious," she said.

"I know you are," he said. "But you don't have to give me a million reasons. While I appreciate the earnestness, honestly, all you have to do is ask."

"Stay?" She leaned closer to him, reaching up to brush her fingers along the sharp line of his jaw. "Please?"

This time when they kissed, there was no sorrow in it, and no doubt about her feelings for him. But when she pulled away, his eyes sparked with mischief.

"I don't know, Bretty." His voice was rough and low, as he traced his finger down her arm. "I think you better ask me again tomorrow."

ACKNOWLEDGEMENTS

A heartfelt thank you to the following people who supported me and cheered me on during the writing and publishing of this book: Ken Brayton, Joyce and Ralph Allen, Suzanne and Mike Geary, Erin Geary, Caitlin Doughty, Jarilyn Wilson, Ali Conley, Florence Beard, and every single one of my enthusiastic VIP Readers who keep coming back for more.

Extra thanks are owed to Caroline Starr Rose, my ride or die in this business. And to Alisa Callos, who never ceases to amaze me with her editing skills and story instincts. Also thanks to Sam Callos for helping out with a few important details.

Parts of this book came together in a park under a shade tree with a writer who never lets anyone tell her what to do. Thank you, Elle Mitchell, for the tea, sympathy, and commas. And thank you, too, for encouraging me to explore other parts of my writerly self and to chase my wild ideas.

And finally, and always, thank you to Ryan, who goes through all the ups and downs with me. Thank you for the brilliant covers. Thank you for double-checking the small details. Thank you for being a one-man IT department and troubleshooting my computer issues. Thank you for the dinners and snacks and tea times and second breakfasts. Thank you for the long walks and even longer bike rides. Thank you for reminding me to breathe.

About the Author

VALERIE GEARY is the author of the Brett Buchanan Mystery Series in addition to *Everything We Lost* and *Crooked River*, which was a finalist for the Oregon Book Award. She lives in the Pacific Northwest with her husband where they enjoy hiking favorite trails and discovering new ones together. Connect with her on Facebook, Instagram, or YouTube to find out what she's reading. Or sign up on her website to become a VIP Reader. You'll be the first to hear about new releases as well as receive discounts, free books, reading recommendations, and more.

Want to go behind-the-scenes with the author, receive exclusive content, pre-order information, reading recommendations, and more?

Sign up to be a VIP Reader today!

valeriegeary.com